The Revised Complete Chronology of Bronze

THE REVISED COMPLETE CHRONOLOGY OF BRONZE

RICK LAI

COVER BY
KEITH WILSON

BOSTON
ALTUS PRESS
2010

© 2010 Rick Lai and Altus Press

INTERIOR PHOTO CREDITS:
Doc Savage: The Lost Radio Scripts of Lester Dent and *The Red Spider* ©1979, 2009, 2010 Bob Larkin; *Escape From Loki* ©1991, 2010 Steve Assel; *Python Isle, White Eyes, The Frightened Fish, The Jade Ogre, Flight into Fear, The Whistling Wraith* and *The Forgotten Realm* ©1991-93, 2010 Joe DeVito; all other interior images ©1933-49, 2010 Condé Nast Publications.

Printed in the United States of America

First Revised Edition — 2010

Visit AltusPress.com for more books like this.

THANKS TO
Scott Cranford & Keith Wilson

ALL RIGHTS RESERVED

No part of this book my be reproduced or utilized in any form or by any means, electronic or mechanical, without permission in writing from the publisher.

Set in Caslon.

TABLE OF Contents

Introduction i

Chapter I: Chronology of Recorded Exploits. 1

Chapter II: Apocryphal Adventures. 250

Chapter III: Parallel Lives: Doc Savage and The Shadow 280

Chapter IV: The Literary Works of Clark Savage, Jr., A Partial List . . .314

Chapter V: Chronological Checklist 316

Chapter VI: Alphabetical Entry Cross-Reference 322

Introduction

Doc Savage's pulp adventures were published by Street and Smith in the 1930s and 1940s. Under the pen name of Kenneth Robeson, Lester Dent and other writers regularly produced exciting exploits featuring Doc Savage, also known as the Man of Bronze. Dent also wrote scripts for a 1934 Doc Savage radio show. Bantam Books reprinted the entire series in paperbacks beginning in the 1960s. Bantam also continued the series with a "lost" novel by Lester Dent *(The Red Spider)*, and new novels by Philip José Farmer and Will Murray (as Kenneth Robeson).

This book is my third version of a Doc Savage chronology. I first wrote *The Bronze Age: an Alternate Doc Savage Chronology* (Fading Shadows, 1992). I then heavily revised my findings into *The Complete Chronology of Bronze* (Aces Publications, 1999). The late Philip José Farmer was the first writer to approach the Herculean task of constructing a chronology of the then published Doc Savage novels in the hardcover edition of *Doc Savage: His Apocalyptic Life* (Doubleday, 1973), a biography of the pulp hero. In the first paperback edition (Bantam Books, 1975), Mr. Farmer revised his chronology even further. In a later and slightly revised edition (Playboy Paperbacks, 1981), Mr. Farmer indicated that he was "not satisfied" with his chronology and was working on a revision Eventually other projects distracted him from pursuing this grand endeavor. In a letter published in *The Bronze Gazette* #13 (October 1994), Mr. Farmer conceded that he had abandoned all intentions of revising his chronology. In fact, he would eliminate the chronology if the book was ever reprinted.

Although my conclusions differ widely from Mr. Farmer's, his earlier chronology proved invaluable to me. His citing of numerous quotes relative to seasons, months and years indicated to me the specific chronological evidence from the majority of the novels. Mr. Farmer's calculation of the exact number of days for each exploit is extremely strong. I have only calculated the number of days for less than twenty novels. Otherwise, I have relied on Mr. Farmer's estimates. Many of these time estimates require some guesswork. For example, Lester Dent's *The Sea Angel* had Doc spending "several days" inside a submarine (chap. 18). A guess has to be made as to how many days transpired during Doc's underwater sojourn. The main events of *The Giggling Ghosts* occurred over eleven days, and then Doc spent an unspecified amount of days working in a hospital. Doc could have spent anywhere from a week to two days in the hospital. With the exception of certain items marked with an asterisk ("*"), all time estimates in my chronology come from Mr. Farmer's earlier conclusions. Since the original publication of *Doc Savage: His Apocalyptic Life*, there have been numerous articles on the Doc Savage series by other scholars in various pulp fanzines. The most significant of these articles have been authored by Will Murray, a man universally acknowledged to be the world's greatest living expert on Doc Savage. Of particular interest from a chronological point of view is "The Secret Kenneth Robesons" from *Duende* #2 (Winter 1976-77). Besides providing an invaluable guide to the authorship of the original pulp novels, Mr. Murray's article listed the original order in which the novels were submitted by the authors to the publisher as well as the submission dates.

Another milestone by Will Murray was "Tracking Doc Savage's Men" from *The Pulp Collector* (Vol. 2, #3, Winter 1987). This article listed the various travels of Doc Savage's assistants. When the novels are viewed in the correct order of submission, these travels are revealed to be strikingly consistent. Dale Balmer, another pulp scholar, wrote a later article on virtually the same subject, "The Adventures of Doc and the Fabulous Five: An Appearance Listing of the Major Characters from the Savage Saga" in *The Bronze Gazette* #7 (August 15, 1992). Mr. Balmer also wrote me a helpful letter pointing out some discrepancies in my original chronology relative to the whereabouts of Doc's assistants. I have made the necessary corrections based on Mr. Balmer's observations.

For various reasons, Philip José Farmer dismissed certain of the original pulp novels as "entirely fictional" exploits and refused to include them in his chronology. In the first version of his chronology, Mr. Farmer only extended this line of reasoning to *World's Fair Goblin* and *Land of Long Juju*. The second version of his chronology further removed *The Monsters*, *Land of Always Night* and *The Red Terrors* from the list of Doc's supposed genuine exploits. I have included all those novels in my chronology.

Doc Savage was presented as a world figure, who often became involved with foreign leaders and international disputes between countries. Sometimes these countries were unnamed, but various hints were dropped about their identities. On other occasions, a fictional name was used for a real-life leader or country. In some cases, the fictional rulers and states were fashioned from two sources. For example, Mungen, the dictator from *Peril in the North*, was probably a composite character based on Benito Mussolini and Vice-Premier Horia Sima of Rumania. In my analysis, I have indicated the real-life counterparts behind the fictional geopolitics of the Doc Savage series. I have also tried to reconcile the differences between known history and the deliberate distortions done in order to fictionalize actual people and events.

In creating this chronology, I have followed the pretense that Doc Savage is not a pulp character but actually a real-life person whose exploits have been slightly fictionalized. This line of reasoning had previously been followed by Mr. Farmer.

Of course, this premise is totally bogus. However, it is accordance with the traditions of the pulp magazine in which Doc Savage originally appeared. The original pulp novels often indicated that they were supposedly the "recorded" exploits of an "actual" person. *Rock Sinister* (chap. 1) professed that the real name of the South American country visited by Doc Savage can not be used. In *The Purple Dragon* (chap. 3), Doc Savage's magazine is on sale while he is having an adventure. In *No Light to Die By*, a letter is printed from Doc to the author of the pulp novels, Kenneth Robeson. Of course, Robeson is really a house name used to hide Lester Dent and the other authors of the series.

I now come to a very important point. Every chronological study of a fictional character is an exercise in accommodating reality to fiction. How many concessions should be made to reality? The biggest question here is the relationship between the chronological entries and their official months of publication. Mr. Farmer went to great lengths to discuss this whole issue in his chronology. First, he was going to apply a rigid rule that three months must separate a novel's placement in the chronology and its official month of publication. Then the rule was altered for two months for *The Squeaking Goblin*. Will Murray's "The Secret Kenneth Robesons" revealed all of the dates the novels were submitted to the publisher by Lester Dent and the other writers. Maybe we should use those dates to figure out when the novels took place. An iron rule could be adopted that no chronological entry could be made after a novel's submission date. I tried such a line of argumentation when I was doing an early draft of the original version of this chronology. This draft was a noble failure. Surprisingly, the chronological entries for the 1930s were not too bad. The major problem resulted when I attempted to place the novels written by Dent after Pearl Harbor (December 7, 1941). The first three novels written by Dent after America's entry into the war *(The Three Wild Men, The Fiery Menace* and *The Laugh of Death)* were set during the spring and summer of 1942.

Dent submitted the first of these novels in January 1942, the second in February and the third in April. I was faced with the prospect of either ignoring the seasonal references in the novels or placing them before the Pearl Harbor attack. The latter approach was out of the question. All of the novels contained firm affirmations of America's entry into World War II. Therefore, I decided to ignore the submission dates as inconvenient facts that would severely complicate matters.

There is another curious aspect about the Doc Savage novels from the 1940s. Many novels written during 1944-45 seemed to be set months after their submission. Novels written months before the Nazi surrender (May 1945) have references to the occupation of a defeated Germany and postwar reconstruction. An excellent example is *Cargo Unknown*, submitted in September 1944. Looking at these postwar references written long before Germany's defeat, I was coming to the conclusion that Lester Dent was doing a superb job of predicting the immediate future. A more likely explanation is that these postwar references were often editorial insertions made by the management at Street and Smith to keep Dent's manuscripts in tune with current events.

On the issue on how much distance to place between a novel's official month of publication and its chronological placement, I have adopted a simple rule. I will only forbid the glaring anomaly of a novel being placed after its official month of publication. I am well aware that the facts of the publishing would usually means that an issue dated August was available in July. On the other hand, an overabundance of such factual data prevents the establishment of a secure middle ground between fiction and reality.

The issue of editorial tampering with the various novels written by Dent and other writers should be addressed. *Doc Savage Magazine* was a team effort, and editors like John Nanovic did play an important role in its success. Therefore, I am generally going to accept obvious editorial alterations as gospel unless they butcher a novel beyond recognition. Some of the editorial alterations do affect chronological placement. For example, Will Murray's "The Secret Kenneth Robesons" revealed that a statement about the quarantine of Chemistry, the pet ape of Ham Brooks, in Dent's *The Metal Master* (chap. 15) was actually an editorial insertion.

Two of the novels, *Fear Cay* and *The Squeaking Goblin*, contain statements that imply that they transpired in 1934. If I accepted these references and then followed the submission order with a minimum amount of juggling, my chronology would have fallen apart by the time my entries reached the year of 1939. *Poison Island* would have ended up in September-October 1939. Even if the question of the official publication month was ignored (the novel was in the September 1939 issue), the novel's plot revolved around a scheme to cause a war between the United States and an unnamed country meant to be Nazi Germany. The novel described Europe as being at peace. This description rules out 1939 as the year of the novel because the fact that World War II broke out on September 1. In order to put the entire Doc Savage series in any coherent order, I had to dismiss the references to 1934 in *Fear Cay* and *The Squeaking Goblin*, and place them in 1933. Please note that many of Doc's adventures are extremely long. The longest, *The Red Terrors*, transpired during a period of 140 days. For me to be consistent with the length of Doc's pulp exploits, I would have to begin placing his adventures in at least 1932. A reference in *Quest of the Spider* to the events of *The Man of Bronze* transpiring a year ago forced me to begin in 1931.

My chronological decision to begin Doc's pulp exploits in 1931 did not give me much leeway to accommodate some of the references in Will Murray's novels. *Python Isle* clearly states that its events transpired in 1934. *The Jade Ogre* and *White Eyes* are intended to be set in 1935, although neither novel contains a direct reference to the year of their respective events. I was unable to place these novels in those years, and they are placed in the corresponding prior year. *Python Isle* was placed in 1933, *The Jade Ogre* and *White Eyes* in 1934. I was able to be more in accordance with Mr. Murray's intentions when it came to placing his four other novels *(The Whistling Wraith, The Forgotten Realm, Flight into Fear* and *The Frightened Fish)*.

Will Murray feels that editorial tampering interfered with many of the dates in the original pulp novels. There is much evidence to support this position. *The Purple Dragon* appeared in the September 1940 issue and contains a reference to "August 1, 1940" (chap. 2). *Five Fathoms Dead* was in the April 1946 issue, and is set in April. The year of the novel has to be 1946 because there are references to the end of World War II. Mr. Murray strongly believes that the month in which the novel was submitted by Lester Dent and the other pulp writers gives a better indication when the authors intended the novel to transpire. There is also evidence to strongly support Mr. Murray's view. The original pulp version of *The Sea Angel* contains footnotes missing from the paperback reprint. One of the footnotes connects the novel to sighting of an alleged monster in July 1936. Dent submitted the novel on July 31, 1936. Dent wrote *The Too-Wise Owl* in September 1941. Published in the March 1932 issue, the novel was set in September. The text also contained dates consistent with September 1941. These two novels by Dent apparently did not undergo any editorial alteration of their chronological references. On the other hand, Dent does seem to have set some novels consistently in periods that do not correspond to the months in which he wrote them. For example, *Poison Island* (submitted March 21, 1939) is set in September. Due to the fact that the novel was published in the September 1939 issue, it would be logical to assume that the September references were editorial alterations. When the novel was viewed in submission order, such an interpretation would appear to be incorrect. Dent submitted *Poison Island, The Stone Man, The Angry Ghost* (ghosted by William G. Bogart) and *The Dagger in the Sky*. The novel ghosted by Bogart was set in the summer, but all of Dent's original work was set in the autumn. Editorial tampering could have accounted for the autumn references in *Poison*

Island, but not for those in *The Stone Man*. That novel mentioned a college football game that only could have happened in autumn.

Some of the seasonal references in these novels were important elements of the plots. For example, *The Polar Treasure* was set in the summer because the Arctic ice would be more difficult to walk on (chap. 11). Dent wrote this novel in the winter of 1933. If he had set it in the winter, it would have been possible for Doc to reach civilization because the ice would be frozen. Another example is Dent's *The Squeaking Goblin*, a novel written in March 1933. The novel is set in a summer resort at the height of the tourist season. I suspect that Dent was aware of the publication schedule of the magazine, and tried to include seasonal references to coincide with it. Novels such as *The Polar Treasure*, *The Squeaking Goblin* and *The Stone Man* were all published in the seasons that matched the references inside the novels.

Although Lester Dent was the primary author of the pulp novels, he frequently used ghostwriters. Will Murray revised his findings about the role of the ghost writers since the original publication of "The Secret Kenneth Robesons." An updated version of his research into the authorship of the pulp novels was published as "An Index to the Doc Savage Novels" in *The Frightened Fish* (Bantam Books, July 1992). Based on that article, I have listed the author(s) of each novel for in the respective chronological entries. In addition to the ghost writers employed by Dent, Street and Smith contracted three writers to write novels independent of Dent's supervision. These writers were Laurence Donovan, Alan Hathway and William G. Bogart. Earlier Bogart had functioned also as a ghost writer for Dent, but three of his novels *(The Disappearing Lady, Target for Death* and *The Death Lady)* were written directly for the publishers.

Will Murray was extremely helpful and responsive when I discussed my chronological observations with him. He pointed out thing that I missed in several novels such as *The Sea*

Angel, *The Midas Man*, *The Giggling Ghosts* and *The Swooning Lady*. I am very grateful for all his help. Will Murray's assistance, however, should not be viewed as an endorsement of my entire chronological arrangement of the Doc Savage series. The chronological judgments made in this article are solely my decisions.

I should also single out the observations of Julian Puga Velasquez who has written insightful articles for *The Bronze Gazette* as Julian Puga V. After reading the previous 1999 version of the chronology, this skilled theorist pointed out to me certain factors that I overlooked in *The Devil Genghis* and *The Talking Devil* as well as a blatant error in the discussion of *Cargo Unknown*.

Unfortunately, I have indirectly spawned a myth about *Cargo Unknown*. The novel featured a crook, Merry John Thomas, who was twenty-eight years old. At one point, Renny noted that Thomas was about the same age as a character named Clark (chap. 6). This Clark was not Doc Savage (whose first name is Clark). I foolishly stated that Renny was referring to Doc in the 1999 edition of my chronology. This error was caught by a Doc Savage fan who had a copy of the pulp magazine. Since I was using the Bantam paperback edition, the fan assumed that the paperback reprint must have changed a reference to "Clark" from "Doc." A false story has since circulated that an editor at Bantam altered the pulp text. This inaccurate tale has surfaced in a least one important scholarly work on Doc Savage. Let me correct this misstatement of fact. There is no editorial alteration in the Bantam reprint of *Cargo Unknown*. The Bantam text is fine. I simply made a mistake.

Doc Savage has appeared in various unauthorized pastiches. If you examine Philip José Farmer's complete works, you will find Doc disguised under such aliases as Doc Caliban *(A Feast Unknown, The Mad Goblin)*, Doc Fauve ("The Grant-Robeson Papers") and even Shart the Shirtless *(A Barnstormer in Oz)*. I have not included any of the unauthorized pastiches by Mr. Farmer or other writers as canonical exploits in my chronological discussion. However, I do discuss some of them in a separate section. These pastiches, as well as a few theories that Doc may have played a role in other famous stories and one historical event, are discussed in a section called "Apocryphal Adventures." I have also included a section called "Parallel Lives: Doc Savage and The Shadow," which notes similarities between the lives of Doc and another notable pulp hero.

The most important factors in my chronology are references to months and seasons, the length of Doc's adventures, historical allusions and parallels, and the internal coherence of the series (e.g. appearances by Pat Savage, Habeas Corpus and Chemistry). Of less concern to me are exact matches between chronological placements and the various writers' description of foliage. For example, the majority of factors in the series as a whole pointed to the placement of *The Midas Man* in late October 1934. However, that novel contained references to "ivy vines" that were "thick and green," as well as "lawn grass" that was "uncut" (chap. 11). These remarks imply a different season than autumn, but they are overridden by other factors. Although meteorological data is important, its significance should not be an overwhelming factor in chronologies dealing with fictional characters. In the chronology argued in William S. Baring-Gould's *The Annotated Sherlock Holmes*, you will find superb examples of meteorological extremism. For example, Sir Arthur Conan Doyle's "The Adventure of the Lion's Mane" was set in July 1907. Although there are many chronological contradictions in the Holmes stories, there is nothing wrong with Doyle's date of 1907 in this story when it is compared to other tales in the series. The tale mentioned a "severe gale" off the coast of southern England. The late Mr. Baring-Gould assigned this story to July 1909 in his chronological arrangement of the Sherlock Holmes saga. The rationale for this placement was that Doyle's description of the gale was more consistent with a storm that transpired in July 1909. With the Doc Savage series, we are dealing with 190 novels written by more than one person. To apply arguments involving exact meteorological data could cause more problems than this chronology is seeking to solve. There are also meteorological impossibilities in Doc Savage. Laurence Donovan's *Murder Mirage* had snow in July. I am not concerned with an exact match between the fictional exploits of Doc Savage and real meteorological events. Lester Dent's *The King of Terror* was set sometime after the Japanese attack on Pearl Harbor. The novel mentioned that it was snowing on a Saturday. I placed this novel in a period of time where it could have snowed, but I didn't bother to check if it really snowed on the Saturday consistent with my chronological placement. In his chronology, Philip José Farmer placed *The Headless Man* by Alan Hathway on an exact date because of its reference to "a fingernail moon" (chap. 9). Since I placed this novel in a different year than Mr. Farmer, I did not concern myself with finding when the exact date when the new moon began.

A much different approach to meteorological data in the Doc Savage series is exercised in Jeff Deischer's *The Adventures of Doc Savage: A Definitive Chronology* (Green Eagle Publications, 2000). a book published after the first two versions of my Doc Savage chronology. In 2008, Mr. Deischer's text was revised and made available through Lulu. Mr. Deischer adopts a more rational perspective than the Sherlockian scholars, but I still have philosophical differences with the overall approach. However, one can not deny that Mr. Deischer's research was a major addition to Doc Savage scholarship. Of particular value is this formidable scholar's analysis of the "midnight sun" reference in *Peril in the North*.

How much was I influenced by Jeff Deischer in my revisions? Besides *Peril in the North*, I also shifted *Mad Eyes* based on his observations. I examined all his remarks about the radio plays before assigning them, but we differ widely on our placement of them.

Mr. Deischer was the first chronologist to include the original Doc Savage radio scripts done by Lester Dent for a program broadcast in 1934. These plays were not all finally published until recently. Half the plays appeared in print in *The Incredible Radio Exploits of Doc Savage: Volume 1* (Odyssey Publications, 1982). There was no "Volume 2." The first complete edition of the radio dramas was *Doc Savage: The Lost Radio Scripts of Lester Dent* (Moonstone, 2009). I have likewise included twenty-four of the twenty-nine radio plays in this revised Doc Savage chronology. Five radio dramas ("The Red Death," "The Golden Legacy," "The Valley of the Vanished," "Gray Spider" and "Polar Treasure") are actually adaptations of pulp novels. They aren't discussed in my chronology.

While consistent with Dent's pulp novels, the radio plays present a somewhat watered down version of Doc Savage. He battled more mundane threats than the great menaces of the 1930s. I have opted to place the bulk of these dramas early in Doc's career (sometimes even before the first pulp novel, *The Man of Bronze*). A few radio plays do involve events that reflected 1933-34 (e. g. actions against gold-hoarding in the United States). Inserting a couple of the radio plays caused me to adjust the months assigned to novels in early 1934. Besides the 1934 entries, the placements of *Mad Eyes, Peril in the North* and *The Talking Devil* are the only significant adjustment to the chronological arrangement of the novels that I proposed in 1999. I shifted *The Talking Devil* based on information from Julian Puga Velasquez about the original pulp magazine text. I did expand the commentary on *The Man Who Shook the Earth, Dust of Death, The Whistling Wraith, Fortress of Solitude, The Devil Genghis* and *The Yellow Cloud*. Some information was added to the "Apocryphal Adventures" and the "Parallel Lives" sections.

In many of the radio dramas, Doc's headquarters was situated in a skyscraper. Could this be different skyscraper from the unnamed structure generally believed to be the Empire State Building in the pulp novels? The Empire State Building didn't open until May 1931. The building from "The Sniper in the Sky" was clearly the same skyscraper that Doc utilized in the pulps, but the other radio scripts don't describe Doc's headquarters in any great detail. Therefore, I have utilized a theory (originally proposed by Albert Tonik) that Doc was once based in the Chrysler Building.

Throughout the series, there are many references to skills that Doc learned during various unrecorded travels around the world. Some of these trips would have occurred in Doc's youth before he enlisted in World War I. Others would have occurred during Doc's unrecorded adventures of the 1920s. In this chronology, I have tried to indicate which of Doc's travels transpire in this gap. These unrecorded activities included Doc's student days in Vienna, observations of jungle cats, and various adventures aboard his yacht. References to Doc being taught by the mystics of Asia, South Sea pearl divers and other unusual teachers are assumed to be relevant to the special training that he underwent from his birth to his decision to become a soldier in World War I. Doc's history before *Escape from Loki* is not covered in this chronology, but this period is occasionally commented on.

In the original pulp novels, there were usually little previews of the next adventure attached to the end of each novel. In most of the Bantam paperback reprints, these previews have been edited out. Those previews contained statements that would affect the chronological placement of novels. Like Philip José Farmer before me, I have generally ignored the chronological references in these previews. However, the previews at the conclusions of *The Three Wild Men* and *The Fiery Menace* are so tightly woven into the dialogue of the characters that they warranted discussion at the very least.

Doc supposedly would disappear for months to conduct experiments in the *Fortress of Solitude*. With all the adventures that he had in the 1930s, it is impossible for Doc to spend these long intervals at the Fortress. At best, he spent days or weeks there. I managed to allow Doc a stay of over a month before *Quest of the Spider*, and allocated a month for him to transform the Fortress from the version depicted in *Python Isle* to the Blue Dome presented in *Fortress of Solitude*. A reference in Harold A. Davis' *The Living Fire Menace* to Doc returning from a six-month stay at the Fortress was dismissed as an impossibility in my discussion of that novel. Besides the difficulty of creating a six-month gap in Doc's adventures during 1937, Davis' reference to a six-month stay would have placed Doc at the Fortress during the time when John Sunlight was encroaching upon the secret sanctuary in Lester Dent's *Fortress of Solitude*.

Due to so many writers being associated with the character of Doc Savage, blatant discrepancies with Lester Dent's primary facts crept into the description of the characters. Lawrence Donovan inaccurately described Habeas Corpus as being from Australia rather than Arabia. Because Harold A. Davis only read the early Doc Savage novels, he was unaware that Johnny had surrendered his glasses for a monocle once his damaged eye was cured in Dent's *The Man Who Shook the Earth*. Davis endowed Johnny with glasses in novels like *The Golden Peril*, *The Living Fire Menace*, *The Green Death* and *Merchants of Disaster*. Eventually Davis realized his error, and gave Johnny a monocle in *Devils of the Deep*. William Bogart inexplicably depicted the short Long Tom as tall in *The Death Lady*. I offer no complex theories to reconcile the above discrepancies. I merely ignore them because they are simply mistakes.

I generally cite chapters in order to allow the astute reader to verify my quotes. I originally used chapters because I reasoned some readers would have the original pulp while other would have the Bantam paperback reprints. The Doc Savage novels are currently being reprinted by Anthony Tollin's Sanctum Books. Will Murray has been revising the text to be in accord with Lester Dent's original manuscripts. In at least two reprints *(Mystery Under the Sea* and *Devil on the Moon)*, an extra chapter was inserted. I have indicated the dual chapters when necessary in my discussion.

In what order should the pulp novels be read? They should be read in the order that the novels ere submitted to the publisher. If you don't have a list of the novels in submission order, it's readily accessible in Jeff Deischer's book (available on www.lulu.com). I considered including such a list in this revision, but I didn't want to be accused of stealing the thunder of my talented fellow chronologist.

CHAPTER I
Chronology of Recorded Exploits

1. Escape from Loki
Published: August 1991
1918: March 31 to mid-July (107 days)
Author: Philip José Farmer

The date on which the novel began is clearly indicated: "The bright French afternoon sun of March 31, 1918, dazzled him" (chap. 1). "It was mid-June" when Doc plotted his escape from the German POW camp (chap. 17). The novel ended in mid-July when Doc and his friends got to the Italian lines (chap. 21). The dates mentioned in the novel are also consistent with the outline of Doc's World War I career in *Doc Savage: His Apocalyptic Life*.

There is an interesting connection between this novel and an event in Doc's later life. In *The Golden Man*, Paul Hest, a high intelligence official of a country that seemed to be Germany, knew the secret details of Doc's birth (chap. 13). Hest claimed to have a "complete dossier" on Doc and his men (chap. 18). In *Escape from Loki*, Baron Von Hessel revealed that German Intelligence had a lengthy dossier on Doc and his father (chap. 8).

There are at least two references to other pulp series from the 1930s. One of Doc's tutors is revealed to have been Dekka Lan Shan of Tibet, a man with a grandson bearing the same name (chap. 16). The grandson is a character from "The Sapphire Death," a serial that ran in *Argosy* (starting June 10, 1933). "The Sapphire Death" is part of the Peter the Brazen series written by George F. Worts (under the pseudonym of Loring Brent). The entire series has been collected in a two volume set, *The Compleat Adventures of Peter the Brazen* (The Battered Silicon Dispatch Box, 2003).

Doc and his men were joined in their escape by Beeton of Australia, O'Brien of Ireland and Cohen of Brooklyn (chap. 18). Cohen is further described as a member of the French Foreign Legion. He also bore the nickname of "The Fighting Yid." I don't know if Beeton is derived from any characters in the pulps, but Cohen is meant to be Abraham Cohen from W. Wirt's Jimmie Cordie series in *Argosy*. Although most of Cordie's assistants served in the Foreign Legion, Mr. Farmer erred in making Cohen a former member of that military association.

As for O'Brien, there are two possible candidates. An adventurer named O'Brien was a member of the French Foreign Legion in G. K. Chesterton's "The Secret Garden" from *The Innocence of Father Brown* (1911). There was also a former World War I soldier, O'Brien, who assisted the title character of Eustace Hale Ball's *The Scarlet Fox* (1927), a collection of pulp stories that first appeared in *Black Mask* during 1923.

Escape from Loki also mentioned that one of Doc's tutors was "a Persian Sufi, Hajji Abdu el-Yezdi" (chap. 14). Christopher Carey's "Farmer's *Escape from Loki*: A Closer Look" from *The Bronze Gazette* #17 (February 1996) identified Hajji as a philosopher created by Sir Richard Francis Burton in his book, *The Kasidah of Haji Abdu* (1880). Mr. Farmer changed the spelling of Haji's first name slightly, and added the "el-Yezdi" because Burton's character was a native of Yezd Province. Burton pretended that Haji was a real person, and the book was merely a "translation" of the fictitious philosopher's Persian writings. Another one of Doc's tutors was supposedly an Australian aborigine, Writjitandel of the Wantella people (chap. 12). This aborigine is a character in Arthur Upfield's

No Footprints in the Bush (1940), a novel in the Inspector Napoleon Bonaparte series. Mr. Farmer altered one letter in the spelling of the name of Upfield's character. Upfield called the aborigine Writjitandil.

Escape From Loki (chap. 3), mentioned that Clark Savage Sr. was "exploring deep inside Brazil." For a discussion of exactly what Clark Sr. found there, see the "Apocryphal Adventures" section.

Note: From 1919 to April 1931 are largely Doc's missing years. After World War I ended with the armistice of November 1918, Doc returned to his medical studies. *Resurrection Day* revealed that Doc could bring a man back to life. This process involved "the use of a new element in a combination which takes at least ten years to develop" (chap. 2). I have placed Doc's adventure in early 1936 (see entry #81). The interval of a decade would means Doc, or possibly his father, had begun developing the element in 1926. It may be relevant that 1926 was also the year when Doc received his M. D. (according to Philip José Farmer's *Doc Savage: His Apocalyptic Life)*.

References in the novels indicate that he spent part of his time studying subjects in Vienna. Mr. Farmer believed that these studies happened after Doc got his M. D. According to *The Man Who Was Scared* (chap. 14), Doc studied neurology in Vienna with a friend named Gaines (chap. 16). In *Repel* (also known as *The Deadly Dwarf)*, Doc conferred with a group of noted scientists (chap. 18). The spokesman of this group was one of Doc's former teachers. The scientist was described as "a renowned specialist in electrochemistry as applied to astronomy, from Vienna." Among Doc's scientific friends was Baron Orest Karl Lestzky, a surgeon living in Vienna *(The Golden Man,* chap. 13).

Hell Below mentioned that Doc as a student at a Vienna university had encountered as rather sinister individual (chap. 11). Among Doc's fellow students was Vogel Plattenheber alias Der Hase ("the Hare"). Plattenheber would supposedly rise years later to an important role in the Nazi propaganda machine. Plattenheber was an emaciated man falsely rumored to be crippled in one foot. By contrast, the real-life Nazi Propaganda Minister, Paul Joseph Goebbels, was an emaciated man with a genuine clubfoot. Since Goebbels was a student at Heidelberg instead of Vienna, it would appear that Plattenheber merely resembled Goebbels instead of really being that notorious figure. The Nazi leaders were rumored to employ doubles. Perhaps Plattenheber was Goebbels' double.

While studying in Vienna, Austria, Doc may have taken an occasional holiday in Switzerland. *The Speaking Stone* (chap. 9) revealed that Doc was familiar with Swiss mountains: "It reminded the bronze man of the marvelously engineered tunnels and mountain paths on Pilatus and the Jungaru in Switzerland." Doc had originally climbed Swiss mountains in his youth (*Escape from Loki*, chap. 16).

Doc's yacht, the *Seven Seas*, appeared in three adventures of the 1930s, *The Fantastic Island*, *The Land of Fear* and *The Red Terrors*. According to *The Red Terrors* (chap. 9), the yacht "had broken through arctic ice after lost explorers, hauled refugees out of the Orient and gone to the South Seas for marine exploration." Since the yacht did none of these things in its two earlier appearances, we can assume that these activities were unrecorded adventures in the 1920s. Doc rarely relied on his yacht for transportation in the 1930s. He generally traveled by air during that decade. The Asian refugees were probably fleeing China which was experiencing turmoil caused by the various feuding warlords of the 1920s. It is possible that another of Doc's aides, Renny Renwick might have been involved in the struggles between the various warlords. In *The King Maker* (chap. 9), Renny remarked "I've been in a few wars in my time…" We know Renny was in World War I, but what other struggles could he have participated before the early 1930s? The conflict between the Chinese warlords would be the obvious candidate. Renny also superintended the installation of a nitrate plant in Chile and "handled many engineering jobs in many parts of the world before joining Doc's crew of trouble-busters" *(The Man Who Shook the Earth*, chap. 13). Renny also worked on "a South American bridge job" *(The Red Skull*, chap. 15) during this period. In his visits to the South Seas, Doc may have renewed his acquaintance with the South Sea pearl divers who taught him how to hold his breath for long period sometime before World War I. Doc's familiarity with the pearl divers was first mentioned in *The Man of Bronze* (chap. 19).

In *The King Maker*, Doc Savage assumed the identity of a pilot named Champ Dugan in order to join the air force of a Balkan country. Doc had references for his false identity supplied to him by prominent men from China, India, Persia (Iran) and Turkey (chap. 15). These men were "indebted" to Doc. Services for these prominent men were probably performed by Doc in the 1920s. On the other hand, Doc could have befriended at least some of these men before his service in World War I. Doc had at least one powerful patron during his boyhood adventures. According to *Mystery Under the Sea* (chap. 2), the Khedive of Egypt gave Doc a valuable rug as a token of appreciation. The Egyptian dynasty abandoned the title of Khedive for that of King in 1914. The last Khedive of Egypt was Abbas II (1892-1914). Doc could not have received the rug any later than 1914. Doc would have been then thirteen years old. Another of Doc's friends in the Middle East was Hafid the Syrian, who lived in Amman, Jordan (known in the 1930s as Transjordania or Trans-Jordan). In *Murder Mirage* (chap. 14), Hafid mentioned that Doc had been "of great service" to his people in the past. This service was probably done around the same time Doc befriended the Khedive of Egypt. At that time, Amman would have been part of the Ottoman Empire.

Various prominent European individuals befriended by Doc were formed into an informal network of information during the 1920s. Doc alluded to this informal network in *The King Maker* (chap. 8): "Long ago, I arranged with certain men, closely in touch with the political situation in each European country, to keep me informed by cable of developments."

It was sometime in the late 1920s that Doc constructed his Arctic retreat, the Fortress of Solitude. He may have discovered the original site of the Fortress during his search for lost explorers in the Arctic. His long periods of scientific research at the Fortress for periods of months mainly happened in the 1920s. In the 1930s, he didn't have time for long stays there.

Doc also spent some times in the jungles of the world during these missing years:

"He had seen great jungle cats slide through dense leafage in that strangely noiseless fashion, and had copied it himself" (*The Man of Bronze*, chap. 4). "Doc had devoted study to this business of stalking; he had observed the great predatory creatures of the jungle, masters of the hunt" (*The Lost Oasis*, chap. 9). Doc's studies of jungle cats probably began in his youth, but he most likely perfected his method of copying their movements in the 1920s. There are references in *The Derelict of Skull Shoal* that Doc had visited the jungles in of South America for a different purpose, the study of native dialects: "I've spent many months exploring the jungles of northern Brazil, and in the Guineas. And I have studied the language before that" (a remark by Doc Savage, chap. 12). "The truth was that he had spent many months doing exploration work in the northern Amazon section, the Guinea back jungles, the whole territory. Part of his work had been making sound transcripts of the native dialects, studying them, classifying them. Later, he had lectured on the subject, and done a short book and a few scientific articles" (chap. 13). Doc probably studied native dialects first during the training of his youth.

I must confess being initially misled by the "Guineas" comment. Guinea is a country in Africa. The resourceful Jeff Deischer straightened me out. "Guineas" is actually meant to represent the Guiana countries in South America. Doc must have visited these South American in Brazil and the Guianas in the 1920s to study both jungle cats and native dialects. Monk Mayfair and Ham Brooks probably accompanied Doc on these expeditions. Monk mentioned that he saw piranha eat a native once *(The Men Vanished,* chap. 10). This incident could have happened in the Amazon jungle during Doc's study of native dialects. Ham made a remark that he had been in "a lot of tropical jungles" *(Brand of the Werewolf,* chap. 10). This statement suggests that Ham was with Doc during these jungle travels. Renny also seems to have been with Doc during these jungle adventures: "Renny had penetrated the thick jungles of the upper Amazon. He had explored in rankest Africa" *(The Land of Terror,* chap. 17). Renny's African journeys may have been without Doc.

Resurrection Day (chap. 1) mentioned that Ham almost got a crooked lawyer, Proudman Shaster, disbarred. This incident probably transpired in the 1920s. An unrecorded incident involving Ham also probably tool place during the 1920s. In *The Munitions Master* (chap. 10), Ham "recalled a case he had once prosecuted in Haiti." The case concerned "Zombi legends" in some fashion. Haiti was under the military occupation of the United States from 1915 until 1934. Although Ham was with the French Foreign Legion in *Escape from Loki* (chap. 6), he must have eventually transferred to the American army. Ham probably did not leave the United States army immediately when World War I ended. In his role as a Brigadier General, he was possibly assigned to Haiti in the early 1920s. There his training as a lawyer must have caused him to be assigned as a prosecutor in a military court martial. Another of Doc's men may also have been involved in this case. Johnny Littlejohn had "made an extensive study of voodoo in the southern United States, Haiti and Africa" *(Quest of the Spider,* chap. 8).

Johnny also led "an expedition into northern Tibet to hunt dinosaur eggs" *(Meteor Menace,* chap. 11). This probably happened in the 1920s. In 1923, Roy Chapman Andrews had stunned the scientific community by discovering fossilized dinosaur eggs in Mongolia, a palace not noted for fossils. Johnny must have been trying to repeat the same feat in Tibet. Several references in the early novels indicate that Johnny was head of the natural science department at a well known university during this period.

By 1929, Doc had created the Crime College in upstate New York. The college was a unique institution that reformed criminals through radical means. Doc abducted crooks and had them secretly taken to the College. There surgeons performed brain operations which destroyed the memories of the criminals. The former crooks were taught a useful trade and given new identities. Most of them were employed by Doc in different parts of his financial empire. Several belonged to a private intelligence network which gathered information for Doc.

The Crime College's existence since at least 1929 was established in *The Purple Dragon*. In 1929, Doc had tangled with a gangster whom the novel called Pal Hatrack. This gangster had been "one of the really big shots of prohibition days" and possibly "the brains behind organized crime in all parts of the country" (chap. 5). Hatrack employed minions in Chicago and New York. Many of them were sent to the Crime College in 1929. *The Purple Dragon* was set in 1940. By this time, Hatrack had died in prison after serving several years, and criminal associates were seeking the crime czar's wealth which had been stashed in various safety deposit boxes around the country. Harold A. Davis ghosted this novel for Lester Dent. The plot of a gangster's hidden wealth had been borrowed by Dent from another of his pulp series. Dent had written a series of tales about a detective named Lee Nace. In "The Diving Dead" from *Ten Detective Aces* (September 1933), Nace fought gangsters who were looking for a stash of hidden loot which belonged to Mel Caroni, a Chicago gangster recently jailed for tax evasion. Caroni was clearly a fictionalized version of Al Capone. "The Diving Dead" was later reprinted in *Pulp Review* #11 (July 1993). The reader is now left with an intriguing question Can we pretend that Pal Hatrack was "really" Capone? Capone was jailed for tax evasion in 1931. Unlike Hatrack, he didn't die in prison. He was released from prison in November 1939. Although Capone was very much alive in 1940, his mind had been destroyed by syphilis during his imprisonment. He could not distinguish truth from falsehood. If he had hidden loot in secret places throughout the United States, he would not have remembered their locations.

The Capone mob was primarily based in Chicago, but the organization had ties to New York gangsters. In July 1928, Capone's operatives in New York successfully murdered a local gangland boss, Frankie Yale.

1929 is an important year in Capone's criminal career. In May, Capone allowed himself to be arrested for carrying a gun in Philadelphia. Sentenced to a year in prison. he was released in March 1930, and was eventually convicted of tax evasion in October 1931. It is generally believed that Capone arranged his 1929 imprisonment because he was fearful that gangland rivals were planning to kill him. Prison was a safe haven from assassination. However, making him the same person as Pal Hatrack gives us a different explanation. Capone concocted his own incarceration to prevent Doc Savage from sending him to the Crime College. Prison was preferable to the fate suffered by the crime czar's henchmen. It was probably during his 1929 battle with Al Capone that Doc spent "two weeks working on the eyes of a blind apple peddler in Chicago" *(Repel*, a.k.a. *The Deadly Dwarf,* chap. 6). After Doc made the beggar see, he turned down "an offer of a quarter of a million to do a plastic surgery job on a rich guy who wanted a younger looking face."

Another of Doc's assistants, Monk Mayfair, spent some time among the Ojibway Indians of Michigan probably in the late 1920s. Monk was familiar with the Ojibway language and their tribal dances *(The Devil's Playground*, chap. 13).

By 1931, Doc had gained an important friend in the political circles of New York City. In The *Land of Terror*, It was stated that Doc had performed a delicate heart operation upon "the leading political boss, the most influential man in city government" (chap. 4).

Doc also became involved in the construction of his skyscraper headquarters as the 1920s ended. Although it is never actually identified as such, it is clear that the skyscraper was meant to be the Empire State Building, which opened on May 1, 1931. Doc's role in the building's design is explained in *Spook Hole* (chap. 6): "When this extremely modern skyscraper had been erected not many years before, Doc had taken a considerable part in its design. As a matter of fact, the architectural designs had been prepared by his colleague, Renny." *The Too-Wise Owl* (chap. 1) would also assert that Doc owned the building.

Doc's father, Dr. Clark Savage Sr., played an important role in all of Doc's activities up until early 1931. Doc apparently attended performance at the New York Metropolitan Opera with his father during this period. The Savages maintained a regular box there *(The Spook Legion,* chap. 8).

Sometime in the 1920s, Doc first met Charlotte d'Alaza, a ruthless female financier. Doc was "a very young man, his ideals blooming like tulips, when he first met Charlotte" *(King Joe Cay*, chap. 5). It is possible that Clark Sr. was romantically involved with Charlotte. According to *Escape from Loki* (chap. 15), Doc's father had mistresses.

Clark Sr. was murdered "three weeks" before the events of Doc's first recorded exploit *(The Man of Bronze,* chap. 1). By my chronological arrangement, Doc's father died in April 1931. Doc was at the Fortress of Solitude at this time. In *The Land of Terror* (chap. 5), Doc stated that he now occupied "the offices formerly used by my father on the eighty-sixth floor." One of the friends of Doc's father, Oliver Wording Bittman, claimed to have even been there when the elder Savage was alive. In early April 1931, Clark Sr. must have shown some friends around the eight-sixth floor before the building was officially opened to the public. Bittman was one of these friends. Clark Sr. also arranged for the floor to be furnished with equipment and possessions belonging to him and his son in April. Clark Sr. would have discussed the proposed layout with Doc before he went to the Fortress. When Doc returned to New York in *The Man of Bronze*, he found the Empire State Building already officially opened. His father had fully equipped the eighty-sixth floor shortly before his demise.

I have placed some of the he radio plays in the missing years of the 1920s. In these dramas, Doc had his headquarters in a New York skyscraper, but this isn't necessarily the disguised portrayal of Empire State Building that appeared in the pulp novels.

2. "Monk Called it Justice" (radio play)
Air Date: June 23, 1934
1928 (1 day)
Author: Lester Dent

Doc was described as a "young scientist." He would be about twenty-seven years old. Only Monk accompanied him on this adventure.

The story was set in Rhodesia (the future Zimbawe) and involved an attempt to cause a native revolt by a foreign power unfriendly to Britain. The agent of this unnamed foreign power, Von Guytersmith, was a German. However, this doesn't necessarily mean that Germany was behind the unrest. Von Guytersmith could have easily been working for the Soviet Union. Since I assigned this drama to 1928, then the Soviets are the likely culprits. The Nazis didn't achieve power until 1933.

Furthermore, Hitler's ideology would have precluded causing trouble in the British colonies in 1933-34. His book, *Mein Kampf*, argued that Britain was Germany's natural ally. Hitler also viewed Africans as racially inferior. In the early years of the Third Reich, Hitler courted the British Empire.

Monk was wounded in the shoulder. Doc and Monk weren't wearing any of the bullet-proof clothing that appeared in the pulp novels.

I must divulge an ulterior motive in dating this radio episode. In this adventure, Doc stopped a native revolt in Rhodesia. In 1930, the Land Apportionment Act was passed that laid the foundation of segregation in Rhodesia. If the radio play was assigned after 1930, Doc could be accused of supporting apartheid in Rhodesia. In 1928, Doc must have hoped that a peaceful solution in Rhodesia would cause the white settlers to adopt more tolerant policies. Unfortunately, Doc was wrong.

3. "The Box of Fear" (radio play)
Air Date: May 19, 1934
1929: April (1 day)
Author: Lester Dent

Doc and Monk were accumulating evidence against gangsters based in New York and Chicago. I view this exploit as part of the conflict between Doc and "Pal Hatrack," discussed at length in the **Note** after entry #1. The choice of April as the month of this adventure is based on Al Capone's incarceration on a concealed weapons charge in May 1929. This must have transpired early in Doc's career because he utilized tear gas rather than his customary sleep gas. Tear gas was used as early as 1915.

4. "The Phantom Terror" (radio play)
Air Date: May 26, 1934
1929: June (1 day)
Author: Lester Dent

Doc, Monk and Ham were in this exploit. Friends of a New York gangster Chuck Andrews sought revenge on Doc. A "few weeks ago," Anderson had been convicted in New York "when Doc started to clean up the rackets." Chuck Anderson was probably Chuck, the crook captured by Doc in "The Box of

Fear." I've allowed for the passage of some extra weeks in order for Chuck to be tried and sentenced. Although the Crime College was in existence in 1929, Chuck Anderson wasn't sent there. Doc must have felt that a public trial for Anderson would do more to reduce crime in New York.

Ham noted that the evening was "jolly warmish."

Part of this drama was set in Doc's laboratory, but the text doesn't identify it as being located in a skyscraper.

5. "The Red Lake Quest" (radio play)
Air Date: February 24, 1934
1929: December (1 day)
Author: Lester Dent

Doc, Monk and Ham visit northern Canada during a blizzard. As Jeff Deischer has skillfully pointed out, the two chemicals used by Doc in this radio play also surfaced in *The Polar Treasure* (chap. 6). When the two chemicals were mixed together, they form a terrible odor.

6. "Needle in a Chinese Haystack" (radio play)
Air Date: May 26, 1934
1930: February (1 day)
Author: Lester Dent

Doc and Monk were in China searching for Henry Lucknow, a corrupt American banker who had embezzled the money of his investors. Lucknow's financial irregularities were probably exposed during the stock market crash of October 1929.

7. "Mantrap Mesa" (radio play)
Air Date: June 2, 1934
1930: March (1 day)
Author: Lester Dent

Doc and Monk investigate counterfeiting along the American-Mexican border.

Although Ham was absent from this exploit, it's possible that he later met Nola Stanborn, the heroine of this drama. Maybe she made a future visit to New York. In *Measures for a Coffin* (chap. 14), Ham rambled incoherently about a woman named Nola.

Doc continued to employ tear gas instead of sleep gas.

8. "The White-Haired Devil" (radio play)
Air Date: June 30, 1934
1930: April (1 day)
Author: Lester Dent

Doc and Monk were in Venezuela. The case was tied to lawsuits that began at the start of the Depression in October 1929.

9. "Poison Cargo" (radio play)
1930: May (1 day)
Author: Lester Dent
Air Date: July 21, 1934

Doc and Monk were in Brazil. The plot of this episode concerned a poison plant called *rotonne*. They were references to recent discoveries concerning its toxic nature. I have been unable to verify anything about this plant. If *rotonne* really exists, then historic scientific experiments concerning it would affect the chronological placement of this adventure.

Note: On May 28, 1930, the Chrysler Building was completed. Doc made this structure his headquarters before moving into the Empire State Building in 1931. This assertion is a modified version of a theory expounded in Albert Tonik's "Chronology of *The Man of Bronze*" from *Doc Savage Club Reader* #7 (1979?).

10: "The Evil Extortionists" (radio play)
Air Date: March 10, 1934
1930: June (1 day)
Author: Lester Dent

Only Doc and Monk appear.

Doc's usage of a private airplane hangar rather than the Hidalgo Trading Company warehouse is consistent with my placement of this novel in 1930. Doc also utilized tear gas (as in "The Box of Fear") rather than the sleep gas from the pulp novels.

11. "Death Had Blue Hands" (radio play)
Air Date: March 31, 1934
1930: June (1 day)
Author: Lester Dent

Doc and Monk travel to Wyoming. The murder victim, Jud Harmon, hoarded gold. The Gold Confiscation Act of 1933 outlawed such hoarding, but nothing in the radio script indicated such procedure was considered illegal. Therefore, the law could arguably be set before the congressional legislation was passed.

12. "Find Curly Morgan" (radio play)
Air Date: July 28, 1934
1930: July (1 day)
Author: Lester Dent

Only Monk appeared with Doc. Usage of tear gas again by Doc (employed earlier in "The Box of Fear," "Mantrap Mesa" and "The Evil Extortionists") suggested that Doc had not yet perfected his sleep gas.

Doc had a file on all crooks living in New York City. His telephone number in this adventure was Empire 1-7900. According to my theory, this would be his number at a Chrysler Building address.

13. "The Sinister Sleep" (radio play)
Air Date: April 7, 1934
1930: July (1 day)
Author: Lester Dent

The story only featured Doc and Monk. Jeff Deischer conceived a brilliant theory about this episode. The "artificial sleep" developed by Jerebella Collins, a female chemist, in this exploit may have been modified by Doc to become his anesthetic gas featured in the pulp novels.

14. "Radium Scramble" (radio play)
Air Date: March 24, 1934
1930: August (1 Day)
Author: Lester Dent

Only Doc and Monk appear. Doc was now using sleep gas rather than tear gas. I am assuming that was an improved version of the gas from "The Sinister Sleep."

15. "The Too-Talkative Parrot" (radio play)
Air Date: April 28, 1934
1930: August (1 day)
Author: Lester Dent

Doc and Monk visited a "summer hotel" in Maine.

16. "The Growing Wizard" (radio play)
Air Date: August 4, 1934
1930: August (1 day)
Author: Lester Dent

The storyline revolving around the growing of rubber plants seem to transpire in the spring on summer. References were made to the "late Burbank." This was Luther Burbank, the botanist who died in 1926.

Only Monk appeared with Doc.

17. "The Blue Angel" (radio play)
Air Date: May 6, 1934
1930: September (1 day)
Author: Lester Dent

As usual, Monk was the only assistant to appear. He met a female detective, Mabel. James of the Middle States Detective Agency. This may be the Mabel whom Monk mentioned in *The Monkey Suit* (chap. 4). In that later novel, Monk muttered Mabel's name while regaining consciousness.

18. "The Green Ghost" (radio play)
Air Date: May 12, 1934
1930: September (1 day)
Author: Lester Dent

Monk was the only aide present. He shot a crook twice in the shoulders. This adventure clearly preceded Doc's usage of mercy bullets (first mentioned in *The Phantom City*).

19. "The Impossible Bullet" (radio play)
Air Date: April 21, 1934
1930: October (1 day)
Author: Lester Dent

Monk and Doc were in the Ozark Mountains near the Oklahoma-Arkansas border Monk may have been returning to his roots. According to *Jiu San* (chap. 5), Monk was born in Tulsa, Oklahoma.

20. "The Oilfield Ogres" (radio play)
Air Date: July 7, 1934
1930: October (1 day)
Author: Lester Dent

Doc and Monk were in Oklahoma. I have placed "The Impossible Bullet" and "The Oilfield Ogres" together in order to make them part of the same trip.

In the conclusion, Monk ticked a crook into burning to death. Doc indicated concern. But does not openly criticize Monk. The announcer then concluded the adventure by staying that it is Doc's policy not to take human life. This was true in 1934 when the radio play was set, but it wasn't true in 1930.

Doc would later go through a violent period after the death of his father (in *The Man of Bronze*) and one of his teachers

(The Land of Terror). Probably before these shocking deaths, Doc was more restrained in handling criminals. Therefore, it would be logical for Doc to be stunned by a ruthless act of Monk in 1930. Later Doc would become more vicious. Eventually, he controlled these brutal tendencies and evolved a non-lethal methodology of crime-fighting.

21. The Man of Bronze
Published: March 1933
1931: May (25 days)
Author: Lester Dent

There have been some very erudite debates about the opening scenes of this novel. A sniper climbed a skyscraper under construction, and attempted to shoot Doc who was in his own neighboring skyscraper headquarters. If Doc was in the Empire State Building, then what was the neighboring skyscraper? Philip José Farmer placed this novel in March-April 1931 by arguing that Doc had moved into the Empire State Building before its official opening in May. The unfinished structure where the sniper lurked was identified by Mr. Farmer as the unfinished tower atop the Chrysler Building.

Albert Tonik's "Chronology of *The Man of Bronze*" from Doc *Savage Club Reader* #7 (1979?) made some important modifications to Mr. Farmer's theories.

Because the tower on the Chrysler Building had really been completed in July 1930, Mr. Tonik came up with the clever idea that Doc initially made his base in the Chrysler Building during the events of *The Man of Bronze*, and then moved to the Empire State Building for all subsequent novels. The sniper was situated on the then incomplete Empire State Building. Mr. Tonik also shifted the entire novel to the month of March through some rather ingenious usage of the meteorological data in the novel. Mr. Tonik's evidence for this belief was based on references to phases of the moon and other factors too lengthy to repeat here.

Although I once sided with Mr. Tonik's theories, I now assert that Doc always resided in the Empire State Building from *The Man of Bronze* onwards. I place the novel's events in May shortly after the building opened. What was the other skyscraper utilized by the sniper? It was a building destroyed before it was ever completed. In the pulp world of Doc Savage, the bronze adventurer occasionally encountered master criminals with super-weapons capable of destroying skyscrapers. As we will shortly see, there is a gap of about a year of unrecorded activity from July 1931 to May 1932.

During this time period, Doc fought a criminal who committed the crime of obliterating a neighboring skyscraper under construction *The Man of Bronze* was the first novel to feature the fictional Central American country of Hidalgo, the source of Doc's hidden treasury of Mayan wealth. Hidalgo is the name of a state in Mexico, but it is quite clear that Doc Savage's Hidalgo is meant to be a separate country. Although Will Murray has found evidence in Lester Dent's notes that Hidalgo was based on Nicaragua, I have opted to identify Hidalgo with Guatemala. This identification results mainly from the fact that Guatemala, the only country besides Mexico and Belize (British Honduras in 1931), with a large population of Mayan Indians, was economically sound during the 1930s. In fact, it was operating on a balanced budget from 1933 to 1944. When Jorge Ubico assumed power in 1931, Guatemala was on the verge of economic collapse. Yet, he managed within a couple of years to put Guatemala ion a sound financial footing. In the Doc Savage series, fictional Hidalgo was financially prosperous due to secret shipments of Mayan gold. It is fairly easy to pretend that Guatemala's economic stability was due to the Mayan gold from Doc's secret hoard.

Jorge Ubico was inaugurated as President of Guatemala on February 14, 1931. He ruled until 1944, I theorize that Dent's fictional President Carlos Avispa of Hidalgo was "really" Ubico. Both Ubico and his fictional counterpart were noted for their friendship with Mayan Indians. One major objection to pretending that Ubico was Avispa is that the real-life historical figure was short while Avispa was tall. The significant difference in height can be "rationalized" as part of the effort to "disguise" the true location of Doc's wealth. On other points, Avispa and Ubico do resemble one another. Both were athletic men. Avispa's age was given as "near fifty" in *The Man of Bronze* (chap. 10). Ubico was fifty-three in 1931. Another objection is that the Avispa regime had been in power for "two years" at the time of *The Man of Bronze* (chap. 9). During the events of Doc's first adventure, the Ubico regime would only have been in power for three months. I will speculate that Dent changed months into years in a further effort to hide the identity of Hidalgo. Twenty years prior to the events of *The Man of Bronze* (chap. 2), Doc's father discovered a hidden Mayan civilization, the Valley of the Vanished, in Hidalgo. According to my chronological arrangement, this discovery would have taken place in 1911. In the same time period, Doc's father supposedly used his medical skill to save the life of Carlos Avispa. The novel claimed that this event happened when Avispa was "an unimportant revolutionist hiding out in the mountains" (chap. 10). The real-life Ubico was never a revolutionary, but he was the governor of Retalhuleu, a Guatemalan state near the Mexican border, during 1911-19. During his administration, he launched a successful campaign to eradicate yellow fever in the area under his jurisdiction. He performed this endeavor at much risk to his personal health. It could be speculated that Doc's father used his medical knowledge to prevent Jorge Ubico from succumbing to yellow fever. The theories advanced here about Jorge Ubico and Guatemala were derived from my article, "The Search for Hidalgo," in *Golden Perils* #18 (Summer 1991).

Although I argue that the country of Hidalgo was really Guatemala, what does this mean for the name of Doc's warehouse, the Hidalgo Trading Company, from later novels? Was it really called the Guatemala Trading Company? No, I think it was still called the Hidalgo Trading Company. Rumors of Doc's hidden wealth would eventually reach the criminal underworld. By naming his warehouse after a Mexican state, Doc was hoping to create the belief that his secret Central American wealth emanated from Mexico instead of Guatemala. As Albert Tonik has noted, *The Man of Bronze* makes reference to an "epidemic known as 'parrot fever' that swept the United States a year or two ago" (chap. 17). "Parrot fever" was an epidemic in 1929-1930.

Note: *The Land of Terror* (chap. 1) mentioned that Doc had "some weeks ago turned over to the surgical profession a new and vastly improved method of performing delicate brain operations." Doc must have done this in the early days of June 1931.

22. The Land of Terror
Published: April 1933
1931: June 12-July 8 (27 days)
Author: Lester Dent

The novel was set in the spring: "The balmy spring breeze, whipping along the narrow concrete path, wafted the vile gray cloud to one side" (chap. 1). The novel began on a Friday (chap. 1). The death of Doc's father happened "recently" (chap. 5). Doc employed his most violent methods of fighting crime in this novel. He slaughtered criminals right and left. The violence would be toned down in the next exploit (almost a year later), but Doc didn't finalize his non-lethal methods of fighting crime until *The Phantom City*.

Note: for the remainder of July 1931, Doc was involved in an unrecorded adventure. This happened in New Zealand, where Doc went at the conclusion of *The Land of Terror* (chap. 22). Doc gained the gratitude of the New Zealand government for some unknown service. The grateful government granted Doc a commission that was valid in their Pacific protectorate of Western Samoa. See the discussion of *Repel ((The Deadly Dwarf)*, entry #82). It would be logical to assume that Doc's commission was valid in New Zealand as well This New Zealand adventure must have happened in July 1931.

23. "The Sniper in the Sky" (radio play)
Air Date: March 3, 1934
1932: August (1 day)
Author: Lester Dent

In the manner of the assassination attempt from *The Man of Bronze*, another sniper tried to shoot at Doc from the nearby unfinished skyscraper A Jeff Deischer has noted, "The Sniper in the Sky" had to transpire after *The Man of Bronze* because the glass in Doc's headquarters was now bullet-proof.

There can't be too much distance between *The Man of Bronze* and "The Sniper in the Sky." The skyscraper used by the different was at the same level of completion. In both exploits, it had reached the eightieth floor.

Note: During the gap from the remainder of August to May 1932, Doc was involved in unrecorded adventures. The first of two unrecorded adventures are hypothetical due to my need to explain chronological inconsistencies in the Doc Savage saga. One adventure involved the destruction of the unfinished skyscraper used by the snipers in *The Man of Bronze* and "The Sniper in the Sky." It is possible that the skyscraper was eliminated by former associates of the deceased criminal Kar from *The Land of Terror*. Kar's weapon, the Smoke of Eternity, was an incredibly powerful acid. One of Kar's associates made the following claim about the Smoke of Eternity: "Enough of it, about a suitcase full, could turn the Empire State Building into that queer smoke" (chap. 4). Although Doc destroyed the island where the Smoke of Eternity was discovered, Kar could have sent a secret supply of it to New York shortly before his demise. There his associates could have planned to use it to destroy Doc's headquarters, but their resulting conflict with Doc resulted in the weapon being used instead on the neighboring skyscraper under construction. Plans to construct a skyscraper were consequently abandoned.

It is not farfetched to have a skyscraper destroyed in a Doc Savage adventure. Cadwiller Olden attempted to destroy the Empire State Building in *Repel (The Deadly Dwarf)*. He only succeeded in dislodging the dirigible mooring mast (chap. 19). Var tried to blow up the Empire State building with his Cold Light explosive *(Cold Death*, chap. 18). The gang in *The Metal Master* (chap. 17) was conspiring to cause the collapse of "a huge office building" in New York. In *The Angry Ghost* (chap. 4), foreign agents caused the Treasury Building to topple in Washington D.C.

The second hypothetical adventure transpired in Chile (see entry #35). Doc performed a service for a Chilean millionaire who in gratitude agreed to finance the construction of a hospital Other adventures consigned to this period are alluded to in the novels. In *The Thousand-Headed Man* (entry #39), It is mentioned that "some years ago" Doc did an unrecorded "great service" for the British Secret Service (chap. 8). Since I placed *The Thousand-Headed Man* in 1933, Doc probably aided the British Secret Service in the second half of 1931. The Service rewarded Doc with honorary membership and the identification number of SX73182. This unrecorded adventure may be connected to a remark about Doc Savage by Lady Nealia Sealing in *The Lost Oasis* (chap. 11): "He once did a great favor for an acquaintance of mine in England…" The exploit with the British Secret Service is probably the same adventure which caused Doc to "have once been tendered an honorary commission from Scotland Yard as an expression of gratitude for services rendered" *(The Sea Magician*, chap. 4). A British crook named Smith remembered how one of his friends was sent to the Crime College by Doc Savage (chap. 6). Smith's comrade was probably caught by Doc while he was assisting the British Secret Service and Scotland Yard. *The Majii* (chap.

13) also mentioned that Doc had been of assistance to the British Empire "on other occasions." *The Devil Genghis* (chap. 9) also asserted that Doc had rendered Scotland Yard "a service in the past."

Doc had visited Mantilla in the Luzon Union (an alias used by Lester Dent for Manila in the Philippine Islands) in 1931. There he met Juan Mindoro, one of the most influential men in the islands, at the home of Scott S. Osborn, an American sugar importer (*Pirate of the Pacific*, chap. 3). Ham apparently was present with Doc during this meeting because he recognized Osborn's brother (chap. 5). I have placed *Pirate of the Pacific* in the summer of 1932, and Ham figured that he had last seen Osborn's brother "perhaps a year ago." As for Doc's activities during this trip, Doc was visiting a "a number of islands in the Pacific, studying tropical fevers and their cures" (chap. 8). Doc met Mindoro because he was the sponsor of a medical clinic.

It is also during the unrecorded period of mid-1931 to mid-1932 that Doc saved the life of New York's police commissioner. *The Phantom City* revealed that Doc saved the commissioner's life through his surgical skill (chap. 7). About the same time, Doc served as a consulting expert for the police department *(Quest of Qui*, chap. 6). Doc designed the police department's radio system and "the teletype hook-up between the various stations." As a result of these services, Doc and his men received honorary commissions in the New York police department.

For other unrecorded adventures, Doc was granted additional honorary commissions by the states of Maine *(The Squeaking Goblin*, chap. 6) and New York *(Death in Silver,* chap. 7). New York State commissions also would appear to have been granted to all of Doc's men as well. Monk had a New York State commission in *Colors for Murders* (chap. 7). According to *Poison Island* (chap. 9), Doc also received an honorary commission from the Coast Guard. This commission must have been granted early in Doc's career because of an incident in *The King Maker* (chap. 3). The coast guard informed a ship to cooperate fully with Doc Savage. Probably, all three commissions were related. Doc must have solved a smuggling case in Maine. This case resulted in commissions from the Coast Guard and Maine. Maine was probably the first state to grant Doc Savage a commission. Maine's actions would have embarrassed Governor Franklin Delano Roosevelt, who had been negligent in not granting a state commission to Doc earlier. Planning a run for the Presidency, Roosevelt quickly defused this public relations fiasco by quickly granting Doc an honorary commission in his home state.

Doc's adventure in Maine was probably a sequel there to his visit there in June 1930 during the events of "The Too-Talkative Parrot." Perhaps Doc decided to do something about racketeer Jimmie the Knife, Jimmie had probably beaten a murder rap due to the killing of a witness in "The Too-Talkative Parrot."

The Three Wild Men (chap. 13), a novel set in 1942, mentioned that Doc's surgical prowess permitted a crippled man named James Cromwell to walk again. The operation was "some time ago" (chap. 14). The operation was probably performed during this unrecorded period.

Brand of the Werewolf (chap. 11) mentioned a Spanish rumor that Doc Savage was "gifted with everlasting life" and that "he could not be killed." Doc's fame had clearly penetrated Spain, and he must have had an unrecorded exploit there. This gap would seem the most likely time period for such an adventure to occur.

Doc also gave a loan to a San Francisco company, which owned the ocean liner *Malay Queen*, to prevent it from laying off workers. This loan happened "some months" prior to *Pirate of the Pacific* (chap. 11).

See the "Apocryphal Adventures" section for the possibility that Doc witnessed the death of King Kong in New York during October 1931.

If I correlate Doc's adventures with those of another pulp hero, I can place the adventure with the Chilean millionaire in September 1931, the adventure involving Scotland Yard and the British Secret Service in December of the same year, and Doc's operation on the police commissioner in February 1932 (See the section entitled "Parallel Lives: Doc Savage and the Shadow" for the justification). Because of these decisions, I can give a probable outline of Doc's activities during this gap.

1931:	Aug.	Criminals (possibly former associates of Kar) destroyed an unfinished skyscraper not far from the Empire State Building.
	Sept.	Doc performed a service for a Chilean millionaire, who promised to build a hospital in his home country.
	Oct.	Did Doc witness the death of King Kong?
	Nov.	Researching tropical diseases in the Pacific, Doc met Juan Mindoro in the Luzon Union (the Philippines).
	Dec.	Both the British Secret Service and Scotland Yard become incredibly indebted to Doc in the course of a highly classified adventure in England.
1932:	Jan.	Doc had an unrecorded adventure in Spain.
	Feb.	Doc saved the life of the police commissioner of New York. He also designed the police department's communications system. The honorary New York City police commissions held by Doc and his men resulted from these activities.
	Mar.	Doc performed services that resulted in honorary commissions from the Coast Guard as well as the states of Maine and New York. He operated on James Cromwell, and approved a loan to a San Francisco shipping company.

24. "The Southern Star Mystery" (radio play)
Air Date: April 14, 1934
1932: Early April (1 day)
Author: Lester Dent

Doc's honorary New York police commission was mentioned. Only Monk appeared.

Note: Shortly before the events of *Quest of the Spider*, the new recorded adventure, Doc made a long visit to the Fortress of Solitude. I place this sojourn in April and May. This stay left an indelible impression in his assistants' minds. In future exploits, they will constantly claim that Doc spent months at the Fortress, even though none of his future visits would exceed a month.

25. Quest of the Spider
Published: May 1933
1932: June (7 days)
Author: Lester Dent

The novel was set in the summer: "A comet hurtled through the cloudy summer sky" (chap. 1). Ham remarked to a millionaire "that during the past year Doc Savage has probably spent on worthy causes more millions than you possess" (chap. 2). As the conversation continued, Ham mentioned Doc's hidden source of wealth, but withheld that it was located in Hidalgo. Ham's reference to "the past year" indicated that a year had passed since the events of *The Man of Bronze*.

Doc returned to New York from his secret Arctic sanctuary, the Fortress of Solitude, at the start of the novel. He had been there for the "past weeks" (chap. 2). There has been much speculation about this visit in Mr. Farmer's *Doc Savage: His Apocalyptic Life* and a few articles in the fanzines. In most of this speculation, it has been erroneously stated that Doc Savage gave up the direct killing of criminals after his Arctic sojourn. Although Doc was much less lethal in *Quest of the Spider*, he still took human as demonstrated in his battle with pygmy assassins (chap. 4). Doc's retreat from killing his fellow human beings was gradual. It would not be finalized until November 1932.

Quest of the Spider (chap. 3) mentioned the destruction of Doc's advanced airplane in the South Seas during the events of *The Land of Terror*. A replacement plane exactly like it had only recently been manufactured. In the early adventures, it must have taken Doc nearly a year to replace one of his aircraft. When Doc realized that his airplanes ran the likely risk of being destroyed on a frequent basis, he must have arranged for several functioning models of his airplanes and dirigibles to be manufactured in advance in order not to wait so long for a replacement.

Doc made up Johnny Littlejohn to look like a Voodoo high priest. Doc claimed that it would take "six months" for the makeup to disappear from Johnny's skin (chap. 9). Doc was probably joking since Johnny seemed to have a normal appearance in all future novels.

Doc persuaded the governor of Louisiana to make Renny "a special forest ranger" (chap. 8). The governor was O. K. Allen, who had assumed the office in May 1932. Allen was a political ally of Huey Long, the former Louisiana governor who had become a senator in January 1932. Allen did whatever Long wanted. Long must have instructed Allen that it was in their political interest to cooperate with Doc.

26. The Polar Treasure
Published: June 1933
1932: Late June to late July (35 days)
Author: Lester Dent

The novel clearly took place in the summer. It has to be at least near the end of July in the novel's closing chapters because there is a reference to the summer having lasted for two months (chap. 13): "Summer, such as it was, was in full swing. The sun had been shining steadily for two months." When it comes to seasons in chronologies, I try to give some flexibility to my arrangement regarding the months in which a season changes. Technically summer only begins in late June. In some entries, I will consider June to be completely a summer month. In other entries, I will consider the beginning and middle of June to be part of spring. I allow myself similar leeway regarding the start of autumn, winter and spring. Counting June as a full summer month, then the end of July 1932 would be nearly two months into the summer.

The revised text in the recent 2007 reprint by Sanctum Books has a reference to "the summer of 1933" (chap. 14). I have to set the novel in 1932 to fit all of Doc's adventures in a cohesive framework.

Philip José Farmer mentioned the novel's early reference to the Sharkey-Schmeling fight (June 21, 1932): "You t'ink Sharkey had just kayoed Schmeling or Sometin'!" (chap. 1). Mr. Farmer also noted the conversation two policemen had about Doc (chap. 1):

> "*The sergeant chuckled mysteriously. 'Me lad, yez know what they say about our new mayor-that nobody has any pull wit' him?'*
> *'sure,' agreed the rookie. Everybody knows our new mayor is the finest New York has ever had, and that he can't be influenced. But what has that go to do with the big bronze fellow?'*
> *'Nothin,' grinned the sergeant. 'Except that, begorra, our new mayor would gladly turn a handspring at a word from that bronze man!'*"

Mr. Farmer commented that this new mayor could be John P. O'Brien, who was elected in November 1932 to fill out Jimmy Walker's expired term. However, a placement of this novel in June-July 1933 would make it impossible to fit all the remaining novels in any coherent order. *The Polar Treasure* clearly precedes the novels published afterwards. Mr. Farmer ignored the apparent reference to Mayor O'Brien, even though he was astute enough to point it out. Therefore, I am interpreting the reference to the "new mayor" very loosely in the context of the New York politics of June 1932. Mayor Walker had been charged with doing countless political favors in exchange for bribes. Under investigation by late June, Walker was adopting a low profile, and not doing any favors for anyone. In short, he was almost acting like a "new mayor." The two policemen could have been ironically commenting on Walker's change of character. The charges against Walker eventually resulted in his resignation in September.

In the novel's conclusion, Doc directly caused the death of

the villains by melting the ice out from under them. In later novels, he will indirectly cause the demise of villains by tricking them into falling into their own death traps.

The novel's plot involved the search for a British ocean liner, the *Oceanic*, which had been lost in the Arctic during World War I "more than fifteen years ago" (chap. 2). Setting the novel in 1932 would place the loss of the *Oceanic* around 1916.

The New York police had been very cooperative with Doc in the earlier novels, but *The Polar Treasure* was the first novel to mention that Doc and each of his men had honorary police commissions (chap. 6). These honorary commissions were for the rank of captain. These commissions will be temporarily suspended in later novels, and the honorary rank held by Doc will vary from inspector to even that of deputy commissioner throughout the series.

The novel gives up a look at the different tastes in cars possessed by Doc's men. Ham drove "an elaborate and costly" car (chap. 4). Johnny was driving an old touring car from the early 1920s. The car looked run down, but it had a special engine (chap. 5). Long Tom Roberts owned an "extremely flashy car" equipped with gadgets (chap.6). This was the first novel to mention that Long Tom was working on a device to kill mosquitoes with radio waves (chap. 6).

Doc gained possession of the *Helldiver*, a submarine equipped for polar exploration, in the course of this adventure

27. Pirate of the Pacific
Published: July 1933
1932: Very late July to mid-August (22 days)
Author: Lester Dent

The novel is a direct sequel to *The Polar Treasure*. Before the events of *Pirate of the Pacific*, there was a gap of "several days" (chap. 2) during which Doc had his submarine, the *Helldiver*, meet with an ocean liner to drop off three passengers from his earlier adventure in the Arctic.

The plot involved an attempt by Tom Too, a Chinese pirate to take over the Luzon Union, an island chain that had recently achieved independence. The Luzon Union was based on the Philippines. Luzon is the largest island in the Philippines. The Philippines did not become independent of the United States until 1934, the year after the novel was published. When Lester Dent submitted this novel (March 10, 1933), the U.S. Congress had recently approved a bill granting independence to the Philippines. However, the Philippine legislature refused to ratify the bill because it granted the United States permanent naval bases. A new bill was negotiated and approved in the following year. Under the terms of the 1934 bill, the Philippines became independent in 1935. Since the Philippines, the obvious alter ego of the Luzon Union, was not independent until after the novel was published, all references to the independence of the island chain should be viewed as distortions and exaggerations. In the time period where I place the novel, the Philippines was on the road towards independence. The House of Representatives had passed the original version of the independence bill in April 1932, and sent in on to the Senate where it became stalled during the summer. The Luzon Union, better known as the Philippines, was still a possession of the United States when Doc Savage battled Tom Too.

Tom Too had been a warlord in China "a year or two" earlier (chap. 8). The armies of Chiang Kai-shek's Chinese republic drove him into Manchuria. There he sought to build up a power base, but his dreams were shattered by the Japanese. The Japanese invaded Manchuria in 1931.

Doc's attitude towards the taking of human life was still evolving in this novel. Doc instructed his assistants to repel pirates by shooting them in the arms and legs, but his strategy was not based on humanitarian grounds: "There was psychology behind Doc's command not to kill. One wounded Oriental, yelling bloody murder, could do more to spread fear among his fellows than three or four killed instantly" (chap. 21).

Doc had put a steel door on his office to prevent Renny from punching out its panels (chap. 6).

28. The Red Skull
Published: August 1933
1932: Late August (4 days)
Author: Lester Dent

Criminals read a newspaper account of Doc's previous adventure, "a yarn about this Doc Savage savin' the Pacific island republic, the Luzon Union, from a lot of pirates who had come down from the China coast and were tryin' to take over the government" (chap. 2).

Doc's view of the taking of human life had considerably altered. In *Pirate of the Pacific* (chap. 6), Long Tom fatally shot a pirate without a word of reproach from anyone. In *The Red Skull*, there is the first evidence that Doc was annoyed by Monk Mayfair's bloodthirsty attitudes. Monk deliberately allowed a prisoner to escape in order for the criminal to perish in a death trap (chap. 22). Considering his own treatment of the novel's main villain, Doc really wasn't in a position to chastise Monk. Doc trapped his opponent in the same death trap that ensnared Monk's victim. The bronze adventurer went out of his way to bring about opponent's demise. He even allowed a valuable dam to be needlessly destroyed in the process. Nor did Doc issue a warning to the villain that his actions would bring about his own destruction. In later novels, Doc will allow the villain one last chance to surrender or suffer the consequences of his own misdeeds.

Earlier novels, *The Land of Terror* (chap. 6), *Quest of the Spider* (chap. 13) and *Pirate of the Pacific* (chap. 3) briefly mentioned Monk's beautiful secretary who handled his correspondence in his Wall Street laboratory. She finally played a prominent role in *The Red Skull* and her name is revealed to be Lea Aster. She would either be mentioned or briefly appear in these later novels: *Python Isle* (chap. 4), *Quest of Qui* (chap. 5), *Mystery Under the Sea* (chap. 8 (chap. 9 in the Sanctum Books text)), *The Metal Master* (chap. 13) and *The Derrick Devil* (chap. 4). In these subsequent novels, she only played a minor role. She was never referred to as Lea Aster in those novels, but only identified as Monk's secretary.

In *The Red Skull* (chap. 4), the panel on the door to Doc's headquarters read "Doc Savage." In future novels, the panel would read "Clark Savage, Jr."

29. The Lost Oasis
Published: September 1933
1932: September (13 days)
Author: Lester Dent

Doc returned to New York after a stay at the *Fortress of Solitude* for "many days" (chap. 5). Lester Dent doesn't mention the exact length of Doc's Arctic visit, but it could not exceed a week to fit into my chronology. The novel's plot involved the mystery surrounding the disappearance of a zeppelin, the *Aeromunde* which vanished "more than a dozen years ago" (chap. 6). By placing this novel in 1932, I have indicated that the *Aeromunde* disappeared in 1919. Dafydd Neal Dyar's "Phantom Airship" from *Megavore* #12 (December 1, 1980) noted the similarities between the disappearance of the fictional *Aeromunde* and a real-life zeppelin, the *Dixmude*. However, the *Dixmude* disappeared in December 1923. Of course, the discrepancy of time could be just one of Dent's deliberate "distortions." The *Dixmude* was originally a German warship, the LZ 114, which was turned over to France shortly after World War I as part of the war reparations imposed on Germany. The ship was re-christened the *Dixmude* in 1920. Its disappearance in the Mediterranean in 1923 eventually led to France's decision to abandon the use of zeppelins in 1925. Doc's Hudson River warehouse first appeared in *The Lost Oasis* (chap. 6).

30. The Sargasso Ogre
Published: October 1933
1932: Late September to Mid-October (28 days)
Author: Lester Dent

The novel is a direct sequel to *The Lost Oasis*.

31. The Czar of Fear
Published: November 1933
1932: Late October (4 days)
Author: Lester Dent

The novel contained a reference to *The Sargasso Ogre*, Doc "had seen passengers on a great ocean liner aghast at approaching disaster" (chap. 7). There is also a reference that Doc "had seen savage tribesmen in far countries living in apprehension of something they did not understand" (chap. 7). Among theses tribes visited by Doc was a pygmy tribe in Africa. Lester Dent mentioned Doc's unrecorded visit with the pygmies in *Quest of Qui* (chap. 15). Will Murray's *The Forgotten Realm* (chap. 16) revealed that Doc had visited the pygmies when he was a boy. Doc had also spent some time in his youth with the Mok tribe in the Amazon jungles *(The Man Who Fell Up*, chap. 13), a tribe from the Ubangi River in the Belgian Congo (*Mystery on Happy Bones*, chap. 9) and Australian aborigines *(Escape from Loki*, chap. 12). Doc also visited jungle tribes in the 1920s (see the "**Note**" after entry #1).

At one point, Doc sent a group of five prisoners to the Crime College. Lester Dent wrote that "it was fully a year before the five prisoners were again seen" (chap. 17). Dent wrote this novel in 1933. His comment about an event that transpired one year after the main events of the novel would indicate that *The Czar of Fear* was set in 1932. *The Czar of Fear* was the first novel to identify Doc's Hudson River warehouse as the Hidalgo Trading Company (chap. 5). The warehouse had appeared earlier in *The Lost Oasis* (chap. 6).

32. The Phantom City
Published: December 1933
1932: November to early December (40 days)
Author: Lester Dent

A newspaper, *The Evening Comet*, contained a "feature story" (chap. 1) about how Doc Savage "went into this manufacturing town of Prosper City with his five helpers, and mopped up an outfit that had murdered no tellin' how many people!" The newspaper story was about *The Czar of Fear*. *The Phantom City* featured the *Helldiver*, the submarine, from *The Polar Treasure*. The villain of *The Phantom City*, claimed that the events of *The Polar Treasure* transpired "some months ago" (chap. 3).

The Phantom City would take Doc and his men to the Rub' Al Khali (also called the Rub-El-Khali). Johnny made the following comment about the Arabian desert (chap. 9): "An Englishman made perhaps the most ambitious attempt at exploration a few years ago, when he took an exploration across a portion of the desert." Two Englishmen had made such an expedition when this novel was published. The first was Bertram S. Thomas in 1930-31. The second was Howard St. John Philby in 1932-33. Since I am placing this novel in 1932, I will assume that Johnny was referring to the Thomas expedition.

With the introduction of mercy bullets in *The Phantom City* (chap. 6), Doc's non-lethal methods of crime-fighting become finalized. In the four adventures that followed *The Red Skull*, Doc trapped the main villains in their own death traps. In *The Lost Oasis* and *The Czar of Fear*, he didn't really have time to issue warnings to his chief antagonists. He did issue warnings in *The Sargasso Ogre* and *The Phantom City*.

A short period of time would have separated *The Czar of Fear* and *The Phantom City*. At the conclusion of *The Czar of Fear* (chap. 19), Doc announced his intention to remain in Prosper City for "a few days."

The Phantom City introduced Habeas Corpus, Monk's pet

pig. Monk acquired the pig in Arabia. Monk had been reading about how to raise pigs in *The Polar Treasure* (chap. 7). He now had the opportunity to put his knowledge into practice.

33. Brand of the Werewolf
Published: January 1934
1932: December (9 days)
Author: Lester Dent

This novel is the first appearance of Doc's cousin, Patricia ("Pat") Savage. She lived on the coast of western Canada where Doc and his aides had gone for a fishing and hunting trip. Pat Savage must have lived in British Columbia. Fish such as the steelhead are still in season during December. Most hunting seasons in British Columbia end in December. It rained during the novel (chap. 10). Winters in British Columbia are wet and mild. It usually rains rather than snows.

The novel also contains a reference (chap. 8) to *The Phantom City*: "Aren't you the man who just got back from Arabia, where you took a submarine and followed an underground river under the desert?"

Long Tom lost two of his front teeth in a fight during this novel (chap. 15). *The Man of Bronze* (chap. 6) mentioned that Long Tom already had a gold tooth. According to Lester Dent's *The Doc Savage Files* (Odyssey Publications, 1986), the gold tooth was often knocked out in fights. The story of the origin of the gold tooth was actually told in a small biography of Long Tom which was printed as "filler" inside at least one issue of *Doc Savage* magazine. This short biography was later reprinted in *Doc Savage Inside & Out* #1 (Flying Tiger Graphics, 1989). The relevant section from this short biography is produced below:

"Long Tom did not get his name because he is 'long,' but from an incident in the past, when he tried to repel an enemy attack by loading a 'long tom' cannon. Such as the ancient privateers used, with nails, tacks and pebbles. The 'long tom' blew up. The fiasco earned Long Tom his name, and he wears a gold tooth in front, where a piece of the demolished cannon struck on that ill-fated occasion."

According to Scott Cranford's "Long Tom Roberts Profile" from *Aces* #9 (1998), the "filler" biography quoted above was printed in the October 1937 issue, which featured *Repel (The Deadly Dwarf)*. Presumably, one of the teeth knocked out in *Brand of the Werewolf* was the gold tooth that originated from the cannon incident. In the later *Spook Hole* (chap. 7), Long Tom (posing as a criminal named Sass) would have two gold teeth.

34. The Man Who Shook the Earth
Published: February 1934
1933: Early January (6 days)
Author: Lester Dent

This novel is set in the winter (chap. 8): "In New York, it was winter. Here in Chile, it was summer." During World War I, an injury had caused Johnny to lose sight in his left eye. In this novel, Doc's surgery restored sight to Johnny's eye.

The villains in this novel worked for a European secret society that was planning a coup in their own country. This is how their country was described (chap. 15): "The country in question is a certain European one which is considered a possible instigator of a future war." The coup would set their nation on the path to war (chap. 16): "In another month, we will be ready to eliminate the leaders in our country who do not desire war." The villains were probably Nazis. In early January 1933, Adolf Hitler was negotiating to be appointed German Chancellor. He was appointed Chancellor on January 30. In February, he used the Reichstag fire as an excuse to establish a dictatorial regime. Further evidence that the secret society was of German origin lies outside the Doc Savage series. The aim of the secret society was to gain control of the Chilean nitrate industry in order to fuel their own country's armament. A similar conspiracy during World War I was foiled by Craig Kennedy, a popular detective whose methods influenced Doc Savage. Kennedy's foiling of the German plot is told in "The Nitrate King" from Arthur B. Reeve's *The Panama Plot* (1918). If the villains were indeed Nazis, then words uttered by the Little White Brother, the secret society's leader in Chile, indicate that he harbored plans to supplant Adolf Hitler as the chief Nazi leader (chap. 16): "I, the First Little White Brother, will be elevated to dictator of my country when the great war comes… Perhaps I shall be dictator of all nations in the world. Mussolini—Hitler—they will be as nothing compared to me!"

This statement also raises the possibility that the Little White Brother may have been an Austrian Nazi as opposed to a German Nazi. Before being absorbed by the Third Reich in 1938, there was a Nazi party in Austria that was supporting unification with Germany. The Austrian Nazis made one failed attempt to seize power in the early 1930s. In July 1934, they assassinated the Austrian Chancellor, Engelbert Dollfuss, in an unsuccessful coup.

Doc was nearly killed with a poison gas, "similar to mustard gas," with which he had a previous encounter (chap. 6). Doc had faced the deadly vapor in *Quest of the Spider* (chap. 7).

35. Meteor Menace
Published: March 1934
1933: January-February (50 days)
Author: Lester Dent

At the conclusion of *The Man Who Shook the Earth*, Doc Savage announced his intention to construct a hospital in Chile. However, he declared that he would be absent from the dedication. In *Meteor Menace*, the hospital was "possibly half finished" (chap. 1), and the dedication ceremony was being performed with Doc Savage secretly attending. The speaker at the ceremony mentioned that Doc's "most recent accomplishment was here in Chile, when he wiped out a gang of fiends who were seeking to get control of the Chilean nitrate industry in order to supply ingredients for explosives to a European nation who contemplates war" (chap. 2). Clearly, Doc's last adventure was *The Man Who Shook the Earth*. Philip José Farmer has skillfully pointed out that there is a chronological problem here. It would take many months to build a hospital. Mr. Farmer's solution was to theorize that Doc spent six months at the Fortress of Solitude between *The Man Who Shook the Earth* and *Meteor Menace*.

I propose a different theory. In earlier adventures like *Pirate of the Pacific* (chap. 22), *The Red Skull* (chap. 22) and *Brand of the Werewolf* (chap. 19), it was mentioned that the building of hospitals was the common remuneration which Doc received from wealthy people who benefited from his intervention. In fact, Doc told General John Acre, the head of the Chilean secret police, that it was his "usual procedure" to do so at the conclusion of *The Man Who Shook the Earth* (chap. 17). By my chronological arrangement, there is a large gap between *The Land of Terror* and *Quest of the Spider*. During this gap, Doc must have performed an unrecorded service for a Chilean millionaire, who was then required to build a hospital as remuneration. General Acre wanted Doc to attend some sort of ceremony after *The Man Who Shook the Earth*. When Doc used the words "usual procedure," Acre remembered a hospital being built in Chile by a resident millionaire not previously known for philanthropic activities. Acre contacted the millionaire, and discovered that the hospital was actually a reward for one of Doc's previous exploits. With the millionaire's concurrence, the half-finished hospital was publicly dedicated to Doc Savage as recognition for his role in foiling the nitrate conspiracy. Doc attended the ceremony, but not publicly like General Acre hoped. Another hospital was later built in Chile as Doc's real reward for his role in *The Man Who Shook the Earth*.

Meteor Menace must have transpired no later than December 1933. The devious John Mark Shrops claimed to be the emissary of the Dalai Lama (chap. 6). The thirteenth Dalai Lama died in December 1933. The position was vacant until a boy, only four years old, was proclaimed the fourteenth Dalai Lama in 1939.

36. The Monsters
Published: April 1934
1933: Early March (5 days)
Author: Lester Dent

The early scenes in the novel involved the disappearance of circus "pinheads." These scenes must have been set in late spring since there was a reference to "the coming of summer" (chap. 1). Shortly before Doc become involved in the story, Lester Dent gives the impression that "ten weeks" have passed (chap. 2) since the "pinheads" disappeared. However, Dent contradicted himself later by stating that "almost a year" had elapsed (chap. 8). When there is a chronological contradiction in a novel, I favor accepting the statement which makes my role as a chronologist easier. The interval of nearly a year would place *The Monsters* in late winter or early spring, a place where other factors in the series are forcing me to locate the novel. The reference to "ten weeks" is ignored. The presence of owls and other birds in Michigan (chap. 16) and a cool climate there (chap. 14) confirm my designation of late winter or early spring (chap. 3).

The events of *The Man Who Shook the Earth* were mentioned in a magazine article read by one of the characters from *The Monsters* (chap. 3): "For he had judged Doc Savage to be a detective, for the story was one telling how Doc and a group of five assistants had ferreted out a group of villains seeking to seize the nitrate industry of the government of Chile."

37. The Mystery on the Snow
Published: May 1934
1933: Mid-March (8 days)
Author: Lester Dent

The novel would seem to be set in early spring (chap. 8): "On northern hill slopes, patches of unmelted snow were discernible. Spring was not far along." At another point in the novel, Doc in New York was contemplating traveling to northernmost Canada (chap. 11): "It's spring here, but only a little past the worst of the winter up there."

Headlines clipped from newspapers (chap. 1) refer to the respective events of *Meteor Menace* and *The Phantom City*: DOC SAVAGE SMASHES TIBETAN MENACE and DOC SAVAGE ON MYSTERY MISSION GOES TO ARABIA.

The Mystery on the Snow was the first of the original pulp novels where Johnny used big words. In *Escape from Loki*, Philip José Farmer depicted Johnny using big words during World War I. Later in *The Mystic Mullah* (chap. 2). it was mentioned that Johnny had demonstrated his usage of big words when he "once held the chair of natural science research in a famous university." Johnny's love of big words was a longtime habit, but he refrained from exhibiting this trait in his adventures with Doc in the early 1930s. Maybe he felt matters were too serious to engage in such levity. However, the restoration of sight to his left eye seemed to have lifted his spirits so much that he couldn't resist utilizing his enormous vocabulary even more in the presence of his close associates.

Note: In late March 1933, Doc did some unrecorded service for James Farley, the Postmaster General of the United States. As a reward for this service, Doc was given a card with Farley's signature identifying Doc as "a fully commissioned postal investigator" *(Fear Cay,* chap. 10). Farley was Postmaster General from 1933-40. He was also the manager of Franklin Roosevelt's first two presidential campaigns. Postmaster General was then a Cabinet position, and it was generally held by the President's senior political advisor. Farley had received Senate confirmation of his Cabinet position in early March.

38. The King Maker
Published: June 1934
1933: April (23 days)
Author: Harold A. Davis and Lester Dent

In this novel, Doc Savage traveled to the fictional Balkan kingdom of Calbia. Although the name Calbia, suggests Albania, Calbia was based on Yugoslavia, I first made this observation in "This King Maker Business" from *Golden Perils* #3 (March 1986). At the time I wrote that article, I was unaware that Will Murray had found among Lester Dent's notes a paper where the words "Calbia" and "Yugoslavia" appear next to each other. Dent stated that Calbia's population was "ten or twelve million" (chap. 8). A 1931 census indicated that Yugoslavia had a population of fourteen million. Like Yugoslavia, Calbia had a seacoast accessible through the Mediterranean. The fictional King of Calbia, Dal Le Galban, would correspond to King Alexander I. The King of Calbia was "near fifty" (chap. 16). King Alexander was forty-five in 1933. Unlike the fictional Calbian monarch, Alexander did not have a beautiful daughter named Gusta. However, but he did have a beautiful wife, Queen Maria, who was thirty years old in 1933. A member of the Rumanian royal family, Maria was the sister of the monarch who inspired "the playboy prince" in *Fortress of Solitude*. Accept the slight differences between Alexander and Dal Le Galban as Dent's literary distortions, and it isn't too difficult to imagine that Doc "really" visited Yugoslavia.

There was much internal unrest during King Alexander's reign due to ethnic tensions between Serbs and other nationalities. King Alexander, a Serb, was particularly despised by the Croatian separatist movement. In 1929, internal strife in

Yugoslavia caused Alexander to abolish the constitution and rule as a dictator. On October 9, 1934, King Alexander along with Louis Barthou, the French Foreign Minister, was assassinated in Marseilles by a terrorist with ties to Croatian separatists as well as the governments of Italy and Hungary. Italy had a rivalry with Yugoslavia over Albania, and Hungary desired territory surrendered to Yugoslavia as a result of World War I.

39. The Thousand-Headed Man
Published: July 1934
1933: Early May (8 days)
Author: Lester Dent

The events of *The King Maker* are mentioned in *The Thousand-Headed Man* (chap. 1): "a few weeks ago… there was a revolution in the Balkan kingdom of Calbia. This Yankee put a stop to it." References in the novel to an unrecorded adventure involving the British Secret Service (chap. 8) are discussed in the "Note" following "The Sniper in the Sky" (entry #23).

The Soviet Union was portrayed sympathetically in this novel. Doc was warmly greeted by Russian officials when his plane landed there (chap. 11).

40. Fear Cay
Published: September 1934
1933: Mid-May (4 days)
Author: Lester Dent

In this novel, Pat Savage made what is clearly her second appearance in the series. Doc Savage "had last seen her in western Canada months before" (chap. 4). There was a reference to Doc's previous adventure in Calbia (chap. 1): "They say he has accomplished fabulous things, feats that range from stopping a revolution in a European country to—." A strong argument can be made to place this novel in 1934, Dan Thunden's age was given as a hundred and thirty-one, and he was "exactly forty" in 1843 (chap. 6). For reasons explained in the introduction, the placement of this novel in 1934 would wreck havoc with the entire series. Either Thunden was forty-one in 1843, or he was only one-hundred and thirty years old.

There may be some connection between the newspaper known as the *Morning Comet* (chap. 8) and the *Evening Comet* from *The Phantom City* (chap. 1). Maybe they are different editions of the same paper. Neither New York newspaper should be confused with the *San Francisco Comet* from *The Jade Ogre* (chap. 8).

41. Death in Silver
Published: October 1934
1933: Mid-May (2 days)
Author: Lester Dent

This was the first novel to feature Pat Savage's Park Avenue beauty salon (chap. 6). The placement of *Death in Silver* is related to Pat Savage's appearance and the novel's relationship to the next entry, *Python Isle*. However, if viewed in isolation from the entire series, an astute reader would be forced to come to the conclusion that *Death in Silver* transpired in December, January, February or March. Consider this statement by a character named Lorna Zane about her employer, Paine L. Winthrop (chap. 6): "Last spring, Mr. Winthrop gave all his regular employees a five-month vacation with pay… I came back four months ago." Adding the five months' vacation to the four months (since Lorna's return) gives us nine months. The spring vacation would have begun in March, April, May or even June. Depending on which month the vacation began, nine months later would be sometime in December, January, February or March.

However, we don't need to assume that Lorna got the same

vacation deal as Winthrop's other employees. Maybe she got a longer vacation, or maybe she had to take an extended leave of absence just after her vacation because one of her close relatives was ill. Perhaps she was gone seven or eight months before returning to Mr. Winthorp's service. I freely admit the above discussion is intellectual trickery, but a chronologist must be allowed some leeway.

The novel featured the return of the *Helldiver* and mentioned its two prior appearances (chap. 14): "Doc and his little group of aides had seen two great adventures aboard the Helldiver -the first under the polar ice, and the second through an underground river into a fantastic phantom city in the Arabian desert."

Death in Silver was the first novel to involve significant traveling by Doc's associates. Johnny was "filling a special lecture engagement at a famous university" in London, Long Tom was in Europe working on a device to "kill insects with ultrasonic or electric waves," and Renny was overseeing construction of a particularly difficult hydro-electric plant" in South Africa (chap. 4).

This novel revealed that Doc also had an honorary commission as a New York State Trooper (chap. 7). Since it would be stated much later that Monk also had a New York State commission (*Colors for Murder*, chap. 7), we can assume that all of Doc's men possess Trooper commissions.

42. Python Isle
Published: October 1991
1933: First half of June (10 days)*
Author: Will Murray

Although the year in which this novel was set is clearly given as 1934 (chap. 1), this designation has to be adjusted to 1933 because of my placement of other novels in this chronology. The novel began in "early June" (chap. 2) and the events of

Death in Silver took place "only weeks before" (chap. 6).

Renny became involved in *Python Isle* while he was working on the hydroelectric plant in Africa mentioned in the previous adventure. Renny had been in Africa for "several weeks" (chap. 3), but my chronological arrangement only allows him to be in Africa for at most three weeks since the events of *Fear Cay*. Johnny was still lecturing in London, and Long Tom continued to work on his insect killer in Europe (chap. 4). Monk's secretary was briefly mentioned (chap. 4).

The novel also featured the *Aeromunde* (chap. 8) from *The Lost Oasis*. The ship had been returned to the country which rightfully owned it at the conclusion of *The Lost Oasis*. Assuming that the *Aeromunde* was really the *Dixmude*, then Doc would have returned the airship to France. However, the *Aeromunde* apparently had a German crew led by a captain named Adler in *Python Isle*. Since the French government had abandoned zeppelins in 1925, that country would have had no need for the returned airship. They probably would have sold it back to Germany, the country which had relinquished ownership of the airship after World War I.

43. The Sea Magician
Published: November 1934
1933: Late June (3 days)
Author: Lester Dent

The novel opened with Johnny in London "where he had been lecturing for some weeks before the Fellowhood of Scientists" (chap. 1). Four days before the adventure began, Doc sent Johnny a telegraph that he would be arriving in London (chap. 1). There has to be at least a gap of four days between this novel and the previous adventure.

The villains tried to establish a base on Magna Island. Great Britain had a protectorate over this island, but it was paid no taxes. The island was ruled by an "independent monarchy" (chap. 7). Magna Island was based on Sark, one of the Channel Islands. Since the sixteenth century, Sark has been ruled by a hereditary line of seigneurs. The island controls its own taxes.

References to *Death in Silver* are present in *The Sea Magician* (chap. 6): "Just recently, there had been an affair in which some clever criminal had hit upon using a submarine in New York as a get-away vehicle, and Doc Savage had put him out of business." A subsequent remark indicated that *The King Maker* transpired before *Death n Silver*: "A bit earlier than that, Doc Savage had, it was rumored, put down a revolution in one of the Balkan countries."

Will Murray noted two topical references in *The Sea Magician* in his: "Intermission" column for the recent 2007 reprint of the pulp novel by Sanctum Books. There was mention of "an American utility king who was running away from the law" (chap, 7). This was Chuck Insull, who fled America for Europe in 1932 when he was indicted for fraud. He was eventually extradited to the United States in 1934. There was also a reference to the Loch Ness Monster as the subject of the "sea serpent tales given some wide publicity some months ago" (chap. 1).

My chronological placement of *The Sea Magician* in June 1933 does not conflict with the Insull reference since his apprehension was never noted by Dent. I'm not totally consistent with the Loch Ness reference. On May 2, 1933, the *Inverness Courier* carried a story of a sighting of the alleged beast by Mr. and Mrs. John Mackay. This would be weeks rather than months before my placement of *The Sea Magician*. However, the MacKays actually made their sighting on April 14, and it took over two weeks to get into the newspapers. Since the sighting was in April, a "months" reference in June could be justified.

Renny and Long Tom were absent.

Note: In *Python Isle*, Doc had visited the Fortress of Solitude (Prologue). The version of the Fortress depicted by Will

Murray was the crater described in Lester Dent's notes published as *The Doc Savage Files* (Odyssey Publications, 1986). Dent depicted the Fortress entirely differently as a Blue Dome when he wrote *Fortress of Solitude* years later. In *Python Isle*, Doc announced his intention to remodel the Fortress (chap. 6). Doc must have redesigned the Fortress in July 1933.

44. "Black-Light Magic" (radio play)
Air Date: March 17, 1934
1933: August (1 day)
Author: Lester Dent

Doc and only Monk were involved in this case. John MacDavid was involved in illegally hoarding gold. MacDavid was violating the Gold Confiscation Act (April 5. 1933). When the miserly villain was apprehended, Monk suggested that the malefactor would be turned over to a judge and jury. Monk wanted to see the skinflint stripped of his wealth. Doc probably sent MacDavid to the Crime College.

45. The Squeaking Goblin
Published: August 1934
1933: August (7 days)
Author: Lester Dent

The novel was set in a summer resort in Maine. The plot concerned a fictional book, *The Life and Horrible Deed of That Adopted Moor, Black Raymond*, which was published in 1834, "one hundred years ago" (chap. 6). For reasons explained in the introduction, 1934 can't be accepted as the chronological year of this exploit. The book about Black Raymond must have been published ninety-nine years before Doc's exploit.

The novel revealed that Doc held a police commission in Maine (chap. 6).

The events of *The King Maker* were alluded to in *The Squeaking Goblin*: "...you once stopped a revolution in some European country" (chap. 8).

Note: In *The South Pole Terror* (chap. 19), there is a reference that Doc and his men visited Death Valley (see entry #67). This reference would seem to indicate an unrecorded adventure. The same reference mentions Doc's known exploits in *The Lost Oasis* and *The Phantom City*. I would assume that the Death Valley episode transpired as close as possible to those earlier exploits. The most likely time that this Death Valley adventure happened would be in September 1933.

This unrecorded Death Valley exploit probably involved Meander Surett, an eccentric inventor who was friendly with Doc. Surett had been living in Death Valley for ten years at the time of *The Pirate's Ghost* (chap. 2). Since I place *The Pirate's Ghost* in March 1937, Surett would have been living there since 1927.

In *The Yellow Cloud* (chap. 6), an unrecorded incident in which Monk gave Pat Savage a package and told her to take it to the mountains and guard it with her life. After guarding it for a week, Pat opened the package and found a picture of a goat. Monk did this to get Pat out of danger. This incident sounds like something that would have happened to Pat early in her association with Doc. East of Death Valley are the peaks of the Amargosa Range. If this incident happened during the unrecorded Death Valley episode, the mountains where Pat hid would have been the Amargosa Range.

It could be that Doc had originally traveled to the Western United States to help American Indians before becoming embroiled in the unrecorded Death Valley episode. *The Devil's Playground* (chap. 13) mentioned that Doc "once defended Western tribes of the red men." His intervention prevented the Indians "from being defrauded of their oil lands."

Since Death Valley is in California, Doc and his men was not too far from Hollywood. Monk apparently took a side trip there around the time of this adventure.

There an incident mentioned in *The Devil Genghis* (chap. 4) happened. A Hollywood producer told Monk that he would make a fortune as an actor. Monk was ready to accept until the film executive uttered these words: "…you'd make Frankenstein and King Kong look like pets for babies." The movie *Frankenstein* was released in 1931, and *King Kong* in March 1933.

46. Land of Always Night
Published: March 1935
1933: Late September to October (32 days)
Author: W. Ryerson Johnson and Lester Dent

The novel contains various references to "a golden autumn haze:" "As softly as a leaf falling through a golden autumn haze, the dirigible cam to rest on the crevice floor" (chap. 11). "She stood like a fairy-book figure seen through a golden autumn haze" (chap. 15). It may be incorrect to read these references as meaningful. The "golden autumn haze" may just be a poetical metaphor for the mysterious phenomenon produced by the Cold Light utilized by the lost civilization featured in this novel. A comment by Monk implied as much (chap. 15): "It's lie when the sun is slanting rays over the earth in the autumn." However, I see no real harm in placing this novel in the autumn.

47. The Annihilist
Published: December 1934
1933: Early November (2 days)
Author: Lester Dent

The novel was set in the fall. There are references to the "the first chilly day of fall" (chap. 2) and "hard snow" caused by "the first gale of Fall" (chap. 4). It has to be either November or December because a character "wore a rather light suit for so late in the Fall" (chap. 6).

Inspector Clarence "Hardboiled " Humboldt was appointed by the "new mayor" (chap. 2). Mayor John P. O'Brien was elected mayor in November 1932 to finish Jimmy Walker's remaining term. On November 7, 1933, Fiorello La Guardia was elected mayor, but he wasn't inaugurated until January 1933. In my chronological arrangement, the "new mayor" would be O'Brien. I would argue that *The Annihilist* must have transpired before Election Day. Since O'Brien had only been in office for a year, he still could be considered "new." Humboldt had once gotten into a fight with a previous mayor (chap. 1), when one of the mayor's friends broke the speed limit. The earlier mayor was almost certainly meant to be Jimmy Walker, who resigned under a cloud.

Doc's accomplishments in *The King Maker* were alluded to by a policeman in *The Annihilist* (chap. 1): "He saves thrones for king and stops wars."

Long Tom was in Chicago "attending an exposition of electrical inventions in which he had exhibits," and Johnny "was filling the chair of natural science research at a famous university during the illness of a professor who regularly occupied that position" (chap. 4). Long Tom must have been at the 1933 Chicago World's Fair.

Doc's honorary rank with the New York police is now inspector (chap. 1). This is a demotion from the rank of captain given in *The Polar Treasure* (chap. 6).

48. The Mystic Mullah
Published: January 1935
1933: November 7-21 (15 days)
Author: Lester Dent

The second day of this novel was a Wednesday (chap. 8). After Doc defeated the Mystic Mullah, there were "months" of internal strife in the Asian city of Tanan, which is located somewhere near Outer Mongolia. Doc supposedly stayed in Tanan until "conditions had attained moderate stability" (chap. 18). Doc could only have stayed a few days to help set up a stable government in Tanan. The length of his later adventures prohibits allowing a sojourn of months in Tanan.

Will Murray informed me of an interesting historical parallel with this novel. The ruler of Tanan was Khan Nadir Shar, who died violently in the novel. Nadir Shah, the ruler of Afghanistan, was assassinated on November 8, 1933. There is the possibility of a theory here, but the geographical distance between Afghanistan and Outer Mongolia precludes speculation that Khan Nadir Shar and Nadir Khan were the same man. To a serious literary scholar who treats Doc Savage solely as a fictional character, Nadir Shah was clearly the inspiration for Khan Nadir Shar. To a speculative theorist seeking to merge fact and fiction into a coherent mixture, the similarity of names between the two rulers should be treated as a coincidence equivalent to the fact that Clark Savage Jr. has the same first name as Clark Gable.

While the political structure of Tanan resembles Afghanistan, its geographical location is similar to Tannu-Tuva, originally part of China. Tsarist Russian troops established a protectorate over Tannu-Tuva (also called Tuva) in 1914. After the October revolution in 1917, Bolshevik and White (counter-revolutionary) soldiers fought for control of the territory. Chinese troops became embroiled in this battle. In 1921 the Bolsheviks established a puppet government in Tannu-Tuva. Existing as technically a country independent of Russia for two decades, Josef Stalin formally annexed Tannu-Tuva into the Soviet Union in 1944. Known as the Tuva (or Tyva Republic), Tannu-Tuva remains part of Russia today.

The Mystic Mullah's poison came from the "neotropical rattlesnake" (chap. 18). This species of snake actually exists, and is more formally called *Crotalus durissus*. It is also known as the Central American rattlesnake.

49. Red Snow

Published: February 1935
1933: December (10 days)
Author: Lester Dent

The novel was set in December: "It was a very warm December day in Florida" (chap. 1).

The unnamed country for which the spies were working in this novel was meant to be Japan. The Japanese invasion of Manchuria in 1931 had raised tensions between the United States and Japan. The villains were planning to murder the Secretary of State as a prelude to a sneak attack (chap. 15). Cordell Hull was Secretary of State from 1933 to 1944.

Renny, Johnny and Long Tom were "abroad at the moment" (chap. 6). Perhaps they had stayed in Tanan to help stabilize the situation. On the other hand, Long Tom may have gone to Argentina (see entry #50).

Note: *Quest of Qui* (entry #58) mentioned an unrecorded adventure involving Habeas Corpus and a lion: "Only other time that I ever seen Habeas act that scared was when he happened on a lion unexpected like down in—" (chap. 5). A possible explanation was offered in Will Murray's *The Forgotten Realm* (chap. 21). Monk remembered that he once experimented with chemical depressants on a lion in his laboratory. The most likely time for the lion incident in late December after returning from Florida.

Around early January 1934, Doc had a couple of brushes with death. I believe this month saw an unrecorded adventure mentioned in *The Majii* (chap. 10): "…an enemy had once tried to poison Doc Savage by tapping the city water main which supplied the bronze man's headquarters."

In *The Roar Devil* (chap. 11), Lester Dent armed Doc with a metal skullcap which protected his head from possible bullets. The skullcap had artificial hair on it. Laurence Donovan would utilize the skullcap frequently in his novels. In *Murder*

Mirage (chap. 14), Donovan claimed that Doc had made the skullcap "after being wounded by a bullet." Dent never had Doc wounded in the head in any of the earlier novels. The head wound probably happened during Doc's unrecorded activities in early January 1934.

50. Dust of Death
Published: October 1935
1934: January (7 days)
Author: Harold A. Davis and Lester Dent

The novel would seem to be set during summer in South America (chap. 12): "Long Tom had ridded himself of opinions concerning the hot weather…" Summer in South America translates into winter in New York.

Besides the description of the weather in South America, the placement of this novel in early 1934 stems from the historical basis for the fictional South American war depicted in this novel. The authors based the war on two concurrent South American conflicts, the Leticia border dispute between Peru and Colombia (September 1932-May 1934) and the Chaco war between Bolivia and Paraguay (1932-1935). The Inca in Gray, the novel's villain, was trying to intervene in a war between two fictional countries, Santa Amoza and Delezon. Santa Amoza was governed by President Carcetas, and Delezon was ruled by General Vigo, who died in the novel. Santa Amoza was modeled on Peru. Santa Amoza has a capital city, Alcala, on the coast (chap. 1). Alcala's location corresponds to Peru's capital, Lima. Neither Bolivia nor Paraguay has a seacoast. Delezon may have been based on Bolivia. The major component borrowed from the Leticia border dispute was modeling one of the combatants in this fictional war on Peru. The ferocity of the fighting and references to oil concessions in disputed territory were lifted from the Chaco War. President Carcetas, a man twice exiled from his homeland (chap. 15) has a totally different background than either of the two men who ruled Peru during the Leticia dispute, Luis Sanchez Cerro (1931-33) or Oscar R. Benavides (1934-39). General Vigo does not strongly resemble either Daniel Salamanca (1931-34) or Luis Tejada Sorzano (1934-36), the rulers of Bolivia during the Chaco War. The only way to reconcile this Doc Savage adventure novel would be to view it as a distorted account of a plot to cause a war between Peru and Bolivia when those two countries were already engaged in separate conflicts with other nations. By this theory, General Vigo would have to be demoted from dictator to the Bolivian general charged with patrolling the Peruvian border. I first identified the actual South American wars which influenced this novel in my article, "Savage Wars in South America," from *Echoes* #61 (June 1992).

In this novel, Ham acquired Chemistry, his pet ape, in the Amazon jungle. The ape will not re-appear in this chronology until the entries for October 1934 because it would be put in quarantine by U. S. Customs officials. Before appearing in this novel, Long Tom had recently completed work at a hydroelectric plant in Argentina (chap. 2).

Renny and Johnny were absent.

51. The Spook Legion
Published: April 1935
1934: February (27 days)
Author: Lester Dent

The fact that the weather was "very chilly" (chap. 12) would be consistent with my placement of this novel in late winter.

Renny and Long Tom were in Europe, and Johnny "was in the western part of the United States investigating a new cliff dwelling discovery" (chap. 12).

Monk had been training Habeas Corpus "over a period of years" (chap. 12). Monk would have owned Habeas for two years.

The villains framed Doc for their crimes. While on the run,

Doc received help from an unnamed police official whom he was able to convince of his innocence (chap. 16 and chap. 18). We never saw the official, and Doc communicated with him by phone. The official was clearly not the police commissioner. Who was he? Possibly he was Inspector Humboldt from *The Annihilist*. In the previous novel, Humboldt had initially adopted an antagonistic attitude towards Doc, but this changed to respect by the conclusion of the adventure.

52. The Secret in the Sky
Published: May 1935
1934: Early March (4 days)*
Author: Lester Dent

The novel revealed that Doc also had an honorary commission as a Federal agent (chap. 8) in addition to his New York City, New York State and Maine commissions. Doc must have been an agent of the Bureau of Investigation, the government agency founded in 1924, and renamed the Federal Bureau of Investigation on July 1. 1935. Later novels such as *The Three Wild Men* (chap. 9) associated Doc with the FBI. Doc probably got his Federal credentials as a result of his rescue of Secretary of State Hull in *Red Snow*. Doc had not worked with the Bureau of Investigation in that earlier novel. He had cooperated with the Secret Service (chap. 13) whose leader, O. Garfew Beech, avoided publicity. In order to hide the existence of Beech's identity, the Roosevelt administration must have pretended that Doc had worked with J. Edgar Hoover's Bureau of Investigation. Hoover would have been a willing participant in such a deception. He loved publicity.

Monk had trained Habeas Corpus "for years" *(The Secret in the Sky,* chap. 9).

53. Spook Hole
Published: August 1935
1934: March-early April (15 days)
Author: Lester Dent

The novel was set in the spring (chap. 10): "It had been cold spring in New York…" It snowed early in the adventure, and the snow was identified as "the hard late spring snow" (chap. 9). "Late spring" would suggest April or May. Having lived in either New York City or neighboring Long Island all my life, I have never known it to snow in May. However, an April snowfall does happen on rare occasions.

Renny was "engaged in a railway building project in a remote Asian province," and Long Tom, who did play an active role later in the novel, had gone to Washington to testify before a Congressional committee on his insect killing device (chap. 6). Renny's project may be synonymous with the "great tunnel in western China," which *Haunted Ocean* (chap. 4) mentioned as one of his earlier construction jobs. Renny could have been building a railway tunnel.

Spook Hole revealed that all Crime College graduates received ten thousand dollars to start a new life. This feature of the "course" was recently implemented (chap. 11).

Doc asked Pat Savage to assist him in this adventure because "he cannot imitate a woman's voice with any great success" (chap. 5). This statement contradicts an earlier assertion in *The Phantom City* (chap. 11): "Moreover, he could simulate what defied most male mimics, the voice of a woman." *Mystery Under the Sea* (chap. 5) attempted to reconcile the discrepancy by asserting that Doc could imitate a woman's voice "fairly well," but without total success.

54. "Fast Workers" (radio play)
Air Date: June 9, 1934
1934: April (1 day)
Author: Lester Dent

After boarding an ocean liner or an unknown destination, Doc and Monk became entangled in a jewel mystery. I opted to make this ocean voyage the trip to Germany described below. Doc and Monk were actually tricked into boarding the ship just as it was sailing. Since they were on a trans-Atlantic ship, they decided to make some inquiries in Europe.

55. "The Fainting Lady" (radio play)
Air Date: July 14, 1934
1934: April (1 day)
Author: Lester Dent

Monk was singing that it was springtime. All other assistants were absent.

Doc and Monk were in an unnamed country which was clearly Nazi Germany. Besides German being spoken in this nation, a new government with "radical ideas" had recently come to power. Hitler became Chancellor of Germany in January 1933. Reference was also made to currency restrictions ("a law forbidding anyone from taking any sizeable amount out of the country") that were recently implemented by the Nazis. Doc also checked the status of "a little bit of property" that he owned in Germany.

56. Cold Death

Published: September 1936
1934: May (3 days)
Author: Laurence Donovan

References to *Land of Always Night* appeared in *Cold Death* (chap. 6): "Like the illumination created by the inhabitants of the Land of Always Night." This previous adventure had transpired months earlier (chap. 11): "You knew, we had visited, months ago, the caverns of the strange race in the Arctic ice field." One of the major characters in the novel was Charles Arthur Vonier, a noted Arctic explorer. Although Doc met Vonier for the first time in this novel, Vonier apparently visited the Land of Always Night in an Arctic expedition launched after Doc's. Doc remarked that Vonier was "one of perhaps only seven men in New York who has seen Cold Light, even though it is of a far different variety" (chap. 11). The other six men are Doc and his assistants. Doc seemed to have learned of Vonier's experiences from a paper which he wrote on his "last trip into the Arctic."

The novel featured an appearance by the unnamed police commissioner of New York. He was described as "a stocky red-faced man" (chap. 24).

Johnny was in Casper, Wyoming, "investigating a new discovery of prehistoric bones" (chap. 4). He had been there "several weeks." A telegraph stated that Johnny was planning to spent another "fortnight" (2 weeks) there, However, the telegraph is a forgery send by the master criminal battling Doc. Johnny could have returned to New York just after this exploit concluded in the time for the following adventure. In my chronological arrangement, Johnny could have gone to Wyoming in early April. He must have been there at least three weeks when *Cold Death* began.

57. The Roar Devil

Published: June 1935
1934: Late May (2 days)
Author: Lester Dent

The novel was set in the spring (chap. 1): "It had been a wet spring in this mountain section of New York State…" It is also mentioned that "the aroma of spring was in the air" (chap. 7). The novel is getting close to the summer because a character was dressed like "a sporty summer visitor" (chap. 17). Villains also made their headquarters look like a "little summer camp" (chap. 4). These references can be interpreted as indicating that the summer business season was approaching upstate New York.

A remark recalled the events of *The King Maker*. A character in *The Roar Devil* asserted that Doc Savage "makes kingdoms and things like that" (chap. 3).

An absent Long Tom was "abroad" (chap. 16).

58. Quest of Qui

Published: July 1935
1934: Early June (10 days)
Author: Lester Dent

June would be the best time to set this novel because conflicting references were made to summer and spring. We are told that "down in New York, it was early summer" (chap. 2). At another point in the novel, Renny remarked that it was "merry old springtime" (chap. 8). When Doc and his men arrived in northern Canada, the following statement was made: "Most of the inhabited world called this season spring" (chap. 9).

Long Tom was "down in South America superintending some kind of an electrical project" (chap. 5).

Monk's secretary made a brief appearance in the novel (chap. 5).

A reference to an unrecorded adventure involving Habeas Corpus and a lion was also made in this novel (see the "**Note**" following entry #49).

The novel mentioned that Doc had visited African pygmies (chap. 15). Will Murray's *The Forgotten Realm* (chap. 16) explained this reference as an episode of Doc Savage's youth.

Monk recalled the events of *Land of Always Night* in *Quest of Qui* (chap. 8): "I got some left from that last dizzy trip we took up there, that time we found that fantastic place underground."

In the course of this adventure, the airplanes used by Doc and the villains to reach northern Canada were all destroyed. The impression is given that Doc and his men were stranded in the lost civilization of Qui, somewhere southwest of Greenland, with the Viking descendants discovered there. In the final chapter (chap. 19), a Viking ship arrived in New York mysteriously "four months later." The Viking ship was examined by Johnny, and later ended up in a museum. Although Lester Dent does not explicitly state it, the impression is given that Doc and his men had taken one of the Viking ships from Qui and used it to return to civilization four months later. Considering the time intervals of later adventures, it is impossible for Doc to have taken four months to return to Qui. Therefore, a theory must be concocted to explain this discrepancy. Doc was known was for always preparing for a possible emergency. He must have transported an extra radio in his plane to Qui. He took the radio and hid it outside in the snow before his plane was destroyed. After the villains were defeated, Doc radioed for help. He called Charles Arthur Vonier, the Arctic explorer from *Cold Death*. Vonier took a plane to pick up Doc and his men. However, Vonier decided to stay in Qui to study the lost civilization there while Doc and his men took the plane back to New York. Vonier used the Viking ship to return to New York because he wanted to donate the ship to a local museum. Vonier and Doc had promised to keep the discovery of Qui secret. Therefore, the voyage of the Viking ship was handled in a mysterious manner which baffled the public.

59. The Jade Ogre

Published: October 1992
1934: Mid-June to early July (15 days)*
Author: Will Murray

The novel began in the spring. There is a reference to a "late Spring chill" (chap. 1). Although Will Murray didn't specify the year of Doc's adventure in the novel, he had indicated to me that it was set in 1935. In fact, there is a remark which implies that the year is indeed 1935. The captain of the Mandarin made reference to "that fool maritime strike last year" (chap. 7). This reference was to the 1934 San Francisco maritime strike. Why then does my chronology place this novel in 1934? As I stated in the introduction, references to 1934-35 in some of Will Murray's novels are ignored to keep the proper sequence of the adventures. The novels by Will Murray only make references to the novels with which Lester Dent was involved. You won't find any references to Laurence Donovan's novels. Many of Donovan's work were set in the spring and summer, and featured a very experienced Pat Savage. While Mr. Farmer mixed Dent's and Donovan's output together in his prior chronology, I have put the bulk of Donovan's output in the spring and summer of the same year. This decision resulted in keeping Lester Dent's and Will Murray's novels together in 1933 and 1934, while nearly all of Laurence Donovan's novels ended up in 1935.

Mr. Murray has indicated that he envisioned *The Jade Ogre* as transpiring after *The Majii*. However, *The Majii* contains no references to spring unlike the other Dent novels *(Spook Hole, The Roar Devil,* and *Quest of Qui)* which precede it in submission order. Considering the length of *The Majii* (29 days), it is impossible to set both it and *The Jade Ogre* in June, the last of the spring months. Therefore, I moved *The Majii* after *The Jade*

Ogre. Since *The Jade Ogre* contains no direct references to *The Majii*, I don't view this shifting as a problem.

The Jade Ogre (chap. 12) mentioned that Pat Savage's last chronological adventure with Doc Savage was *Spook Hole*. The events of *The Thousand-Headed Man* were also recalled (chap. 25). A remark that "the ways of the Orient were unknown" to Pat (chap. 20) also indicates that *The Jade Ogre* transpired before *The Motion Menace* in which Pat visited China. Johnny, Renny and Long Tom were missing from the events of *The Jade Ogre*. Johnny was in Europe, while the other two were working at an Argentine hydro-electrical project (chap. 22).

There may be a reference to an unrecorded adventure of Monk Mayfair's in this novel. Monk told Ham Brooks that he once saw a woman hanging from a tree the last time he was in China (chap. 36). However, Monk quickly made a joke from this remark which could indicate that he was only pulling Ham's leg. If the anecdote about the dead Chinese woman was true, Monk's experience could have happened during the trip to Asia in "Needle in a Chinese Haystack."

In Hong Kong, a policeman remarked that Doc Savage "had rendered certain services to His Majesty's government in the past" (chap. 17). These unknown services are probably the same which were mentioned in *The Thousand-Headed Man* as having earned Doc membership in the British Secret Service. For a discussion of this reference, see the "**Note**" following entry #23.

Lester Dent had originally called Pat Savage's business "Park Avenue Beautician" *(Death in Silver*, chap. 8). A totally different name, "Patricia, Incorporated," was given in *The Yellow Cloud* (chap. 9). *The Jade Ogre* (chap. 9), which is intended by Will Murray to transpire years before *The Yellow Cloud*, uses the abbreviated form of the second name, "Patricia, Inc." We must conclude that Pat used the name of Park Avenue Beautician for only a year.

Doc had recently purchased an airline in *The Jade Ogre*

(chap. 2). This was probably the same airline in which he had only owned "goodly portion" of the stock in *The Secret in the Sky (*chap. 7). Doc must have expanded his stock holding of the airline to become the majority shareholder.

Doc's meeting with the police chief of San Francisco in *The Jade Ogre* (chap. 4) was based on a statement in *The Feathered Octopus* (chap. 13).

60. The Majii
Published: September 1935
1934: July to early August (29 days)
Author: Lester Dent

The novel is set largely in Jondore, a fictional princely state of India. Jondore was ruled by a prince with the title of Nizam. The Nizam was famous for his large collection of jewels, and reputed to be the richest man in the world. He was also very short. Jondore is based on the Indian princely state of Hyderabad. Its hereditary rulers were known as Nizams. In 1911, Osman Ali Khan Bahadur became the seventh Nizam of Hyderabad. In 1948, troops loyal to new Indian central government took control of Hyderabad. Osman Ali continued as a figurehead monarch until 1956 when Hyderabad was incorporated into the Indian state of Andhra Pradesh. The Nizam officially retired, and the position as monarch of Hyderabad was abolished. Osman Ali was often described as the richest man in the world. He had some many jewels that some of them were used as paperweights. He was only five feet and three inches tall. The Nizam of Hyderabad was known for this loyalty to the British government which he demonstrated through two World Wars.

This was true of Kadir Singh, Dent's fictional Nizam of Jondore. However, Kadir Singh had supposedly recently replaced his half-brother, who plotted to lead a rebellion to oust the British. The anti-British half-brother had supposedly died, but this death was later revealed to be a hoax.

The pro-British Nizam of Hyderabad succeeded his father in 1911. To pretend that Jondore was "really" Hyderabad, it would have to be imagined that Dent distorted the "true" events. The ruler disguised under the alias of Kadir Singh had always occupied the throne since the death of his father. The half-brother never succeeded to the throne, but just remained a power in the court. The pro-British Kadir Singh and his half-brother greatly resembled each other. It could be speculated that something like Dumas' *The Man in the Iron Mask* happened in Hyderabad prior to the events of *The Majii*. The anti-British half-brother imprisoned the rightful Nizam, and then sought to impersonate him on the throne. The plot was eventually exposed and the rightful ruler restored to power, but the Nizam's half-brother escaped by faking his death only to come into conflict later with Doc Savage.

Renny was in Germany "attending an international association of engineers conclave," Johnny was in Central America, and Long Tom, although he participated in this exploit, was considering an offer of fifty thousand dollars to superintend construction in South America (chap. 5).

The novel made reference to an unrecorded adventure involving the poisoning of the water supply of Doc's building (chap. 10). I place this adventure in January 1934 (see the "Note" after entry #49).

61. The Fantastic Island
Published: December 1935
1934: August (10 days)
Author: W. Ryerson Johnson and Lester Dent

While all assistants participated in this adventure, Johnny was leading an expedition to the Galapagos Islands, and Ham and Monk along with Pat Savage were on "a vacation cruise" off the coast of Panama (chap. 1). Johnny could have left for the Galapagos Islands from Central America, his location in *The Majii*.

62. Mystery Under the Sea
Published: February 1936
1934: September 1 to October 10 (40 days)
Author: Lester Dent

The novel began "on the first Saturday of September" (chap. 1). Johnny was in Europe, and Long Tom was in South America (chap. 5). Throughout the chronological entries for 1934, Long Tom was involved in South American projects which involve either construction or hydro-electrical work. In *Dust of Death* and *The Jade Ogre*, the project was identified as an Argentine project. Long Tom probably worked only on one South American project, the construction of a hydro-electrical plant in Argentina. He started work in Argentina around December 1933, and returned to Doc Savage's service in January 1934. He went back to Argentina in June, and returned to New York in July after finishing his assignment there. At that time, he received an additional offer of fifty thousand dollars to continue with the Argentine project. Long Tom eventually accepted the offer, but he didn't return to Argentina until late August. He spent all of September in Argentina, and returned to New York sometime during October, but then became involved in a project in Cuba (see entry #65).

63. The Seven Agate Devils
Published: May 1936
1934: October 15-18 (4 days)
Author: Lester Dent

The novel began "on one particular Monday morning" (chap. 1). Renny, Long Tom and Johnny "were practicing their various professions in other parts of the world" (chap.

1). Chemistry made his second appearance here (according to the original submission order). Although Chemistry appeared here and in the next entry, *The Midas Man,* the explanation for his lengthy absence will be examined in the discussion of *The Metal Master* (entry #65).

International spies assassinated an Asian diplomat in the novel. The diplomat was killed while on "a good-will mission" to the United States (chap. 14). The diplomat was probably from Japan. He would have been trying to improve American relations because of the damage done by Japan's invasion of Manchuria in 1931. In Doc's fictional world, the diplomat may also have been attempting to ease tensions caused by his country's activities in the earlier *Red Snow*.

64. The Midas Man
Published: August 1936
1934: October 23-24 (2 days)
Author: Lester Dent

Doc Savage became involved in this novel "the next day" after a bank examiner found an irregularity on "Monday morning" (chap. 1). Therefore, Doc's case started on a Tuesday.

The events of *The Fantastic Island* are remembered by Johnny in *The Midas Man* (chap. 17): "He thought of an incident, months in the past, when he had gone through some hair-raising encounters with what had first appeared to be monsters, but which had later turned out to be nothing but oversize lizards."

Renny and Long Tom were absent "because their professions called them for the time being" (chap. 9).

Chemistry was described as "lately acquired" (chap 10). Although Ham had acquired the simian in January, he was able to get his pet out of quarantine only recently. Chemistry's quarantine was described in the next adventure, *The Metal Master*.

In *The Midas Man* (chap. 14), the villains discovered that the senate's committee on tariff revision intended to alter the tariff on Cuban sugar. The villains then proceeded to buy up all available sugar to making a financial killing later. Doc discovered this plot, and convinced a prominent senator to "pigeonhole" the bill (chap. 16). In October 1934, Congress was in recess until January. However, the Senate committee may have already made its plans for tariff recommendations that would be presented in January. The villains could have acted in October in order to have ample time to gain control of the sugar supply. Even though Doc had two months to foil the villains before their sugar scheme bore fruit, the bronze adventurer couldn't assume that he would have the criminals defeated by January. As we shall later see, some of Doc's adventures took longer than two months (e. g. *The South Pole Terror)*. Therefore, Doc's telephone call to the senator should just be viewed as a wise precaution.

Note: In late October, the Viking ship mentioned in the final chapter of *Quest of Qui* made its appearance in a New York harbor and was examined by Johnny (see entry #58).

65. The Metal Master
Published: March 1936
1934: November (3 days)
Author: Lester Dent

The time has to be late autumn or early winter (chap. 1): "It was sleeting a little. Cold." An argument could be made that the novel occurred in either February or March. A telegraph was received containing the sentence RETURN OVERLAND ON MARCH 7 (chap. 12). However, the message written in code, and didn't make any sense to those reading it at face value. The code was to take the first letter of every word.

RETURN OVERLAND ON MARCH 7 translated into "Room 7." The usage of "March 7" in the message should not be taken seriously.

Johnny was "in Europe excavating a cave in which a farmer had found the fossil of a prehistoric man" (chap. 10). Renny and Long Tom entered the novel while they were in Cuba. Renny "was ostensibly engaged in superintending the laying of a narrow gauge railway to a sugar plantation" (chap. 5). Actually, Renny and Long Tom were "investigating the various ramifications of the narcotics smuggling racket" (chap. 6). Long Tom and Renny had been in Cuba for a least "two weeks" (chap. 6). Their presence on the island for weeks would be consistent with their absence from New York since mid-October.

The absence of Chemistry from February until October can be explained by a remark in this novel (chap. 15): "Ham had been without his pet for a few months, due to regulations of the United States. Customs that demanded that an animal be in quarantine until it could be declared free of any contagious or infectious diseases before being brought into the country."

Monk's secretary was briefly mentioned (chap. 13).

In *The Midas Man* (chap. 9), crooks rented the eighty-fifth floor to attack Doc on the floor above. In *The Metal Master*, Doc was renting the floor below his (chap. 7). However, Doc's stated reason for doing so was not to prevent potential enemies from using the eighty-fifth floor. His reason for renting the floor in *The Metal Master* was to prevent the building from losing money. No one wanted to be in such a risky location where dangerous things could happen because of the proximity to Doc's headquarters. Most likely, Doc rented the floor for two reasons. No honest people would rent the floor because of the risk, and crooks could use it to attack him. *The Metal Master* asserted that the eighty-fifth floor "had been without a tenant for a long time." This remark would seem to contradict *The Midas Man*. However, the crooks in *The Midas Man* only occupied the floor for one day to attack Doc. Probably they only rented the floor for one day. They were probably were not considered tenants in the true sense by the building's management.

66. White Eyes

Published: March 1992
1934: Early December (5 days)*
Author: Will Murray

The novel opened on "a cold Winter day" when it was snowing in New York (chap. 1), and policemen were thinking of Christmas bonuses (chap. 20). The United States went off the gold standard "a few years ago" (chap. 4). The gold standard was abandoned in 1933. The reference to the passage of "a few years" would imply 1935 rather than 1934. As I mentioned earlier in my discussion of *The Jade Ogre*, the need to keep the whole series chronologically coherent forces me to sometimes backdate the events in the new novels by a year.

In *White Eyes*, Doc used a Cuban sugar plantation to receive his Central American gold and convert it into cash. This was probably the same plantation used by Renny and Long Tom as a cover for a narcotics investigation in *The Metal Master*. *White Eyes* also featured the mind-reading device from *The Midas Man* which Doc had acquired "some months ago" (chap. 16).

Renny and Johnny were "currently pursuing their respective professions in different European capitals" (chap. 17), and were absent from this adventure.

The police commissioner of New York in *White Eyes* was not a political appointee, but a man who rose through the ranks (chap. 21).

Long Tom's had taken a patent on his insect killing device "over a year ago" (chap. 30). Long Tom had been working on the device since *The Polar Treasure* (entry #26), which I have placed in 1932.

67. The South Pole Terror
Published: October 1936
1934-35: December to early March (82 days)
Author: Lester Dent

It was summer at the South Pole (chap. 16): "The water was free of ice for the South Pole summer was beginning." Summer at the South Pole would mean winter in New York.

Renny and Johnny became involved in the story while they were in London. Johnny had been busy "translating some old tablets for the English national museum" (chap. 4).

There is an intriguing reference to the travels of Doc Savage and his men: "…they had been in the Sahara, Death Valley, and that most unknown of all deserts, the Rub-El-Khali of Arabia" (chap. 19). They had visited the Sahara in *The Lost Oasis*, and the Rub-El-Khali in *The Phantom City*. However, there is no record of a previous visit to Death Valley. Doc visited there later in *The Pirate's Ghost*, but that novel was written much later and should be placed in the late 1930s. For when this unrecorded Death Valley episode most likely transpired, see the "**Note**" after entry #45.

68. Haunted Ocean
Published: June 1936
1935: March (7 days)
Author: Laurence Donovan

There is an apparent reference to winter (chap 15): "But the winter air was clear and cold." The air was in Lapland where the climate is dominated by winter. Water freezes in November and does not thaw until May.

Johnny entered the novel while serving as an American delegate to an international peace conference. The delegates met in London, and then departed for Calais. This conference's alleged purpose was o conclude "a pact that would include not disarmament of any nation, but the immediate super-armament of the six member nations against all others" (chap. 3). The six nations were the United States, Great Britain, Italy, France, Germany and Spain. Taken at face value, this conference would seem to be aimed at Japan and the Soviet Union, the two major absentees. The geopolitical realities of 1935 would not have permitted the convening of a "super-armament" conference. In July 1934, Germany and Italy nearly went to war over Austria. Italy and Germany were bitter enemies until British and French condemnation of the Italian invasion of Ethiopia (October 1935) convinced Mussolini to seek Hitler as an ally. More likely, this peace conference was an effort by the four neutral nations to mediate the dispute between Italy and Germany. The German delegates probably tried unsuccessfully to transform the meeting into a "super-armament" discussion in order to sanction the Nazi rearmament program which violated the Treaty of Versailles.

Among the novel's villains were representatives of San Tao, "an isolated little known, but immensely wealthy province of southern China" (chap. 4). San Tao was probably based on Szechwan in southwest China. Szechwan was then self-sufficient in resources. It has lofty mountains everywhere. Chiang Kai-shek had very little control over matters in Szechwan, until the Japanese invasion of 1937 forced him to make that province his central base of operations. The remoteness of Szechwan appealed to pulp writers like George F. Worts ("Loring Brent"), whose Peter the Brazen stories in *Argosy* influenced Lester Dent. I don't know whether Laurence Donovan was familiar with Worts' work. Worts populated Szechwan with evil masterminds like the Gray Dragon and the Blue Scorpion.

69. Mad Eyes

Published: May 1937
1935: Late March (3 days)
Author: Laurence Donovan

Ham was wearing the "latest in spring fashions" (chap. 6).

Prior to the opening of this novel, Doc hadn't been seen by Ham or Monk for "three days" (chap. 2). This was the only novel written by Laurence Donovan in which Chemistry appeared.

70. He Could Stop the World

Published: July 1937
1935: April (19 days)
Author: Laurence Donovan

The best time to place this novel would be in the spring due to the following reference (chap. 5): "At this season, the snow laid many feet deep on all of Mount Shasta's upper ranges and in the valleys." The snow would have accumulated on Mount Shasta in California during the winter. The snow would have stopped falling in the spring, but the large accumulations would remain.

Monk and Ham were absent for only the early portions of the novel because they were attending conventions in Salt Lake City. Monk went to a meeting of the World Society of Chemists, and Ham was at a gathering of the American Bar Association. Renny was offstage "in Japan on a project that was to make him a wealthy man" (chap. 2).

Note: Doc began working on the *Zephyr*, a new dirigible for the United States Navy (see entry #76).

71. Land of Long Juju
1935: Late May (4 days)
Published: January 1937
Author: Laurence Donovan

In the first version of his chronology (in the Doubleday hardcover), Philip José Farmer dismissed this novel as "all fiction and bad fiction at that." The novel is full of inaccuracies about Africa. The reason for all these mistakes was explained in Dafydd Neal Dyar's "The Switcheroo Revisited" in *Doc Savage Quest* #8 (February 1982). This novel was set in either Central or South America, but editorial changes shifted the locale to Africa. This action resulted in such anomalies as piranha fish in Africa and a Mayan-speaking African. This novel should be viewed as a distorted view of a Latin American adventure.

An absent Long Tom "was attending a convention on the Pacific coast" (chap. 3). Wherever this novel happened, Renny was there trying to survey a railroad. He had been there "nearly six weeks" (chap. 1). Renny had been in Japan at the start of *He Could Stop the World* in early April, but he could have gone to Latin America for the railway survey sometime during the course of that long adventure.

72. The Men Who Smiled No More
Published: April 1936
1935: First half of June (3 days)
Author: Laurence Donovan

The novel was set in late spring (chap. 17): "As it often does in late spring, the heat broke with a violent thunderstorm." Ham was wearing the "latest in spring togs" (chap. 5). "More than a week" had passed since Doc's last adventure (chap. 5). Monk had been buying ducks on Long Island for that length of time. Pat Savage hadn't seen Doc for "several days." She had participated in *Land of Long Juju*.

73. Murder Melody

Published: November 1935
1935: June 16-20 (5 days)
Author: Laurence Donovan

The novel would have to have transpired in the summer or very late spring. The novel contained references to "summer residents" living on the coast of British Columbia (chap. 1). The summer residents could have begun to take up residence in early June. The date of the month on which the novel began was clearly given. The novel also mentioned the "dry summer season" (chap. 3). The novel started with Doc responding to a message to be in Vancouver, British Columbia, on the "16th" of the month (chap. 1).

Doc remembered "the earth-shaker in Chile" (chap. 4) encountered in *The Man Who Shook the Earth.*

74. Murder Mirage

Published: January 1936
1935: July 4-13 (10 days)*
Author: Laurence Donovan

The novel was quite explicit on when it began (chap. 1): "To be exact, it was the midnight of July 4th. In a mater of minutes, it would be the morning of July 5th."

When Pat Savage was contacted, she was unaware of Doc's true whereabouts. She heard rumors that he may be in Malaysia or Yucatan (chap. 6). This statement would indicate that Doc and Pat hadn't been in contact for at least a brief period. By my chronological arrangement, it would have been almost a month since Pat assisted Doc in *The Men Who Smiled No More*. Pat must have heard the false rumors about his whereabouts when he disappeared off the face of the earth in *Murder Melody*.

Throughout the novel, there was unusual weather. It was

snowing in July. The text doesn't offer any precise explanation for this phenomenon. The villains used a weird element which blasts people into shadows, and the novel hinted that usage of the element may be causing the unusual weather by somehow affecting the atmosphere. The element was radioactive in nature, and the unusual snowfall may have been Donovan's version of "nuclear winter." An elevator operator was held hostage by Bedouins who invaded Doc's headquarters. It is mentioned that this was "the second time that he had a run-in with some of Doc's peculiar visitors" (chap. 8). Perhaps this operator was the same one nearly killed by a poisonous centipede in *The Fantastic Island* (chap. 4). On the other hand, he could have been one of the elevators overcome by gunmen in either *The South Pole Terror* (chap. 7) or *White Eyes* (chap. 28).

75. The Black Spot
Published: July 1936
1935: August (3 days)
Author: Laurence Donovan

The novel would seem to be set in the summer or late spring. A character named Cedric Cecil Spade was at his "summer house" in Manhasset (chap. 9).

The novel was set in 1935. Ronald Doremon had been the assistant to General Manager Congdon of the Electro-Chemical Research Corporation for "five years" (chap. 8). Doremon had starting working for Congdon in 1930 (chap. 16).

76. The Terror in the Navy

Published: April 1937
1935: Late August (7 days)
Author: Lester Dent

There are references to "green shrubbery"(chap. 6), and a man was mowing the lawn (chap. 7). Summer would be consistent with these references. At least a week passed since Doc's last adventure. Long Tom, Renny and Johnny had been watching suspicious characters on the water front for "almost a week" (chap. 4).

Monk fooled Ham with a "trick nickel with heads on both sides" (chap. 15). Monk had earlier used a coin with tails on both sides to trick Ham in *The South Pole Terror* (chap. 22).

An important reference is made to *The Man of Bronze* in *The Terror in the Navy* (chap. 11) by Long Tom: "There's been bulletproof glass in these windows a long time… Ever since some guys on the tower of an unfinished skyscraper tried to shoot Doc, almost three and a half years ago." By my chronological arrangement, it would be four years and nearly three months ago. I justify the discrepancy by asserting that Long Tom simply made a mistake. He really should have said "almost four and a half years ago." The statement by Long Tom also contained one other inaccuracy. Who were "the guys?" There was only one Mayan sniper. However, it could be argued that Long Tom was also referring to the assassin from "The Sniper in the Sky." The bulletproof glass windows had been mentioned earlier in *Pirate of the Pacific* (chap. 6) and "The Sniper in the Sky."

In this novel, we learn that Doc wrote a book entitled *The Armor Plate Value of Certain Alloys* (chap. 1). It was also indicated that Renny was writing his autobiography (chap. 10).

The novel featured a U.S. Navy dirigible, the *Zephyr*, which Doc had "worked for months" designing "with a crew of the world's leading experts" (chap. 13). Doc really didn't have time to work consistently for months on such a project, but he could have allocated a significant amount of time during May 1935, and then kept in touch with the other dirigible designers during the gaps between his adventure in the summer of 1935. Doc had earlier utilized dirigibles of his own design in *Land of Always Night, Dust of Death, The South Pole Terror* and *Murder Mirage*. Doc would later utilize more of his own dirigibles in *Ost* (also known as *The Magic Island), The Green Death, The Crimson Serpent* and *The Headless Men*.

The *Zephyr*'s catwalks were said to be superior to those of the *Los Angeles* and the *Macon (The Terror in the Navy*, chap. 13). The *Los Angeles* was a dirigible built by Germany for the United States in 1924. After 331 flights, it was decommissioned in 1932. The *Macon* was built for the U.S. Navy by Goodyear. It was launched in April 1933. On Feb. 12, 1935, the *Macon* crashed into the sea off the California coast.

Doc met with the Secretary of the Navy (chap. 11). This position was held during 1933-39 by Claude A Swanson.

Note: There is a theory in Philip José Farmer's *Doc Savage: His Apocalyptic Life*. Johnny, whose full name was William Harper Littlejohn, was the college professor called William Dyer in two tales by H. P. Lovecraft, "At the Mountains of Madness" and "The Shadow Out of Time." Dyer was on an Antarctic expedition from September 1930 to mid-February 1931, and on an Australian expedition during March-July 1935. The identification of Dyer with Johnny appears to be incorrect. Although Johnny could have been in Antarctica before the events of *The Man of Bronze*, there is now way that he could have participated in the Australian adventure without it interfering with his activities with Doc Savage during 1935. Mr. Farmer may be on firmer ground when he asserts that Johnny was the head of the natural science department at Miskatonic University, a center of learning featured in Lovecraft's writings, before his adventures in the 1930s with Doc. There is nothing inconsistent between Miskatonic University and the unnamed university where Johnny once headed a department. It could be that Johnny was Dyer's predecessor as Professor of Geology at Miskatonic. Johnny could have resigned his position sometime in the late 1920s, and Dyer was hired to replace him. By leaving Miskatonic University, Johnny would have missed participating in some incredible research regarding man's true role in the cosmos. It also has to be noted that *Doc Savage: His Apocalyptic Life* alters the chronology of "At the Mountain of Madness" from 1930-31 to 1929 for no apparent reason.

77. The Derrick Devil
Published: February 1937
1935: Mid-September (6 days)
Author: Lester Dent

Doc made a brief trip to the Fortress of Solitude (chap. 4). References to "insects" and "birds" (chap. 3) would still be consistent with September.

The novel contained the last appearance of Monk's secretary (chap. 4).

An old submarine was probably the same "one that was showed at a fair in Chicago" (chap. 9). The Chicago World's Fair had been in 1933.

78. The Vanisher
Published: December 1936
1935: Late September (5 days)
Author: Lester Dent

The novel seems to be set in early fall: "The early fall issue of a magazine of national circulation had carried a feature write-up about Doc Savage" (chap. 1). In *The Derrick Devil*, a magazine featured a photo of Doc Savage (chap. 3). This was probably the same magazine mentioned in *The Vanisher*. Early fall issues have been known to be published in September.

An argument could be made that this novel should be placed closer to *Dust of Death*. *The Vanisher* described Chemistry as "acquired not many months before" (chap. 6). However the placement of the novel in the autumn of 1934 would still make it at least eight months since Chemistry was acquired. Eight months would still be "many months." The reference to "not many months" is still an inaccuracy even if I place the novel a year earlier.

In *The Vanisher*, a top government official was murdered by the novel's villain (chap. 13). The victim was described in the following manner: "He was a big shot in the U. S. Department of Investigation. A fellow who had made a remarkable record. He had been something of a dictator in the organization, a man who ran everything personally." This description could fit J. Edgar Hoover, the director of the Federal Bureau of Investigation. Since Hoover didn't die until 1972, it could be theorized that the murdered man was an ill-fated actor whom the real FBI director had hired to impersonate him.

Doc had problems with the New York police in this novel. These difficulties were ascribed to "a change of police commissioners" (chap. 13).

Renny, Long Tom and Johnny were offstage in Europe (chap. 13).

79. The Land of Fear

Published: June 1937
1935: October (5 days)
Author: Harold A. Davis and Lester Dent

Arriving on the S. S. *Gentina* in New York, Virginia Jettmore wore "a cape around her shoulders, despite the warmth of the day" (chap. 1). Miss Jettmore's dress implied that she expected the weather to be cold. She probably arrived in the autumn when warm and cold days alternate.

Doc and his men used "breathing pills" in *The Land of Fear* (chap. 11). Similar pills would appear later in *Resurrection Day* (chap. 18), *The Submarine Mystery* (chap. 16), *The Green Death* (chap. 11), *Merchants of Disaster* (chap. 4), *The Devil's Playground* (chap. 17) and *Devils of the Deep* (chap. 17). As noted in Will Murray's "The Secret Kenneth Robesons," Doc's pills were probably derived from the oxygen pills discovered in a lost civilization during the events of the earlier *Mystery Under the Sea*.

The Land of Fear mentioned that Doc "had known cases before where girls had been member of gangs" (chap. 14). Doc had encountered female crooks earlier in *Mad Eyes* and *Murder Mirage*.

Whatever Doc problems were with the police commissioner of New York in *The Vanisher*, they were solved by *The Land of Fear*. A policeman claimed that the commissioner said Doc's "all right" (chap. 5).

Johnny, Renny and Long Tom were absent from *The Land of Fear*.

Note: In *The Men Vanished* (entry #118), it is asserted that Doc had an unrecorded adventure in which he saved the lives of Carl Voorheis, a plantation owner in Hidalgo (i.e. Guatemala) and his family. This even happened "four or five years" prior to the novel (chap. 11). Since I place *The Men Vanished* in 1939, this unrecorded episode transpired in either 1934 or 1935. The gap in November 1935 would seem to be the best place to put Doc's rescue of the Voorheis family.

In The *Freckled Shark* (chap. 5), it is mentioned that Monk had once gone swimming nude in a tropical river. A naturalist mistook him for an ape and shot at him with a rifle loaded with mercy bullets. This episode probably happened in Hidalgo during the same adventure where Doc saved the Voorheis family. An incident mentioned in *Mystery on Happy Bones* (see entry #152) may be related to Doc's unrecorded exploit. Doc recalled swinging in jungle trees like Tarzan with Ham on is back.

80. The Mental Wizard

Published: March 1937
1935: December (8 days)
Author: Lester Dent

The novel transpired during the New York winter (chap. 10): "It was bitterly cold in New York which meant summer and heat down here."

The novel opened with Doc and his assistants visiting Colombia. Monk recalled the events of *Dust of Death* in the Colombian scenes of *The Mental Wizard* (chap. 4): "Doc ain't been in this country recently. All he ever done was stop a war between a couple of their neighbors in which they might have been involved." Monk also stated that the earlier exploit transpired "over a year ago." Monk's statement is consistent with my placement of *Dust of Death* in January 1934. It would be a year and eleven months since that earlier exploit.

The Prologue of *The Mental Wizard* alluded to the disappearances of Colonel Percy Fawcett in 1925 and Paul Redfern in 1927. Both men disappeared in the Matto Grosso jungle.

81. Resurrection Day

Published: November 1936
1936: January 3-February 28 (57 days)
Author: Lester Dent

There were "storm clouds" in the Nubian Desert (chap. 17). These clouds would imply that it was now the rainy season in Egypt. The season lasts from December to February. The third day of the novel was a Sunday (chap. 2).

82. Repel

Published: October 1937
Bantam Reprint Title: The Deadly Dwarf
1936: March to early April (38 days)
Author: Lester Dent

Johnny recalled a ride on a Tibetan yak. This ride probably occurred when Doc and his men visited Tibet in *Meteor Menace*. When the evil Cadwiller Olden tried to sabotage the gas tank of Doc's airplane in *Repel* (chap. 14), Doc remarked that "we have had experience with stuff in the gas tanks before." Doc must have been thinking of how villains sabotaged his planes in *The Thousand-Headed Man* (chap. 11) and *The Man Who Shook the Earth* (chap. 12).

Repel began on Fan Coral Island in the South Pacific. Doc "had a kind of commission from the government, which had a protectorate, so-called, over Fan Coral" (chap. 5). This commission "had been given Doc for a past service, and was supposed to entitle him to almost any type of cooperation." The League of Nations had granted four countries Pacific protectorates after World War I. In 1920, the Japanese had been granted a protectorate over the Carolines, the Mariannas and the Marshalls. In 1921, Australia received a protectorate over northwestern New Guinea, the Bismarck archipelago and the northern Solomons. New Zealand was granted a protectorate over Western Samoa. The governments of Great Britain, Australia and New Zealand shared a protectorate over the island of Nauru. Fan Coral Island was a fictional name for an island in one of these Pacific protectorates. Doc traveled by plane from San Francisco to Hawaii to Tahiti to Fan Coral Island. The closest of the Pacific protectorates to Tahiti was Western Samoa. The two largest islands of Western Samoa, Savai'i and Ulopo, are mountainous islands of volcanic origin, with coasts surrounded by coral reefs. The same description can be applied to Fan Coral Island. Fan Coral Island must be based on one of these two islands. Savai'i would seem the more likely of the pair to be Fan Coral Island. A volcano erupted in *Repel* (chap. 1). Savai'i had a volcanic eruption also. Unfortunately, it happened in 1911 instead of 1936, but this fact is probably what inspired Lester Dent to fashion the fictional Fan Coral Island. Doc must have performed a service for New Zealand immediately after *The Land of Terror*. See the "**Note**" after entry #22.

When crooks were normally sent to the Crime College, they had their memories totally erased and were given new identities. However, there was an alternate procedure where the corrupt individual just had his personality changed. The subject was then returned to his normal life. This procedure was utilized with the Baldwin siblings in *Repel* (chap. 21), as well as with the shady financiers of *The Sea Angel* (chap. 23), *The Dagger in the Sky* (chap. 17), and *The Magic Forest* (chap. 18).

83. The Motion Menace

Published: May 1938
1936: Mid to late April (15 days)
Author: W. Ryerson Johnson and Lester Dent

Doc was being watched by the villains in New York during "the last few weeks" (chap. 3). Some of this surveillance would have coincided with the closing weeks of *Repel*. Doc probably assumed that the people following him worked for Cadwiller Olden. When Olden was defeated, Doc must have realized that the individuals stalking him worked for some other mastermind.

Throughout the novel, the Russian secret police was called the OGPU. In July 1934, the secret police changed its name from the OGPU to the NKVD. I toyed with placing this novel in 1934, but references in Will Murray's *The Jade Ogre* and *The Whistling Wraith* deterred me from doing so. Therefore, the usage of the name OGPU should just be treated as a mistake by the authors. Perhaps the error resulted from the fact that Doc had done a service for the secret police earlier (chap. 18). This service was probably a reference to the assistance which Doc rendered a Soviet agent, Oscar Gibson, in *The Mystic Mullah*. In that earlier adventure, Gibson's employer would have been known as the OGPU. *The Mystic Mullah* depicted Gibson, an American born in Texas, as one of "the four highest ranking officers" of the secret police (chap. 13). Gibson was probably the "OPGU chief" who sent Doc a telegram in *The Motion Menace* (chap. 8).

This novel revealed Doc's super-machine pistols have "two different secret safeties" (chap. 12). Furthermore, it was claimed that there were "occasions when enemies captured one of the guns, only to spend hours in futile efforts to make it function." The fact that the guns had safeties had been mentioned briefly in *The Mystery on the Snow* (chap. 5). The only previously recorded instance of a capture of Doc's guns was in *The Mental Wizard* (chap. 17 & 18). However, Doc probably turned the safeties off because he wanted the villains to find the guns. Doc had set a booby trap that only someone possessing his pistols could set off. There are no other recorded instances prior to *The Motion Menace* of crooks having trouble with the safeties on Doc's guns. Probably the instances mentioned in *The Motion Menace* transpired in some of the unrecorded adventures of July 1931-May 1932, September 1933, January 1934 and November 1935.

Renny was at "an engineering project in South Africa," and Johnny was "in the South Seas conducting researches into the historical past of certain mystifying statues in some remote island" (chap. 6). As Will Murray noted in "Tracking Doc Savage's Men," the description of Johnny's whereabouts fits Easter Island.

84. Ost

Published: August 1937
Bantam Reprint Title: The Magic Island
1936: April 30 to July 14 (76 days)*
Author: Lester Dent

The third day of this adventure is a Sunday (chap. 9). Monk tricked Ham a using a fake nickel with two heads (chap. 9). Monk had used similar trick coins earlier in *The South Pole Terror* (chap. 22) and *The Terror in the Navy* (chap. 15).

Doc and his men "held a special commission from the California governor designating them as special investigators with police authority" (chap. 8). Doc and his assistants could have earned these commissions as a result of their successful investigations of the strange doings around Mount Shasta in *He Could Stop the World*. Doc did not have this California commission at the time of *The Jade Ogre* because the San Francisco police were only shown Doc's New York commission (chap. 4). Doc's commission was granted by Frank F. Merriam, who was governor of California during 1934-39.

Ost (chap. 15) contained a reference to *The Land of Terror*: "Reminds me of the time we found some prehistoric monsters in a volcanic pit."

In *Ost* (chap. 11), Doc had "special engine fuel" which required less refueling stops on long flights across the Pacific. Doc "probably had the only supply available." Doc's fuel explained why some of his aerial trips across oceans seem so quick.

85. The Whistling Wraith

Published: July 1993
1936: July 23 to August 3 (12 days)
Author: Will Murray

Doc became involved in the novel on a Thursday (chap. 1).

The novel was set during the summer (chap. 7): "It was a warm summer's day…" Will Murray has indicated in interviews that he intended his novel should follow *The Sea Angel*. However, there is nothing in the text of *The Whistling Wraith* to indicate such. As I will discuss in the following entry, textural evidence in *The Sea Angel* would place it in August. That fact left the only other summer month available to be September, but another novel, *The Red Terrors*, would swallow that month whole. Therefore, I have placed *The Whistling Wraith* in front of *The Sea Angel* since I had a sizable gap in July.

The kingdom of Merida was based on Albania. King Goz of Merida was derived from King Zog of Albania. Goz is Zog spelt backwards. In the novel, Merida was virtually a satellite of another country, Santa Bellanca, which was ruled by an unnamed dictator. Santa Bellanca was clearly meant to be Italy, and the dictator was Benito Mussolini. The relationship between Italy and Albania in 1936 was identical to their fictional counterparts Reference is mad to the dictator's conquest of "a defenseless African country" (chap. 27). The African nation was Ethiopia, which Italy conquered during October 1935 through May 1936.

In the novel, Santa Bellanca nearly went to war over Merida with one of that country's Balkan neighbors, Carullana. Italy had rivalries with two other countries, Yugoslavia and Greece, over Albania. Considering that Yugoslavia was already the basis for Calbia in Lester Dent's *The King Maker*, Will Murray used Greece as the basis for Carullana. An incident in Albania in 1923 nearly led to war between Italy and Greece, and Italy would eventually attack Greece in 1940 during World War II. A misunderstanding between Will Murray and myself unfortunately led to Yugoslavia being falsely identified as the model for Carullana in a previous version of this chronology. Carullana was said to be ruled by a president (chap. 27). This statement would imply that Carullana was a republic as opposed to a monarchy. Actually Greece was technically a monarchy, but the ultimate power was held by a Prime Minister, Ioannis

Metaxas. On August 4, 1936, Metaxas created a dictatorial regime that paralleled Mussolini's in Italy. Both Metaxas and Mussolini were nominally subordinate to kings. Will Murray's reference to a president is merely a deliberate distortion on his part intended to cloak the historical basis for the fictional Carullana.

Although King Zog was a virtual puppet of Mussolini's, Italy invaded Albania in April 1939. Zog fled the country with a large fortune In Will Murray's novel, Zog's fictional alter ego, Goz, realized that his dictatorial patron would eventually turn on him. Goz tried to flee his Balkan nation with a fortune in bonds. He tried to hide his flight by staging his own disappearance in the United States. The fictional Goz came to a violent end. He was shot in the head by a rebellious subordinate. There seemed little doubt as to his death. Nobody bothered to examine his corpse due to the large "quantity of brain matter" lying about (chap. 27).

Did Goz really die? If he faked his own disappearance, couldn't he fake his own death. Perhaps the man who supposedly shot him was participating in an elaborate illusion involving fake bullets, phony blood, and stage makeup. The man known as Goz could have sneaked away while everyone was ignoring his supposed corpse. Maybe he fled back to his Balkan kingdom only to be ousted by his untrustworthy patron in April 1939.

Earlier remarks about Doc's super-machine pistols were incorporated into *The Whistling Wraith*. *The Motion Menace* (chap. 12) had mentioned hidden safeties, and *The Mental Wizard* had indicated the Doc had recently secreted radium in the grips "to locate the deadly weapons if they were stolen" (chap. 18). *The Whistling Wraith* mentioned both the safeties (chap. 4) and the hidden radium (chap. 7).

The events of *The King Maker* were cited in *The Whistling Wraith* (chap. 1). *The Motion Menace* was also mentioned in *The Whistling Wraith* (chap. 6). *The Motion Menace* transpired "weeks before." Considering the length of *Ost* (76 days), the novel which immediately followed *The Motion Menace* in both the original submission order and my chronological order, it would have been more accurate if the distance between *The Motion Menace* and *The Whistling Wraith* had been given as months rather than weeks. However, the statement regarding "weeks" is still an accurate one in conformity with the chronology presented here.

Doc was still renting the floor below his headquarters (chap. 15) as he did in *The Metal Master*. *The Whistling Wraith* (chap. 15) revealed that the last regular tenant was an insurance company, which moved because of the danger of being so close to Doc. Except for the crooks in *The Midas Man*, who probably only rented the floor for a day, we can assume no one else rented the lower floor from the time the insurance company left and Doc started to pay rent.

Although Doc healed his misunderstanding with the police commissioner of New York shortly after *The Vanisher*. *The Whistling Wraith* (chap. 15) had the installation of "a new commissioner" resulting in the temporary suspension of Doc's honorary commission.

86. The Sea Angel
Published: November 1937
1936: August (17 days)
Author: Lester Dent

The Bantam paperback edition of this novel omitted several footnotes which were in the original magazine version. I would be unaware of these footnotes if Will Murray had not called them to my attention. Among the missing footnotes is a discussion of the theory that glandular irregularities cause criminal tendencies, the citing of a radio program on the usage of hypnotism to relieve pain, and a familiar explanation of Doc's Crime College. Three other notes cite actual events in 1936 which Dent tied into the novel. All of these three notes will be reproduced here.

The first relevant footnote is connected to a conversation between Doc and a woman named Nancy Quietman. Nancy asked Doc if anyone had previously seen a strange monster known as the Sea Angel (chap. 2). Doc did not reply, but the footnote explained his silence:

"New York newspapers of the date of July 25, 1936, carried the story of a fantastic monster seen near Wading River, Long Island N. Y. Stories of persons seeing the monster were garbled, some declaring it was just an incredible shape which left footprints like those of a human hand. On Saturday, July 25, 1936, a newspaper carried the story of a man who had shot at it, but without the bullet having any appreciable effect. Doc Savage had undoubtedly read these items As Doc Savage is to discover later in this incredible adventure, one of the stamping grounds of the Sea Angel was on Long Island."

This first note is the most important. Doc's adventure had to transpire after July 25. 1936 since he had prior knowledge of this news story, In the next note, Dent tried to give justification to how the villains acquired a submarine. The submarine was an old German U-boat that sank due to a propeller malfunction during World War I. Decades later, the U-boat rose to the surface. Dent's note mentioned a similar occurrence involving a real-life vessel in the North Sea (chap. 16):

"In the spring of 1936 almost all United States newspapers carried the story about a sunken wartime vessel rising mysteriously to the surface of the North Sea. Nor was this the first time such a thing had happened."

Dent did not intend his phantom submarine to be the vessel which surfaced in the North Sea, but he did try to identify it with another mysterious vessel sited in the newspapers. The third note is tied to a claim by the ringleader of the submarine gang. He indicated that the submarine had been seen twice before by spectators (chap. 17):

"Close readers of the newspapers will recall items printed

early in 1936 about a mysterious submarine being sighted off the coast of the United States. The headlines were to the effect that a foreign submarine had been sighted near the U. S. Coast. An explanation which would actually occur to account for the appearance of a submarine in American waters, a submarine which was manifestly not a U. S. navy craft."

In the course of the novel, Monk attempted to purchase "the crown of King Emanuel Alfredo, one-time monarch of Spain" (chap. 12). Emanuel Alfredo was probably an alias for Alfonso XIII, the Spanish king who went into exile in 1931.

87. The Red Terrors
Published: September 1938
1936-37: September-January (140 days)
Author: Lester Dent

In the early section of the novel, Doc spent nine weeks in Salisbury, Maryland, the center of the oyster industry (chap. 3). Doc was attempting to find a way to fight a plague of starfish which was threatening to destroy the oysters. The oyster season begins in Maryland in the autumn in either late September or early October. If they are predators threatening oysters, they are generally detected shortly before the season starts. Doc must have averted the outburst of a starfish because the 1936-37 season saw no significant losses due to starfish. However, another predator, the drill snail did cause important loses. Doc's method of combating starfish must have lost its effectiveness after one season. Starfish caused losses in the 1937-38 season. Although one can't deny the importance of the oyster industry, predatory starfish seem too mundane a problem for Doc Savage to spent nine weeks solving. The possibility arises that Doc was secretly working on some other problem. There is some discussion in the novel of Doc's attempts to find a cure for cancer. Perhaps Doc was really working or a cure for that horrible disease.

Another possibility arises that Doc was never in Salisbury at all. Later in *The Laugh of Death* (chap. 6), Doc hired an actor to impersonate him. Doc could have used a similar ploy in order to undertake a secret mission elsewhere. For a discussion of an ingenious theory advanced by Albert Tonik that Doc Savage operating under an alias in John W. Campbell's "Who Goes There?" rescued mankind from a horrible fate during September 1936, see my section on "Apocryphal Adventures."

The events of *Mystery Under the Sea* were cited in *The Red Terrors* (chap. 14): "You remember we found a kind of vault under the sea with a lot of remarkable scientific things in it, and we decided that it had been left by some prehistoric race... ." *The Red Terrors* mentioned another of Doc's adventures (chap. 12): "In the past, Monk and Ham had seen him go through a thing where houses were blown up, ships sunk and dozens of enemies perished, then heard Doc dismiss it as a 'slight difficulty.'" I am unsure exactly which adventure is being alluded to here. *The Terror in the Navy* comes pretty close, but no houses were blown up in that novel. The villains of *Death in Silver* hit a skyscraper with a canon shell, sank an ocean liner, wrecked Doc's submarine, and exploded an incendiary device inside another building. Nearly all of these miscreants died in the explosion of a tramp steamer. It may be that the "slight difficulty" was *Death in Silver*.

In *The Red Terrors* (chap. 8), the *Sea Mist* had been suspected of "shipping guns into Nicaragua and Cuba a few years back." In Nicaragua, rebels led by Cesar Augusto Sandino fought the government until 1934, when General Anatasio Somoza, head of the Nicaraguan National Guard, had Sandino assassinated. Somoza arranged the overthrow of Nicaragua's president, Juan Bautista Sacasa in 1936, and then formally became president himself in early 1937. In August 1933, President Gerardo Marchado y Morales was overthrown in a popular revolution, which led to a period of violence and unrest. There were frequent changes of government until 1936, when Federico Laredo Bru became president.

88. Devil on the Moon
Published: March 1938
1937: February (13 days)
Author: Lester Dent

The novel's villain, the Man in the Moon, described a past service to an ambassador of an unnamed foreign country: "Some months ago, your nation was grabbing another small country. Another nation tried to put a stop to the hogging, and your government hired me to start riots and a little revolt in the nation's colonies" (chap. 9 (10 in the revised Sanctum Books text)). The ambassador country was meant to be Italy, which conquered Ethiopia during October 1935 through May 1936. The other nation with the colonies was Great Britain. The Man in the Moon was probable responsible for unrest in India, Egypt and Palestine.

A character in the novel is a munitions dealer known for his "sales of used planes, arms and ammunition in the Chinese, Ethiopian and Spanish troubles of recent years" (chap. 11 (chap. 12 in the revised text)). The Chinese "troubles" started with the Japanese invasion of Manchuria in 1931. The Italian invasion of Ethiopia has already been discussed. The Spanish Civil War began in 1936.

The Man in the Moon imprisoned prominent people with valuable information. One of these prisoners "was a prominent judge from the City of New York, who had vanished unexpectedly, and for no reason that anyone had been able to discover" (chap. 16 (17 in the revised text)). As I pointed out in "Crater on the Moon" from *Golden Perils* #5 (July 1986), the judge had to be Joseph Force Crater, who vanished on August 6, 1930.

An objection could be raised about my placing this novel in February. There are references to a "bird" (chap. 2) and "rabbits" (chap. 5). However, these references were relative to scenes set in Virginia.

Doc's headquarters was supposed to be on the eighty-sixth floor of a skyscraper clearly based on the Empire State Building. According to this novel, the owners of Doc's skyscraper headquarters had recently renumbered the floors by eliminating the number thirteen (chap. 12 (13 in the revised text)), and hid Doc's location by making the floor below appear to be eighty-sixth floor. In real life, the observatory, where onlookers can view the skyline, is the eighty-sixth floor of the Empire State Building, and it would have to be above Doc's floor. Lester Dent was aware of this, and tried to accommodate this fact in a passage from *The Terrible Stork* (chap. 8), which suggested that more than just the observatory would be above Doc Savage's floor:

"There was quite a battery of elevator shafts. The eighty-sixth floor was called the top floor, but actually it was only figuratively the top. Above it was located a roof restaurant and night club, an observation tower, and a shop which sold gimcracks to sightseers. There was also the machinery, enough to fill a young factory, of the elevators, and a water tower and the other stuff found on the top of buildings."

Shortly before *Devil in the Moon* began, Renny was sent to France to investigate an incident in which the Man in the Moon used a dirigible for espionage purposes.

There were references to "services rendered past to the French government by Doc Savage" (chap. 6). These services probably included Doc's activities in World War I as well of his discovery of the missing *Aeromunde* (i.e. the *Dixmude*) in *The Lost Oasis*.

In *Devil on the Moon* (chap. 10 (11 in the revised text)), Doc had "a rather high honorary commission in the navy." Doc must have earned this commission for the services performed in *The Terror in the Navy*. Doc certainly did not have this commission in *The Terror in the Navy*. In that earlier novel (chap. 9), Doc got passed a navy sentry by displaying "a document given to him by the U. S. navy as a gesture of appreciation for presenting the United States government with a device that would guide a torpedo to any ship afloat within an area of miles." It would have been much simpler to display an honorary commission, if Doc had owned one, in that previous exploit.

Doc received information for "the espionage department of the U.S. Government—there wasn't supposed to be a United States spy system, of course" (*Devil on the Moon,* chap. 12 (13 in the revised text)). This organization was probably the same agency whose leader, Leslie Thorne, was assassinated by Japanese spies in *Red Snow* (chap. 6).

89. The Golden Peril
Published: December 1937
1937: Early March (6 days)
Author: Harold A. Davis and Lester Dent

Renny and Johnny became involved in the novel's events while they were in South America (chap. 5). Renny had been directing an engineering project. Johnny was "making archaeological surveys at the same place."

Doc returned to the fictional Central American republic of Hidalgo, the site of his first published adventure, *The Man of Bronze*. Hidalgo also played an important role in three later novels, *Poison Island*, *They Died Twice*, and *The King of Terror*. When Doc and his men returned to Hidalgo in *The Golden Peril*, the capital city, Blanca Grande, looked quite different. There was a new National Palace and a modern hospital (chap. 8). Continuing my speculation that Hidalgo was really Guatemala, I must note that there were massive construction projects underway in the capital, Guatemala City, during the regime of Jorge Ubico (1931-44). The block-long National Palace in Guatemala City would have been under construction in 1937. The construction project began in 1931. This building, which housed the major ministries and presidential offices, took years to build and did not become operational until the final year of Ubico's reign. The Offices of the Public Health Department, complete with a clinic and medical facilities, opened in 1937. The Ubico regime constructed several major hospitals throughout Guatemala.

The government of Hidalgo was nearly overthrown in a violent military coup during this novel. If you look through newspapers in 1937, you will find no mention of any trouble in Guatemala, Hidalgo's real-life counterpart. How could the news media have overlooked these events? In 1934, American reporter Lowell Thomas had falsely reported on the radio that Jorge Ubico had been overthrown in a revolt. The actual truth was that Ubico had arrested all the participants in a plot against his regime. The rebels never got a chance to launch their revolt. This misstep by Thomas caused a diplomatic incident between Guatemala and the United States. In 1937 reporters would have been reluctant to quickly spread any news of trouble in Guatemala due to the earlier Lowell Thomas fiasco. This reluctance probably enabled Doc Savage to suppress all news reports through his economic empire, which did include a few newspapers. Doc didn't want any news of his Mayan gold being printed in the press.

Doc was not above manipulating the news. In *The Jade Ogre* (chap. 36), Doc used his ownership of the *San Francisco Comet* to kill a story. In *The Motion Menace* (chap. 10), "it had cost Doc an enormous sum to have two national network news commentators spread false reports that the bronze man was on his way across the continent by plane." In *The Laugh of Death* (chap. 7), Doc purchased a small town newspaper in order to plant a fake news story.

Doc used a device that shot "atomic blasts" to outwit the villains in *The Golden Peril* (chap. 19). An earlier version of this device appeared in *The Motion Menace* (chap. 18).

90. The Pirate's Ghost
Published: April 1938
1937: March 15-27 (13 days)
Author: Lester Dent

The novel began on "the advent of a certain fifteenth day of March" (chap. 1).

Monk mentioned "the time Doc found that lost island of prehistoric dinosaurs" and "the devilish goings-on we found in the Louisiana swamps" (chap. 7). These remarks were respective references to *The Land of Terror* and *Quest of the Spider.*

The Pirate's Ghost (chap. 12) briefly featured "a spectacular, noisy, flamboyant and notorious female evangelist." She was meant to be Aimee Semple McPherson (1890-1944).

Sagebrush Smith remembered reading a magazine article (chap. 2), which said that Doc hit fifty dimes, thrown in the air, in a row with a six-shooter (Doc was given time to reload). Doc even repeated the feat for Smith (chap. 16). This demonstration is a variation of a feat that Doc had done for his assistants. *The Polar Treasure* (chap. 18) mentioned that Doc shot a handful of twelve pennies tossed up in the air with two pistols.

In *The Pirate's Ghost* (chap. 12), Doc's assistant used credentials identifying themselves as "Federal agents." These credentials had earlier been used by Doc in *The Secret in the Sky* (chap. 8). These credentials had probably been updated. They would have been issued originally by J. Edgar Hoover's Bureau of Investigation. In July 1935, Hoover's organization was renamed the Federal Bureau of Investigation.

Note: Renny worked on the Lincoln Tunnel in April 1937 (see entry #108 for a detailed discussion). *The Flaming Falcons* made reference that Doc had spent part of his time helping American steamship lines (chap. 12): "A year or two ago, when unscrupulous foreign competition was about to break the steamship lines financially, Doc invested part of his money and some of his time, and put them on a sound financial basis." As a result, Doc owned parts of several steamship lines. The term "unscrupulous competition" can mean a lot in a Doc Savage novel. Villains throughout the series engaged in murder and kidnapping to ruin competitors. Since I have placed *The Flaming Falcons* in 1938, then Doc's involvement with the steamship lines happened in either 1936 or 1937. I have no gaps for unrecorded adventures in 1936, so I must place Doc's involvement with the steamship industry in April 1937. There also is a reference in *The Feathered Octopus* (chap. 6) about Doc taking over "decrepit steamship lines." Therefore, Doc's heavy investment with steamship lines probably began before that novel's events.

Doc involvement with steamships had begun even earlier than the incident alluded to in *The Flaming Falcons*. In *The South Pole Terror* (chap. 15), a novel assigned to the winter of 1934-35, Doc was revealed to be the secret owner of "one of the largest Atlantic steamship concerns." Perhaps Doc expanded his steamship holdings to the Pacific in the unrecorded adventure.

Doc owed a "great favor" to a man named Jonathan Treat in a post-World War II novel, *Target for Death*. This favor was done "a few years before the war" (chap. 10). Treat "made his money discovering copper and tin and stuff" on Pacific islands (chap. 11). It could be that Treat did his favor for Doc when he was reorganizing the steamship companies.

Doc may also have done a tremendous favor for a fellow named Wilbur C. Tidings during this involvement with steamship companies. The favor was mentioned in *Trouble on Parade* (chap. 1). See entry #184 for a full discussion of this unrecorded service.

In April 1937, Johnny went to Britain for the purpose of being knighted (see entry #93).

91. The Munitions Master
Published: August 1938
1937: May (15 days)
Author: Harold A. Davis

Ten men were executed in Japan for planning an insurrection "supposedly for a political faction dissatisfied with the government's policy in China" (chap. 14). The only violent protests against Japan's China policy were done by military cliques favoring war. Japan eventually made that decision in July 1937. Therefore, the novel had to transpire before the outbreak of the Sino-Japanese War.

Renny and Johnny were "in the Arctic, far from civilization, on an exploration trip of their own" (chap. 4).

The novel's main villains, Carloff Traniv and Pecos Allbellin, controlled a network of agents. Each of these agents had a device in his belt. The device would allow the agent's masters to incinerate him if he failed to carry out orders. Among these agents was Morvan Zagor, the huge second-in-command to a powerful European dictator of an unnamed country. Traniv and Allbellin have the dictator killed, and Zagor assumed control of the country in order to carry out his masters' pan to launch a World War. Zagor was preparing to order his country's air force to attack Britain. Before the order could be carried out, Doc tricked Traniv and Allbellin into activating the execution device in all of their loyal agents' belts. Zagor was killed before the attack on Britain could be carried out. Morvan Zagor was a thinly disguise portrayal of Hermann Goering, the second most important man in the Third Reich. The murdered dictator was clearly meant to be Adolf Hitler. Unfortunately, both Hitler and Goering lived long enough to really ordered the bombing of Britain and other countries. How do we reconcile the supposed deaths of these two notorious figures in *The Munitions Master* with historical reality?

The Nazi leaders were rumored to have doubles who impersonated them when they were occupied elsewhere. Hitler must have left Germany to have a secret meeting with Benito Mussolini in Italy. Hitler left a double in his place. Goering stayed in Germany, but the agents of Traniv and Allbellin abducted him. Traniv and his partner had convinced Goering's double, a man whose real name was Morvan Zagor, to work for them. It could be said that Zagor was truly a double agent. Zagor impersonated Goering while the genuine article was held captive by other agents of Traniv and Allbellin. The fake Hitler was killed, and Zagor sought to seize power before the real Hitler could return to Germany. When Zagor died, the activation of the belt devices slew Goering's captors as well. With Hitler's return and Goering's liberation, the genuine Nazi leaders resumed control of Germany. This theory had earlier been presented in "Doc Savage and the Murder of Adolf Hitler" in *Echoe*s #59 (February 1992).

92. The Feathered Octopus
Published: September 1937
1937: May 25 to June 4 (11 days)
Author: Lester Dent

The novel was set in the spring (chap. 1): "It was spring. Spring with sunlight soft and warm, with birds nest-building in Central Park, and an occasional colored butterfly astray among the skyscrapers of New York. This adventure began on a Tuesday (chap. 2). Monk and Ham had been interviewing people, who wanted to see Doc, for three days (chap. 1) when the novel opened.

On Thursday, Renny Johnny and Long Tom returned from a vacation in Bimini (chap. 4). The trio had gone there to fish for marlin. After finishing their Arctic exploration in the previous chronological entry, Renny and Johnny must have spent a few days in the tiny island off Florida, where Long Tom joined them.

Misbehavior by the press corps caused Monk to remark that this was "a sample of why Lindbergh left the country" (chap. 12). Aviator Charles Lindbergh left the United States to live in Europe in 1935 due largely to the press coverage of the 1932 kidnapping and murder of his son.

The minions of High Lar and Lo Lar had been observing Doc secretly for "months" (chap. 5). They must have been spying on Doc since the events of *The Golden Peril*. The villains in *The Feathered Octopus* took advantage of Doc's policy to buy out financially troubled companies (chap. 6). Doc would gain control of the stock of a company, put the business on a sound basis, and then sold it back at the original price to the former owners. Doc doesn't have the time to become deeply involved personally in turning around all these companies. He must have had a team of brilliant business managers working for him. This team would have to move from company to company as Doc acquired them. Doc's financial subordinates didn't inform him of all their detailed transactions. According to *The Mental Monster* (chap. 12), Doc owned holding companies, which often brought and sold smaller companies as part of their regular business transactions: "Quite a lot of time, Doc does not know what he owns." High Lar was trying to use Doc's name to gain a monopoly on the airline industry. At various times in his career, Doc owned one or two airlines. He may not have always kept control of the same airlines. He may have bought one, put in on a profitable basis, then resold it to buy another failing airline. Doc's ownership of airlines is mentioned in other novels such as *The Secret in the Sky* (chap. 7), *The Jade Ogre* (chap. 2), *The Whisker of Hercules* (chap. 2), *King Joe Cay* (chap. 5), *Terror and the Lonely Widow* (chap. 2), *Fire and Ice* (chap. 2) and *Target for Death* (chap. 5). In *The Disappearing Lady* (chap. 4), a novel assigned to 1946, Doc "owned a couple of well-known airlines."

The fictional World-Air Air Lines in *The Feathered Octopus* (chap. 6) sounds like an alias for Trans World Airlines (TWA). High Lar gained control of the company by pretending to be acting in Doc's name. With High Lair's demise, Doc could have kept control of the company. However, the initials TWA originally stood for Transcontinental and Western Air when the name was adopted in 1930. The name was changed to Trans World Airlines in 1950. However, there is firm evidence that Doc had some involvement with the real-life TWA. According to *Colors for Murder* (chap. 10), Doc knew a TWA pilot named Al Jinson in the post-World War II years. If Doc ever secretly owned TWA, it would have been only in the 1930s. In 1940, Howard Hughes gained undisputed control of the company. In 1959, Hughes was forced to relinquish control to a consortium of bankers.

The police chief of San Francisco was described as "an acquaintance of Doc Savage" in *The Feathered Octopus* (chap. 13). Doc met the police chief in *The Jade Ogre* (chap. 4).

93. The Forgotten Realm
Published: November 1993
1937: June (17 days)
Author: Will Murray

The novel transpired during the summer (chap. 1): "One summer's morn, a window had been left open." In order to fit all the novels into a coherent time period, June is considered totally a summer month in this chronological entry.

The Spanish Civil War (1936-39) was mentioned as "the recent Spanish troubles" (chap. 14).

Johnny was in Britain again giving lectures before the Fellowhood of Scientists (chap. 2). This was the same organization for which Johnny lectured in *The Sea Magician*. Johnny was supposedly lecturing before the Fellowhood for "several weeks" (chap. 2) by the time *The Forgotten Realm* began. Johnny was now extremely bored. Unfortunately, I can't fit an uninterrupted interval of "several weeks" into this chronology. Therefore, I must engage in some creative speculation. The novel revealed that Johnny had been "knighted for outstanding accomplishments in his field" (chap. 2). Although Johnny was an American, the British crown can give foreigners the honorary title of Grand Knight of the Most Honorable Order of the Bath to foreigners. Among Americans honored in such a fashion have been Dwight D. Eisenhower, Ronald Reagan and George H. W. Bush. Since I have a gap in April, Johnny must have journeyed to England in April to receive this honor. He also agreed to lecture before the Fellowhood for a lengthy period. After an interval of weeks, Johnny became bored. He contrived the excuse that he had to go on an important Arctic expedition with Renny in May in order to withdraw from his commitments. Johnny and Renny only proceeded with their expedition for a few days, and then abandoned it to go on a vacation to Bimini where they would later be joined by Long Tom. Somehow the Fellowhood learned of Johnny's detour from the Arctic to Bimini, and became extremely irate. Johnny felt compelled to return to Britain to resume his lectures shortly after the events of *The Feathered Octopus* concluded. Johnny then got caught up in the events of *The Forgotten Realm*. Therefore, the reference to "several weeks" in *The Forgotten Realm* was taking into account the fact that Johnny had originally begun his lectures two months earlier. Johnny was supposed to return to Britain to resume his lectures after this adventure concluded (chap. 28). Since there is no chronological room for Johnny to do so, we can assume that the Fellowhood canceled his lectures in dismay over Johnny's continued absences.

The events of *Devil on the Moon* happened "a few months" before the events of *The Forgotten Realm* (chap. 4). There was also a reference to *Python Isle* in *The Forgotten Realm* (chap. 22). A reference to Doc's visit with an African pygmy tribe in *Quest of Qui* (chap. 15) was explained as one of Doc's boyhood experiences in *The Forgotten Realm* (chap. 16). The novel also mentioned that Doc had "done the Crown a good turn or two in the past" (chap. 9). At the very least, the good turns would include Doc's foiling a revolt in India during *The Majii* as well as the unrecorded services for the British Secret Service and Scotland Yard (see the "**Note**" after entry #23). Doc's honorary commission from Scotland Yard cited originally in *The Sea Magician* (chap. 4) was also mentioned in *The Forgotten Realm* (chap. 9).

Note: According to *The Yellow Cloud* (chap. 3), a novel which I have placed in late March 1938, an incident transpired on the Fourth of July: "The previous Fourth of July, Monk had lighted a nickel firecracker and threw it, and the cracker hit a tree limb and bounced back and hit Monk on top of the head, exploding just as it struck."

94. The Living Fire Menace
Published: January 1938
1937: Early July (2 days)
Author: Harold A. Davis

The novel would seem to be set in the summer (chap. 1): "At Palm Springs... The thermometer was well over a hundred." When this novel began, Doc was supposedly returning from a visit to the Fortress of Solitude which lasted "six months" (chap. 3). Such a visit can not be made to fit in any chronological arrangement of the novels. Doc must have gone somewhere to turn over the submarine (which he acquired in *The Forgotten Realm*) to the United Stated government. At the conclusion of *The Forgotten Realm*, Doc had sworn to keep secret the existence of the lost civilization that he found in Africa. Therefore, he must have forbidden his chroniclers from making references to this adventure in the 1930s.

Another explanation had to be contrived for Doc's absence from New York at the start of the novel. Doc's trip to the Fortress is a total falsehood. Doc's absence for six months would seem to be confirmed by the fact that he needed to go to a newspaper morgue to lookup news stories for the last six months (chap. 4). However, it should be noted that Doc was distracted by his adventures for most of the last six months. For example, he was away for most of January in a lost civilization during the events of *The Red Terrors*. In *The Living Fire Menace* (chap. 4), Doc was unaware that a man named Darren Meeker had escaped prison "about four months ago." Probably the escape happened when Doc was in Central America during *The Golden Peril*.

Doc normally wore a vest equipped with pockets for gadgets in his exploits. Instead of the vest, Harold A. Davis had Doc wear the "emergency kit," a belt with pockets, in *The Living Fire Menace* (chap. 16). The kit may have been the inspiration for Batman's utility belt, and Doc was depicted wearing it on the magazine cover for this novel. The belt had originally been introduced by Lester Dent in *The South Pole Terror* (chap. 11), and re-utilized by Davis when he ghosted *The Golden Peril* (chap. 18).

In *The Living Fire Menace* (chap. 3), Johnny mentioned that he had been in the army with a Department of Justice agent known as Z-2. In *Escape from Loki*, Johnny was not a member oft the U. S. army during World War II. Johnny may have joined the army after escaping from the German POW camp with Doc, and only served in the army for the closing days of the war.

95. The Mountain Monster
Published: February 1938
1937: July 12-14 (3 days)
Author: Harold A. Davis

The date on which Doc became involved in the novel was clearly stated (chap. 3): "Chicago, July 12." Renny and Johnny were "in distant China working on a commercial project of vast importance" (chap. 16). The project was probably canceled due to the outbreak of war between China and Japan during July 1937.

Monk and Ham were engaged in telepathic experiments (chap. 8). They would engage in similar experiments in *The Devil's Playground* (chap. 17) and *The Headless Men* (chap. 15). Harold A. Davis apparently originated this idea, and Alan Hathway then incorporated it in his novels.

In *The Mountain Monster* (chap. 9), a character was reading *The Shadow* magazine. The existence of this magazine does not prevent The Shadow, the other great crime-fighter of the 1930s and 1940s, from existing in Doc's fictional world. Doc's own magazine was read by characters in his stories, and The Shadow series featured scenes with characters reading *The Shadow* magazine. Fortunately, no master criminals read these magazines. Otherwise, they would have discovered enough information to enable them to defeat these crime-fighters.

96. Mad Mesa
Published: January 1939
1937: Mid-July to August (42 days)
Author: Lester Dent

The novel was set in the summer (chap. 3): "The summer sun beat down on the place…" (chap. 3).

Doc always used an X-ray machine on his packages received in the mail as early as *The South Pole Terror* (chap. 1). In *Mad Mesa* (chap. 5), it was mentioned that the bomb percentage had been high during the last year." By the mid-1930s, Doc had made a lot of enemies. They included Al Capone's former associates (such as Frank Nitti), the Nazi Party, the Japanese intelligence network, Benito Mussolini, the King of Albania, anti-monarchists from Yugoslavia, Colombian revolutionaries, the Cuban narcotics syndicate, the ruling elite of a remote Chinese province, advocates of a Czarist restoration in Russia, exiled opponents of the President of Guatemala, and former disciples of the Mystic Mullah of Outer Mongolia. The bombs must have emanated from these various sources.

Note: In *The Mental Monster*, a novel set during World War II, it was mentioned that Renny had worked with Bill Keely on an African dam "before the world got so crazy" (chap. 1). In *Birds of Death*, a novel which I have placed in 1940, another character, Ollie Saff, worked with Renny on "the Nile job," a British government project, three years prior to the start of the novel (chap. 3). The African dam and the Nile job were probably the same project. Renny must have worked on this Nile job in September 1937.

In *The Freckled Shark* (chap. 10), an unrecorded adventure was mentioned where Doc rescued a detective from the "Albergold kidnappers" in Key West, Florida. The kidnappers were stuffing the detective in a canvas bag and attaching a weight to it when Doc intervened. The detective had been tortured horribly before Doc appeared. This unrecorded exploit most likely transpired in September 1937. The adventure involving the Albergold kidnappers may be synonymous with an unrecorded adventure alluded to in *The Devil's Playground* (chap. 6). A crook named Dutch Scorvitch had been "involved in an air-kidnapping that spread across the front pages of the nation's newspapers." Doc "had helped unravel" the case, and Dutch had "nearly gone to the chair." It could be that Doc apprehended Scorvitch, but was forced to turn him over to the local authorities rather than send him to the Crime College. Scorvitch then must have eventually escaped from incarceration.

This case involving aviation and abduction may have brought Doc Savage into contact with Charlotte d'Alaza, the ruthless female tycoon from *King Joe Cay*. Charlotte had considerable holdings in the aviation industry. Doc had known Charlotte in the 1920s (see the "**Note**" after entry #1).

97. The Submarine Mystery
Published: June 1938
1937: October to early November (33 days)
Author: Lester Dent

The novel had to have taken place after September 1937. The Spanish Civil War (1936-39) was alluded to as "that Spanish trouble" (chap. 11). Attacks by submarines, generally believed to be part of the Italian navy, had occurred on ships carrying supplies to the Spanish Loyalists throughout August-September 1937. These attacks were cited in the novel: "The newspapers had carried, from time to time, stories about mysterious attacks on ships which were made by submarines of unidentified nationality. First attacks had occurred in the neighborhood of the Mediterranean." The novel also made reference to the "mess in China" (i.e. the Japanese invasion which started in July 1937).

Renny, Johnny and Long Tom were in Europe (chap. 4).

Doc used a chemical, originally designed to frighten off sharks, to scare dogs (chap. 15). The chemical had been used against sharks in *The Pirate's Ghost* (chap. 15).

98. The Green Death
Published: November 1938
1937: Late November (4 days)
Author: Harold A. Davis

The novel would seem to have transpired when it was either summer or late spring in South America (chap. 1): "The hot moist air was ominous...."

A character in the novel was Scotty Falcorn, an American flyer who had disappeared in the Matto Grosso jungle the year before the novel's events (chap. 2). Falcorn had been looking for Paul Redfern, a real-life American aviator who had disappeared in the same vicinity in 1927. In 1935, reports reached the United States that Redfern had been cited in Dutch Guiana as wither the prisoner or ruler of a South American tribe. Extensive search parties searched the area from 1936 until 1938, but they failed to find Redfern. In 1938, Redfern was declared legally dead by the American courts.

The "*Hindenburg* disaster" (chap. 6) was also mentioned. The *Hindenburg* blew up on May 6, 1937.

Johnny had been missing for "three weeks" in the Matto Grosso (chap. 3) when the novel began. Long Tom was in Europe "studying a new electrical development there" (chap. 18).

A new book by Doc Savage, *Atomic Research Simplified*, was published when the novel began (chap. 2). Doc had mentioned his experiments with "cracking the atom" in *The Land of Terror* (chap. 8).

Ham's pet, Chemistry, was an ape unclassifiable by science. Philip José Farmer's *Doc Savage: His Apocalyptic Life* speculated that Chemistry was a refugee from Maple White Land, the Amazon plateau discovered by Professor George Edward Challenger in Sir Arthur Conan Doyle's *The Lost World*. If this theory is true, then over a score of Chemistry's species fled Maple White land for another locale in the Amazon. Ham and Monk encountered two dozen apes like Chemistry in *The Green Death* (chap. 12).

99. Fortress of Solitude

Published: October 1938
1937-38: December to very early January (31 days)*
Author: Lester Dent

The novel was set in the winter when Doc became involved (chap. 3):

"Only dark cold night and the gloomy clumps of shrubbery, which was evergreen, and hence unaffected by the fact that the time was winter." I could place this novel in December, January or February. In order to fit all the novels in a coherent fashion, December has to be chosen. However, there is a reference which would seem to indicate either January or February as the month. Before, I mention that reference, I need to re-construct the history of the novel's villain in chronological fashion based on references in the first two chapters.

1935:	Aug.	An ice-breaker took John Sunlight, who had been convicted of blackmailing superior officers in the Soviet army to a Siberian prison camp.
1936:	Aug.	The ice-breaker made another trip to the Soviet prison camp.
	Oct.	The Soviet authorities discovered the prison camp in ruins. The ice-breaker was missing.
1937:	Feb.	The icebreaker, which had been seized by Sunlight and the Siberian inmates, became stuck in the Arctic ice.
	May	Food began to run out on the icebreaker.
	July	John Sunlight first saw the Strange Blue Dome in the Arctic, and made contact with neighboring Eskimos.
	Sept.	Sunlight broke into the Dome, and discovered that it was really Doc Savage's Fortress of Solitude.

It isn't until the winter that Doc reached the Fortress. He asked an Eskimo, Aput, when Sunlight first come. Aput replied with "akkane," the Eskimo word for "last year" (chap. 18). The time has to be at least five months since Sunlight made contact with the Eskimos. Aput's comment implied that the winter setting in *Fortress of Solitude* transpired after the passage of New Year's Eve. However, *The Devil Genghis* (chap. 10) claimed that the word "akkane" could mean any duration from one month to twenty-five months. My chronological arrangement has a duration of five months between the first citing of Sunlight by the Eskimos (July), and Doc's meeting with Aput (December). The novel ended three weeks after Doc's defeat of Sunlight. This time interval will carry the remainder of the adventure into early January.

John Sunlight plotted to sell deadly inventions to rival Balkan nations. One of Sunlight's prospective customers was ruled by "the playboy prince" (*Fortress of Solitude*, chap. 13). This ruler was meant to be King Carol II of Rumania (also spelt Romania or Roumania). Carol ruled his nation from

1930 until his abdication in 1940. He lived openly with his mistress, Magda Lupescu, during his reign. Carol's private life was a scandal even during his days as Crown Prince. Lester Dent's decision to cast Carol as one of the villains in a Doc Savage may have been inspired by Leslie Charteris' Saint series. Charteris had based a recurring villain, Crown Prince Rudolf, on Carol II. The fictional Rudolf consorted with nefarious munitions dealers with access to super-weapons. In first battle with the Saint, *The Saint Closes the Case* (1930, British title: *The Last Hero*), Rudolf was involved in a scheme which involved a machine capable of creating "electron clouds" which electrified people. In Dent's *Fortress of Solitude*, Sunlight was trying to sell the playboy prince a machine called an electron stopper. The evil Crown Prince Rudolf also appeared in *The Avenging Saint* (1930, British title: *Knight Templar*) and *Getaway* (1932, also known as *The Saint's Getaway*). A more detailed discussion of Carol II and his fictional counterparts occurs in my article, "The Playboy Prince," from *Nemesis Incorporated* #21 (March 1986).

A dead body ravaged by a grenade was identified as that of "the playboy prince" (chap. 20), Since Carol II eventually died in exile during 1953, we can assume that the identification was in error. "The playboy prince" must have escaped the Arctic and returned to Rumania.

The other nation with which Sunlight dealt had a representative named Baron Karl. His country was based on Hungary. Rumania and Hungary had a dispute over the territory of Transylvania, which had been ceded to Rumania in December 1918. In a pure geographical sense, Rumania is only a borderline Balkan state. Only its southeastern portion is considered part of the Balkan Peninsula. Hungary wouldn't be considered part of the Balkans after the treaty of Trianon (1920). Before this treaty, Hungary (then an autonomous part of Austria-Hungary) extended into the northern portion of the Balkans. The revolution in which Baron Karl shot at least fifty people (chap. 11) was based on the "White Terror" of 1919-20, a counter-revolution against the short-lived Hungarian Communist regime led by Bela Kun. About 5,000 Hungarians lost their lives in the "White Terror." Hungary's head of state was Admiral Horthy, who came to power as a result of the "White Terror" with the title of Regent. Horthy appointed prime ministers to run the country for him. The fictional Baron Karl was a close friend of his country's prime minister.

Lester Dent characterized the prime minister as a man who was "as bloodthirsty and intolerant a tyrant as ever seized life-and-death control over an unsuspecting population" (chap. 10). This would be an extremely harsh assessment of Kalman Daranyi, a colorless politician who was Horthy's prime minister from October 1936 to May 1938 (Dent submitted the novel in March 1938). Perhaps Dent confused Daranyi with Gyula Gombos, an extreme fascist and major organizer of the "White Terror." Gombos was prime minister from October 1932 until his death in October 1936. On the other hand, American newspapers portrayed Hungary as a reactionary country in the 1930s. and some of that criticism probably rubbed off on Darayni. Possibly Dent's fictional prime minister may have been meant to be simply Horthy. Dent may have just changed Horthy from a regent to a prime minister in his fictionalized version of Hungary in the same fashion that Will Murray changed Metaxas from a prime minister to a president in his fictionalized version of Greece from *The Whistling Wraith*.

Hungary deserved some of its negative press during the 1930s. It was aligning itself with Hitler during that decade. As a result of Hungary's allegiance, it was awarded large chunks of Czechoslovakia, Rumania and Yugoslavia during 1939-41. The alliance with Nazi Germany even prompted Hungary to declare war on the United States following Pearl Harbor.

In spite of the 1938 submission date for *Fortress of Solitude*, there is a line of reasoning that supports the nameless prime minister being Gombos. The sequel, *The Devil Genghis*, was also submitted in 1938. The second John Sunlight novel has a statement indicating that "years": transpired (chap. 20) since the battles between Doc and Sunlight. If this statement was accepted at face value, *Fortress of Solitude* would have transpired no later than 1936, the final year of Gombos' life. My reasons for rejecting a 1936 time frame for the Sunlight novels are discussed in entry #100.

Besides Hungary, Rumania also had a rivalry with Bulgaria, a nation firmly in the Balkans. I considered Bulgaria as Baron Karl's country, but ruled it out for various reasons. While Rumania also had a territorial dispute with Bulgaria, the border area in question, Dobruja, was much smaller then Transylvania. Consequently, Bulgaria's rivalry with Rumania was less intense than Hungary's. The major figure in Bulgarian politics was Tsar Boris III. In 1934, Boris had been reduced to a figurehead in a military coup. In 1935, Boris launched a countercoup that re-established his authority. Although not a flawless advocate of democratic rule, Boris permitted the formation of political parties and a limited parliamentary government. The 1934 coup against Boris is the only event that could correspond to the "revolution" in which Baron Karl murdered fifty people. That Bulgarian coup was far less violent than the White Terror in Hungary. Therefore, the identification of Hungary as the model for Baron Karl's country stands unchallenged.

Sunlight's trial in the Soviet Union could be viewed in the context of Josef Stalin's purge trials of the mid-1930s. It is claimed that the Soviet "jury" was lenient with Sunlight *(Fortress of Solitude,* chap. 1) There was no such thing as "trial by jury" in the Soviet Union. The judge or judges must have decided Sunlight's fate. Scores of people were accused of espionage in the Soviet Union in the purge trials. The Jeeves sisters in the novel were American citizens accused of espionage. There were quite guilty in the novel, and presumably spying for another country (possibly Germany or Japan) other than the United States. The overwhelming majority of defendants accused of espionage in the Soviet Union were innocent. In this novel, Lester Dent was almost an apologist for the Soviet Union. Unlike Walter Gibson, the creator of The Shadow, Dent would seem to be pro-Soviet in the 1930s. Doc Savage received friendly cooperation in refueling his plane on Soviet soil in *The Thousand-Headed Man* (chap. 11), helped a Soviet agent in *The Mystic Mullah*, and prevented ex-Czarists from launching a counter-revolution in *The Motion Menace*. Dent's pro-Soviet views would change considerably by the late 1940s as shown by such novels as *Terror Wears No Shoes* and *The Red Spider*. Viewed in the context of the 1930s, it should be remembered that the Soviet Union seemed to be the only country standing up to fascism until the notorious Non-Aggression Pact of 1939. There are also far worse literary sins. Dent's sympathy for the Soviet Union in the 1930s was more understandable than the anti-Semitism practiced by anti-Soviet British writers of adventure fiction in the 1920s and early 1930s (e.g. H. C. "Sapper" McNeile, the author of the Bulldog Drummond series).

The chronology of Stalin's purge trials has some bearing on the proper placement of *Fortress of Solitude*. The justification for the mass arrests was the assassination of Soviet leader Sergei Kirov on December 1, 1934. Allegedly Kirov was slain by counter- revolutionaries. Conspiracy theorists argue that Stalin actually masterminded Kirov's death in order to justify the subsequent reign of terror. In supposed retaliation for Kirov's death, Stalin executed over a hundred people in December 1934. A long series of arrests followed. The first infamous "show" trial of prominent "traitors" began in Moscow in 1936. Since I have placed the trials of Sunlight and the Jeeves sisters in 1935, their convictions must be seen as forerunners of the more publicized trials that followed.

Renny was in France working on "new flying fields designed for high-speed modern transport planes," and Johnny was in Egypt "opening another Pharaoh's tomb" (chap. 13).

Note: At the conclusion of *Fortress of Solitude*, Doc Savage announced his intention to retrieve the darkness machine which John Sunlight had sold Baron Karl (chap. 21). Doc with at least Monk and Ham probably spent some considerable time in Eastern Europe during early 1938 fighting Baron Karl. Two of Doc's World War II adventures contained references to travel by Monk and Ham in Eastern Europe during peacetime. In *Death Had Yellow Eyes* (chap. 6), it was stated that Ham had met Edera Mendl "in Bucharest, before Roumania got into the war." This meeting was "at a reception of King Carol's" (Ham must have learned very quickly that "the playboy prince" had not perished in the Arctic. In *The Shape of Terror* (chap. 8), it was revealed that Ham and Monk met a treacherous chorus girl, Jiln, on a "pre-war visit to Prague." This chorus girl may have secretly betrayed Monk and Ham to Baron Karl, a man who "was quite a hand with the chorus girls" *(Fortress of Solitude,* chap. 11). If Will Murray's contract had been extended by Bantam Books, he would have written a novel (tentatively titled *The War Maker)* which would have shed light on Doc's unrecorded battle with Baron Karl.

Doc also moved the location of the Fortress of Solitude during this period. During the gap between *Fortress of Solitude* and *The Devil Genghis*. *The Men Vanished* (chap. 3) mentioned Doc had moved the Fortress after "some guys found it."

According to *Men of Fear* (chap. 11). Doc had been corresponding for two years with Professor Jellant of Vienna on a "fear vitamin." Doc had never met Jellant (chap. 5), but perhaps they shared mutual friends since Doc studied in Vienna in the 1920s. The correspondence must have begun in 1938, and probably started before the Nazis overran Austria in March 1938. After Hitler annexed Austria, Doc and Jellant used invisible ink to fool the Nazi censors (chap. 11).

100. The Devil Genghis
Published: December 1938
1938: March (18 days)
Author: Lester Dent

The novel mentioned John Sunlight's supposed death in the Arctic (chap. 11): "But John Sunlight was supposed to have died in the Arctic those many months ago—" Although *Fortress of Solitude* ended in January 1937, Sunlight supposedly perished in December. I would have liked the gap between Sunlight's alleged demise (December) and his next confrontation with Doc (March) to have been longer to accommodate the reference to "many months" better, but the length of Doc's later adventures narrowed my options on the size of the gap. When John Sunlight fled the Arctic, he indirectly caused the death of an Eskimo named Kummick. Johnny Littlejohn interrogated Eskimos about Kummick's demise (chap. 10). He asked the Eskimo when did Kummick perished. They replied with the enigmatic phase "akkane" ("last year") which could mean any duration from on to twenty-five months. Johnny eventually concluded that Kummick died more than six months ago from interrogating the Eskimos. Johnny was unaware of John Sunlight's involvement in this adventure, and his estimate could have been incorrect. Since it is impossible to accommodate a gap of over six months, it would be assumed that Johnny was mistaken.

The argument could be made that this novel and the earlier *Fortress of Solitude* should be placed around 1935-36. Once Doc defeated John Sunlight in *The Devil Genghis*, he left Sunlight's followers with a codified set of laws. Dent wrote that "explorers in later years" were surprised to find these Asians in possession of such commandments (chap. 20). This statement implies that years have passed since this novel's events and its publication in 1938. However, moving these novels down a few years would cause a tremendous set of problems. Doc's men finally learned the location of the Fortress in Doc's first duel with Sunlight. Many novels including *The Red Terrors* (chap. 3) asserted that Doc's men didn't know the location of the Fortress. The reference to "later years" should be read as a mistake. Explorers must have encountered the Asians in later months.

Consistent with the indications of over six months, *The Devil Genghis* was meant to take place in the autumn (chap. 10): "Beyond the window was a park, with green grass and trees having leaves which had already turned the bright color of fall." The direct reference to "fall" was brought to my attention by Julian Puga Vasquez. However, I have opted to set this novel in the spring.

The novel featured a roadhouse usually "patronized during the summer months" (chap. 3). The roadhouse was closed because it was "the off season." I freely admit that I am ignoring the blatant "fall" reference. The other references would be consistent with spring although they were meant for autumn.

Here are my reasons for blatantly dismissing the "fall" reference. When Renny and Johnny participated in *The Devil Genghis*, they were in the exact places where the previous novel had placed them. Renny "was in France serving as a consultant in the establishing of a chain of ultramodern airports suitable for high-speed planes," and Johnny was in Egypt reading hieroglyphics in "another Pharaoh's tomb" (chap. 5). A totally absent Long Tom was involved in an Alaskan hydroelectric plant.

If a gap of six months or more is created between *Fortress of Solitude* and *The Devil Genghis*, then a chronologist would be forced to fill it with other novels. Johnny and Renny would be elsewhere than France and Egypt. It would be very odd for Renny and Johnny to leave their respective locales during the first Sunlight case, travel all over the world, and then return to those exact same spot for the next battle for Sunlight. Also presence of other novels in the gap would cause different contradictions and complications. In *Fortress of Solitude*, Doc's assistants don't know where Doc's Arctic retreat was situated. They learn the location in the first Sunlight novel. Therefore, it's inconsistent to put earlier novels in the gap. Using later novels in the gap might violate a beautiful interpretation of Doc's character development advanced by Will Murray in "Reflections in a Flake-Gold Eye" from *Reflections in Bonze*. (Odyssey Publications, 1978). The central idea of this brilliant essay was that Doc was unnerved by his final battle with Sunlight. Dazed by the similarities between himself and Sunlight, Doc became less aloof in later novels *The Freckled Shark* and *The Gold Ogre*. Therefore, I narrow the gap and only have unrecorded activity inside it. A reference in *The Yellow Cloud* (see the next entry) supports this decision.

In this novel, John Sunlight sought to establish himself as the ruler of a remote corner of Asia. Sunlight may have been inspired to take the this strategy by the real-life activities of the psychotic Baron Roman Von Ungern-Sternberg. In October 1920, the Baron invaded Outer Mongolia with his own private army of mercenaries. He captured the capital of Ulan Bator in February 1921. Soviet forces apprehended the Baron in August and executed him in September. During his service with the Soviet army, Sunlight could have read of the Baron's exploits in the military archives.

The mountainous region where Sunlight established his base was located "not far from Afghanistan" and "not distant from Tibet." Dafydd Neal Dyar concluded that the territory was the Chinese province of Sinkiang (Xinjiang) in his article, "Sunlight, Son Bright," from *The Doc Savage Club Reader* #8 (1979?).

Johnny was reminded of coyotes in Wyoming in *The Devil Genghis* (chap. 12). He had visited Wyoming during the events of *Cold Death*.

Other novels had mentioned that Doc had authored books. In *The Devil Genghis* (chap. 10), we learn that he had several surgical treatises published.

Monk was still using trick coins. Having fooled Ham with a coin with heads on both sides in *The South Pole Terror* (chap. 22) and *Ost* (*The Magic Island*, chap. 9), as well as a coin with two tails in *The Terror in the Navy* (chap. 15), Monk in *The Devil Genghis* (chap. 5) kept a coin with two heads in one pocket and a coin with tails on both sides in the other.

In *The Devil Genghis* (chap. 9), Doc borrowed a London police car "because he held an appointment to Scotland Yard, result of a service rendered in the past." For a discussion of how Doc became so cozy with Scotland Yard, see the "**Note**" after entry #23 and the "Parallel Lives: Doc Savage and The Shadow" section. Doc "had not been in London for some time." Doc had last visited London in June 1937 during *The Forgotten Realm*.

101. The Yellow Cloud
Published: February 1939
1938: Late March (4 days)
Author: Lester Dent and Evelyn Coulson

The fact that the night was "a little chilly" in North Carolina (chap. 1) would be consistent with setting this novel in the spring.

There was a comment on the prior romantic efforts of Ham and Monk (chap. 3): "During the last two or three adventures in which Doc Savage had been involved, Monk and Ham had been unfortunate. They had fallen for feminine wiles. Three times in a row, a pretty girl associated with an enemy made fools of them." The women were the Jeeves sisters (*Fortress of Solitude*), Toni Lash (*The Devil Genghis*) and probably a Czech chorus girl in the unrecorded adventure involving Baron Karl.

In submission order, *The Green Death* and *Mad Mesa* were between *The Devil Genghis* and *The Yellow Cloud*. The female character in Lester Dent's *Mad Mesa*, Nona Idle, was not working for the villains of that novel. Neither was the heroine of *The Green Death*, a novel written by Harold A. Davis. Dent and/or Coulson must have been thinking of at least the two Sunlight novels.

Pat's new plastic surgeon was a refugee from Vienna, Austria (chap. 9). The Nazis had invaded Austria on March 13, 1938.

An absent Johnny Littlejohn was said to be in Central America (chap. 9), but later it was asserted that he was in South America (chap. 11).

Spies stole an agreement a briefcase from a Japanese diplomat. The briefcase contained "the details of a secret military agreement between his country and a couple of European nations" (chap. 15). The other nations must have been Germany and Italy. In 1936, Hitler had established the Rome-Berlin Axis with Mussolini, and signed the Anti-Comintern Pact with Japan. In 1937, the two agreements became linked.

The spies in this novel sold their services to the highest bidder. They were hired by a foreign power to steal new American airplanes (chap. 16). The unnamed power was probably Nazi Germany even though the spies also took the opportunity to steal a secret agreement between Germany and two other countries. The only loyalty these spies had was to money.

The Yellow Cloud revealed that Doc had written a book on corporate law (chap. 10). Ham wondered how Doc could have found the time to write it. There were several other books or treatises written by Doc (these are all listed in a separate chapter of this chronology). Looking at my chronological arrangement, I wonder like Ham how Doc found time to write these books. The man was truly superhuman.

Note: See the "Apocryphal Adventures" section for a discussion of Doc's involvement with Dave Stevens' comic book character, the Rocketeer, during April 1938 for a period of nine days.

102. The Giggling Ghosts
Published: July 1938
1938: April (18 days)
Author: Lester Dent

The plot of *The Giggling Ghosts* concerned a swindle involving land adjacent to the structure described in the following passage (chap. 19): "Several months ago... a new vehicular tunnel was completed from Manhattan under the Hudson River to that part of New Jersey directly opposite thickly populated New York." This tunnel was the Lincoln Tunnel, which opened in December 1937.

Both Monk and Ham "had barely escaped getting married in the course of a recent adventure" (chap. 4). These marriages had nearly happened at the conclusion of *The Submarine Mystery* (chap. 19). A newspaper in *The Giggling Ghosts* described "the international situation" as "calm" (chap. 9). In April 1938, the crisis caused by Hitler's invasion of Austria in March was generally viewed as defused when the majority of Austrians voted in favor of union with Germany.

This novel revealed that Ham ran a law firm (chap. 16): "Ham maintained a law firm of his own that was so expertly staffed that it could run itself for months while Ham was off adventuring." Considering the constant adventures experienced by Ham, his law firm was extremely autonomous.

Doc made a visit to the grounds of the New York World's Fair while it was under construction (chap. 19): "The fair would not open for some months, but many of the exhibits were already complete." The fact that Doc made a trip to an unopened World's Fair supports a theory which I have advocated about a later adventure, *World's Fair Goblin* (entry #110).

The Giggling Ghosts mentioned Doc's atomic research (chap. 1): "There was a story in the newspapers, a while back about a man named Doc Savage who had discovered something new about atoms or molecules or some such thing." The news story could have been about the publication of Doc's new book, *Atomic Research Simplified*, mentioned in *The Green Death* (chap. 2).

In *The Giggling Ghosts* (chap. 2), Doc discussed the devices in his elevators to warn if any harm overcame the operators. Doc remembered earlier "trouble in elevators which lead up here." Elevator operators had suffered mishaps at the hands of Doc's enemies earlier in *The Fantastic Island* (chap. 4), *Murder Mirage* (chap. 8), *The South Pole Terror* (chap. 7) and *White Eyes* (chap. 28).

103. Merchants of Disaster
Published: July 1939
1938: Early May (5 days)
Author: Harold A. Davis and Lester Dent

The novel opened with Johnny and Long Tom in Mexico. Johnny "had been investigating Mayan ruins," and Long Tom "had been called for consultation of a big power project" (chap. 3). Mention was made of "the Far Eastern powers at present engaged in a slight 'misunderstanding'" (chap. 17). The two powers were China and Japan, which had been at war since July 1937.

The novel featured "a flying fortress" (chap. 12). The U.S. military had conducted their first test flight of the first version of a Flying Fortress, otherwise known as an YB-17, in December 1936.

The climax of the novel was set on the Golden Gate Bridge. The structure was completed in 1937.

The independent spy ring in this novel gained possession of a model of "an automatic bomb-sighter" (chap. 19), which was a closely guarded American military secret. This was supposed to be the Norden bombsight. In real life, the Abwehr, the intelligence section of the German military, had managed to construct a model of the Norden bombsight during 1937-38.

It was noted that "Monk and Ham had been in Chinese hideouts before" (chap. 18). This was certainly a reference to *The Mountain Monster*, and possibly also *Pirate of the Pacific*, *The Thousand-Headed Man* and *The Feathered Octopus*.

104. The Flaming Falcons
Published: June 1939
1938: Mid-May to early June (20 days)
Author: Lester Dent

Doc revisited Indochina in *The Flaming Falcons*. He had previously been there in *The Thousand-Headed Man*, *The Jade Ogre,* and *Ost* (also known as *The Magic Island*). *The Flaming Falcons* contained references which could be viewed as tie-ins to all those earlier adventures. There was a saying in Indochina that the tigers go hungry from hiding in the caves when Doc was in the jungle (chap. 10). Doc had spent considerable time in the jungles of Indochina in his previous exploits particularly *Ost* (chap. 21), where Doc and his men took three weeks to travel through the jungle back to civilization. He had encountered a tiger in *The Thousand-Headed Man* (chap. 16). *The Flaming Falcons* (chap. 13) mentioned that Doc had visited an unnamed Asian port in Indochina "on previous occasions." It was probably the same port where Doc and his men reached after their jungle trek in *Ost*. Doc and his men probably dropped off the survivors of the Copeland Expedition at the same port shortly after the recorded events of *The Thousand-Headed Man*. Viewing ruins in *The Flaming Falcons*, Doc remembered "similar ruins" (chap. 16). He had previously seen the City of The Thousand-Headed Man, the Temple of the Jade Ogre and the lost civilization of Ost.

Renny, Johnny and Long Tom were in Europe (chap. 11).

105. The Freckled Shark
Published: March 1939
1938: Second half of June (5 days)
Author: Lester Dent

Key West was "identified as a "winter resort" (chap. 1), but this doesn't necessarily mean that the novel transpired in winter. A "college boy" was on a Florida vacation (chap. 1). This could have been during the winter recess, but it could also have been during the summer recess. The fact that there were pigeons in New York, as well as "thick" shrubbery (chap. 3), strongly suggested that the season was not winter.

Tex Haven, a daring adventurer, had once been chased by the Japanese army in Manchuria (chap. 3). He also eluded the German and Italian navies to run guns to Spain. The Japanese had invaded Manchuria in 1931, and the Spanish Civil War, in which the Spanish rebels received support from Germany and Italy, had begun in 1936. Haven had also received "a very elaborate Chinese mandarin's robe" from "the Korean Emperor before the Japanese took possession of that country" (chap. 6). In 1910, the Japanese annexed Korea, and removed the reigning Choson dynasty from power.

The novel's villain was Senor Steel, dictator of the fictional South American country of Blanca Grande. He was a relatively young man with an athletic build. Steel had looted his country of eighteen million dollars (chap. 18). His country had nationalized the property of American oil companies (chap. 14). Steel imprisoned his indigenous political opponents in a secret prison. The prison was located on Matecumbe, an island in the Florida keys. Senor Steel was probably based on a real-life President of Bolivia. In March 1937, the Bolivian government nationalized the seventeen million dollar investment of the Standard Oil Company. Notice how close the holding of the American company are to the eighteen million dollars accumulated by Steel.

Although the Bolivian government was led by Col. David Toro, the chief architect of the oil nationalization was Toro's assistant, Lt. Col. German Busch. In July 1937, Busch overthrew Toro in a coup. Busch was about thirty-three years old when he seized power. A democratic constitution was passed in 1938 limiting Busch's power. Despite the constitutional limitations, Busch's political opposition accused him of dictatorial aspirations. In April 1939, Busch fulfilled the prophecies of his critics by abolishing the constitution. The *New York Times* quickly branded him the first "totalitarian" ruler of the Western Hemisphere. Because Bolivia's army was trained by Germans, speculation centered on Busch being a potential ally of Adolf Hitler. Bush then imprisoned his political opposition on Coatl Island, an island in Lake Titicaca, Bolivia. Bush then embarked on a campaign to nationalize the Bolivian tin industry. He met formidable opposition to this plan from the tin companies. In August 1939, Busch was found dead with a bullet in his head. The official verdict was suicide, but rumors persist that Busch was murdered by his political enemies.

Senor Steel's youth and the oil nationalization issue would point to Busch as the real-life model for this fictional villain. If this is true, it is remarkable that Dent wrote this novel in the autumn of 1938, months before Busch revealed his true dictatorial nature. Also Dent had Steel incarcerating his political opponents on an island months before Busch did so. It would not be too difficult to pretend that Busch was really Steel. We could envision that the whole Matacumbe episode was a secret operation necessitated by the fact that the 1938 constitution hampered him from oppressing people openly inside his own country. The man known as Senor Steel was supposedly slain by poison gas at the novel's end. Maybe he faked his death by stealing some of Doc's oxygen tablets when he captured Ham and Johnny. The oxygen tablets had recently been utilized in *Merchants of Disaster* (chap. 4). The dictator then fled Matacumbe for his own South American country only to die under mysterious circumstances months later. A slightly different version of the theory presented here appeared in "Alias Senor Steel," my article from *The Pulp Collector* (Vol. 2, #4, Spring 1987).

While Blanca Grande was used as alias for Bolivia in *The Freckled Shark*, the same name was used later to mask a fictionalized portrayal of Uruguay in *Rock Sinister*. Neither Blanca Grande should be confused with Blanco Grande, the capital of the fictional Central American republic of Hidalgo, featured in *The Man of Bronze* and other Doc Savage novels.

Renny and Long Tom were in "Czechoslovakia trying to build a dam and electrify it" *(The Freckled Shark,* chap. 4).

106. The Crimson Serpent
Published: August 1939
1938: Early July (6 days)
Author: Harold A. Davis and Lester Dent

At the start of the novel, Renny was doing a survey for a flood control project in Arkansas (chap. 1). Johnny was "with an expedition in Egypt," and Long Tom was on "a job for the government in Panama" (chap. 7).

At the annual dinner of the Scientific Adventurer's Club in Chicago, Doc related the events of a previous adventure (chap. 4). The adventure was *The Living Fire Menace*. In *The Crimson Serpent* (chap. 4), Doc's wrist radio had been "acquired as the result of a previous adventure." The case was *Merchants of Disaster*.

In *The Crimson Serpent* (chap. 8), Gerald Pettybloom, a reporter, remembered "another Chicago crime reporter who hadn't kept on living, but been shot down because some of his 'connections' thought he knew too much." Pettybloom was thinking of Jake Lingle, a reporter friendly with Al Capone. Lingle was murdered in 1930.

107. The Gold Ogre
Published: May 1939
1938: July (15 days)
Author: Lester Dent

The boys helping Doc Savage in this novel were at a summer camp. Therefore, the novel transpired in the summer. Ham and Monk spent the early part of the novel on vacation in Maine. Renny, Johnny, and Long Tom "were serving as consulting specialists for foreign governments" (chap. 6).

Johnny could have been working for the Egyptian government, and Long Tom for the Panamanian government. Such service would be consistent with the previous chronological entry.

We learn that Doc had written "a book on psychology and philosophy" (chap. 2).

108. Tunnel Terror
Published: August 1940
1938: July 30 to August 2 (4 days)
Author: William G. Bogart

The novel began on a Saturday (chap. 1). On the fourth and last day of this adventure, there was a newspaper dated "August 3rd" (chap. 15). Normally, I would have concluded that this adventure began on Saturday, July 31, and ended on Tuesday, August 3. Such dates would then imply that the year was 1937. However, there is a reason why this novel can not be placed in 1937. Renny met Hardrock Hennesey when they both worked on "that Hudson River tunnel job" (chap. 2). Both men had been involved in "that fight one day in the heading." It appears that Renny was called in as a consultant during the construction of the Lincoln Tunnel under the Hudson River. Renny's involvement with the Lincoln Tunnel probably happened in April 1937. Work had begun on the tunnel in 1934, and the tunnel was completed in December 1937. Hennesey left New York because "there were no tunnels being constructed at the moment in New York" (chap. 1). This statement implies that the Lincoln Tunnel was completed. Therefore, *Tunnel Terror* could not have happened during the summer of 1937 because the Lincoln Tunnel was under construction then. Hennesey's statement that there were no tunnels under construction in New York after the Hudson River tunnel is inaccurate. The Queens-Midtown Tunnel was under construction from the autumn of 1936 until the autumn of 1940. Renny also worked on this structure (see entry #115). Consequently, I am interpreting "August 3rd" as a misprint of "August 2nd." The reference to August could be viewed as an editorial insertion because the novel was published in that month. Nevertheless, other references place the novel clearly in the summer. The temperature was eighty at night in an unnamed western state (chap. 11). It is also noted that "a bee buzzed in the heat of late afternoon" (chap. 10).

Johnny and Long Tom were missing from *Tunnel Terror*.

109. The Angry Ghost
Published: February 1940
1938: August (5 days)
Author: William G. Bogart and Lester Dent

The novel was set in the summer (chap. 15): "…being summer and warm, many of the places were opened all night."

Before the novel began, Doc, Long Tom and Renny were working on a diving-bell device for "some days" (chap. 5). Johnny was missing from the novel.

The unnamed foreign country running a campaign of sabotage from a submarine was "one of those which borrowed heavily from America during the World War, then repudiated its debt" (chap. 19). The Soviet Union had done so, but the nameless nation was later called "a little half-baked European country" in the same chapter. Whatever one thought of the now defunct Soviet Union, it would never be described as "little." Most likely, the country was Italy, which also defaulted on its World War I debt. The name of Ambrose Zoanisti, the inventor of the deadly weapon in this novel, has a vaguely Italian ring.

Doc Savage now had an honorary commission as a member of the American Secret Service (chap. 9). Doc probably received this commission due to his cooperation with the Secret Service in *Merchants of Disaster* (chap. 8). Doc had worked with the Secret Service even earlier in *Red Snow*, but its then leader, O. Garfew Beach, avoided publicity and wouldn't have granted Doc a commission. However, I suspect Beech convinced J. Edgar Hoover's organization to make Doc an honorary Federal agent.

Doc's honorary naval commission, cited earlier in *Devil on the Moon* (chap. 10 (11 in the revised text)), was described in *The Angry Ghost* (chap. 19) as "a commission as a naval officer, retired."

Ham gave an indication of his political beliefs in this novel. He went to Washington to advocate the passage of "free public-hospital care" (chap. 2). In other words, Ham believed in universal health care.

110. World's Fair Goblin
Published: April 1939
1938: August 25-26 (2 days)*
Author: William G. Bogart and Lester Dent

The novel began on the thirteenth day of the New York World's Fair in 1939 (chap. 1). The World's Fair opened on April 30, 1939. Philip José Farmer rightfully adopted the position that this novel could not have happened in the time when it was supposedly set. The novel was published before the World's Fair opened, and set during May 12-13, 1939.

Consequently, Mr. Farmer viewed this novel as an impossible adventure. On the other hand, the novel could be viewed as a distorted account of an adventure which took place during the construction of the Fair in 1938. As noted earlier, *The Giggling Ghosts* (chap. 19) had Doc visiting the Fair during its construction. The spectators in *World's Fair Goblin* could have been construction workers. The exhibits shown before live audiences could have been test demonstrations to small groups. The Trylon and the Perisphere, the landmarks of the World Fair, played a major role in the novel. They were completed on August 12, 1928, and turned over to the custody of Mayor La Guardia after a ceremonial final riveting. I place this novel thirteen days after the buildings' completion. My theory was first presented in "When did Doc Savage Visit the New York World's Fair?" from *Echoes* #58 (December 1991).

Johnny and Renny were absent from the novel.

Note: Annie Linders had once gone with a surgeon to hear Doc lecture in New York *(The Screaming Man,* chap. 1). The audience was a group of "famous surgeons."

Doc probably gave this lecture a few days after performing the operation filmed in *World's Fair Goblin* (chap. 2). The lecture would have been in late August or early September, 1938

111. Poison Island
Published: September 1939
1938: September 4 to October 24 (51 days)*
Author: Lester Dent

It was clearly stated when the novel began (chap. 1): "On the morning of September 4th…" Reference was made to a ship which vanished in 1937 (chap. 18). The disappearance happened "a year or so ago." The novel has to be set in either 1938 or 1939.

As mentioned in the introduction, the geopolitics of the novel match 1938 and not 1939. Europe was clearly at peace in this novel. Jurl Crierson, the novel's villain, was the exiled follower of a European dictator. Crierson had organized a bloody purge for the despot (chap. 11). The dictator was meant to be Adolf Hitler. The purge was the "Night of the Long Knives" in which Hitler had Ernst Roehm and other Nazis murdered during 1934. Crierson later had a falling out with the dictator, and he fled in order to avoid execution by the secret police "a year or two ago" (chap. 21). By my chronological arrangement, Crierson fled in either 1936 or 1937. I have set *The Munitions Master* in 1937, a novel in which Hitler was supposedly murdered. In my discussion of that novel (entry #91), I concocted the theory that the murdered man was Hitler's double. Crierson may have been responsible for security when Hitler's double was slain. Hitler could have blamed Crierson for failing to prevent the strange goings-on in *The Munitions Master*. Consequently, Crierson fell out of favor as a result.

Poison Island (chap. 9) revealed that Doc held "a high commission in the Coast Guard, the result of some work he had done for the service in the past." Doc's past service for the Coast Guard apparently happened during the long gap between *The Land of Terror* and *Quest of The Spider*. See the "**Note**" after entry #23.

Doc didn't have any oxygen pills in *Poison Island* when he needed to stay underwater for a long time. Instead, he used a pellet "which did not supply his lungs with oxygen," but "did enable him to stay under much longer than would have been possible otherwise" (chap. 15).

Reference was made to Doc owning a lot of steamship lines (chap. 18). This fact had been mentioned earlier in *The Flaming Falcons* (chap. 12). See the "**Note**" after entry #90. There is a gap of "six weeks" early in *Poison Island* (chap. 4). During this gap, Pat Savage was held captive by Crierson, and Monk did "two days work" as "a consulting expert for a chemical plant" (chap. 5). Monk earned ten thousand dollars. Doc could have had an unrecorded adventure during this gap.

Long Tom was in Africa "superintending the construction

of a hydroelectric project" (chap. 9).

American newspapers reported news of a brief aborted revolution in Hidalgo on September 4 (chap. 1). I couldn't find any news reports of a similar occurrence in Guatemala, Hidalgo's fictional counterpart. However, the revolt was easily crushed, and probably a poorly planned effort. The overwhelming amount of respectable newspapers probably felt the news wasn't worth mentioning, or suspected the reports might be false. False reports of revolts in Guatemala had been carried by the *New York Times* in January and February 1938. These earlier incidents must have convinced the *Times* not to carry the story. However, the standards of journalistic conduct would have been far lower at New York papers like the *Planet* (see entry #134), the *Classic* (see entry #122) and the *Blade* (see entry #170).

Note: On Saturday, October 29, 1938, Ham enacted the infamous Harvard football game prank. Monk and Renny had bet Ham that "Harvard wouldn't win last Saturday" (*The Stone Man*, chap. 4). In the 1938 football season, Harvard had experienced four straight loses at the start of the season. On October 29, they faced Princeton and won their first victory (26 to 7). Monk and Renny had been listening to the game on radio. Having rigged a microphone in the radio, Ham cut in and described a totally fictitious game where Harvard lost. Ham then walked in, and pretended not to know the results of the game (chap. 6). He goaded Monk and Renny into betting against Harvard. The bet was that the losing side would bark for a week.

In the interval between *Poison Island* and *The Stone Man*, Doc addressed "a mass meeting of police." The subject was "crime-prevention methods." This was about a "week before" the events of *The Stone Man* (chap. 6).

112. The Stone Man
Published: October 1939
1938: Early November (7 days)
Author: Lester Dent

It was "some days" (chap. 6) after the football bet described above.

An early murder victim was a refugee from Austria (chap. 1). The Nazis had invaded Austria in March 1938.

The villainous Spad Ames had wanted to recruit mercenaries "who had experience in Spain or China" (chap. 3). The Spanish Civil War lasted from 1936 until 1939. American volunteers had fought on the Loyalist side. Americans also served with the Chinese military following the Japanese invasion in July 1937.

Pat Savage's yacht, which had made its debut in *Poison Island*, was now in the Hidalgo Trading Company warehouse (chap. 9).

Johnny was in Mongolia "trying to prove or disprove somebody's claim that the human race had first appeared in that part of the world" (chap. 8).

113. The Dagger in the Sky
Published: December 1939
1938-39: December 11 to January 13 (34 days)
Author: Lester Dent

The time was late fall: "This was a late fall day" (chap. 1). The fact that it was snowing in New York (chap. 4) has influenced me to put this novel as late as possible in the fall. Normally, I would consider December a winter month. The second day of this adventure was a Monday (chap. 7). The adventure must have begun on a Sunday. I also want to create as long a gap as possible between this novel and *The Stone Man*. If Will Murray is ever given the chance to continue the Doc Savage series again, there will be a novel (*The Ice Genius*), involving Johnny's activities in Mongolia, which falls inside this gap. The second day of this adventure was a Monday (chap. 7). The adventure must have begun on a Sunday.

The novel can't have taken place any earlier than 1938. One of the characters in the novel was a financier named Lord Dusterman. His "munitions-factory holdings… had been somewhat abbreviated when Germany absorbed Czechoslovakia" (chap. 7). The Munich Conference (September 29, 1938) permitted the Nazi conquest of Czechoslovakia. The munitions center of Czechoslovakia was Pilsen, a city which the Nazis didn't occupy until March 1939. However, Pilsen bordered the Sudetenland, the region which the Munich conference immediately awarded to Germany in 1938. The Nazis then slowly encroached on the rest of Czechoslovakia, and finally gained control of the entire country in March 1939. Dusterman's holdings could have just been only in the Sudetenland for this novel to be set in late 1938. Doc made a comment that the policy of one nation claiming that its nationals had been mistreated in another "was used fairly successfully in Europe" (chap. 8). Doc was thinking of Hitler's claim that the Czechs mistreated Germans in the Sudetenland.

Dusterman was one of a group of ruthless financiers who had bribed one South American country to make war on another. The war supposedly resulted from "a border dispute" (chap. 8). Lester Dent based his fictional war on the border dispute between Peru and Ecuador. There was sporadic fighting between the two countries during the late 1930s. The dispute eventually resulted in the military seizure of the disputed territory by Peru in 1941.

A ship's captain had "experience running arms into Spain during the revolution" (chap. 10). The "revolution" was either the overthrow of Alfonso XIII in 1931 or the fascist revolt in the Spanish Civil War (1936-39).

Ecuador was known for its wonderful climate. This was true

of Cristobal (chap. 14). The political history for Cristobal was quite different than that of Ecuador.

Cristobal had enjoyed political stability since 1930 (chap. 4), but the 1930s were a tumultuous time for Ecuador. The other country in this fictional dispute was christened Hispanola by Lester Dent. Although Hispanola's aggressive behavior echoed Peru, Dent didn't model this country on Peru. Dent made Hispanola a agricultural country like Colombia, Ecuador's other neighbor. To ensure that Hispanola would not be identified with Peru, Dent even made a reference to Peru as co-existent with Hispanola (chap. 2). The President of Cristobal did not resemble the President of Ecuador in the late 1930s, not did the fictional President of Hispanola resemble either of the Presidents of Peru or Colombia. The historical basis for this fictional war was earlier disclosed in my article, "Savage Wars in South America," from *Echoes* #61 (June 1992).

In the novel, Doc Savage exposed the financiers' plot to fund a war of conquest. The President of Hispanola was overthrown in a revolution. There was no revolution in either Peru or Colombia in 1938 or 1939. To make this adventure reconcile with known historical facts, it could be argued that the published exploit is a distorted account of how financiers bribed Peruvian government officials and military officers to provoke fighting along the Ecuadorian border in 1938. Doc exposed this scheme which led to the apprehension of the corrupt officials and officers, but the conspirators never included Peru's chief executive among their ranks. It should be noted that the President Oscar Benavides of Peru easily crushed a coup directed against him in February 1939.

Perhaps the instigators of that coup attempt were former confederates of Lord Dusterman and his associates.

Note: Doc may have spent February-March 1939 conducting experiments at the Fortress of Solitude in the Arctic In *According to Plan of a One-Eyed Mystic* (also known as *One-Eyed Mystic),* Doc encountered Fritz Renntier, an important

German official, during World War II. Doc and Renntier recalled that their last meeting had been at a "diplomatic" affair in London" before the war (chap. 12). Renntier recalled Doc's advice from that earlier meeting: "You said that we were unequipped by psychology to administer the conquered peoples, and that our failures would drive us to a hysteria of force, which would bring the world down on our heads, and we would lose everything."

This meeting must transpired after the Nazis finalized their control of Czechoslovakia in March 1939 in violation of the agreement reached earlier at Munich (September 1938). Doc and Renntier probably met in London during April 1939.

In *Mystery Island* (chap. 4), Doc mentioned that he once heard Elvo Sinclair Lively, a British subject, lecture once at a geological society. This lecture probably happened during the same period when Doc met with Renntier in Britain.

114. The Other World
Published: January 1940
1939: First half of May (9 days)
Author: Lester Dent

There was trouble between Russia and Japan (chap. 6): "... I didn't know how much about Russia to tell him, except that them and the Japanese have been makin' faces at each other" (chap. 6). In May 1939, there transpired the Nomonhan Incident in which Japanese forces in northern China fought Russian forces in Outer Mongolia. Fighting continued throughout the summer of 1939. On September 16, Japanese and Russian diplomats negotiated a settlement.

The presence of "birds" (chap. 8) would suggest that it was not winter.

Doc discovered a lost land of dinosaurs in this novel. He decided to keep its discovery a secret to prevent the dinosaurs from being made extinct by hunters in the same way that the buffalo were (chap. 18). Doc's decision may have been prompted by guilt. Earlier in *The Land of Terror* (chap. 22), Doc needlessly destroyed another dinosaur colony just so he could have the satisfaction of killing Kar, the mastermind responsible for the death of an old friend. Discovering a third colony of dinosaurs later in *The Time Terror*, Doc would also decide to keep its existence a secret.

115. The Spotted Men
Published: March 1940
1939: Second half of May (3 days)
Author: William G. Bogart and Lester Dent

While Doc and the others were on this adventure, Johnny and Long Tom were offstage at the New York headquarters (chap. 18). Renny joined in the adventure, but he joined late because of distractions caused by his job as "consultant on a new tunnel job beneath the East River" (chap. 19). The tunnel was the Queens-Midtown tunnel, which was under construction during 1936-40.

116. Hex
Published: November 1939
1939: Early June (6 days)
Author: William G. Bogart and Lester Dent

Lilacs were growing in New England (chap. 1).

When the novel began, Renny was in Boston (chap. 2). Long Tom was absent without explanation. Viewed in the submission novel, *Hex* fell between *The Flaming Falcons* and *The Crimson Serpent*. The basic plots of *Hex* and *The Crimson Serpent* are identical. A construction project was threatening to reveal the secret base of a criminal organization. The crime syndicate responded by manufacturing seemingly supernatural manifestations. Due to the duplication of plot, I have felt it wise to put a distance of a year between *The Crimson Serpent* and *Hex*. When I mentioned the plot similarities to Will Murray, he informed me that Street and Smith didn't want to publish *The Flaming Falcons* and *Hex* too close together because both novels involved plants.

Hex (chap. 11) mentioned that Doc could duplicate every escape trick performed by Harry Houdini (1874-1926). Houdini may have been one of Doc's teachers.

Note: June 1939 would be the most likely time that Doc attended "a special meeting of metallurgists in New York City" *(The Exploding Lake,* chap. 1). Doc lectured on "The Molecular Structure of Several Lesser Known Metals." One of the attendees was Juan Russel of Argentina. In June 1939, the New York's World Fair, opened since April 30, would have attracted people from all over the world. One of the main exhibits was Mines and Metallurgy (also known as Metals). Argentina was one of the countries represented at the Fair. Metallurgists probably scheduled their meeting to coincide with the Fair. This meeting happened "several years" before the events of *The Exploding Lake*, a novel assigned to January 1946.

117. The Devil's Playground
Published: January 1941
1939: July (4 days)
Author: Alan Hathway

The novel had a summer setting (chap. 4): "In all probability, the most unhappy man on the shores of Lake Superior that fine summer morning was Brigadier General Theodore Marley Brooks." Johnny had been in the North woods for about a month (chap. 2) before the novel started. I have to construct a gap of about that size between *Hex* and *The Devil's Playground*. The best place to this novel could have been the summer of 1940. However, the placement of Lester Dent's

The Golden Man (entry #129) precluded such a decision. Doc made a remark which seem to imply that World War II was in progress in Europe: "In a world at war, possession of nickel is vital" (chap. 18).

World War II did not start until September 1, 1939. Therefore, I must interpret Doc's statement as an allusion to the inevitability of "a world at war" based on the diplomatic situation in July 1939.

The novel's villain was a Russian spy seeking control of nickel deposits in the United States. The spy "knew that his country needed it and could not get it from the British Empire" (chap. 18). In July 1939, the Soviet Union was fighting a limited war with Japan in the Far East (see entry #114). At the same time, Germany was threatening to invade Poland, the Soviet Union's neighbor. The Soviet Union was conducting negotiations with the British and French to form an alliance against Germany. The Soviets asked for assistance against Japan, but the British and France refused to give it. This refusal was one of many factors in Josef Stalin's decision to conclude the notorious Non-Aggression Pact with Adolf Hitler in August 1939.

118. The Men Vanished

Published: December 1940
1939: Late July-early August (15 days)
Author: Lester Dent

The novel transpired during either January, February, July August, September or October (chap. 10): "This, fortunately, he thought, was not the time of the igapo. Twice each year, once in November, and December, and once in March to June, the great flood came down and hundreds of thousands of square miles of the Amazon valley were under water. These floods were known as the igapo." Since November was mentioned first rather than March, the reader gets the impression that November is closer in the future. This impression is also enforced when a woman named Junith Stage falsely claimed that she would be married in November (chap. 6).

During the events of *The Men Vanished*, Renny and Long Tom were "installing a new system of mining diamonds in the Kimberly district" of South Africa (chap. 3).

There was a reference (chap. 3) to the events of *Fortress of Solitude*. Doc has moved the Fortress since his first battle with John Sunlight, and his assistants no longer know where it was located.

119. Bequest of Evil
Published: February 1941
1939: August 21-September 5 (16 days)*
Author: William G. Bogart

The novel began on a Monday (chap. 2). On the eighth day of the adventure it was August when Doc Savage flew to Death Island off the cost of Greenland (chap. 10): "In the summer months-it was August now-the climate here was fairly mild." On the thirteenth day of the adventure, Doc confronted his adversary, Lucky Napoleon. The evildoer revealed that he was constructing a device for "a European dictator whose country was already at war in Europe" (chap. 17). The dictator must have been Adolf Hitler, who ordered the invasion of Poland on September 1, 1939. The day on which Lucky Napoleon made his remark would have been September 2.

Johnny and Pat Savage were "away from New York" (chap. 4).

120. The Headless Men
Published: June 1941
1939: Mid-September (5 days)
Author: Alan Hathway

The novel was set in the autumn: "It was early fall… (chap. 1). The month was September: "That particular September…" (chap. 1).

The novel mentioned a recent event (chap. 15): "The amazing situation of the Mexico oil expropriations was too fresh in the minds of everyone who could read." Mexico nationalized all foreign-owned oil properties in 1938.

The title of the ninth chapter mentioned a famous 1937 disaster: "Blast a La Hindenburg,"

While Doc and four of his associates were in Central America, Johnny returned to New York from parts unknown (chap. 16).

San Roble, the Central American republic in this novel, bore no resemblance to any actual independent country. The republic was depicted as "a small country south of Mexico… little known… .no exports or imports of importance " (chap. 7). San Roble was probably an autonomous community in Quintana Roo, a remote and isolated Mexican territory.

There were supposedly "Inca ruins" (chap. 13) in San Roble. It would have made more sense if these had been Mayan or Aztec ruins because the Inca Empire never extended to Central America. On those other hand, considering that ancient Egyptians founded a colony in South America in Lester Dent's *The Mental Wizard*, it would be conceivable that the Incas founded a colony in Central America. In fact, such a claim would later be made in Dent's *The Green Master*, in which Doc discovered a lost Inca civilization in Peru. A representative of that civilization asserted that some of his ancestors had traveled "as far north as Mexico" (chap. 10). For a fuller examination of San Roble, see "Three From Doc Savage," my article in

Echoes #52 (December 1990).

Doc's honorary title in the New York police department was given as "commissioner" in *The Headless Men* (chap. 9). In *The Mindless Monsters* (chap. 8), Alan Hathway would clarify this remark by giving Doc the rank of "honorary deputy commissioner." Doc's rank had been "inspector" in Lester Dent's earlier novels such as *The Annihilist* (chap. 1) and *The Vanisher* (chap. 6). One would assume that Hathway's reference to the rank being "deputy commissioner" was a temporary promotion because Doc's rank was again "inspector" in Dent's later novels, *The Invisible-Box Murders* (chap. 3) and *Trouble on Parade* (chap. 2). See my discussion of the New York police commissioner in the "Parallel Lives: Doc Savage and The Shadow" section.

121. The Evil Gnome
Published: April 1940
1939: September 21-23 (3 days)
Author: Lester Dent

The novel unquestionably too place while World War II raged in Europe (chap. 2): "She glanced over the headlines, noted among items the wars were still going full blast in Europe and a new neutrality debate had started in the Senate." This newspaper was published on a Thursday (chap .2), the day when Doc Savage became involved in the adventure. On Thursday, September 21, a special session of Congress convened to debate neutrality. On the previous Monday, it was "a warm summer day," but it was "a cold day" on Thursday. The month sounds like September when summer ends and autumn begins.

A large part of the novel was set in Missouri where it was snowing (chap. 16): "Since the day was rapidly turning into a blizzard..." September seems an odd month to have snow, but Lester Dent also featured snow in September during the events of *The Too-Wise Owl* (chap. 13).

A subplot of the novel involved "Prince Axel Gustav something-or-other" and his attempts to persuade the United States to intervene in an European crisis. The Prince's country was backing a small neighboring country, which was the enemy of a much larger nation (chap. 17). The Prince was afraid that own his country would eventually be "gobbled up" by the larger power. The Prince persuaded the United States to "send some very threatening notes" which caused the larger power to back down (chap. 18). The notes were sent after Doc had defeated the villains and dispatched them to his Crime College. Prince Axel Gustav was based on Crown Prince Gustav of Sweden. In September-October 1939, Sweden was supporting Finland against the territorial demands of the Soviet Union. The Prince was afraid that Sweden would be next if the Soviets overran Finland. On October 10, President Franklin Roosevelt received a letter from Prince Gustav Adolf asking that an American plea be made to Josef Stalin to respect Finland's territorial integrity. Roosevelt felt that his influence with Stalin was close to zero, but sent a very mild message to the Kremlin on October 11. Lester Dent heard about this when writing *The Evil Gnome* (he delivered his manuscript to the publishers on October 26), and probably assumed that Roosevelt's note influenced Stalin to back off. Dent was wrong. The Soviet Union attacked Finland on November 30. The war ended in March 1940 when a peace treaty, which surrendered a large chunk of Finnish territory to the Soviet Union, was signed. Stalin's failure to conquer Finland removed any chance of a Soviet invasion of Sweden. The identification of the real-life counterpart pf Axel Gustav first appeared in my article, "Doc Savage and the Winter War," in *The Pulp Collector* (Vol. 1, #4, Spring 1986).

Doc's victory over the novel's villains happened "long before" Prince Axel Gustav convinced the United States to intervene diplomatically (chap. 18). If we imagine Axel Gustav and Gustav Adolf to be the same man, then Doc's adventure happened before October 11, 1939. The phrase "long before" is subjective It could means days or weeks. In this chronological entry, the phrase means weeks. Dent created a very unsympathetic view of the visiting Prince in this novel. The principal author of the Doc Savage series was apparently embracing the cause of isolationism in this novel. Like Charles Lindbergh, Dent may have felt in 1939 that the United States should not be drawn into foreign conflicts. The sentiment also pops up later in Dent's *The Golden Man*. The fact that Doc Savage "didn't approve" of the Prince's activities would suggest that he was a bit of an isolationist too in October 1939. Another possibility is that Doc may have just felt that it was foolish diplomacy for the United States to be drawn into the Russo-Finnish controversy. An astute observer of the international scene would have concluded that the Nazi-Soviet Non-Aggression Pact wouldn't last in the long run. By supporting Finland, Doc may have concluded that the United States would just be pushing Stalin closer to Hitler and delaying the inevitable rupture between the two dictators. Such an analysis would be more consistent with Doc's earlier statement to a German diplomat that the world would unite to defeat the Third Reich (see the "**Note**" after entry #113).

Johnny returned from "excavating a village of the early basket-weaver era" in the Painted Desert (chap. 8). Long Tom was in England working on a "superdetector for submarines" (chap. 12). Since he was assisting the British to detect U-boats, we can absolve Long Tom of any isolationist taint.

According to a newspaper, the governor of Missouri was fatally stabbed in the novel (chap. 2). Since the governor of Missouri wasn't murdered in September 1939, we can assume that the governor was only seriously wounded and the newspaper was in error. After all, newspapers erroneously reported Doc's death in *The South Pole Terror*.

Lester Dent lived in Missouri. I have the distinct impression the incumbent governor of Missouri in the fall of 1939 was someone whom Lester Dent refused to vote for. In case any reader is curious, the incumbent governor was Lloyd C. Stark. He was a rising star in 1939 of the Democratic Party. He was mentioned as a possible Senator, Vice President, or Secretary of the Navy. His political aspirations faltered when he lost the Democratic Senate Primary in Missouri to incumbent Harry S. Truman during the summer of 1940.

122. The Mindless Monsters
Published: September 1941
1939: Early October (2 days)
Author: Alan Hathway

The novel was set in the autumn (chap. 8): "While not late in the fall, there was little bay traffic. The summer residents had long since put their boats up in winter storage."

Johnny had just returned from Ohio where he had been involved with "a new discovery of North American Indian relics unearthed in a burial mound that had just been found" (chap. 13).

This novel featured a quote from a New York newspaper called the *Classic* (chap. 2). In Street and Smith's other great pulp series, The Shadow, a recurring character, Clyde Burke, worked for the *New York Classic*.

Before the novel began, Renny was "inspecting some intricate highway engineering jobs that were eliminating grade crossings on Long Island" (chap. 6).

The novel featured the governor of New York (chap. 13). He was Herbert H. Lehman, who was governor from 1933 to 1942.

Monk had a special laboratory in Queens as a backup for his regular laboratory in Wall Street (chap. 16). This must be the same Long Island laboratory featured in Lester Dent's *The Pink Lady* (chap. 6). Laurence Donovan had described a Long Island laboratory owned by Monk in *The Men Who Smiled No More* (chap. 5). However, the laboratory was much further east on Long Island. The earlier lab was located in the Shinnecok Hills in Southampton, which is part of Suffolk county. Protests by the neighbors concerning the slaying of ducks by Monk's pet pig must have caused the chemist to move the lab to Queens.

123. The Boss of Terror
Published: May 1940
1939: Mid-October (3 days)
Author: Lester Dent

The novels' chief mastermind had left Europe "when all that trouble started over there" (chap. 17). The "trouble" was World War II.

Renny and Johnny were absent.

Note: It was probably during late October and November of 1939 that Doc Savage tracked down Birmingham Jones, "gangster, outlaw, murderer" *(The Flying Goblin,* chap. 4). Jones would be taken to the Crime College, but the brain operations performed there would only destroy his memories and not remove his lust for killing. Jones was once associated with John Dillinger (chap. 1), the notorious bank robber slain by the FBI in 1934. However, Doc's capture of Jones transpired "only recently" (chap. 4) before the events of *The Flying Goblin* (entry #126).

In the next entry, *Devils of the Deep*, Doc was returning from an unrecorded adventure in Central America. This exploit started "two weeks ago" (chap. 1). It was a "confidential mission for the government" (chap. 2). This secret exploit must have transpired during the second half of November and may have extended into early December. Doc's secret mission for the American government lasted 14 days.

124. Devils of the Deep

Published: October 1940

1939-40: December to early January (36 days)

Author: Harold A. Davis

The novel would seem to be set in the winter (chap. 2): "Doc had just returned from two weeks where the weather was hot. It was cold in New York." The novel clearly took place after the outbreak of World War II (chap. 7): "Still others blamed the warring nations, declaring the guilty side was ready to sacrifice lives of its own countrymen in an attempt to win support of the world's most powerful neutral." The novel mentioned "the neutrality zone established by Pan-American nations after war started in Europe" (chap. 5). The neutrality zone was created by the Declaration of Panama (October 3, 1939).

Johnny returned from Mexico (chap. 11). It is possible that Johnny's presence there had something to do with Doc's unrecorded secret mission in Central America (discussed in the previous "Note").

The events of *The Crimson Serpent* were recalled in *Devils of the Deep* (chap. 15): "Reminds me of the dungeon we were in when we were hunting the 'Crimson Serpent'..." The special wrist watches, which were acquired by Doc in *Merchants of Disaster* and featured in *The Crimson Serpent* and *The Purple Dragon*, reappeared in *Devils of the Deep* (chap. 11). The unnamed submarine utilized by Doc (chap. 12) was unquestionably the *Helldiver*. Doc hadn't taken a voyage in it since *Death in Silver*.

Note: Doc and Johnny spent part of January 1940 in England. We don't know whether they got to England by air or sea, but they returned by ship (see the next entry). It could be that Doc was testing the submarine detector invented by Long Tom for the British (in *The Evil Gnome*) during the voyage home. Doc could have gone to England to turn over to the British government the plans of the sub-catching device, which he captured and later modified with Long Tom during the events of *Devils of the Deep*. Doc had already given a copy of the plans to the U. S. government The theory that Doc gave the sub-catcher to the British would explain Doc's familiarity with the Morenta organization later in *The Man Who Fell Up*. This organization was "a branch of the English espionage service" (chap. 13). Its primary purpose was "developing or securing war inventions."

Doc probably had his first of three meetings with Winston Churchill during this visit. Churchill was then First Lord of the Admiralty. On January 9, 1940, Churchill had returned to London after a trip to France. Churchill later became Prime Minister on May 10, 1940. For Doc's other meetings with Churchill, see the discussion of *The Lost Giant* (entry #169).

125. The Awful Dynasty
Published: November 1940
1940: January 23 to March 2 (40 days)
Author: William G. Bogart

The novel began on a Tuesday (chap. 1). The year has to be 1940 because there were 366 days in it. Princess Amen-Amen firmly noted that it was "Leap Year" (chap. 16). As the novel began (chap. 1),

Doc and Johnny were sailing on an ocean liner from Southampton, England, to New York. The reason why this novel contained no references to World War II was because it happened during the period known as the "Phony War" in which there were no major land battles between the Allies and Germany (see entry #129).

Doc wrote "a treatise on a new type of brain surgery" during the novel (chap. 1).

Princess Amen-Amen professed to be a descendant of King Tutankhamen (chap. 12). The ancient ruler died when he was eighteen. Although history does not list any offspring of the Egyptian monarch, it is not impossible that he sired offspring.

126. The Flying Goblin
Published: July 1940
1940: March 6-13 (8 days)
Author: William G. Bogart

The novel took place during World War II (chap. 1): "It sounded as though as part of the war in Europe had suddenly been moved to the wilderness of upstate New York" (chap. 1). However, there was another war going on besides the struggle against the Nazis. When Doc and his crew arrived in Europe, there was a war in Europe involving two nations in which "thousands of men continue to be killed wantonly" (chap. 16). After Hitler's conquest of Poland ended in October 1939, there was no major fighting between the Allies and Germany until April 1940. However, the Winter War between the Soviet Union and Finland transpired from November 30, 1939, to March 12, 1940. On the last day of the adventure, Monk mentioned that the war between the two unnamed nations was over. For more historical details on the Winter War, see the discussion of *The Evil Gnome* (entry #121).

The evil Birmingham Jones had been caught by Doc in an unrecorded adventure prior to the events of *The Flying Goblin*. See the "**Note**" following entry #123.

Renny and Johnny were already in Paris before the novel began (chap. 13). They probably flew to France from Egypt while Doc and the others flew back to New York after the conclusion of *The Awful Dynasty*.

127. The Awful Egg
Published: June 1940
1940: Second half of March (11 days)
Author: Lester Dent

The novel revolved around a German vessel, the *South Orion*, which was "one of the first ships sunk in the war" (chap.

11). World War II began on September 1,1939. The *South Orion* "went down months ago."

Johnny entered this novel in the Painted Desert, but he got there by trailing a crook from New York (chap. 5). This novel revealed that Johnny was "an inveterate writer of articles for the scientific magazines" (chap. 6). Johnny was also a great proofreader of articles. In *The Land of Terror* (chap. 6), Johnny read an article written by Long Tom for a technical magazine. Johnny noticed that Long Tom had "made a mistake any ten-year old could catch." For more on Johnny's literary output, see entry #133 *(Mystery Island)*.

128. The All-White Elf

Published: March 1941
1940: Early April (3 days)
Author: Lester Dent

An argument between Monk and Ham implied that the war between the Soviet Union and Finland was a recent event (chap. 3). The pair had each been trying to date a "little Finnish girl." Ham told the girl that Monk was "a Russian commissar."

Doc now had a Washington D.C. honorary police commission (chap. 6). He may have been given this due to his successful investigation of the collapse of the Treasury Building in *The Angry Ghost*.

129. The Golden Man

Published: April 1941
1940: April (after the 9th) to July (109 days)
Author: Lester Dent

The novel opened with Monk and Ham in Portugal. They were about to get involved in the European hostilities when

Doc ordered back to America. Monk and Ham took passage on an American ship. There "were scores of Americans on the ship who should have been overjoyed to be there instead of in Europe, dodging bombs, bullets and blitzkriegs" (chap. 1). Philip José Farmer's earlier chronology had placed the start of *The Golden Man* in September 1939. He logically assumed that the American war refugees were fleeing Europe because World War II had started. This view makes perfect sense only if *The Golden Man* is viewed in isolation from other novels. This adventure was extremely long because Monk and Ham spent "fourteen weeks" in a South American jail (chap. 6). The references to World War II in *The Evil Gnome*, as well as its veiled discussion of tensions between Russia and Sweden in October 1939, make it impossible for Monk and Ham to have been in Europe at the start of the conflict, and then subsequently thrown in a South American jail for a lengthy period.

It should be noted that the period from the late autumn of 1939 to the early spring days of 1940 was called the "Phony War" by the public. Many American did not leave Britain or France because they saw that there was no major fighting on the Western front. On April 9, the Nazis invaded Norway and Denmark. This action showed that Hitler was serious about soon launching an offensive against France, and many Americans reevaluated the wisdom of staying there. On May 10, Hitler launched his offensive against France and the Low Countries. Either of these two offensives could have caused Americans to flee Europe in 1940. I have chosen the Scandinavian campaign as the cause of the American exodus in *The Golden Man* because of the need to fit certain novels into August 1940. Viewed in the context of April 1940, it could be argued that Monk and Ham may have traveled to Portugal with the intention of continuing on to Scandinavia. They may have been chasing the Finnish girl over whom they were arguing in *The All-White Elf*.

In *The Golden Man*, one of the warring nations tried to frame its opponent for a submarine attack on an American vessel. The nation doing the framing was apparently meant to be Great Britain, and its enemy would seem to be Nazi Germany. It may shock modern readers that Britain was meant to be one of the mischievous unnamed nations in a Doc Savage novel. It should be noted that the novel was written during a period of isolationist fervor in which Britain was being publicly accused of trying to trick the United States into entering the war. As a consequence of the fall of France in June 1940, many isolationists rethought their stance and embraced military assistance to Britain. Later in *Men of Fear* and *The Man Who Fell Up* (submitted before the Japanese attack on Pearl Harbor), Dent returned to the anti-Nazi sentiments that he had earlier embraced in the 1930s (e. g. *The Man Who Shook the Earth, Poison Island*).

The title character of the novel was apparently a high-ranking Nazi official. His real name was given as Paul Hest (chap. 18). This name is reminiscent of Rudolf Hess, a member of Hitler's inner circle who went on a secret airplane mission to Britain in 1941. Hest went on a secret airplane mission to the Atlantic Ocean in *The Golden Man*. For the theoretical implications of some connection between Paul Hest and Rudolf Hess, see the "Apocryphal Adventures" section.

During the period in which Monk and Ham were in prison, Doc must have been engaged in other activities. In the later *Men of Fear*, it was indicated that Doc had done a lot of defense work on aircraft (chap. 6): "During the past year, as the international situation became more crucial, Doc had devoted a great deal of time to designing airplanes of high speed and maneuverability and long range." Doc probably did the bulk of this work during the imprisonment of his two aides. Doc may even have had an unrecorded adventure during this gap of fourteen weeks. See the "Apocryphal Adventures" for the theory that Doc struck a crippling blow against a contemporary master criminal of equal scientific stature during April 1940.

130. The Purple Dragon
Published: September 1940
1940: August 1-3 (3 days)
Author: Harold A. Davis and Lester Dent

A newspaper was dated "August 1, 1940" (chap. 2). The newspaper's content was consistent with that date: "Most of it seemed to be about fighting some place in Europe or Asia." There was an interesting ad in this story (chap. 3): GET THE LATEST DOC SAVAGE MAGAZINE. The latest issue would have been *Tunnel Terror*, the August 1940 issue.

Long Tom was working "on a gigantic power project in South America," and Johnny "was with a scientific expedition in far-off Asia" (chap. 6). Since Johnny was back in New York by the next chronological entry. I suspect military movements by the Japanese caused Johnny to cancel his expedition.

This novel revealed that the Crime College was operating since 1929. For a discussion of Doc's activities in 1929, as well as the true identity of the Prohibition "crime czar" called Pal Hatrack in this novel, see the "**Note**" after entry #1.

Monk and Ham wore special watches that were "often used by Doc and his men since an adventure long before" (chap. 6). The adventure was *Merchants of Disaster*. After acquiring these watches from the villains of that novel, Doc utilized them himself in *The Crimson Serpent*.

131. The Pink Lady
Published: May 1941
1940: Early August (3 days)
Author: Lester Dent

The weather was "hot" (chap. 6).

The novel featured some important data regarding Monk Mayfair. On Long Island, Doc visited an old summer house "purchased by Monk Mayfair once when he'd gotten the idea that he wanted rural solitude for some chemical experiments" (chap. 6). The place "had not been used for a long time." Could this place be Monk's Long Island residence featured in Laurence Donovan's *The Men Who Smiled No More* (chap. 5)? A comment in one of Alan Hathway's novels would suggest otherwise (see entry #122).

The Pink Lady (chap. 10) mentioned Monk's false teeth. Monk used the teeth to house two chemicals. If the chemicals were mixed together, an explosive would result. Monk had originally created the chemicals for Doc, who had housed them in his own mouth before his wisdom teeth grew in. Doc had used the chemicals hidden in his teeth during *The Polar Treasure* (chap. 8), *The Lost Oasis* (chap. 16) and *The Sargasso Ogre* (chap. 3). Monk's false teeth would play a key role later in *Rock Sinister*. Although Doc ceased to use the chemicals, he later wrapped a tiny steel saw around one of his wisdom teeth in *The King of Terror* (chap. 9).

132. The Green Eagle
Published: July 1941
1940: Late August (5 days)*
Author: Lester Dent

Doc was in Wyoming for about "a little more than a week" (chap. 6) before the novel began.

133. Mystery Island
Published: August 1941
1940: Early September (3 days)
Author: Lester Dent

World War II was in progress. Miss Wilson could not go back to England because of "the horrid old war" (chap. 4).

At the start of the novel, Doc "was serving in a consulting capacity for that new fortified zone in Charleston, South Carolina" (chap. 2).

Johnny was identified as the author of a "book on movements with a horizontal component, involving some of the most difficult problems of modern geology" (chap. 4). We also learn that he has an uncle named Ned (chap. 5).

134. The Invisible-Box Murders
Published: November 1941
1940: September 13-17 (5 days)
Author: Lester Dent

The novel started on a Friday (chap. 1): "Today is Friday." The fact that the weather was "hot" (chap. 5) would be consistent with September. World War II was raging in Europe because Ted Parks had studied "in Europe before everyone had started shooting at everybody else over there" (chap. 4).

The police commissioner was a man named Stance. He was described as "the acting head of the police department" (chap. 3). This description would imply that his position was transitory. Either the permanent police commissioner had not be appointed, or Stance was filling in for someone on temporary leave Stance's background, a career policeman who rose from pounding a beat in Gravesend, would be consistent with the unnamed police commissioner mentioned in Will Murray's *White Eyes*. His attitude towards Doc was very different from the actions of the unnamed police commissioner in other novels. Stance didn't cut any slack at all for Doc when the intrepid adventurer was being framed for murder. By contrast, the unnamed commissioner from *The Purple Dragon* (chap. 17) released Monk and Ham to Doc's custody even though Doc hadn't fully produced the evidence to refute the false murder charge with which they were charged. Certainly Stance wasn't the commissioner from that earlier novel. For an in-depth study as well as solution as to the identity of the police commissioner of New York in the Doc Savage novels, see my section on "Parallel Lives: Doc Savage and The Shadow."

In addition to Stance, another public official causing problems for Doc in *The Invisible-Box Murders* (chap. 8) was the Manhattan District Attorney, who badly wanted to be governor. Dent gave this character the fictional name of Einsflagen, but he was modeled on the politically ambitious Thomas E. Dewey, who was Manhattan District Attorney from 1937 to 1941. Dewey achieved his ambition to be elected governor in 1942, and he would be re-elected in 1946 and 1950. However, he would lose two presidential elections as the Republican candidate in 1944 and 1948.

While driving a car, Ham was trapped by the bad guys (chap. 7). The crooks pushed his car into the back up of a van. Ham remarked that this "happened to us once before!" Ham was remembering how Doc was trapped in similar fashion by a different group of opponents in *The Submarine Mystery* (chap. 2).

The Invisible-Box Murders (chap. 5) featured a New York newspaper called the *Daily Planet*. Such a fictional newspaper was featured in the Superman comic strip at the time Dent wrote this novel. However, Dent was borrowing from himself rather than Superman, whose series borrowed the Fortress of Solitude among other items from the Doc Savage novels. Dent had created a New York paper identified only as the *Planet* for the trio of Foster Fade detective stories published in *All Detective Magazine* during 1934. These tales were collected in *The Crime Spectacularist* (Pulpville Press, 2006).

The Submarine Mystery (chap. 1) also featured a newspaper called the *Planet*, but it was published in Tulsa, Oklahoma, rather than New York City. Will Murray's *Python Isle* (chap. 8) had a scene where Monk consulted the latest edition of the *Planet* (the New York version as opposed to the Tulsa version). Monk liked the *Planet*, but Renny characterized its reporters as "stinkers" in *Terror and the Lonely Widow* (chap. 8). Monk and later posed as reporters from the *New York Planet*, depicted as "a particularly noisy tabloid," in *Death is Round Black Spot* (chap. 3). The *Daily Planet* from *The Invisible-Box Murders* must be the same newspaper identified elsewhere as the *New York Planet*.

The same newspaper must also be the *New York Evening Planet* featured in the radio play "The Box of Fear."

135. Birds of Death
Published: October 1941
1940: September 19-25 (7 days)*
Author: Lester Dent

On the first day of Doc's involvement, Liona Moldenauer informed him that her father had been in a coma since a week from Monday. Doc observed that the coma started "ten days ago" (chap. 3). The novel had to begin on a Thursday.

Johnny had just got back from Westchester County where he had been examining spurious pre-Inca tablets (chap. 4).

It was mentioned that Doc composed music for the violin (chap. 1). Doc had done this for violinist Victor Vail in *The Polar Treasure* (chap. 2).

136. Men of Fear
Published: February 1942
1940: October 9-13 (5 days)
Author: Lester Dent

The novel was set during the hurricane season (chap. 8): "This happens to be the hurricane season." The novel began on a Wednesday (chap. 1).

The novel took place during World War II as demonstrated by references to "war-mad Europe." The villains belonged to an unnamed nation which was clearly Nazi Germany. It was frequently mentioned that the unnamed country controlled Vienna. Professor Jellant of Vienna and Doc Savage had been communicating on the "fear vitamin" since "two years ago" (chap. 11). The communications with Jellant probably started before the Nazi invasion of Austria in March 1938. It continued through the use of invisible ink up to 1940. If the Nazi agents had not happened upon the scene, Doc and the gang would have gone on a scientific expedition to the Inirida River in Colombia (chap. 1). The expedition "wasn't very important," and Doc may have canceled his plans for it when the adventure concluded.

A woman saw a movie of Doc Savage performing a delicate brain operation (chap. 5). The operation had been filmed in *World's Fair Goblin* (chap. 2) at the fairgrounds. In my chronological arrangement, Doc actually performed the operation before the Fair really opened (see entry #110). I speculate that Doc utilized the facilities of the Hall of Medicine before the building officially opened. The spectators were actually a special audience of prominent doctors.

Note: In *Jiu San*, Monk commented that he had visited Japan before the attack on Pearl Harbor (chap. 6): "… they hired me to put in an efficiency system in a chemical plant before the war… I worked here four months and got their chemical plant in a worse mess every day. I could see Pearl Harbor coming up." The lengthy stay in Japan must have transpired from November 1940 through February 1941. Monk had been at Yokohama (chap. 5).

Doc may also having been traveling in the Pacific area. In *Pirate Isle* (chap. 6), Doc mentioned that he had "twice" met the novel's villain, Lord London alias Faustin Archibald Montclan Herford. On both occasions, Lord London looked totally different. Since Lord London's base of operations was in the South Seas (chap. 9), Doc may have been made visiting there. It is unclear whether Doc's previous two meetings with Lord London were two separate adventures, or two incidents in the same adventure. Like many Doc Savage villains,

Lord London had a dual identity. The reason why Lester Dent mentioned the two meetings was to offer a subtle clue to the criminal's true identity. Earlier in the novel (chap. 3), a character mentioned that he had seen Doc before. The same character also implied that he had "a couple of friends" sent to the Crime College. This character would be revealed to be Lord London. In addition to Faustin Archibald Montclan Herford, Lord London was also known as Joe Gatter, Elmer Stone and John Doe (chap. 2).

Rumor had it that Lord London had been a warlord in China, who fled when China united against Japan. Lord London would have fled around 1937 when Japan sought to conquer all of China. Lord London then became a pirate in the South Seas. Tom Too from *Pirate of the Pacific* had a somewhat similar background. He had become a pirate after his career as a Chinese warlord was terminated by the Japanese invasion of Manchuria in 1931.

Without Monk to argue with, Ham did some legal work for a change during this gap of four months. A song writer was being sued and accused of plagiarism by another writer. Ham had to prove that his client "stole the song that he was being sued over from a pre-Revolutionary War song, instead of the later copyrighted one" (*Weird Valley*, chap. 7). Ham also began to teach an evening law course that would be regularly scheduled in February. Ham would teach this course during 1941, 1942 and 1943 (see entry #164).

137. The Magic Forest
Published: April 1942
1941: March to April (47 days)
Author: William G. Bogart and Lester Dent

The novel was set in the spring (chap. 4): "It was shortly after dawn, and there was the cold chill of spring in the air." A woman dressed "in expensive spring furs" (chap. 2).

Long Tom had "just returned from a convention of electrical engineers being held in Chicago," and an absent Johnny was "in South America on some sort of expedition" (chap. 5).

138. The Rustling Death
Published: January 1942
1941: May 10-11 (2 days)
Author: Alan Hathway

The date on which the novel began was clearly indicated (chap. 9): "The last statement was contained in a letter dated May 1st. It was now the 10th." A reference to the New York World's Fair (which opened on April 30, 1939) implied that the year was 1941 (chap. 2): "the device was an artificial lighting machine. Similar to the one which had been on display at the World's Fair for two years." The fair had actually closed in the fall of 1940.

Renny and Johnny were present in this novel, but they initially went on "a routine engineering inspection trip to the Southwest" (chap. 5). Ham was preparing for a appearance before the Supreme Court (chap. 1).

The foreign spies in this novel probably worked for Nazi Germany, The leader of this group was a distinguished diplomat who disguised himself as an American named Flathead Simpson. At the novel's end, the man posing as Simpson was killed. Doc removed the disguise from what remained of the body, and recognized the diplomat.

In his real identity, Simpson wore a monocle. Baron Karl, the evil diplomat of an unnamed country in *Fortress of Solitude* also wore a monocle. Assuming that Baron Karl survived the unrecorded adventure where Doc recovered the darkness machine (see the "**Note**" between entries #99 and #100), then he could have been Flathead Simpson. Baron Karl was apparently working for Hungary in *Fortress of Solitude*. He could have either switched his loyalty to Nazi Germany, or the covert operation in *The Rustling Death* was a joint scheme by Germany and Hungary. This is a distinct possibility because Hungary was a minor member of the Axis powers in World War II.

139. Peril in the North
Published: December 1941
1941: Late May (3 days)
Author: Lester Dent

Jeff Deischer deserves kudos for pinpointing the chronological slot for this novel. The "midnight sun" in Greenland was mentioned (chap. 11). This phenomenon would have only happened during May 25 to July 25.

The novel's villain, Mungen was the deposed dictator of a fictional country called Monrovia. Mungen was described as "the biggest limelight hog of the dictator crop," "the Mad Dog of Europe" and "the most hated man in this century" (chap. 10). His populace eventually revolted against him. Faking suicide in a chancellery, Mungen fled his nation with a large fortune. In *Peril in the North*, Mungen went to Portugal, where he embarked on a ship that was then chased into the Arctic by a warship. Both ships belonged to Mungen's own country (chap. 15).

Bucharest, the capital of Rumania, was mentioned (chap. 7). An Italian passport was examined (chap. 6). It would seem unlikely that Monrovia was based on Rumania or Italy, but Mungen was a composite of prominent leaders from both nations. There are clear similarities with Mussolini. The Rumanian politician who influenced Mungen was Horia Sima. In Rumania, there were two right-wing groups competing for power in January 1941. The first was the military. The Rumanian army's leader, General Ion Antonescu, had been appointed Premier. The other was an indigenous fascist party, the Iron Guard, led by Horia Sima. The Iron Guard was also called the Green Shirts. Antonescu attempted to control the

Green Shirts by making Sima Vice-Premier. However, Sima launched a revolt against Antonescu. When his insurrection failed, Sima disappeared. It was rumored that he had fled the country with a fortune, but he was actually being held secretly in Nazi Germany. Rumania had been forced by Hitler to allow. German troops to be garrisoned in Rumania. When the struggle between Antonescu and Sima reached a critical point, the Nazis supported the Rumanian military. The German troops in Rumania played no active role in quelling the revolt. Nevertheless, they marched in support of the Antonescu regime once the Rumanian army defeated Sima's forces. Sima was incarcerated in Germany to be held as insurance in case Antonescu ever betrayed Hitler. When World War II ended, Sima found refuge in Spain. He died in Madrid during 1993.

Sima looked nothing like Mungen. Sima was a lean clean-shaven man like John Sunlight. Mungen was an obese bearded man. Various clues point to the Rumanian inspiration for Mungen. The Monrovian ship in which Mungen fled Portugal was called the *Green Guard* (chap. 11). The name is derived from the names given to Sima's fascist followers, the Iron Guard and the Green Shirts. Mungen's flight was exactly four months and three days ago (chap. 11) before the novel. This time frame suggests late January. Sima's ill-fated rebellion, known as the Legionnaires' Revolt, transpired in January 21-23, 1941. About four months and three days later would be late May, the time of the midnight sun.

The whole story of the Legionnaires' Revolt was well known to the editors of Street and Smith. Theodore Tinsley had written a Shadow novel, *Gems of Jeopardy* (September 1), about a leader of the Green Shirts hiding in America. Tinsley's character, the Colonel, was based on Sima. Mungen can't be Sima for various reasons, but he could have been one of the Green Shirt chieftains. Dent just disguised Mungen's Eastern European origin by making him similar to Mussolini and by replacing the failed Rumanian insurrection with a successful Monrovian revolution.

Britain didn't declare war on Rumania until November 30, 1941. Rumanian ships would not have been hampered in the Atlantic by either the Axis or the Allies in early 1941. A Green Shirt kingpin could have easily fled Europe like Mungen.

Peril in the North featured a newspaper with a World War II headline. A newsboy was shouting "Another battle in Europe" (chap. 8). There was significant fighting in Greece in late May. On May 27, Athens was occupied by German troops prompting a Greek surrender. There was also a substantial Nazi offensive to conquer the Greek island of Crete that began on May 20, and lasted for about 10 days.

Doc's birthday was celebrated on the first day of this adventure (chap. 4). The fact that Doc's birthday was recognized as being in May contradicts Philip José Farmer's speculation in *Doc Savage: His Apocalyptic Life* that Doc was born on November 12, 1901. The implications of this contradiction are discussed more fully in the "Apocryphal Adventures" section.

Note: Doc played an important part in the history of American espionage during June 1941. In the World War II adventure, *According to Plan of One-Eyed Mystic* (or *One-Eyed Mystic*), Doc mentioned that he was familiar with the work of a special government agency led by "Curt MacIntell" (chap. 10):

"It's an army department of special nature, very hush-hush. In existence only for the duration of the war, and responsible only, and reporting only, to the chief of staff. The nature of its work is completely secret. Curt MacIntell, who is a man whose name is totally unknown to the American public, is probably one of the most accomplished and experienced secret agents in the world. That is about all I know. I have met MacIntell several times, to discuss organization of an investigative agency such as this one. That was at the beginning, before the war broke, but when it was evident that we were going to get into the fracas."

"Curt MacIntell" is a clever in-joke. The "Intell" stands for intelligence. This actual organization was originally formed as the Office of the Coordinator of Information on June 18, 1941. For some peculiar reason known only to government bureaucrats, the name of this agency was abbreviated as COI rather than OCI. The head of the COI was William J. "Wild Bill" Donovan. The COI was described by Donovan at the time as "a central enemy intelligence organization," which would collect valuable information about "potential enemies." President Roosevelt dissolved the COI on June 13, 1942 in order to allow Donovan to reorganize it as the Office of Strategic Services (OSS). In December 1942, the Joint Chiefs of Staff led by General George Marshall were made Donovan's direct superiors. The OSS was abolished on September 25, 1945.

"Curt MacIntell" could be an alias for Donovan. After foiling the Axis spies in *The Rustling Death*, Doc must made contact with Donovan in May 1941. With Doc's advice and counsel, Donovan persuaded President Roosevelt to create the COI. Although the COI's successor organization, the OSS, was dissolved shortly after the war, the Central Intelligence Agency (CIA) arose from the bones of the OSS in 1947.

In *Pirate Isle* (chap. 4), it was asserted that Doc and Renny "taught an officers' class in military parachuting technique." Doc and Renny probably conducted this course in the second half of June 1941. This course may be related to "a gadget which Renny Renwick had worked out for use by American parachute troopers, a gadget for releasing themselves quickly from the encumbrance of a parachute harness" *(The Talking Devil,* chap. 14).

In *The Three Devils* (chap. 3), it was revealed the Doc attended "the lumberman's convention" in Chicago during 1941. There he displayed "a new bonding method for plywood." Doc probably attended the convention in the first half of July. Also see entry #183.

In *The Devil's Black Rock*, a novel set in 1942, a character remembered that Doc had passed through the town of Mile High, Arizona, the previous year. This was on the seventeenth of the month exactly one year ago (chap. 1). When Donkey

Sam remembered Doc's visit, he witnessed a strange occurrence in Arizona. He later told a crook named Willard Cole about it (chap. 2). It was unclear how much time passed between Donkey Sam's observation of the strange event on the seventeenth of the unspecified month, and his conversation with Cole about it. The interval could be hours, days or even months. The next concrete date given in *The Devil's Black Rock* was "the tenth of October" (chap. 3), and Doc didn't become involved until the nineteenth of the same month (chap. 4). Therefore, the automatic assumption would be that Donkey Sam witnessed the bizarre occurrence on September 17, 1942, and Doc had been in Mile High on September 17, 1941.

However, there is clear evidence that Doc was elsewhere on September 17, 1941 (see entry #143). The same is true of August 17, 1941 (see entries #149 and 150). Since I have a gap in July, it is most likely that Doc visited Mile High on July 17, 1941. Donkey Sam's experience with a strange phenomenon must have happened on July 17, 1942, and he waited about two months before telling Cole about it.

Doc's visit to Mile High on July 17, 1941, involved the inspection of "mining property" which he owned (chap. 3). Two of Doc's men also inspected a mine. In *Hell Below* (chap. 3), it was mentioned that Monk and Renny had once gone to Mexico "to put a mine on a profitable basis." This Mexican trip by Monk and Ham may have been related to Doc's Mile High visit. Maybe Doc was investigating mysterious doings at various mines in July 1941. The best person besides Doc and Renny to inspect a mine was Johnny, the brilliant geologist. However, Johnny was in the Pacific during July 1941 (see below).

140. Pirate Isle
Published: May 1942
1941: August (12 days)
Author: Lester Dent

The novel was set in the summer (chap. 10): "...snowballs in the hottest day of summer...."

Before the events of this novel unfolded, Johnny had mysteriously vanished in the Pacific "almost three months ago" (chap. 6). Johnny was hired to work on Jinx Island when he disappeared. He probably left for Jinx Island in mid-May (shortly after the events of *The Rustling Death)*, and then disappeared soon after his arrival.

Lord London, the villain of *Pirate Isle* had met Doc before under unrecorded circumstances (see the "**Note**" after entry #136 for a detailed discussion).

Ham and Monk were in Tierra del Fuego during this adventure. Ham was "straightening out some legal tangles," and Monk was "serving as consulting chemist in the matter of processing whale by-products" (chap. 8).

Johnny was identified as a member of the Explorers League of New York (chap. 1). This was the same organization, which gave Doc, another of its members, an award in *The Men Vanished* (chap. 1).

In *Pirate Isle* (chap. 15), Johnny erroneously stated that Doc "has never killed a man." Doc had killed men in the early novels, most notably *The Man of Bronze* and *The Land of Terror*. Doc also had slain other human beings during World War I in *Escape from Loki*. Johnny made this unquestionably false statement to explain why he stopped Doc from killing Lord London. Johnny was giving this explanation to an outsider named Charlie Custis. I could view Johnny's statement as a simple inconsistency of the Doc Savage series, but there is another interpretation. Johnny deliberately lied to Custis. Why? The answer may be that Doc developed an addiction to violence in 1931 due to the grief which he experienced over the murders of his father (shortly before the events of *The Man of Bronze*) and his mentor Jerome Coffern (in *The Land of Terror*). Doc may have been brutally slaying criminals during the gap between *The Land of Terror* and *Quest of the Spider*. After spending weeks at the Fortress of Solitude shortly before *Quest of the Spider*, Doc returned to New York and gradually weaned himself away from violence by developing non-lethal methods of fighting crime which were finalized by the time of *The Phantom City*. Doc's near killing of Lord London was apparently prompted by not only the fact that the criminal was about to kill Johnny in a depraved and demeaning way. Lord London talked love to his male victims before killing them, and I am going to gracefully refrain from any further discussion of this matter. Johnny may have recognized that Doc was relapsing into a pattern of behavior which he abandoned years ago. Hence, Johnny stopped Doc. Since he didn't want to give a long discussion of Doc's previous addiction to violence, Johnny told Custis a lie.

141. The Speaking Stone
Published: June 1942
1941: August (6 days)
Author: Lester Dent

This novel, a direct sequel to *Pirate Isle*, had Doc Savage leaving Jinx Island to locate Monk and Ham in South America. It was remarked the Monk and Ham "had spent some time in Egypt" and were "familiar with the pyramids" (chap. 14). The pair had visited Egypt in *The Lost Oasis*, *The Sargasso Ogre*, *Resurrection Day* and *The Awful Dynasty*.

142. The Man Who Fell Up
Published: July 1942
1941: Early September (6 days)
Author: Lester Dent

Doc became involved in a competition between the British and Nazi agents for a new weapon. The British agents didn't cooperate openly with Doc. This fact means that the United States was not directly involved yet in World War II.

For the early part of this adventure, Renny, Johnny and Long Tom were in Washington to attend a "defense-board meeting" (chap. 2). By September 1941, the United States, still not a direct participant in the global struggle, was becoming increasing involved in World War II. In March 1941, Congress had passed the Lend-Lease Act which permitted the dispatch of American weapons to nations fighting the Axis powers. In July, American troops had been sent to postings in Iceland and the Caribbean. Undoubtedly, Renny, Johnny and Long Tom discussed such matters in Washington.

Ham had "a knife scar" on his back (chap. 7) from some previous adventure. The only time when I remember Ham getting stabbed was in *Quest of Qui* but the wound was "a cut on his shoulder" (chap. 8).

In *The Man Who Fell Up* (chap. 10), it was revealed that the newsstand operator in the south lobby of Doc's skyscraper was Bob Caston, a Crime College graduate. Caston was employed on this occasion to follow some crooks. In *The Golden Man* (chap. 7), the newsstand operator across the street from the skyscraper was also one of Doc's undercover agents. This other operative was "an observant ex-detective who lost both legs in an accident." His job was to contact Doc or his men by telephone when suspicious activity was noticed outside the building.

143. The Too-Wise Owl
Published: March 1942
1941: September 16-24 (9 days)
Author: Lester Dent

Philip José Farmer made extremely astute observations when he placed this novel in his original chronology. The novel started on a Tuesday (chap. 1): "It was Tuesday afternoon." The novel was set in September (chap. 13): "Kind of cold for September, ain't it?" The third day of the adventure, Thursday, was the eighteenth: "...the eighteenth of the month... that was yesterday."

A character named Jefferson Shair had been a hunter in Africa. He came back to America "a year or two after the war started over there" (chap. 5). I assume "over there" was meant to mean Europe where World War II started on September 1, 1939. On the other hand, military operations were extended into Africa when Italy entered the war in 1940.

We learn that Ham had a half-brother, Oliver Brooks. He was an English subject who resided in South Africa (chap. 9). He was murdered in the course of the novel.

Note: In the year prior to *The Mental Monster* (entry #151), Monk installed a secret set of tunnels around Doc's skyscraper headquarters. Ham used a stink bomb on Monk, who "went around smelling like a polecat for a month" (chap. 4). To escape Monk's wrath, Ham "had to take a hurried trip to England, on the pretense of studying the rationing over there." I place this incident between Ham and Monk in October 1941. In September 1941, a German submarine had attacked an American destroyer, the *Greer*, in the Atlantic. A series of incidents then followed involving conflicts between American ships and Nazi U-boats. It was becoming apparent that the United States would enter the war, and some government agency must have commissioned a study of rationing in England in order to implement such a policy here when the time arose. Ham volunteered for this project to escape Monk's rage.

Doc visited Ernest Green's bank in Boston once during October-November 1941. Doc's visit was "five years" prior to the events of *The Disappearing Lady* (chap. 1), a novel set in October 1946.

During the same time period, Doc and Monk spent "months" developing a chemical which could be introduced into a plane's engine *(The Talking Devil,* chap. 8). The chemical would leave a vapor out of the plane's exhaust. The vapor could be spotted with ultraviolet and infrared light. Doc hoped that enemy planes could be tracked by this method if Allied spies could secretly introduced the chemical into their gas tanks.

Around December, Monk performed a "production installation job" for a firm called Central-Allied Chemical *(Jiu San,* chap. 5).

The Japanese bombed Pearl Harbor on December 7, 1941. Doc and the rest of the United States were now plunged fully into World War II. At this point, we come to one of the most important secret periods of Doc's life. For years, it has been believed by the majority of Doc Savage fans that this great hero never served officially as a soldier in the American armed forces during World War II. There is evidence to refute this belief.

The evidence of Doc's official military service is in *No Light to Die By*. In that novel, Doc's medals were displayed in a case at his headquarters (chap. 4). There is an excellent discussion of the medals by Philip José Farmer in *Doc Savage: His Apocalyptic Life*.

"The little blue ribbon with the stars on it" was the Congressional Medal of Honor. Doc had lesser medals including four purple hearts. Mr. Farmer concluded that Doc won these medals in World War I. Although he saw plenty of action in World War II, Doc would have been ineligible for medals because he was technically on the inactive list. The purple hearts would have been given to Doc retroactively because the medal, originated by George Washington and neglected after the Revolutionary War, was reactivated by Herbert Hoover in 1932. I don't accept this theory. I believe that Doc was officially and secretly made an officer in the American military shortly after Pearl Harbor. Due to his close friendship with William Donovan, Doc could have been assigned to the COI, the forerunner of the OSS (see the "**Note**" after entry #138). He then went on two secret missions for the United States. None of his five assistants knew of these missions.

The first was to the Middle East. Sometime during December 1941 to March 1942, Doc saved the life of Mustaphet Kemal, a Turkish supplier of secret information, and his "small son" *(The Three Wild Men,* chap. 2). This rescue probably happened in Libya, which was then controlled by Lieutenant General Erwin Rommel, who would later be promoted to Field Marshall in June 1942. The evidence for Doc's presence in Libya can be found in Doc's words from *The Angry Canary* (chap. 8): "The place is south of Barca, in Libya. Bomber base first established by the Nazis, later developed by the Allies. I was in here a couple of times during the war." I believe that Doc's second visit happened during a stop to re-fuel his plane on his flight to Egypt shortly before the events of *The Pharaoh's Ghost*, a novel that I placed in May 1943 (entry #162). However, his first visit transpired when the Nazis were in Barca. In preparation for his North African mission, Doc must have gone to London in December 1941. According to *The Pharaoh's Ghost* (chap. 7), Doc met an English intelligence officer, Richleister, in London two years before the events of that novel.

Doc's second mission took him to Berlin, the heart of the Third Reich. Evidence of Doc's visit is in *The Shape of Terror* (chap. 10): "Once he had been in Berlin on a day when the Fuhrer was dedicating new buildings, and there had been that day cordons of brown and black clothed men like this." Possibly this is a reference to Doc's 1934 German trip (depicted in "The Fainting Lady"), but it could be a different visit to the

Third Reich based on other evidence.

In many previous novels, graduates from Doc's Crime College had acted as members of a private intelligent network (often referred to as "private detectives"). In *The Three Wild Men* (chap. 12), a novel which I place in late April 1942 (see the next entry), the graduates were able to telephone and telegraph messages to Doc from occupied Paris and Berlin (chap. 12), as well as Rome (chap. 15). In *Strange Fish* (chap. 12), a novel which both Philip José Farmer and I put in September 1944, Doc was able to make a telephone call to Berlin from a ranch in Oklahoma! The evidence is inescapable, Doc established secret lines of communications to the heart of Hitler's empire during the early months of American entry into World War II. This communications network would have been of incredible value to the Allies during World War II. Perhaps Doc reorganized his private European intelligence organization from *The King Maker* (chap. 8). Doc would later do something similar in the Soviet Union during the events of *Flight into Fear*.

Although Doc Savage viewed Hitler from afar, he didn't meet him until *Violent Night* (also known as *The Hate Genius)*. Doc didn't meet Herman Goering, and possibly Paul Joseph Goebbels (or at least his double), until the events of *Hell Below*. He possibly earlier met Rudolf Hess or his double in *The Golden Man*. There existed a couple of top ranking Nazi whom we have no recorded encounters with Doc. They were Heinrich Himmler, the head of the SS, and his ruthless deputy, Reinhard Heydrich (possibly the most dangerous Nazi leader). Perhaps Doc encountered them on this Berlin visit. In order to do these two missions, Doc risked his life incredibly. He was wounded four times in four months. When he returned to the United States, the American government concluded that Doc was pushing himself to the extreme. President Roosevelt ordered that Doc be given a medical discharge, and put on the inactive list as a Brigadier General (see entry #155). He remained on the inactive list for all future secret war missions which the government sparingly assigned him *(The Black, Black Witch, The Pharaoh's Ghost, The Shape of Terror, The Derelict of Skull Shoal, The Lost Giant, Jiu San* and *Violent Night).* Doc had other fights with Axis agents *(The Time Terror, The Devil's Black Rock, Hell Below, The Secret of the Su, The Three Devils, Death Had Yellow Eyes, According to Plan of One-Eyed Mystic* and *Strange Fish),* but he was acting on his own initiative on these adventures.

Doc was ordered not to talk about his missions performed during December 1941 to March 1942. He was forbidden even to mention them to his five close assistants. Doc made some excuse probably that he was at the Fortress of Solitude during that period.

After his discharge, Doc fought to get re-instated in the military. His assistants mistakenly assumed that Doc was trying to get into the military for the first time after Pearl Harbor. They didn't know he had been an active officer for four months. Either "Kenneth Robeson" didn't know about Doc's secret wartime missions, or he just kept his mouth shut. For whatever reasons, "Robeson" put distortions in his wartime novels that Doc had never served in uniform during World War II. The evidence leaked out in *No Light to Die By* for a very obvious reason. As clearly stated in the novel's opening section, "Kenneth Robeson" didn't write the novel, but received the manuscript from Sammy Wales, the novel's narrator. Wales wasn't sworn to secrecy like "Robeson." When the war ended, Doc was awarded the Congressional Medal of Honor in recognition of his covert missions in the early months following Pearl Harbor.

After Pearl Harbor, Monk tried to develop "a surefire nerve gas, effective through the skin pores, and confidently tried it on himself, with the result that he turned green as a bullfrog and stayed that way several months" *(Weird Valley,* chap. 8). Monk was in seclusion during this period. Ham taught a law course during February 1942 (see entry #164).

144. The Three Wild Men

Published: August 1942
1942: Very late April (2 days, possibly April 29-30)
Author: Lester Dent

Renny was in South Africa, Johnny was in London (chap. 7), and Long Tom was in Portugal (chap. 9). They were engaged in "war work" (chap. 7).

Doc lost his FBI security clearance (U-93, Department K) temporarily in this novel (chap. 8). Doc had held a commission granted by J. Edgar Hoover since at least the time of *The Secret in the Sky.*.

This temporary loss of would initiate a series of misunderstanding with the authorities over the next few adventures. In *The Three Wild Men*, Wealthy Raymond Cushing's sugar company had once financed a revolution in Central America (chap. 7). Sugar is a crop in both El Salvador and Nicaragua. The government of El Salvador was overthrown in 1931 in a military coup, and a similar fate befell the Nicaraguan government in 1936. Probably either one of these two countries was the one with which Cushing's sugar company had been involved.

The novel's villain was abducting prominent business and political leaders from around the world. A machine caused these leaders to have a nervous breakdown, and made them open to mental suggestion. The leaders were told to behave like "wild men."

One of these "wild men" was abducted in Asia and brought to New York. He was Mehastan Ghan, "the little man, half-English and half-Tibetan, who is the religious leader of millions of Orientals" (chap. 6). For a Tibetan, it seemed strange that Ghan wrote in Hindustani. It would make more sense if Ghan was an Indian. In fact, I am certain he really was an Indian. We have another case of a deliberate distortion by Lester Dent. The name Mehastan Ghan is too close to Mohandas

Gandhi (alias Mahatma Gandhi) for it to be a mere coincidence. The physical description, "little man," also fits Gandhi. The evil mastermind must have kidnapped Gandhi in April 1942. Gandhi had just refused in March 1942 to negotiate with Sir Stafford Cripps about India's future. There can be little doubt that Doc restored Gandhi's mental health. The pacifist leader returned to India only to be jailed by the British in August 1942. Gandhi was arrested for launching a "Quit India" campaign. At the time, the British, concerned with the possibility of a Japanese invasion of India, felt that Gandhi's activities would injure the war effort.

This novel's placement was affected by the preview at its conclusion for *The Fiery Menace* affected its placement (see entry #146 for a full discussion).

145. The Fiery Menace
Published: September 1942
1942: Early May (3 days, possibly May 2-4)
Author: Lester Dent

The events of *The Three Wild Men* transpired "last month" (chap. 2). Johnny and Renny were still in Europe "doing a little in the current war" (chap. 6). In Washington, Doc tried unsuccessfully to get posted to "the war front, personally" (chap. 4). Even lunch at the White House didn't help. Washington would consistently resist Doc's request for regular combat duty in the exploits that followed.

An American cargo ship, the *Domino* was sunk off the coast of Greenland by the Nazis "three months" earlier (chap. 14). Doc had given his formula for sleep gas to the War Department who put it in their secret vaults (chap. 10). However, Doc would later admit that the gas was of limited military value *(The Mental Monster,* chap. 5). Maybe the formula was put in a box next to a crate containing a Biblical artifact recovered by Indiana Jones. The War Department had also received the inertia-increasers from *The Motion Menace* (chap. 18), the oxygen destroyer from *Merchants of Disaster* (chap. 20), and the deadly device from *The Angry Ghost* (chap. 19).

In *The Fiery Menace* (chap. 6) Pat Savage now owned cars named "Clarence," "Tarzan" and "Adolf Hitler" as well as a truck named "Winston Churchill." The criminals in the novel owned a car which had been "built special for a syndicate that had taken a job to kidnap and kill Mussolini" (chap. 3). The syndicate was probably the American branch of the Mafia. Mussolini had been trying to drive the Sicilian branch of the same organization out of business.

The preview at the end of *The Three Wild Men* for *The Fiery Menace* affected its placement (see entry #146 for a full discussion).

Note: According to *The Three Wild Men* (chap. 2), Doc was scheduled to have a meeting with Mustaphet Kemal, a supplier of secret information indebted to him, concerning news of a Baltic scientist who was developing bullet-proof vests. The Baltic scientist was "tied up with a war-mongering clique" (chap. 2). Doc was concerned that the vest would fall into the "wrong hands" (i.e. Hitler's). Kemal went to the Baltic country to find out more information and promised to meet Doc six weeks later. This meeting would have happened in early June and may have involved an unrecorded adventure involving the Baltic scientist. The Baltic country was probably Sweden, which Lester Dent criticized in *The Evil Gnome*. The scientist was probably mixed up with the pro-Nazi lobby in Sweden. This chronological arrangement doesn't give Doc time to travel to Sweden, but maybe Kemal stole the bulletproof vest and brought it to New York. No doubt the scientist and his associates would have gone to New York to retrieve the vest.

146. The Laugh of Death

Published: October 1942
1942: Second half of June (12 days)
Author: Lester Dent

The earliest month where I can place the novel is June because there was a reference to summer (chap. 2): "It was a hot summer afternoon...." A character lost brothers at Pearl Harbor and at Bataan in the Philippines (chap. 14). The fighting around Bataan transpired during January-April 1942.

In *The Three Wild Men* and *The Fiery Menace*, Doc was constantly being falsely accused of crimes. In *The Laugh of Death*, a policeman alluded to those events (chap. 2): "For a couple of months, we had a lot of trouble, and some people got suspicious of you. It got so bad we had to lock you up."

Generally, I have ignored the previews inserted in the Doc Savage series since they have very little to do with the novel and were often arbitrarily based on the editor's choice of which novel to publish next. However, Dent wrote *The Three Wild Men*, *The Fiery Menace* and *The Laugh of Death* in that order, and the previews at the end of the first two novels are tightly woven into the dialogue. In *The Three Wild Men* (chap. 16), Monk and Ham returned to headquarters, and their discussion of the last events of that adventure are disrupted by a disturbance in the lobby which led directly into the opening scene of *The Fiery Menace*. The impression is given that no more than a day separated the two novels. Since *The Fiery Menace* mentioned that *The Three Wild Men* happened in the previous month, and *The Laugh of Death* placed their events over a period of two months. I have placed *The Three Wild Men* in late April and *The Fiery Menace* in early May. *The Fiery Menace* has a tightly woven preview of *The Laugh of Death*. At the conclusion of *The Fiery Menace* (chap. 15), Monk was reading a newspaper about a bank robbery in Mexico where a strange laughing sound was heard. In *The Laugh of Death* (chap. 13), the robbery happened three days after a medical operation was performed on a man named Henry Famous Martin. The operation was three weeks earlier. If I honored the preview in *The Fiery Menace*, then I will have to move it either into June, or push *The Laugh of Death* down into May. However, the preview was later disavowed by an event in *The Laugh of Death*. Monk called up a newspaper friend to find out if any unusual stories had happened recently, and learned about the bank robbery in Mexico (chap. 13). Shouldn't Monk have remembered it if he read it in a newspaper only three weeks earlier? Since Lester Dent ignored the preview in *The Fiery Menace*, I will too.

In *The Laugh of Death* (chap. 1), Doc was in the Fortress of Solitude for over "two days." The Fortress had been remodeled since John Sunlight's visit to look like "a chunk of ice." The events of *Fortress of Solitude* were briefly recalled by Doc in *The Laugh of Death*: "Only once had his men come anywhere near it, and that was long ago."

It was recalled in *The Laugh of Death* how "the Germans took that fort in Belgium" (chap. 17). The Germans had captured Fort Eben Emael in Belgium during May 1940.

Doc owned a pocket periscope, which also functioned as a telescope and a microscope. He had been using it at least as far back as *Red Snow* (chap. 5). The periscope had been built for him by "a specialist who had been chased out of Germany by the Nazis long ago" *(The Laugh of Death,* chap. 11). This specialist was "one of e most skilled of living grinders of optical lenses." The Nazis had assumed power in January 1933, and I placed *Red Snow* in December 1933. Therefore, the logical conclusion would be that the device was constructed for Doc in 1933. However, Doc also briefly used a device called "a pocket microscope" in *The Red Skull* (chap. 17). Either the microscope used in *The Red Skull* was a forerunner of the combination telescope-periscope-microscope used later by Doc, or the German specialist fled Germany in 1931 or 1932, before the Nazis gained control of Germany. The Nazis were intimidating people long before Hitler became Chancellor.

In *The Laugh of Death* (chap. 14), Groves, "an official of army intelligence," displayed discomfort when dealing with Doc Savage. Could this army official be General Leslie R. Groves, the man in charge of the Manhattan Project, the development of the atomic bomb? Maybe Groves' discomfort is a clue as to why Doc never worked on the Manhattan project. As the author of *Atomic Research Simplified (The Green Death,* chap. 2) and the inventor of the "atomic gun" featured in *The Motion Menace* (chap. 18) and *The Golden Peril* (chap. 19), Doc was unquestionably qualified to be approached to work on the Manhattan Project. On of is tutors had been "a Yale expert on atomic phenomena" *(Waves of Death,* chap. 5). Perhaps Doc was offered a position and turned Groves down. Doc may not have wanted to be associated with so devastating a weapon. Groves must have retaliated by helping to arrange the suspension of Doc's security clearance in *The Three Wild Men.*

147. The Time Terror
Published: January 1943
1942: Early July (4 days)
Author: Lester Dent

The time would seem to be summer (chap. 7): "It had not been exactly hot at Trapper Lake, but it had been above freezing, which was the heat of summer for Trapper Lake." The year was clearly 1942. A chemist named Calvin Western had been in Japan "before the war started" (chap. 9). Western was actually spying on Japanese poison gas facilities. When his cover was blown, he and some fellow spies fled Japan by airplane.

Japanese airplanes pursued into the Arctic. All of the planes landed in an unexplored region populated by dinosaurs. The dinosaurs wrecked the planes and marooned Western's party and its Japanese pursuers for "more than a year" (chap. 9).

Renny and Long Tom went to England to work on a "combination electrical and mechanical engineering job" (chap. 1). They intended to be there "several weeks."

148. The Talking Devil
Published: May 1943
1942: July (7 days)
Author: Lester Dent

A reference to "a bright crisp morning" (chap. 4) would be consistent with summer.

An absent Johnny was "preparing some specimens" in Alaska (chap. 14). According to Julian Puga Vasquez, the pulp has a footnote eliminated from the Bantam paperback:

> *The specimens to which Doc Savage refers were some amazing prehistoric life forms which Johnny Littlejohn had collected in the course of another adventure, "The Time Terror."*

Doc came under investigation for his Crime College activities in this novel. The Manhattan D. A. assigned to this case (chap. 16) adopted a more cooperative attitude than D. A. Einsflagen did in *The Invisible-Box Murders* (entry #134). The historical figure on whom Einsflagen was based, Thomas E. Dewey, had abandoned the role of D. A. at the end of 1941 in order to launch his successful 1942 gubernatorial campaign.

149. The Goblins
Published: October 1943
1942: Early August (4 days)
Author: Lester Dent

It was at least six months after the Pearl Harbor attack. The Jumping Toad Dude Ranch had "closed about six months ago, when tourist trade blew upon account of the war" (chap. 8). Parker O'Donnel "had joined the U.S. air force nearly eight months ago" (chap. 1). Assuming that O'Donnel was seized by patriotic fervor immediately following Pearl Harbor (December 7, 1941), the time would have to be either late July or early August.

Doc was revealed to be the author on a book on "electrolysis phenomena" (chap. 10). Doc had been taught "the art of silent movement" by "jungle natives in Africa, men of a fierce tribe who were always hunting and being hunted by their neighbors" (chap. 6). The natives were either the Congo pygmy tribe revealed to be Doc's boyhood friends in *The Forgotten Realm* (chap. 16), or the Ubangi River tribe of the Belgian Congo *(Mystery on Happy Bones*, chap. 9).

Renny, Johnny and Long Tom were absent in *The Goblins*.

150. Waves of Death
Published: February 1943
1942: August 12-14 (3 days)
Author: Lester Dent

The novel began on "Aug. 12th" (chap. 1).

Combined with an airplane motor muffler invented by Doc, Pat Savage devised a set of fans which made the remaining noise sound like a motor car on the highway (chap. 8). Both inventions were given to the War Department. The light beam machine, which is the subject of this novel, was also given to the government (chap. 14).

Note: Monk was outwitted by a clever female during an unrecorded adventure in early August 1942 (see entry #154).

151. The Mental Monster

Published: August 1943
1942: Second half of August (2 days)
Author: Lester Dent

The presence of "insects" in a forest (chap. 6) would be consistent with summer.

Renny was in Africa (chap. 2), where he was "building a highway for the U. S. army" (chap. 1). For unknown reasons, Doc was unable to contact Pat Savage during this adventure (chap. 7).

This novel gave the most comprehensive explanation of how Doc acquired his habit of trilling like a bird (chap. 14). One of Doc's teachers, "an old Hindu" who was "a specialist in mental discipline," had utilized the sound "effectively as part of a system of mind control, a system in which Doc never had much faith." Despite his lack of faith, Doc picked up this habit from his teacher. This teacher was also described in *The Laugh of Death* (chap. 6) as "a Hindu Yogi in India." The earlier novel had credited him with teaching Doc "the art of emotional control early in life." The same Yogi was also mentioned among Doc's instructors in *Waves of Death* (chap. 5). A more abbreviated version of the story involving Doc's trilling and the Yogi appeared later in *The Shape of Terror* (chap. 7).

In addition to his honorary New York City police department commission, Doc had a similar commission from the fire department (chap. 10).

Note: During late August to mid-September, Monk was in England" on a chemical warfare mission." There he met Winston Churchill. On August 24, 1942, Churchill had returned to England from a trip to North Africa. Monk's trip happened "four months" before the events of *The King of Terror* (chap. 10). Doc did not accompany Monk on this mission. According to *Jiu San* (chap. 5), Monk had been "working for the Chemical Warfare Service in the development of poison gases." *The Devil's Black Rock* (chap. 13) mentioned that Monk had "friends in the chemical division of the war department."

The Running Skeletons (entry #157) involved a scientific search for a food substitute. "About a year" (chap. 16) prior to the novel's events. Doc had unsuccessfully conducted his own experiments in this area. Doc probably conducted this research while Monk was in England.

152. Mystery on Happy Bones
Published: July 1943
1942: September 23-24 (2 days)
Author: Lester Dent

The novel began on a Wednesday (chap. 2).

Major Sam Lowell's Emergency Necessity Office was set up "largely for getting badly needed things in a hurry" (chap. 3). One of Lowell's earlier accomplishments was making sure that "arms and equipment were furnished in a hurry to some Eskimos in Northern Alaska." This action may have been a response to the Japanese seizure of three of the Aleutian Islands in June 1942.

Long Tom was in the Soviet Union "serving as consulting expert with the Russian army," and Pat Savage was in California "setting up the physical air-conditioning for a new WAAC camp" (chap. 2). Maybe California was Pat's location when she couldn't be reached by Doc in *The Mental Monster* (chap. 7).

In *Mystery on Happy Bones* (chap. 12), Doc tied Theodora Hannah on his back, and swung through the trees like Edgar Rice Burroughs' Tarzan. Doc recalled an incident from an unrecorded adventure: "Once he had done something similar with Ham Brooks, who was not supposed to have any nerves, and Ham had fainted." This incident may have happened during the unrecorded adventure in Hidalgo that I have placed in November 1935 (see the "**Note**" after entry #79).

153. They Died Twice

Published: November 1942
1942: October 6-16 (11 days)
Author: Lester Dent

The novel was set in early autumn (chap. 3): "Outside, it was a rather biting early-fall afternoon…" The novel began on a Tuesday (chap. 1). This exploit clearly took place after Pearl Harbor. Doc Savage was making "repeated efforts to get into active combat service" (chap. 1). Three members of a criminal gang turned "patriotic" and "even joined the army for the excitement" (chap. 4). The U. S. Navy was flying patrols along the coast (chap. 10). Long Tom made this remark to Renny: "You look like something that had been done to the Japanese navy." Long Tom must have been remembering the defeat of the Japanese navy at Midway (June 1942).

It was mentioned that the Hidalgo Trading Company was "not far from the spot where the *Normandie* capsized" (chap. 10). The liner *Normandie* was destroyed by a fire in 1941.

Doc returned to the fictional Central American republic of Hidalgo, and visited the Valley of the Vanished for the third time. Doc's previous visits to the Valley were *The Man of Bronze* and *The Golden Peril*.

154. The Devil's Black Rock

Published: December 1942
1942: October 19-28 (10 days)
Author: Lester Dent

It was clearly indicated when Doc's involvement in this exploit began (chap. 4): "On the nineteenth day of October, Doc Savage and his group of five associates returned to their headquarters in New York City (chap. 4). They had just returned from the adventure described in the previous chronological entry: "Nothing whatever appeared in the newspapers about the unusual matter which had taken them to Central America" (chap. 4).

The novel took place after Pearl Harbor. A Nazi spy made reference to things changing "since America became involved in the war" (chap. 12). The novel featured "shells for French 75s being shipped around as part of this war" (chap. 10).

Someone shot a bullet at the windows of Doc's headquarters (chap. 10), and Renny alluded to the Mayan sniper from *The Man of Bronze*: "Been a long time since anyone tried to shoot us through the windows!" Seeing that bullets were ineffective, the villains of *The Devil's Black Rock* then shot a cannon shell into Doc's headquarters.

Ham made the following remark about Monk (chap. 4): "Twice within the last few months he's almost gotten my neck broken by snorting around after the wrong girl." One of the two incidents could be from *Mystery on Happy Bones* (chap. 1). Monk foolishly dropped his guard with Theodora Hannah, and was consequently rendered unconscious. Ham revived Monk. Although Ham was never in danger, he would almost certainly exaggerate the incident. Monk's other encounter with a dangerous female must have transpired in an unrecorded adventure during early August.

155. The Black, Black Witch
Published: March 1943
1942: November (6 days)
Author: Lester Dent

The novel was set in the fall (chap. 10): "The snow proceeded to come down in one of these sudden, furious storms which occur in the fall of the year." A radio was "the kind of an outfit that was designed so a Nazi general could talk by radio-telephone to a colleague before Stalingrad" (chap. 6). The Nazis fought at Stalingrad during August 1942 to February 1943.

Renny and Long Tom were in Australia on an "army mission" (chap. 7). Monk held the rank of lieutenant colonel "on detached duty" during World War II (chap. 2). Monk had been a lieutenant colonel in World War I. Doc's rank, also "on detached duty," was higher than Monk's. In *Jiu San* (chap. 3), we learn that Doc's rank is that of a Brigadier General, but Doc was said to be on the "inactive list" instead of "detached duty."

During World War I, Doc had been only a lieutenant in World War I *(Escape from Loki,* chap. 1). It is believed that Doc had a private audience with Winston Churchill shortly before leaving on the mission described in *The Black, Black Witch* (see *The Lost Giant*, entry #169).

Note: In late November, Ham arrived in Japan on a secret mission. He saw an American agent posing as "a prince of the Imperial family in Tokyo" *(The Red Spider,* chap. 9). Ham's mission happened "almost a year after Pearl Harbor." Whether Doc or any of the four other assistants was on this mission is not known. The mission probably also occupied most of the month of December.

156. The King of Terror
Published: April 1943
1943: January 3-10 (8 days)
Author: Lester Dent

The novel began on a Saturday, and it was "winter in New York" (chap. 1).

Renny and Johnny were in Europe "assisting in the war effort" (chap. 2).

Long Tom was in England "installing that new plane detector device" (chap. 1).

The novel's chief villain. Abraham Mawson, was planning to gain powers by replacing world leaders with doubles. He intended to start with the fictional Central American Republic of Hidalgo by using a person whom he mistakenly believed to be a phony Doc Savage. Mawson mentioned that the current president of Hidalgo was Juan Doyle, and Doc had supported his election by influencing the indigenous Mayans (chap. 13) Based on my theory that Hidalgo is really Guatemala (see entry #21), then Jorge Ubico, whom I identified with Dent's fictional Carlos Avispa, would still have been president in January 1943. In July 1944, Ubico was overthrown in a general strike. In December 1944, Juan Arevalo, a prominent leader of Ubico's opposition, was elected president. In January 1943, Arevalo was an internationally known Guatemalan educator living in voluntary exile in Argentina. I speculate that Doyle was really Arevalo, and that Dent just "distorted" the "truth" about him.

In 1943, opposition to Ubico was beginning to crystallize. There can be no doubt that Doc had withdrawn his support from Ubico and given it to Arevalo in late 1942. Hoping to regain Doc's favor, Ubico didn't interfere with the secret gold shipments from the Valley of the Vanished. Ubico is a controversial figure in Guatemalan history. As a leader, he fell somewhere between Huey Long and the early Benito Mussolini. He improved Guatemala with schools and construction projects. He did much to help the indigenous Mayan Indians. On the other hands, he would become gradually corrupted by power. Although democratically elected, he evolved into a dictator and extended his presidential term in 1935 by an amendment to the Guatemalan Constitution. The amendment was approved in a nation-wide plebiscite. Ubico's second term should have expired in 1943. However, Ubico arranged for the granting of a third term by another amendment in 1941. Ubico was now scheduled to leave office in 1949. By 1942, Doc must have realized that Ubico had become a brutal dictator. During his visit to the Valley of the Vanished in October 1942 *(They Died Twice)*, Doc must have conferred with his Mayan allies. Together, they agreed to withdraw support from Ubico, and settled on the exiled Arevalo as the next president. It would take two years for Doc, the Mayans and their democratic allies to overthrow Ubico. Somehow Mawson learned all about this in *The King of Terror*.

When Abraham Mawson examined Guatemala in 1943, he concluded that Ubico's days were numbered. Mawson was more interested in Arevalo (alias Juan Doyle). By similar logic, Mawson chose to create a double for Charles De Gaulle (chap. 10), then leader of the Free French and clearly France's future leader, rather than Marshal Petain, currently in power in France as the leader of the collaborationist Vichy regime.

Note: According to *The Death Lady* (chap. 5), Doc met Captain Dennis "during the war when the man had been in charge of convoys to Casablanca." This meeting took place "four years" before the events of *The Death Lady*, a novel that I have placed in January 1947. Doc probably arrived during the final stages of the Casablanca Conference, which lasted from January 12 to 23, 1943. President Roosevelt and Prime Minister Churchill met there to declare that only unconditional surrender would be accepted from the Axis. Doc did not meet Churchill at this time (see the discussion of *The Lost Giant*, entry #169).

Ham taught a law course during February 1943 (see entry #164). In the closing days of the same month, Doc bought a controlling interest in the Goody-Prest Company, a cereal manufacturer. This was "about three months" before the events of *The Man Who Was Scared* (chap. 14), a novel which I have placed in June 1943 (entry #163).

157. The Running Skeletons
Published: June 1943
1943: Early March (4 days)
Author: Lester Dent

Long Tom "had just returned from England where he had been doing advanced work in electronic plane detection" (chap. 3). This comment is consistent with Long Tom's activities in the previous chronological entry.

Two sons of a chemist had died from starvation in the Aleutian Islands during the war (chap. 15). The Japanese had seized three of the islands in June 1942.

The majority of Doc's special vehicles had been removed from the basement of his skyscraper, and lent to defense plants. The vehicles' special features would be studied in order to see if some of their feature could be incorporated into military transports being used in the war (chap. 10).

158. Hell Below
Published: September 1943
1943: Mid-March (9 days)
Author: Lester Dent

Two Nazi leaders had decided that Germany would lose the war, and fled to Mexico. The Nazis had been in Mexico for "two months" (chap. 10). By my chronological arrangement, they had arrived in Mexico in January 1943. This would have been an appropriate time to reach the conclusion that Germany faced defeat. 1942 had seen the defeat of Rommel at El Alamein, the destruction of the Japanese aircraft carriers at Midway, and the North African landings during Operation Torch. By early 1943, Germany was close to losing the Battle of Stalingrad, the turning point of the Russian campaign. One of the Nazi leaders was called Das Seehund ("the Seal"). He was described in the following passage (chap. 10): "Das Seehund is the fellow who set up the submarine campaign for the enemy. You've seen his pictures-a great fat guy. Enormously fat, and covered with medals. In a different uniform and a different big car every day." Change the word "submarine" to "airplane," and you would have an accurate description of Hermann Goering. There's no question that Dent had Goering in mind. Putting Goering in charge of U-boats rather than the Luftwaffe is merely a minor distortion by Dent.

The other Nazi leader was called Der Hase ("the Hare").

He was supposed to be the head of the Nazi propaganda machine. On the face of it, he would appear to be Paul Joseph Goebbels. However, there are distinct differences. Goebbels had a clubfoot, but Der Hase doesn't. Doc recognized Der Hase as a fellow Vienna student named Vogel Plattenheber (chap. 11). Nothing in Goebbels' background indicated that he ever assumed the alias of Plattenheber or studied in Vienna. Das Seehund and Der Hase differed over why they were in Mexico. Das Seehund wanted to just escape and enjoy his wealth, but Der Hase wanted to start another Reich. This disagreement resulted in Das Seehund fatally shooting Der Hase. Der Hase's real-life counterpart, Goebbels committed suicide in 1945, two years later.

The Nazi leaders were rumored to have doubles. These doubles posed as the Nazi leaders in order for the genuine articles to go to secret meetings. Plattenheber was probably Goebbels'. Goering must have convinced the double to go along with this flight to Mexico. Goering's purpose would have been to have Goebbels' double convince any skeptical Nazi followers that Hitler approved of this scheme. However, Plattenheber came to play his part too well. Goering was forced to kill him. Das Seehund's treachery was being investigated by a loyal Nazi named Schwartz. At the conclusion of the novel, Das Seehund escaped back to Germany. Doc let Schwartz escape in the hope that he would inform Hitler of Das Seehund's treachery. Doc hoped Hitler would execute Das Seehund. Since Goering lived only to commit suicide in 1945 after been tried for war crimes at Nuremburg, we can assume that Das Seehund had Schwartz murdered before he could reach Hitler. An earlier version of this theory appeared in my article, "Three From Doc Savage," in *Echoes* #52 (December 1990).

159. The Secret of the Su
Published: November 1943
1943: Late March (5 days)
Author: Lester Dent

Doc had "cards and letters of authority from the war department" (chap. 7).

Doc was probably given these papers in recognition of his successful mission in *The Black, Black Witch*.

160. The Three Devils
Published: May 1944
1943: April 5-7 (3 days)
Author: Lester Dent

The chapter numbers cited here are from the magazine version of the novel. In the Bantam paperback version, the sixth chapter has the Roman numeral for 4 ("IV") instead of 6 ("VI"). I have heard it claimed by two pulp magazine fans that a chapter was missing, but a comparison of the magazine to the paperback reveals that all the chapters are there, but one is mislabeled.

The novel was set in the spring (chap. 1): "The plane carrying Doc Savage and four of his aides arrived at Mock Lake, which was about two hundred miles northwest of Vancouver, Canada, at two o'clock in the spring afternoon." The novel began on a Monday (chap. 3).

Ham's Harvard roommate, Carl John Grunow, was murdered in the novel. Ham had not seen him for five years (chap. 2). Ham would have last seen Grunow sometime in 1938. Grunow lived in Vancouver, Canada. When *The Yellow Cloud*, a novel which I have placed in late March 1938 (see entry #101), concluded, Ham was somewhere in "the northwestern part of Canada" (chap. 12). Perhaps Ham decided to take a brief side trip to Vancouver to visit his old friend after that earlier adventure concluded.

Nazi spies were trying to sabotage the lumber industry in Canada. The novel discussed the importance of wood pulp in the war effort. The novel was aimed at Doc Savage readers who were complaining that the size of the magazine had shrunk due to the paper shortage (chap. 11): "The average guys kicks because his favorite magazine has to cut itself down to something you can stick in your pocket." The novel explained that wood pulp was important for tri-nitro cellulose and other products used by soldiers.

The German spies had been in Canada for "twenty years" (chap. 14). The spies must have been dispatched by extreme elements in the German military during 1923. The Nazis didn't achieve power until 1933, ten years later. Like Das Seehund (see entry #158), the head of the spy ring had come to the conclusion that Germany "wasn't doing too well" (chap. 14). However, German defeats were making the ringleader work harder for the war effort, rather than save his own skin like Das Seehund. Long Tom was absent from *The Three Devils*.

161. Death Had Yellow Eyes

Published: February 1944
1943: April (8 days)
Author: Lester Dent

The novel was set in the spring (chap. 2): "There had been crispness of spring in the earlier part of the day..."

Renny and Long Tom were in China (chap. 5).

Jan Mereschal, an Axis official in charge of inspecting gold shipments, had concluded that the Axis was going to lose World War II (chap. 13). Mereschal had reached the same conclusion as Das Seehund in *Hell Below*. Fleeing Europe, Mereschal had been in the United States for "about four months" (chap. 10) when the events of *Death Had Yellow Eyes* unfolded. Mereschal would have first arrived in the United

States around January 1943, the same time that Das Seehund came to Mexico, Probably Mereschal had left Europe with the supposed intention to help Das Seehund fund his Mexican operation, but the wily financier decided to take a detour in order to hide in the United States.

In *Doc Savage: His Apocalyptic Life,* Philip José Farmer concluded that Ham Brooks' father must have been English due to the fact that Ham had a half-brother from South Africa in *The Too-Wise Owl.* In *Death Had Yellow Eyes* (chap. 1), there is reference that Ham had a paternal ancestor named Colonel Blackstone Brooks, "a lawyer who in his life had never rubbed more than two dollars in his pocket together." The reference to "dollars" would imply that the Ham's paternal ancestors had been Americans for several generations.

Note: After returning to New York after the events of *Death Had Yellow Eyes,* Monk and Ham engaged in a rivalry over a wealthy chorus girl named Dawn O'Day.

Ham told Dawn that Monk was an undercover IRS investigator trying to get the dirt on her. Dawn dropped Monk in favor of Ham *(The Man Who Was Scared,* chap. 7).

162. The Pharaoh's Ghost
Published: June 1944
1943: Late May (6 days)
Author: Lester Dent

This novel and its sequel, *The Man Who Was Scared*, contradict each other in terms of chronology. *The Pharaoh's Ghost* claimed to have happened sometime "near the rainy season in Egypt" (chap. 9). By contrast, *The Man Who Was Scared*, a novel set in June, said the events of *The Pharaoh's Ghost* transpired in the previous month. Therefore, I advocate the argument that the statement about the rainy season in Egypt be ignored. There was "no longer much enemy action" in the areas of the Mediterranean bordering Egypt (chap. 2). On May 13, the last Axis forces in North Africa surrendered to the Allies.

Jaffa, the novel's villain, was causing trouble for the Allies "in captured territory and in territory not yet captured but would be soon" (chap. 7). Jaffa was causing rebellions and civil wars in Tunisia, Lebanon, Albania, Italy and Greece. By late May 1943, only Tunisia and Lebanon were in Allied hands. However, the Allies were already starting to seize small islands off Sicily, and it was becoming clear that Italy was in danger of being invaded. The British were sending supplies to resistance groups in Albania and Greece, and encountering severe problems with competing factions inside those two countries. These problems mainly resulted from disputes between the Communists and the non-Communists. Jaffa was probably responsible was exacerbating the rivalries among local resistance groups. In fact, Jaffa may have lit the fuse that resulted in the Greek Civil War after the end of World War II.

Long Tom once flew over Monument Valley in the Grand Canyon district of Arizona (chap. 10). Long Tom probably became familiar with this Arizona landmark when visiting that state during the events of *The Red Skull*.

Long Tom also hated camels due to prior exposure to them (chap. 12). Long Tom's earlier experiences with camels would have happened during the visits to Egypt in *The Lost Oasis*, *The Sargasso Ogre*, *Resurrection Day* and *The Awful Dynasty*.

Renny was in "in the interior of China" (chap. 2).

Johnny arrived in Egypt to become embroiled in this exploit. Prior to his arrival, Johnny had been "supervising a geographical seismographic survey of oil possibilities" in Russia. After completing the mission, Johnny had gone to Iran before taking a plane to Cairo. Doc, Ham, Monk and Long Ton traveled to Egypt from New York. At the conclusion of *Death of Yellow Eyes*, Doc, Monk, Ham and Johnny were in Rumania.

They stole a plane with the intention to fly to either Egypt or Turkey. Doc then planned to travel to New York in order to clear up some false murder charges against him. Doc and his group must have flown to Turkey. There Johnny got an assignment from the American government which took him to Russia. Doc, Monk and Ham returned to New York to convince the authorities of their innocence. Renny and Long Tom were in China during *Death Had Yellow Eyes*. Leaving Renny behind in China, Long Tom returned to New York in time to participate in the events of *The Pharaoh's Ghost*.

163. The Man Who Was Scared
Published: July 1944
1943: June (7 days)
Author: Lester Dent

The novel began on "a normal June afternoon" (chap. 1). The events of the previous chronological entry transpired "just last month" (chap. 16). The villain of *The Man Who Was Scared* was the brother of Jaffa, Doc's nemesis in *The Pharaoh's Ghost*.

During *The Man Who Was Scared* (chap. 7), Renny, Johnny and Long Tom "were in China working out a new setup with the Chinese Army."

Both Monk and Ham received invitations to visit Elma Champion at the Lazy-C Ranch in Wyoming (chap. 7). They probably went there when this adventure concluded.

164. The Spook of Grandpa Eben
Published: December 1943
1943: July 26-30 (5 days)*
Author: Lester Dent

The novel began on a Monday (chap. 1). Prior to the start of this novel, Doc had assumed the identity of chauffeur to a wealthy industrialist, Harland Crown Copeland, for "two weeks" (chap. 3). Doc was investigating if Copeland was selling inferior war merchandise to the U. S. government (chap. 2).

Ham had a special solid gold belt buckle which was "a gift from the law class," which he taught "evenings during the winters" (chap. 10). By my chronological arrangement, Ham taught evening classes during February in 1941, 1942 and 1943.

Renny, Johnny and Long Tom were absent.

Note: In *Jiu San* (chap. 3), female reporter Carlta Trotter recalled having seen Doc at "a meeting of scientific bigwigs in New York." Doc gave a lecture about electronics. This lecture probably happened in August 1943. Around the same time, Doc attended the insurance convention in Kansas City. He gave "a talk exposing new types of insurance frauds," and met the beautiful Sethena Williams *(The Thing That Pursued,* chap. 4). Back in New York, Doc also performed a minor good deed while riding the subway between Times Square and Grand Central. Two years before the events of *Fire and Ice* (chap. 3), an Alaskan tourist, known only as Yukon, got robbed of all his money on the New York subway. Doc gave Yukon the money to buy a plane ticket and return home.

165. The Whisker of Hercules
Published: April 1944
1943: Early September (3 days)
Author: Lester Dent

The police commissioner of New York was identified as someone named Boyer (chap. 5).

Part of this novel's plot involved a secret gold shipment (chap. 10): "This gold was being shipped to New York, in preparation for a deal with a foreign government whereby currency over there will be stabilized." In the next chronological entry, we learn the top secret details of this gold shipment.

166. The Derelict of Skull Shoal
Published: March 1944
1943: Mid or Late September (6 days)
Author: Lester Dent

The novel's plot involved a gold shipment "to show those Italian bankers they had better stabilize their currency and stuff" (chap. 14). This shipment would only have been sent if there was a friendly regime in Italy. An armistice between the Italian government and the Allies was signed on September 8, 1943. The gold shipment was probably a secret addendum to the armistice. Preparations for the shipment were underway in the previous chronological entry. The preparations may have begun before the armistice was signed. Mussolini had been overthrown in July 1943.

This novel revealed that Doc had written "a small book and a few scientific articles" on native jungle dialects (chap. 13). This book was probably published in the 1920s (see the **"Note"** after entry #1).

Teresa Ruth "Trigger" Riggert, an undercover naval operative, made this comment about pirates: "But there have been no pirates of any consequence in nearly a hundred years, except on the China coast, twenty years or so ago" (chap. 5). The lady was obviously unaware of the more recent activities of Tom Too *(Pirate of the Pacific)*, Jacob Black Bruze *(The Sargasso Ogre)*, High Lar and Lo Lar *(The Feathered Octopus)*, Prince Albert *(The Submarine Mystery)*, Jurl Crierson *(Poison Island)* and Lord London *(Pirate Isle)*.

In *The Derelict of Skull Shoal* (chap. 10), Doc remembered he had seen Cuban fishermen hunt sharks for their livers off Moro Castle in Havana harbor. *White Eyes* revealed that Doc owned a plantation in Cuba which was utilized in the early 1930s for smuggling in gold from the Valley of the Vanished in Central America. Doc could have visited Moro Castle shortly after *White Eyes* concluded in Cuba, or possibly when he first purchased the plantation after the United States went off the gold standard in 1933.

Johnny and Long Tom were absent from *The Derelict of Skull Shoal*.

167. According to Plan of a One-Eyed Mystic
Published: January 1944
Bantam Reprint Title: One-Eyed Mystic
1943: October 7-12 (6 days)
Author: Lester Dent

The story began on a Thursday when Renny left New York, and the next day was given as "Friday, the first week in October" (chap. 2). Although the first day in October fell on a Friday in 1943, I interpret "the first week in October" to mean the first full week of days in October. I make this interpretation to give Doc and his men time to get back from being stranded in the Caribbean at the conclusion of the previous adventure.

Long Tom and Johnny were absent. Doc held commissions as "a special investigator for half a dozen government departments" (chap. 6). As mentioned elsewhere in this chronology, Doc had commissions from the FBI *(The Secret in the Sky,* chap. 8), the U.S. Navy *(Devil on the Moon,* chap. 10 (11 in the revised text)), the Secret Service *(The Angry Ghost,* chap. 9), the Coast Guard *(Poison Island,* chap. 9), the U. S. Army *(The Black, Black Witch,* chap. 2), the War Department *(The Secret of the Su,* chap. 7), and the State Department *(The Thing That Pursued,* chap. 11). He also held police commissions for New York City (first mentioned in *The Polar Treasure,* chap. 6), New York State *(Death in Silver,* chap. 7), Maine *(The Squeaking Goblin,* chap. 6), California *(Ost (The Magic Island),* chap. 8), Washington D. C. *(The All-White Elf,* chap. 6) and Miami *(Return from Cormoral,* chap. 6). He also owned a New York City fire department commission *(The Mental Monster,* chap.

200   *The Revised Complete Cronology of Bronze*

10). Doc had received a special commission from Postmaster General James Farley as a "fully commissioned postal investigator." *(Fear Cay,* chap. 10). However, this commission may have expired when Farley left the Roosevelt administration in 1940.

Note: "A couple of years" prior to the events of *Three Times a Corpse* (chap. 2), Doc lectured "on the Keeler polygraph for recognizing psychogalvanic reflexes" at the FBI school. This lecture probably transpired around November 1944. Leonarde Keeler developed his first polygraph in 1926.

168. The Shape of Terror
Published: August 1944
1943: December (5 days, after the 7th)
Author: Lester Dent

The novel mentioned "the Teheran conference on any Churchill-Stalin-Chiang-Roosevelt get-togethers" (chap. 4). Churchill, Roosevelt and Chiang Kai-shek met at the Cairo Conference, and then Churchill and Roosevelt met with Stalin in Teheran. These conferences were held from November 23 to December 7, 1943.

The novel's plot mentioned a German secret weapon whose nature was never fully explained. The weapon was probably some form of germ warfare. In *The Mental Monster* (chap. 13), a footnote discussed the dangers of germ warfare.

In *The Shape of Terror*, one of the characters was a British spy named Jones-Jones. There also was a Nazi agent who impersonated Jones-Jones. The genuine Jones-Jones remembered meeting Monk and Ham in Washington, but neither of Doc's men could recall the meeting (chap. 2). Jones-Jones was probably introduced to Monk and Ham briefly when the pair went to Washington with Doc to argue with army officials in *Hell Below* (chap. 1).

In *The Shape of Terror* (chap. 7). it was mentioned that Doc had made "peacetime visits to Prague." He had rented rowboats at the Vltava River when "he wanted to be alone with peace and stillness." Doc probably visited Prague, Czechoslovakia, when he was a student in Vienna, Austria. He also probably accompanied Monk and Ham on the "pre-war visit to Prague" (chap. 8). I believe this visit was connected with the trip that Doc made to Eastern Europe to retrieve his darkness machine from Baron Karl (see the "**Note**" after entry #99).

The Nazis offered a reward of fifty million marks for Doc in *The Shape of Terror* (chap. 5). It was mentioned that a reward had been offered of ten million marks for Mihailovich. The individual in question was Draja Mihailovich, the leader of the Chetniks in Yugoslavia. The Chetniks were initially the most prominent resistance group in Yugoslavia, but were later overshadowed by Tito's Partisans. The Chetniks were eventually accused of collaborating with the Nazis, and Mihailovich would be executed for treason by Tito in 1946.

Rumors that the Nazis had captured a Belgian fort with a secret weapon were remembered (chap. 3). The fort was Eben Emael, which the Nazis seized in May 1940.

Renny, Johnny and Long Tom were absent from *The Shape of Terror*.

169. The Lost Giant
Published: December 1944
1944: January (4 days, before the 14th)
Author: Lester Dent

Jonas House, a Hollywood make-up artist, "was in New York for the winter" (chap. 1). House did the make-up for Doc Savage in this novel. Doc was feeling the strain of the war. Not only couldn't he do his own make-up, but he was also getting clumsy with his lip-reading (chap. 6). I can't resist the opportunity to speculate that Jonas House was "really" Jack P. Pierce, the man who did the makeup for such classic Universal horror pictures as *Frankenstein* and *The Wolf Man*.

A woman who once worked in a doctor's office recalled seeing "a sound picture" of Doc Savage "making a delicate brain operation" (chap. 7). This is the film which Doc made in *World's Fair Goblin* (chap. 2). It has also been mentioned in *Men of Fear* (chap. 5).

The year of *The Lost Giant* would seem to be 1944. A spy, Thaddeus Fay, had been working "on and off" with another agent, Burroughs, since 1939 (chap. 9). After occasional missions with Burroughs, Fay began to work consistently with him since Pearl Harbor (December 7, 1941). Later, a State department official mentioned that Fay and Burroughs had been working closely together for 'about three years" (chap. 12).

In *The Lost Giant* (chap. 12) Doc met an old acquaintance, Lieutenant General Gaines (chap. 12). Doc had last seen Gaines in Cairo "about six months ago" with "a striking blonde Englishwoman named Celia" (chap 12). In my chronological arrangement, Doc was in Cairo during *The Pharaoh's Ghost*, May 1943. The interval between *The Pharaoh's Ghost* and *The Lost Giant* would be eight months, which would be consistent with the statement of "about six months." It isn't clear from the text whether Gaines was British or American. Since he was traveling with Winston Churchill on a transport plane, Gaines was probably British. This Gaines is not the same individual as Gaines the neurologist, Doc's friend in *The Man Who Was Scared*.

Doc rescued Churchill in this novel. Churchill's plane had crashed in the Arctic. Churchill had been aboard a plane probably returning to England. A group of German planes intercepted Churchill's escort. In order to escape the Germans, Churchill's plane ran into a cold front. The cold front threw Churchill's plane off course, and it had to make a forced landing. After the Teheran Conference ended on December 7, 1943, Churchill went to North Africa. According to history, Churchill left North Africa on January 14, 1944, and returned to London on January 18. Since history doesn't give Churchill enough time to get lost in the Arctic and be rescued on Doc, I am forced to speculate upon the facts. Churchill must have "really" left North Africa on an earlier date in January. When Churchill got lost in the Arctic, the British government had to conceal his peril by having an actor impersonate him in North Africa. The British did use doubles in North Africa during World War II. Actor M.E. Clifton-James impersonated Bernard Montgomery in a well-documented case. After Doc rescued Churchill, the actor posing as Churchill left North Africa on January 14.

Why have the British kept this episode so secret? On January 12, 1944, history states that Winston Churchill met with Charles De Gaulle in Marrakech. If a false Churchill had met with De Gaulle, then the future leader of France would have been extremely offended if he ever found out about the deception. The whole episode of Doc's rescue of Churchill was classified top secret in order to protect Franco-British relations.

Doc had met Churchill on two previous occasions in "the man's executive offices" (chap. 12). Doc was at Number 10 Downing Street, the Prime Minister's residence in *The Shape of Terror* (chap. 3). Churchill did not make an appearance in that novel due to the fact he was in North Africa during December 1943. The first meeting with Churchill must have transpired in January 1940 just before Doc became drawn into *The Awful Dynasty* (see the "Note" between entries #124 and #125). Churchill had been only First Lord of the Admiralty at the time. Doc's second meeting with Churchill, now Prime Minister, most likely happened in Downing Street shortly before Doc was parachuted into France at the start of *The Black, Black Witch*. Although Monk accompanied Doc at that mission, he did not meet with Churchill immediately before *The Black, Black Witch*. However, Monk met Churchill separately during an earlier trip to Britain (see the "Note" after entry #151).

Renny, Johnny and Long Tom were absent in *The Lost Giant*.

170. Jiu San

Published: October 1944
1944: March (27 days)
Author: Lester Dent

Doc Savage had been pretending to be a Japanese sympathizer for "six weeks" (chap. 5). Ham had disappeared for a "month" as well. Ham had actually been preparing to impersonate a Japanese (chap. 10). Ham now knew the Japanese language, and claimed to have been studying since "before Pearl Harbor." However, Ham couldn't speak Japanese in *The Time Terror* (chap. 7). Probably it was a long difficult task for Ham to master Japanese.

Jiu San (chap. 5) revealed that Monk had been born in Tulsa, Oklahoma.

Doc's involvement in *The Shape of Terror* was recalled in *Jiu San* (chap. 3): "Just a few months ago, he helped crack one of those German secret war scares…"

Renny, Johnny and Long Tom were absent from *Jiu San*.

Carlta Trotter worked for a newspaper called the *New York Blade* in *Jiu San* (chap. 1). This newspaper may be the same as the *Morning Blade*, which criticized Doc Savage in *The Talking Devil* (chap. 4). In *The Mountain Monster* (chap. 7), Doc met another female reporter, Barbara Hughes, who worked for a newspaper called the *Blade*. She was covering the "Chicago angles" of that case, but it isn't clear where the *Blade* was located. It could have been a New York newspaper in that novel.

In *Jiu San*, the Japanese accepted Doc's pretense that he was pro-Japanese. Why? Doc had fought their agents in *Red Snow*, and been a constant thorn in Nazi Germany's side even before Pearl Harbor. Perhaps Doc had inadvertently done some service for the Japanese during his unrecorded battle (or possibly battles) with Lord London in the South Seas sometime during November 1940 to February 1941.

171. Weird Valley

Published: September 1944
1944: April (4 days)
Author: Lester Dent

The year was 1944 because Methuselah Brown was allegedly a 290-year-old man born in 1654 (chap. 2).

Renny "for some months had been in an engineering job in China" (chap. 8). By this chronological arrangement, Renny would have been absent from Doc's adventures after October 1943. Long Tom was in Russia, and Johnny "was currently trying to open up a tin deposit in northern Canada."

Note: Doc went to the Electrar Corporation during April-May 1944. Doc had been dispatched there by "the War Department to organize a department to produce an advance form of radar" (*The Wee Ones*, chap. 6). This assignment transpired "about a year" before the events of *The Wee Ones* (entry #180). The interval was also given as "more than a year" (chap. 2). I placed *The Wee Ones* in June 1945. Therefore, April-May 1944 would be slightly more than a year. Long Tom was probably involved in this trip for the War Department. Long Tom worked with an engineer named Tremaine on "some advanced radar experiments during the war" (*The Pure Evil*, chap. 8).

172. The Terrible Stork

Published: June 1945
1944: May (2 days)
Author: Lester Dent

The novel was set in the spring (chap. 4): "Spring of-the-year clouds, peaceful as lamb, filled the evening sky."

The plot involved a financier who secretly stored the wealth of spies and enemy aliens during World War II. Renny, Johnny and Long Tom were absent.

173. Violent Night

Published: January 1945
Bantam Reprint Title: The Hate Genius
1944: June (3 days, probably after D-Day (June 6))
Author: Lester Dent

In this novel, Doc captured a man who was supposedly Adolf Hitler. The apprehension of Doc's opponent happened in Switzerland. Hitler was preparing to flee Germany, and leave a double in his place. Hitler had altered his appearance. He was clean-shaven with red hair and freckles. The novel does not explain how Hitler altered his appearance. It could have been plastic surgery. On the other hand, Hitler could have used makeup just as Doc had done to disguise himself and his associates for numerous pulp novels. Lester Dent may have been hinting that Hitler's red-haired appearance was really his true appearance, and that the dictator had been disguising himself with black hair dye and a false mustache. At the end of this novel, Doc left the alleged Hitler in the custody of Allied agents in Switzerland.

I once constructed an elaborate theory that the man captured by Doc was a bogus Hitler, and that the Nazis were trying to lure Doc to Switzerland with a fake Fuehrer in order to capture him. I now disown that theory. Doc really captured Hitler. Unfortunately for the world, Hitler escaped from his Swiss captivity and returned to Germany. If the mishap of his escape hadn't happened, the war in Europe would have probably ended one year earlier. As for how Hitler altered his appearance, I believe he was just using makeup like Doc.

There were two nefarious individuals, one from history and the other from the Doc Savage novels, who could have conspired to rescue Hitler. The first was Otto Skorzeny, an SS commando leader who took orders personally from Hitler. Skorzeny rescued Mussolini from his Italian captors in September 1943, and abducted Admiral Horthy of Hungary in

October 1944. Skorzeny also trained the SS men who posed as American soldiers during the Ardennes counteroffensive in the winter of 1944-45. His confederate in masterminding Hitler's escape was Jonas Sown, who would be revealed as the secret power behind Hitler in *The Screaming Man*.

As for Hitler, he arrived in Germany only to be nearly killed by a bomb in July 1944. On April 30, 1945, he committed suicide in the bunker. June 1944 was the month where Hitler would have wanted to flee Germany. D-Day happened on June 6, and the Western Allies was now in France and heading towards Germany while the Soviets were approaching from the east.

Faced with Hitler, the ultimate in evil, Doc came very close to taking the tyrant's life (chap. 13).

The novel mentioned the Italian surrender after the overthrow of Mussolini (chap. 3). Mussolini was overthrown in July 1943, and the Italians surrendered in September of the same year. The novel also mentioned the assassination a Nazi general named Neufsedt, who was killed "early in the war" after ordering the execution of American prisoners. Neufsedt is an invention of Lester Dent's. His name suggests Von Rundstedt, the leading Nazi general, who survived the war and died in 1953. The assassination of the fictional Neufsedt may have been based on the assassination of Reinhard Heydrich, Heinrich Himmler's top lieutenant, in Czechoslovakia by Allied agents on May 27, 1942.

Renny, Johnny and Long Tom were absent from this novel.

174. Satan Black
Published: November 1944
1944: Early July (9 days)
Author: Lester Dent

The novel was set in the summer (chap. 1): "Early summer darkness lay over Arkansas…" Doc was sent by the War

Department to Arkansas to investigate why a vital oil pipeline was not being completed (chap. 4).

Renny had written articles for engineering journals (chap. 10).

Johnny and Long Tom were absent.

175. Strange Fish
Published: February 1945
1944: September (2 days)
Author: Lester Dent

The novel would seem to be set either in late summer or early fall (chap 5): "It looked as if the grass and the shrubs had grown carelessly most of the summer, then given a thorough job of trimming in the next few days." Paris Stevens, a WAC, had been wounded in Normandy shortly after the invasion (chap. 1). The invasion was on June 6, 1944.

Reference was made to the execution of Count Ciano, Mussolini's son-in-law (chap. 14). Ciano was killed in January 1944.

Doc made a telephone call to Johann Jon Berlitz, the man whom the Allies were considering as the leader of a postwar Germany (chap. 12). The text implied that Berlitz was in Berlin, Germany. Such a communication would seem impossible in September 1944. Allied troops had liberated nearly all of France, but had just begun to penetrate German territory. However, Doc was able to receive messages during 1942 from occupied Paris and Berlin his own private intelligence network in *The Three Wild Men* (chap. 12). Perhaps Doc's agents arranged this telephone call to Berlitz. One would assume that Berlitz was at a secret location to prevent Hitler from finding him. Berlitz would eventually be revealed to be a Nazi mass murderer who was betraying Hitler. I have speculated that Doc set up a communication network in the heart of the Third Reich during early 1942 (see the "**Note**" after entry #143).

In *Strange Fish* (chap. 10), Ham told "a preposterous lie" about an imaginary adventure involving himself, Monk, Doc and their imprisonment by African pygmies.

Ham must have derived this bogus story from his actual experience with pygmies in *The Forgotten Realm*. The pygmies in that adventure were quite pleasant.

At the conclusion of *Strange Fish* (chap. 14), Monk intended to stay at Paris Stevens' ranch for a short period after this adventure. Ham was also trying to stay.

A letter by an Army Intelligence official, Theodore Toms indicated that Doc had "lately" been in England (chap. 3). Toms was probably referring to Doc's presence in England during the events of *The Shape of Terror* in December 1943.

Long Tom was in China (chap. 4). Renny and Johnny were missing.

176. The Ten Ton Snakes
Published: March 1945
1944: October (4 days)
Author: Lester Dent

The novel would seem to have taken place after the Normandy invasion: "…the war near its end…" (chap. 5).

Ham "went to Europe to work on that legal tangle the Nazis left" (chap. 3). Johnny and Long Tom were outside the United States. One of the novel's characters, Bob French, an American soldier, had worked with Renny during his wartime activities in China. Renny and French had been stationed at Yung-shun in the Hunan province of China. Renny had been building "an intermediate field for the B-29's" (chap. 1). Renny had been the supervising engineer, and French "had been with the army engineer group assigned to the project" (chap. 3). Renny and French had been assigned the same quarters, "a Chinese farmer's house." It was suggested that Renny and French also spent took a detour to "the Burma jungles" (chap.

14) during the period that they were working in China.

By my chronological arrangement, Renny was in China from mid-April 1943 to August 1943, and from mid-October 1943 to June 1944. He would return to China in the next chronological entry.

Monk's car was "a second-hand job which had belonged to a Balkan dictator who had been chased out of his country by another dictator" (chap. 6). The former owner of this car was probably King Zog of Albania, who had started out as a dictator and declared himself a monarch. The other dictator who caused his flight was Benito Mussolini.

Renny recalled being in the Amazon jungle before (chap. 10). Renny had been there in *Dust of Death*, *The Mental Wizard* and *The Green Death*.

177. Rock Sinister
Published: May 1945
1944: November (5 days)
Author: Lester Dent

Renny was in China, Johnny in Alaska, and Long Tom in France (chap. 6).

Monk's false teeth played a major role in the novel (chap. 14). Ham learned that Monk had a false set of teeth in this adventure. Monk had removed his false teeth in a scene from *The Pink Lady* (chap. 10), but Ham had not been present.

The president of the fictional South American Republic of Blanca Grande, Andros Lanza made reference to some of Doc's recent adventures in *Rock Sinister* (chap. 12): "You have gone to Japan, representing the United States Department and meddled with Japanese internal affairs. You have meddled with internal affairs in Germany, in the Mediterranean and elsewhere." Lanza was referring to the respective events of *Jiu San*, *Strange Fish* and *The Pharaoh's Ghost*. In all those earlier novels, Doc was trying to ensure that stable honest post-war governments would arise after the end of World War II.

The country of Blanca Grande in *Rock Sinister* was based on Uruguay. It was located near Brazil (chap. 6). Blanca Grande had a large cattle industry maintained by the South American cowboys known as Gauchos (chap. 7). Gauchos are only in Uruguay and Argentina A reference to Buenos Aires (chap. 8) ruled out Argentina.

The novel's plot involved an attempt by the incumbent president to turn his country into a fascist dictatorship. Formerly a strong believer in democracy, Andros Lanza had inexplicably become an advocate of tyranny. Lanza tried to frame Doc as an imperialist agent of the United States in order to create a scapegoat and drum up popular support inside South America. At the conclusion of the novel, Lanza was captured by Doc. Lanza was put in seclusion by indigenous democratic elements inside his own country. He officially resigned because of ill health.

Lester Dent would appear to have based this novel on an event that happened in Uruguay during January 1943. In order to explain the incident properly, I need to digress into Uruguayan history. Gabriel Terra had been elected president of Uruguay. He staged a coup and declared himself a dictator in 1933. A new constitution in 1934 granted the president sweeping powers. In 1938, Terra allowed free elections and his brother-in-law, General Alfredo Baldomir, was elected president. Baldomir wanted to return Uruguay to a democratic path. He scrapped the 1934 constitution, but the possibility of a pro-German coup forced him to briefly assume dictatorial powers in 1942. Baldomir allowed free elections in which he was not a presidential candidate. In January 1943, shortly before his term was to officially end, Baldomir suffered a strange illness that caused his seclusion. He reappeared in February to formally transfer power to his democratically elected successor. Baldomir retired from politics, and died in 1948. I originally discussed this historical background in my article., "Doc Savage in Uruguay," from *Echoes* #57 (October 1991).

Lester Dent would seem to have based Andros Lanza on Alfredo Baldomir. Apparently Dent saw something sinister in Baldomir's illness and seclusion in early 1943. Dent described Lanza as a long lean man who slightly resembled Abraham Lincoln. Actually, Baldomir was a heavyset man who looked more like Grover Cleveland or Theodore Roosevelt.

I toyed with the idea of placing *Rock Sinister* in January 1943, but its relationship to other Doc Savage adventures prohibited such a decision. I view the novel as a "distorted" account of how a former South American President tried to launch a fascist takeover inside his own country. The inexplicable personality change in the South American leader which changed him from a ardent believer in democratic ideals to a scheming fascist may be due to the intervention of a sinister personality well known to Doc Savage readers. Jonas Sown, the villain of *The Screaming Man* and *The Frightened Fish*, had some sort of mind control device that could alter people's personality. Perhaps Sown was exposing a noted South American politician to this device since January 1943, and the final result of utilizing this method of mind control was an aborted fascist coup in October 1944.

Monk's finances were radically changing in the autumn of 1944. In *Strange Fish* (chap. 14), it was mentioned that he was "perpetually broke." *The Ten Ton Snakes* (chap. 8) mentioned that he had been thrown out of an apartment near Radio City for not paying rent. In *Rock Sinister* (chap. 2), Monk was living luxuriously in his old Wall Street laboratory. Monk must have had a sudden financial windfall between *The Ten Ton Snakes* and *Rock Sinister*.

Rock Sinister (chap. 3) offered a totally different explanation for how Theodore Marley Brooks got his nickname of Ham. The traditional explanation was that Monk framed him for stealing hams during World War I. The explanation from *Rock Sinister* was that Ham shouted that he didn't like pork in any form while inspecting a mess hall . Probably the mess hall incident happened after Monk's frame-up, and Ham's stated aversion resulted from Monk's earlier prank. Another modification to the classic origin story of the Monk-Ham feud can be found in *The Wee Ones* (see entry #180).

Dent made modifications to the World War I story about the Monk-Ham feud as the series progressed. In most versions, Ham was brought before a court martial and convicted of the theft. Dent must have later realized that such a conviction would have destroyed Ham's military career. He stopped mentioning Ham's conviction. A "filler" for the magazine stories was produced about the Monk-Ham feud. It appeared in some of the original pulp magazines published in the 1930s. This little write-up was called "Monk, Ham and their Private War." It was reprinted in *Doc Savage Inside & Out* #1 (Flying Tiger Graphics, 1989).

According to this version, Ham was not convicted: "Ham's agile tongue finally got himself out of the scrape, but not before the whole army knew about it, and had a good laugh." This version also gave the details about how Monk planted the evidence against Ham. Monk stole Ham's billfold and left it at the scene of the crime, presumably the room where food supplies was stored. The stolen pork was planted in Ham's private quarters.

Note: In December 1944, Doc journeyed to Moscow. There he heard rumors of a dangerous female Soviet agent, Anna Gryahzyni (*Flight into Fear*, chap. 19). Doc recalled this episode in 1948. He said that it transpired "before the war." However, he also mentioned that the Soviets were on "our side." The "war" would seem to be the Cold War rather than World War II.

In December 1944, Johnny began his pursuit of Jonas Sown (see entry #181).

According to *Cargo Unknown* (chap. 5), Doc "had lectured frequently at the police academy, and at special meetings." Doc was having a lot of problems with the New York police during the United States' early involvement in World War II.

As the war reached its end, Doc must have felt the need to improve his relationship with the police, and started a regular series of lectures at the academy and elsewhere during January 1945 to February 1945. Despite these lectures, Doc would have problems with the police later in *Terror Takes 7*. However, this trouble largely resulted from an ambitious Assistant District Attorney. Doc had addressed mass meetings of New York policeman before. *The Stone Man* (chap. 6) mentioned such a meeting in the autumn of 1938.

Sometime during the first two months of 1945, Doc and Pat Savage took a walk down New York City. They saw "a man in an atrocious green suit" in the distance. Pat assumed that the man was Monk, and she hit him with a snowball. To her embarrassment, she discovered that she was mistaken. The incident was mentioned in *Terror Tales 7* (chap. 6).

178. Cargo Unknown

Published: April 1945
1945: March (20 days)
Author: Lester Dent

Cargo Unknown reads as if the war with Germany was over. Germany surrendered in May 1945, and this novel was published in the April 1945 issue. My only solution to this chronological problem is to place the novel in March, which would be very close to the end of the war in Europe.

This novel's plot involved a secret gold shipment from Germany. The gold was being shipped out of Germany because "the German bankers decided it was too risky to keep all that gold in Germany the way conditions after the war were" (chap. 14). Note the reference to "after the war." Since I could only place this novel before the German surrender, I must assume that German bankers were attempting to curry favor with the Allied troops pouring into Germany. Consequently, the bankers arranged this shipment. Maybe the bankers were afraid that German communists allied with the Soviet Union would get their hands on the gold. The Allies picked up the gold on "the west cost of Schleswig Holstein" (chap. 3). Since the Allies hadn't occupied that area of Germany by the beginning of March 1945, the German bankers must have bribed some official in the German military to arrange the pickup of the gold by the Allies.

At one point in the novel, there was a reference, which suggested that the war with Germany might not be fully over yet. The war was described by a naval officer "as nearly polished off" (chap. 3).

Monk and Ham had been "in France on some kind of a commission, one of the Allied special advisory committees which was currently flitting all over the world telling nations how to run their business" (chap. 2). The pair then went to London where Renny had been serving "as a consultant on industrial conversion back to peace production" (chap. 1). Long Tom and Johnny were absent.

The windows on Doc's headquarters were no longer made of bulletproof glass. A sniper shot through the windows (chap. 6). During the events of *The Devil's Black Rock* (chap. 10) in October 1942, a cannon shell had damaged the windows. Perhaps wartime shortages prevented Doc from replacing them with bulletproof glass. The sniper in *Cargo Unknown* fired at Doc from the "Mercator Automative Building." This name sounds like a fictional alias for the real-life Chrysler Building, which is close to the Empire State Building. *The Devil's Black Rock* failed to identify the building from which the cannon shell was fired, but it was probably the Chrysler Building as well. The Chrysler Building must also be the "near-by skyscraper" from where Var sent his Cold Light beam into the Empire State Building during *Cold Death* (chap. 18). In *The Land of Terror* (chap. 10), the minions of Kar supposedly used "the observation tower" on "the spire of a skyscraper some blocks distant" to spy on Doc's skyscraper. The other skyscraper would have to be the Chrysler building. However, this supposed act of espionage was a theory advanced by Kar himself in his true identity. Kar had actually informed his underlings himself (chap. 22). The Chrysler Building wasn't always guilty of being a haven for Doc's foes. Nevertheless, a totally separate group of crooks did use the "tower of a skyscraper a few blocks distant" to spy on Doc's headquarters in *The Red Skull* (chap. 5). The Chrysler Building was again used as a base by Doc's foes.

In *Cargo Unknown* (chap. 6), Monk was the owner of a car "gaudy enough to satisfy a Balkan dictator." This car would seem to be the same one that appeared in *The Ten Ton Snakes* (chap. 6).

In *Cargo Unknown*, Merry John Thomas, "about thirty-eight" years old, had been known in New York criminal circles as "the gentleman of Sutton Place" (chap 6), and was active in Chicago (chap. 2). A New York policeman mentioned that Thomas was before Doc's time. Thomas had been inactive in organized crime for a while. Considering that Doc was fighting gangsters in New York and Chicago as early as 1929 (see *The Purple Dragon*), then Thomas must have established a formidable criminal reputation by 1928, and then temporarily retired on his ill-gotten gains. Thomas would only have been twenty-one in 1928. He must have either been incredibly successful during the Prohibition Era, or some individual frightened him into a temporary retirement. Thomas had no qualms about taking Doc on. However, Doc wasn't the only formidable crime-fighter during this period. Who knows what evil lurks in the hearts of men? See the section on "Parallel Lives: Doc Savage and the Shadow."

The relationship between Renny and Doc became very strained in A *Cargo Unknown*. Doc nearly punched out Renny when he began to become emotional about the impending danger to Monk and Ham (chap. 7). Renny came perilously close to violating Doc's rule about taking human life (chap. 12). Renny would finally cross that boundary in *The Pure Evil* (chap. 11).

In *Cargo Unknown* (chap. 10), Doc had a special commission as "a special agent, civilian section, United States Navy." This commission was "the survival of some earlier work he had done for the Navy." This commission was probably the same commission (perhaps amended) as the one featured in *Devil on the Moon* (chap. 10 (11 in the revised text)) and *The Angry Ghost* (chap. 19). Doc probably was granted the commission after the events of *The Terror in the Navy*.

A remark in *Cargo Unknown* (chap. 7) about Doc's pre-war gadgets mentioned "chemicals which would do an assortment of things ranging from turning a man's skin green to making a shark afraid of him." This remark recalled a chemical utilized by Doc in *The Czar of Fear*. However, the chemical turned a subject's skin yellow. The chemical for scaring off sharks had been used in *The Pirate's Ghost* (chap. 15).

Note: During April 1945, Doc made a trip to London. Lawrence Morand, a top State Department official, saw Doc in London during 1945 (*Danger Lies East*, chap. 3).

At some point after March 1945, Doc learned the truth about why his father had him trained to become a champion of justice. In adventures of the 1940s, such as *The Man Who Fell Up* (chap. 4), *The Goblins* (chap. 5), *Waves of Death* (chap. 5), *The Mental Monster* (chap. 7), *The Black, Black Witch* (chap. 2), *The Man Who Was Scared* (chap. 3), *The Ten Ton Snakes* (chap. 10) and *Cargo Unknown* (chap. 6), it was stated that Doc was plagued by the mystery of why his father had decided to raise him in such an incredible manner. In *Danger Lies East* (chap. 2), a novel which this chronology places in January 1946, it was asserted that Doc's father "had possibly been a little cracked on the subject of crooks, particularly of the international sort." This statement teases us with a hint that Doc now knew about his father's motivations. A statement from a very authoritative source would later amplify the hint. In *No Light to Die By* ("Statement by Doc Savage"), Doc wrote a letter to Kenneth Robeson" (actually Lester Dent), and gave the clue as to why he had been raised in such a peculiar fashion.

Doc stated that his father had been "victimized by criminals." Both Philip José Farmer and I placed this novel in February 1947. Doc's visit to Britain must have been done to investigate his father's background. *Escape from Loki* mentioned that Doc intended to investigate his father's origins in Yorkshire when the senior Savage died (chap. 12). He must have done so during his 1945 trip.

For whatever reasons, Doc didn't do so in the 1930s even though he visited England on numerous occasions (there is a contradictory statement in a recent Doc Savage pastiche set in the Wold Newton Universe, see the "Apocryphal Adventures" chapter). The implication of the statement from *No Light to Die By* is that criminals persecuted Doc's father. As to who these criminals might be and how they fit in with Philip José Farmer's explanation of the past of Clark Savage Sr., see the "Apocryphal Adventures" section.

179. The Thing That Pursued
Published: October 1945
1945: May (3 days, after V-E day (May 8th))
Author: Lester Dent

The novel mentioned V-E day (chap. 15). V-E day was May 8, 1945. Poison ivy was not in season (chap. 8). Poison ivy is in season during the summer and fall. Hence, the novel had to transpire in the spring.

Alfred Mants had been smuggled out of "occupied Germany" (chap. 14). Allied troops began capturing German territory in September 1944. The impression was given that Mants had been in The United States for a while. He probably fled Germany in 1945 before V-E day. Most likely, Mants fled in February or March.

Mants was trying to sell an invention to Iturbi Sanchez, an influential South American. Sanchez "had formerly occupied the position of Assistant Secretary of War with the regime in his country which had been defeated in the last 'election'" (chap. 9). Dent puts the word "election" in quotes because it "had been more in the nature of a revolution, although with little bloodshed." Sanchez's country had not been at war with Germany (chap. 12). Sanchez's country was probably Argentina. In February 1944, President Jose Pedro Ramirez had been overthrown by a junta, which included Juan Peron, in a relatively bloodless coup. Argentina remained at peace with Germany throughout most of World War II. When Allied victory in Europe was assured in March 1945, Argentina declared war on Germany as a face-saving gesture. Sanchez had probably been associated with Ramirez, and was seeking to regain power.

In *The Thing That Pursued* (chap. 8), Doc utilized a private detective agency headed by C. B. Fay. This agency had been used in the past, and could be part of the intelligence network manned by Crime College graduates.

Doc had a special commission as an investigator for the State Department (*The Thing That Pursued*, chap. 11). Doc could have been given this commission because of a all the World War II adventures in which Doc examined the nature of probable postwar governments (*The Pharaoh's Ghost*, *Jiu San* and *Strange Fish*). These cases were cited within the context of the State Department in *Rock Sinister*.(chap. 12). On the other hand, Doc could have received his commission shortly after the events of *Red Snow* in 1933. Doc had rescued Secretary of State Cordell Hull in that novel. All of Doc's assistants were absent from *The Thing That Pursued*.

180. The Wee Ones
Published: August 1945
1945: Early June (3 days)
Author: Lester Dent

The novel would seem to be set in June because it was "the

season of year when hail storms were occasional" (chap. 5). The villains tried to get Doc to go on a goose chase by claiming to work for a company in liberated France (chap. 3). The Electrar Corporation was engaged in "essential war work" (chap. 10). Although Germany had been defeated by June 1945, Japan had yet to surrender.

The novel mentioned a case of mass hysteria in Mattoon, Illinois (chap. 7). The hysteria resulted from an untrue rumor that an assailant was using a sleep gas. This incident happened in September 1944. It is popularly known as the "Mad Gasser of Mattoon." Although the Internet today has much information about the Mad Gasser, I learned the true details of this odd event from Jeff Deischer some years ago.

In the early novels, it was frequently mentioned how Monk didn't know French in World War I. Ham took advantage of this fact by tricking Monk into using cusswords with a French general. According to *The Wee Ones* (chap. 4), a French chemistry student, had given Monk French lessons. However, the student "as a gag" had only taught Monk cusswords. Perhaps the French student was Ham's accomplice in the World War I prank. Ham and the student may have jointly taught Monk the French cusswords. Monk might have been suspicious of Ham, but he would have trusted the student.

This novel made the shocking revelation that Doc was a horrible cook (chap. 3). He could use a scalpel with great mastery, but no one would let him near a skillet. A remark that his assistants "didn't even consider his jungle cooking safe" would suggest that Monk and Ham first learned of this unbelievable flaw in Doc's skills when they traveled with him in the Amazon jungles during the 1920s.

Renny, Johnny and Long Tom were absent.

181. The Screaming Man

Published: December 1945
1945: June (16 days)
Author: Lester Dent

Johnny had been on a secret mission for "six months" (chap. 3). He trailed the evil Jonas Sown to Japan, to Burma, China and the Philippines (chap. 13). Sown fled to Japan "when Germany fell" (chap. 12). Germany had yet to surrender at the time of Sown's flight, but that country was clearly on the verge of total defeat. Sown must have left Germany when the western Allies were preoccupied with fighting the Ardennes counteroffensive (December 1944 to January 1945). The war was not yet over, it was "on its way to becoming a bad memory" (chap. 8). Japan had not yet surrendered.

Renny and Long Tom were absent.

Note: According to *Target for Death* (chap. 1), Pat Savage once visited a hospital in Manila. The early scenes of *The Screaming Man* happened in Manila. Pat must have gone there in order to barge in on Doc's adventure, but arrived after Doc had left by boat to continue his quest for Jonas Sown. Pat must have gone to the hospital in the belief that Doc might be there.

182. King Joe Cay

Published: July 1945
1945: Early July (6 days)
Author: Lester Dent

"Yuletide 1944 was engraved on a cigarette case" (chap. 2). Near Chicago, "farmers were harvesting their oats" (chap. 3).

As Philip José Farmer has insightfully pointed out, oats are harvested during July 1-15 in northern Illinois. Since Mr. Farmer's chronology was governed by different rules regarding publication dates, he interpreted 1944 as a typographical error (Mr. Farmer felt it should have been "Yuletide 1943"), and then placed the novel in July 1944. A serious objection can be raised against placing this novel in July 1944. The "Allied authorities" caught a collaborator named Fleish, and placed him in a jail inside France (chap. 13). Only if Fleish had taken his 1944 summer vacation in Normandy would the Allies be able to apprehend him in July of that year. Therefore, 1945 fits the novel much better. That year is also compatible with references to upcoming "war guilt trials" (chap. 11).

Monk was in England, Ham in Italy, Renny and Long Tom in China, and Johnny in Iran (chap. 6).

183. Terror Takes 7
Published: September 1945
1945: Mid-July (2 days)
Author: Lester Dent

A group of people met at a "summer house" on an island off the coast of Maine (chap. 10).

Renny was in Russia, Long Tom in China, and Johnny "in occupied Germany" (chap. 6). The reference to "occupied Germany" would imply that this novel transpired after the German surrender in May 1945. Throughout the novel, World War II was spoken in the past tense. For example, Doc told a group of industrialists that they "were active on the wartime industrial stage" (chap. 10). The impression was given that at least Germany was defeated. By July 1945, Germany had surrendered, but Japan remained to be beaten.

It was mentioned that Doc had developed "the thermoelectric bonding process for plywood that came out a few months before" (chap. 5). Doc apparently had actually discussed this bonding process at "the lumberman's convention" in Chicago during 1941 *(The Three Devils,* chap. 3). The process must have taken four years to perfect.

Two days before *Terror Takes 7*, Monk had a fight in a nightclub with a policeman named Clancy Weinberg (chap. 2).

Note: On July 28, 1945, an army B-52 accidentally crashed into the seventy-ninth floor of the Empire State Building at 9:50 a.m. Whether Doc was in the building at that time is unknown.

184. Trouble on Parade
Published: November 1945
1945: August 1-2 (2 days)
Author: Lester Dent

The novel mentioned the day of the week and the month when it began (chap. 1): "It was a hot Wednesday afternoon in August…"

All of the assistants were absent but we do know Monk was in New York (chap. 12). Doc unsuccessfully tried to reach him by telephone there. Monk's number was Central 0-9000.

A man contacted Doc claiming to be the brother-in law of Wilbur C. Tidings (chap. 1). Doc had once performed an unrecorded favor for Tidings. The brother-in-law wanted to sell Doc some "small war surplus steamships" at bargain prices. The steamships in the proposed deal would suggest that Tidings might have been involved with Doc's acquisition of steamship. companies in the late 1930s. Doc's ownership of steamship companies was mentioned in *The South Pole Terror* (chap. 15), *The Feathered Octopus* (chap. 6), *The Flaming Falcons* (chap. 12) and *Poison Island* (chap. 18).

Throughout his career, Doc had been falsely accused of crimes. He had previously endured these accusations with great stoicism. In *Trouble on Parade* (chap. 6), Doc completed lost his temper with the inspector accusing him falsely, and overturned the police official's desk.

185. Se-Pah-Poo

Published: February 1946
1945: August (5 days)
Author: Lester Dent

In the Painted Desert, it was "a hundred and ten" degrees (chap. 1). The time would seem to be summer.

Doc's body must have really ached in 1945. He received bullet wounds in *Cargo Unknown* (chap. 15), *The Thing That Pursued* (chap. 7), *The Wee Ones* (chap. 14) and *Se-Pah-Poo* (chap. 13).

Renny, Johnny and Long Tom were absent from *Se-Pah-Poo*..

186. Terror and the Lonely Widow

Published: March 1946
1945: Late August (7 days)
Author: Lester Dent

World War II had ended (chap. 1): "The best explanation was that the management didn't know the war was over." The Pacific war came to an end on August 14, 1945. This was the day when Japan finally accepted the final terms of surrender. The formal surrender was not signed until September 2.

This novel concerned the search for an atomic bomb that had been lost in the final stages of the war. The bomb on Hiroshima had been dropped on August 6, and the one on Nagasaki on August 9. The missing bomb was lost between those two dates (chap. 6). The novel was set in the summer. There were references to "petunias" (chap. 1) and "sun-glasses" (chap. 3).

Johnny and Long Tom were in Brazil. Johnny was searching "for a ruin somebody found in the jungle," and Long Tom was doing "some radar installation work for the South Atlantic plane routes" (chap. 4).

A woman named Berthena "Bert" Gilroy worked for the Office of Special Investigations (chap. 5). This was probably an alias for William Donovan's Office of Strategic Services (OSS). The OSS would be dissolved in September 1945. Miss Gilroy's agency was in competition with other government agencies, including an unnamed one represented by Brigadier General Theodore Lowell (chap. 8). He is not to be confused with Major Sam Lowell of the Emergency Necessity Office from *Mystery on Happy Bones*.

Note: Doc was awarded the Congressional Medal of Honor after the end of World War II. This medal was given to him for two highly classified unrecorded adventures as an active officer in World War II. These missions happened during December 1941 to March 1942. See the "**Note**" after entry #143 for the details of these missions.

187. Colors for Murder
Published: June 1946
1945: Mid September (4 days)
Author: Lester Dent

The war was over. Reference was made to radar devices which had been released "after the war" (chap. 8).

Renny "was in South America, at the moment, on a private venture of his own, laying out a processing problem for a petroleum concern" (chap. 6). Johnny and Long Tom were absent.

188. Fire and Ice

Published: July 1946
1945: September 23-26 (4 days)
Author: William G. Bogart and Lester Dent

The third day of this adventure was a Tuesday (chap. 10). In Alaska, it "was a warm day" (chap. 2). In New York, it was "a warm, mild night" (chap. 11). Such weather would be consistent with September. The war was spoken as a thing of the past. For example, the Alcan Road was called the Road to Tokyo "during the war" (chap. 1).

The plot involved Nazi war criminals fleeing to South America.

Renny, Johnny and Long Tom "were scattered around the world on various missions" (chap. 9).

Note: In October, Monk arrived in occupied Germany (see the next entry). In *Measures for a Coffin* (chap. 14) contains an intriguing reference about Doc's prestige: "Recently, as another example, he had merely warned a political group in South America who had fascist leanings, and the group had changed its ideas overnight." This might be meant as a reference to *Rock Sinister*, but Doc did not more than "merely" warn the villains from that earlier novel. It is possible that Doc Savage may have been responsible for one of three events in South America during October 1945. In that month, right-wing regimes were easily overthrown in Venezuela and Brazil, and the Argentine military briefly imprisoned Juan Peron. A warning by Doc could have been responsible for anyone of these events (if not all).

189. Measures for a Coffin

Published: January 1946
1945: December 5-9 (4 days)
Author: Lester Dent

The day of the week and the month in which the novel started are specifically mentioned (chap. 1): "It was 2:40 p.m., a Wednesday afternoon in December. The fact that it was snowing in the novel was consistent with December (chap. 12). References to the death of Adolf Hitler (chap. 4) indicate that the year was 1945.

The novel opened with Monk in "occupied Germany" (chap. 3). He had been there for the "past six weeks." He was "functioning as a sort of advisory czar over the German chemical industry." Ham was in "Jugolslavia" (Yugoslavia). There he was trying to teach the Yugoslavians about international law. Both Monk and Ham returned to New York. Pat Savage "was in England somewhere, trying to hire a high-powered Frenchman for her string of beauty shops" (chap. 3). Renny was in China, and Long Tom was on "a radar project" in the Pacific (chap. 1). Johnny was in Sweden (chap. 3).

The novel mentioned the Durwell Agency, Research and Investigations (chap. 7): "The owner, Mike Durwell, had been associated with Doc Savage for a considerable period of time." Durwell, an honest man, sold his detective agency unfortunately to a dishonest purchaser, and then went on an investigative trip to Mexico for the new owner. Durwell's detective agency may be one of those manned by Crime College graduates and used for information gathering by Doc. Maybe Doc made the mistake of not retaining ownership of the agency.

190. Three Times a Corpse

Published: August 1946
1945: Mid December (2 days)
Author: Lester Dent

Doc was in Miami for a vacation (chap. 4). Winter is the perfect time to leave New York and go to Florida.

It had been months after the German surrender in May 1945. Snelling, a former POW in Germany, had "gotten back several months following the end of the war" to the United States (chap. 7). In fact, he had been in the United States for "two months."

Renny, Johnny and Long Tom were absent.

191. The Exploding Lake

Published: September 1946
1946: First half of January (12 days)
Author: Harold A. Davis and Lester Dent

The season of the year was clearly mentioned (chap.9): "…winter in New York, summer in Patagonia…"

The plot of the novel concerned a search for a Nazi war criminal in Argentina. The Germans and the Russians weren't the only people to install sleeper agents in countries years before they were needed. According to *The Exploding Lake* (chap. 15), the Netherlands planted a spy in Argentina before World War II. This spy helped the Allies during the war, and hunted war criminals afterwards. Let's give the Dutch credit for brilliant advanced planning.

Johnny and Long Tom were absent.

192. Danger Lies East
Published: March-April 1947
1946: Late January (6 days)
Author: Lester Dent

The time of year would seem to be winter (chap. 1): "It was cold in Washington…" In Egypt, it was "the rainy season" (chap. 8). The rainy season in Egypt lasts from December to February. Lawrence Morand of the State Department hadn't seen Doc "since London in '45" (chap. 3). The reference to 1945 would imply that the year was either 1946 or 1947. The 1945 visit to London was not recorded in any of the novels (see the "**Note**" after entry #178). The Cold War was starting. Morand mentioned that "the world is split pretty much in two factions" (chap. 3). Reference was made to "the Palestine problem" (chap. 6) which would eventually lead to the creation of Israel in 1948.

Ham's finances were getting as bad as Monk's money problems. Ham was "usually broke no more then once a year" (chap. 1). The plot of the novel involved Nesur, an Arab religious leader. In Egypt, Homer Wickett, an evil American oil tycoon, was trying to find Nesur and force him to provoke a war in the Middle East. Wickett hoped to be able to gain control of the Middle Eastern oil supply in the resulting chaos. Thwarting the tycoon, Doc found Nesur and persuaded him not to provoke a war. The American government had stopped Wickett's oil sales to the Nazis "about seven years ago" (chap. 9). If this novel transpired in 1946, then the oil sales would have been stopped in 1939. The year of 1939 makes perfect sense because World War II started then.

Nesur was not depicted as an evil person. Doc described Nesur as "the leader of a minor religious sect" and "sort of a holy man" (chap. 3). Morand of the State Department corrected Doc. Nesur was "not minor." He was the key to peace in the Middle East.

Rumored to be pro-Nazi, he was forced into exile "a couple of years" before the novel transpired. However, elsewhere in the novel, it was hinted that Wickett persuaded Nesur to come out of exile "two years" previously (chap. 9). Therefore, Nesur either was exiled or came out of exile in 1944. Although quite an effort was made to blacken Nesur's name, Morand believed that he had been treated unfairly. Doc remembered that Nesur had 'been pushed around" by the English and American, but "not until he had started the pushing himself" (chap. 3)

Lester Dent based Nesur on Haj Amin al-Husani, Mufti of Jerusalem from 1921 to 1937. He was an ardent Arab nationalist whose leadership played a major role in sparking the Arab Revolt in Palestine during 1936-39. He fled to Lebanon in 1937, and then to Iraq in 1939. In Iraq, he was allied with Prime Minister Rashid Ali. Concluding that Rashid Ali was pro-Nazi, the British successfully invaded Iraq in 1941. The Mufti fled to Iran, Turkey, and Italy. Near the end of 1941, he arrived in Germany, where he became a propagandist for the Nazis. In 1945, the Mufti went to France. In 1946, he surfaced in Egypt. It isn't too difficult to pretend Nesur was "really" Haj Amin al-Husani. The details of Nesur's exile are told in a contradictory and unclear manner. Morand's somewhat sanitized view of the religious leader's past could be viewed as epidemic of the Cold War mentality. This mindset motivated many American officials to seek deals with prominent foreigners, formerly pro-Nazi, whose influence could counteract the spread of communism.

Doc may have persuaded the religious leader not to provoke a war in 1946. However, Doc's achievement was of brief duration. In 1947, the Mufti led the Arab opposition against the partition of Palestine, which resulted in the first Arab-Israeli War one year later.

Renny, Johnny and Long Tom were absent from *Danger Lies East*.

Note: Perhaps concerned about the unscrupulous activities of the oil industry revealed in *Danger Lies East,* Doc lectured before a meeting of oil chemists *(Terror Wears No Shoes,* chap. 1). This lecture probably transpired in February 1946.

193. Death is a Round Black Spot
Published: May-June 1946
1946: March (2 days)
Author: Lester Dent

The time of year would seem to be early spring. There were sparrows in Missouri (chap. 1), but sleet was also falling (chap. 9). There had been some passage of time since the Japanese surrender (August 14, 1945). Doc saw "American visas and stampings by American occupation authorities in Japan" (chap. 8). A man named Larson was in the Merchant Marine "for some time after the war" (chap. 7).

The criminals in the novel were hiding securities for former collaborators and Axis war profiteers in order to prevent the Allied authorities from confiscating their assets.

Pat Savage was described as being in "her twenties" (chap. 1). Pat must have charmed someone connected with the *Doc Savage* magazine into hiding her true age. She had been "about eighteen" in her initial appearance in *Brand of the Werewolf* (chap. 2). She would have been about thirty-two in 1946.

Renny, Johnny and Long Tom were absent from *Death is a Round Black Spot.*

194. Five Fathoms Dead
Published: April 1946
1946: April 1-10 (10 days)
Author: Lester Dent

The novel was set in "early, very early April" (chap. 4). The year in which the novel transpired was clearly indicated: "A man capable of organizing a band of pirates able to function in this year of 1946" (chap. 8). The novel happened "after the war ended" (chap. 1). The pirates were "fairly well organized by the end of the war with Japan" (chap. 8).

If we are to accept the month of April for this novel's events, then the year can only be 1946. Some one might raise the objection that the novel bore April 1946 as its official publication date. If we pretend that Doc Savage is a real person, then we are pretending several other things as well. We are pretending that in the 1930s and 1940s there existed dinosaurs, death rays, a resurrected Egyptian pharaoh, an earthquake machine, all sorts of lost civilizations and much more. If we are pretending that all these incredible things existed, it isn't too much of a great leap of faith that an issue dated April 1946 came out some time during April rather than the month before. Furthermore, it is not too much to pretend that the fellows at Street and Smith produced the April 1946 issue in an incredibly short space of time after the allegedly real events transpired. Doc Savage could do incredible feats in a brief timeframe. The publishers, writers and artists behind him must also have been capable of such achievements.

Although there is no evidence that Doc directly participated in the creation of the atomic bomb, some of his research helped the scientists who developed the weapons. We have this information from Mr. Ivanitz, "one of the brain-trust which worked out the atomic bomb" (chap. 5). These are Ivanitz's exact words about Doc's contribution: "Why, without his contribution to the development of the mass spectrograph which was used to separate uranium isotopes, the big colutron wouldn't have been—". Mass spectrographs grew out of a device developed by Francis William Ashton, a British physicist, in 1919.

Monk, Johnny and Long Tom were missing from *Five Fathoms Dead*.

195. The Devil Is Jones
Published: November 1946
1946: May (2 days)
Author: Lester Dent

Almost a week prior to the novel's events, Monk and Ham were conducting investigations in the unnamed city (chap. 3), which is the novel's setting. World War II was referred to as "the not-so long ago war" (chap. 2). The time would not seem to be summer because a "summer cabin" was "untenanted" (chap. 14).

Renny and Long Tom were in Europe (chap. 11).

196. Death in Little Houses
Published: October 1946
1946: July (2 days)
Author: William G. Bogart and Lester Dent

The novel began on "a July afternoon" (chap. 1). A crook, James Bridges, left prison in "January 1946" (chap. 11).

Doc had known Daniel Jamison, "an expert on electronics" (chap. 6), for "ten years" (chap. 1). Doc met Jamison in 1936. Their meeting probably transpired in *Repel (The Deadly Dwarf)* when Doc conferred with other scientists (chap. 18).

Doc had been in Chicago before (chap. 6): "Once or twice in his life he had brushed with that part of it that is not gay, boisterous and beautiful. Deep below the surface, as in any great city, there are shifting undercurrents-strange events that happen with swiftness and mystery." Doc fought crooks briefly in Chicago during *The Mountain Monster* and *The Crimson Serpent*. According to *The Purple Dragon*, He also fought gangsters there in 1929 (see the **"Note"** after entry #1). "The Box of Fear" also had Doc returning from Chicago after uncovering evidence against organized crime.

Renny, Johnny and Long Tom were "out of the country" (chap. 6).

Note: Jonathan Treat, an old friend, contacted Doc in July 1946. Treat was going to send Doc a weekly report concerning his status. If the reports failed to arrive, Doc was to investigate. This was "two months" prior to *Target for Death* (chap. 10). Treat once did a great favor for Doc (see the "**Note**" after entry #90).

Around August, Doc attended a convention of physicians in Denver, Colorado *(Let's Kill Ames,* chap. 6). A confidence trickster named Berry skipped town due to Doc's presence.

197. Target for Death
Published: January 1947
1946: September (8 days)
Author: William G. Bogart

Shortly before the novel began, Renny was in Manila as an "adviser on new postwar reconstruction work" (chap. 2). When the novel opened, Renny was in Honolulu. He had been conducting an investigation for Doc for "three weeks" (chap. 10). Renny was investigating why Doc had not received a report from Jonathan Treat.

Johnny and Long Tom were absent. It was not yet 1947. A character had a lodge card that was good until that year (chap. 6).

198. The Disappearing Lady
Published: December 1946
1946: Late October (2 days)
Author: William G. Bogart

The novel was set in "late October" (chap. 1).
Renny, Johnny and Long Tom were absent.

199. The Death Lady

Published: February 1947
1947: January (12 days)
Author: William G. Bogart

It seemed to be summer in South America (chap. 11): "The sticky heat of mid-morning hung everywhere…"

The year would seem to be 1947. Four years prior, Doc met a sea captain who ran convoys to Casablanca (chap. 5). The Allies gained control of Morocco during Operation Torch in November 1942. Casablanca came into prominence when Churchill and Roosevelt met there in January 1943 (see the "**Note**" after entry #156).

The events of *Meteor Menace* were recalled in *The Death Lady* (chap. 5): "Doc had once escaped a band of Tibetan tribesmen with less mental uneasiness."

Renny and Johnny were absent from *The Death Lady*.

200. No Light to Die By

Published: May-June 1947
1947: February 1-2 (2 days)
Author: Lester Dent

The novel was set in February (chap. 6), and began on a Friday (chap. 1).

This was the first of five novels in which the events are described by a first-person narrator. The novel's narrator, Sammy Wales, saw a picture of Doc's father. According to Wales, the elder Savage "didn't look too much like Doc" (chap. 9). By contrast, *The Land of Terror* (chap 5) said something quite different when a picture of Clark Sr. was viewed: "The resemblance between parent and son was marked." Since *No Light to Die By* has a first person narrator and *The Land of Terror* does not, the explanation for this discrepancy is simple. Lester

Dent had a different perspective telling the novel from Wales' viewpoint. Wales did not see any resemblance between father and son, but Lester Dent, writing in the normal third person perspective, did.

Renny, Johnny and Long Tom were absent from *No Light to Die By*.

Note: During February to March 1947, Doc traveled to London, Paris, Bombay and Shanghai. Besides whatever adventures that he experienced in those cities, Doc exchanged a series of telegrams with "Kenneth Robeson" (Lester Dent), Monk and Sammy Wales, the narrator of *No Light to Die By*. The subject was Wales' first-person account of his recent exploit with Doc. These telegrams were published after Dent's Foreword in *No Light to Die By*.

While Doc was traveling, Monk was chasing chorus girls. At one theater, he became friendly with Ancil Mitroff, a recent Russian immigrant and a dance instructor. Ancil mentioned to Monk that he had a sister, Seryi, in Moscow. Ancil asked Monk to look her up if he was ever in Russia *(The Red Spider,* chap. 4).

201. The Monkey Suit
Published: July-August 1947
1947: April (2 days)
Author: Lester Dent

A statement implied that March had passed (chap. 9): "He went to the cottage plant in January of this year, and the Mason plant in March, I think."

Ham, Renny, Johnny and Long Tom were absent.

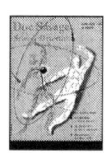

202. Let's Kill Ames

Published: September-October 1947

1947: May (3 days)

Author: Lester Dent

A copy of a state's legal statues was "printed in three volumes for the year of 1947" (chap. 3).

Renny, Johnny and Long Tom were absent. Monk's appearance was very brief (chap. 6).

203. Once Over Lightly

Published: November-December 1947

1947: June (3 days)

Author: Lester Dent

This novel, set in the California desert, would seem to have transpired in the summer (chap. 1): "Outside the temperature must be past a hundred."

A crook named Roy had been seen by Doc years ago (chap. 7). Roy was part of a gang trying to sell uranium to unscrupulous foreign countries (chap. 8). Assuming that Roy had something similar in the past, then he was probably a minor member of the gang which tried to peddle an atomic bomb in August 1945 *(Terror and the Lonely Widow)*.

The criminal gang in *Once Over Lightly* was trying to sell the uranium to one of two foreign nations (chap. 8). One was clearly the Soviet Union. The other may have been Argentina, which was portrayed critically in *The Exploding Lake*.

Ham, Renny, Johnny and Long Tom were absent from *Once Over Lightly*.

204. I Died Yesterday

Published: January-February 1948
1947: July (1 days)
Author: Lester Dent

As noted by Philip José Farmer , the fact that an absent Ham was on vacation (fishing in Quebec, chap. 7), and the vegetation ("green trees," chap. 5) suggested summer.

The novel was narrated by Pat Savage, and was her last chronological appearance in the series. Renny, Johnny and Long Tom were in London (chap. 7).

Note: In August 1947, an unrecorded adventure happened involving Doc and Monk. Doc asked Monk to arrange "a mild unpleasantness" for a crook. Monk did so, and the crook "came near never leaving the hospital" *(Terror Wears No Shoes,* chap. 2). Doc felt Monk had exceeded his instructions.

205. Terror Wears No Shoes

Published: May-June 1948
1947: September (17 days)
Author: Lester Dent

The adventuress Canta had "been go betweening for Moslems who are anxious to ease out of Hindu territory with their property intact" (chap. 3). The British colony of India had been granted independence on August 15, 1947. It was partitioned into Hindu-dominated India and Moslem-dominated Pakistan.

The villains were Soviet spies trying to spread a deadly virus in the United States. Doc was now a soldier in the Cold War. The head Soviet villain, Makaroff, was actually "second in line to head his government," although newspapers incorrectly placed him as "sixth or seventh" (chap. 6). Makaroff didn't succeed Josef Stalin after his death in 1953. Since Makaroff was captured at the end of the adventure, we can assume that Doc eventually shipped him to the Crime College. Makaroff "controlled the man who controlled the security police" (chap. 9). Makaroff had control over Lavrenty Beria, the head of the secret police. Beria would be executed by Kremlin rivals after Stalin's death in 1953.

Stalin was briefly mentioned under the alias of the Leader (chap. 9). It was asserted that the Leader had murdered two of his own brothers. This was untrue of the historical Stalin, but he did order the death of Yagoda and Yezhov, the two secret police chiefs who supervised his most brutal purges in the 1930s.

Long Tom resurfaced in this novel. He had disappeared in Shanghai "a few weeks" before the novel started (chap. 3). It was stated that Long Tom vanished "early in 1942" to do secret government work. Long Tom was absent during January-April 1942, June-July 1942, September 1942, November 1942 to February 1943, April 1943, June-August 1943, mid-September 1943 to December 1946, and February-August 1947.

Renny and Johnny were absent from *Terror Wears No Shoes*.

Note: During October-November 1947, Doc, Ham, Monk, Long Tom, and Canta were in quarantine in "the mountains somewhere" *(Terror Wears No Shoes,* chap. 12). Doc wanted to make sure that none of them had been exposed to the deadly virus created by the Soviet Union. Makaroff and the other prisoners may have been with them, or held in a separate location. Doc figured that they would be segregated for "several weeks." Doc probably studied the virus during this period, and created a vaccine for it.

In December, Long Tom went to South America (see next entry).

206. The Pure Evil

Published: March-April 1948
1948: Late January (2 days)
Author: Lester Dent

It was snowing in New York: "Out of the clouds, or out of somewhere, came the hard shooting pellets of snow…" (chap. 7). Christmas had recently passed. A silken cord from a bathrobe, a recent Christmas gift, was used as a murder weapon (chap. 2).

A man applied "more than a year ago" for funds involving research into spiritualism (chap. 9). The date in which he applied was "January 18" of the previous year. Therefore, that novel has to have happened more than one year since that date.

Johnny was absent without explanation. Long Tom was in South America (chap. 8). He had been there "several weeks laying out blind landing systems for an airline."

Renny deliberately slew a criminal in front of Doc (chap. 11). Renny had nearly done such an act earlier in *Cargo Unknown* (chap. 12).

Note: In February 1948, Monk and Ham established false identities in Moscow.

207. The Red Spider

Published: July 1979
1948: March (13 Days)*
Author: Lester Dent

The weather in Moscow would suggest late winter (chap.6): "The cold front had passed but before morning there was likely to be quite a lot of sleet and perhaps some snow…"

Only Johnny was absent from this adventure. Renny and Long Tom were with Doc in the American zone in Germany at the start of the novel. Ham and Monk had been undercover in Moscow for an unspecified amount of time. For Monk to become a commissar in the Russian Textile Workers' Union (chap. 2), he would have had to be there at least a month.

Doc discovered the existence of Frunzoff Nosh, a faceless bureaucrat whom Stalin was grooming as his successor. Frunzoff must have replaced Makaroff from *Terror Wears No Shoes* as the heir apparent. Makaroff lost his position of top lieutenant when Doc apprehended him. Frunzoff never succeeded Stalin probably because his existence became known to Mahli, a daring Russian anti-communist. After Doc left Russia, Mahli hinted that he would assassinate Frunzoff (chap. 11).

Under the influence of Doc's truth serum, Frunzoff confessed to the murder of a Soviet leader named Uritsky (chap. 5). Doc described Uritsky as "a terrorist leader killed during the early days of the Soviet." Uritsky had been "supposedly murdered by the opposition," but Frunzoff's confession indicated he committed the murder for one of Uritsky's rivals in the party (Stalin?). Frunzoff's victim really existed. Moisei Solomovich Uritsky was Petrograd chief of the Cheka, the Soviet secret police (later re-christened the OGPU, the NKVD and the KGB).. The city of Petrograd (later renamed Leningrad) is today known by its original name of St. Petersburg given to it by Czar Peter the Great. On August 30, 1918, Uritsky was assassinated by the Social Revolutionaries, a popular group of agrarian socialists opposed to Lenin and the Bolsheviks. At least, that's the verdict of history. Due to Doc's interrogation of Frunzoff, we now have the "true" version of Uritsky's death.

The novel dealt with Soviet development of the atomic bomb. Lester Dent was deliberately vague on how far the Soviets had gotten with their atomic research. He never indicated what Frunzoff's answer was to Doc's question about whether the Soviet Union had the atomic bomb. Evidence that the Soviet Union actually had the bomb surfaced in the autumn of 1949, one year after Dent wrote this novel. If Mahli didn't kill Frunzoff, then Stalin may have killed Frunzoff for failing to protect the secrets of the Soviet atomic program.

208. The Angry Canary
Published: July-August 1948
1948: April (7 Days)
Author: Lester Dent

The novel concerned the violence resulting from the partition of India and Pakistan. The two independent countries had come into existence in August 1947. The novel mentioned "raids and violence against the neighboring Kashmir state" from Pakistan (chap. 9). These raids began in October 1947. A cease-fire was arranged in January 1948, but violations continued into April and beyond.

The novel's villain, Plott, was using science to fill human minds with hate and anger. The fact that Plott hated Hindus (chap. 10) may only have influenced him to choose Pakistan as his testing area. His hatred may not have been his sole motivation for these diabolical experiments. Plott's modus operandi was not too different from Jonas Sown, who used a machine which influenced emotions to grant him control over the Axis leaders. Sown had been forced to destroy his device in *The Screaming Man*. When Sown re-surfaced in *The Frightened Fish*, he announced his intention to eventually build another machine (chap. 9). Perhaps Plott was actually working for Sown. Plott may have building another device for Sown, and testing it in Pakistan.

Renny, Johnny and Long Tom were absent from *The Angry Canary*.

209. Return from Cormoral
Published: Spring 1949
1948: May (3 Days)
Author: Lester Dent

The novel was set in the spring (chap. 4): "… it was a crisp spring morning…"

Doc was no longer living in his skyscraper. He was living in hotels, which he changed "frequently as a matter of common-sense precaution" (chap. 4). The reason for Doc's usage of hotels will be given in *Flight into Fear*.

Doc owned "a special commission from the Miami police department" (chap. 6). The commission was possibly "outdated." Doc probably was given the commission after the events of *Red Snow*. The Miami police were most likely trying to make amends for falsely suspecting Doc of the murders committed in that novel.

Macbeth Williams had met Doc "during attendance on a few occasions at a scientific society which they both held membership" (chap. 4). The scientific society was possibly the Scientific Club, which was featured in *The King of Terror* (chap. 1). Back in that earlier novel, Doc was president of the Scientific Club.

Renny, Johnny and Long Tom were absent from *Return from Cormoral*.

210. The Swooning Lady
Published: September-October 1948
1948: June (1 day)
Author: Lester Dent

The novel was set in June (chap. 1): "At this late June season, springtime was very full-bosomed in New York's Central Park."

Doc had made "a recent warning to Monk that he was "a pushover for anything in skirts that was blonde and glittered" (chap. 1). This warning "had followed an episode in such a blonde had nearly been the finish of all of them." The blonde was Audrey from *The Angry Canary*.

Ham was having money problems because of neglecting his law practice (chap. 2). By this time, Ham's law firm mentioned in *The Giggling Ghosts* (chap. 16) must have fallen into disarray.

Renny, Johnny and Long Tom were absent from *The Swooning Lady*.

Note: Doc Savage was approached by the State Department to undertake an important mission involving the Soviet Union. In order to make this mission a success, Doc needed to establish a false identity, Dwight "the Face" Banner. Doc would spend July to September traveling around Europe as Banner. The bulk of this time was spent in Sweden, Norway and the Soviet Union (chap. 4). In Russia, he visited the cities of Moscow and Archangel (chap. 9). In Archangel, Doc as Banner tried to smuggle cigarettes and nylon stockings into Russia. Betrayed by an unscrupulous Russian, Paul Poltov, Doc had to flee from the Soviet authorities by joining up with a group of Russian lumberjacks. As Banner, Doc was also in Prague (chap. 4), Czechoslovakia, and Warsaw (chap. 9), Poland. While traveling in the Iron Curtain countries, Doc set up "several clandestine radio stations" (chap. 8). Unfortunately, all of them "turned up as useful as a hat on a squirrel."

211. Flight into Fear
Published: March 1993
1948: October (13 days)
Author: Lester Dent and Will Murray

About ninety percent of this novel was written by Lester Dent. Will Murray based his other Doc Savage novels on unused outlines and drafts by Dent. *Python Isle* and *The Frightened Fish* were based on outlines for novels that Dent never wrote. *The Jade Ogre* was based on the outline of an unwritten adventure for Curtis Flagg, another pulp hero created by Dent. Many of Dent's early drafts and outlines for published Doc Savage novels differed radically from the final version. *White Eyes* was based on Dent's early ideas for *The Annihilist*. *The Whistling Wraith* bears the same relationship to *The Vanisher*, as does *The Forgotten Realm* to *The Phantom City*.

Flight into Fear was actually a rewrite of an unpublished espionage thriller that Dent wrote during the Korean War. In his afterword, Will Murray explained how he expunged the novel of references to the 1950s and transformed it into an adventure set in the 1940s. Despite the efforts of this extremely meticulous writer, I spotted two references to events of the 1950s. Breckenridge, the American spy, mentioned how he trailed a would-be defector to Czechoslovakia after "the Fuchs case" broke in England (chap. 4). Klaus Fuchs was a real-life German scientist who worked for the British but gave atomic secrets to the Soviets. He was arrested in 1950. There is also a discussion of baseball owner Bill Veeck's plans to move the Browns out of St. Louis (chap. 22). Veeck didn't own the Browns until the summer of 1951. Since I was brazen enough to ignore chronological references in *The Jade Ogre* and *White Eyes* which reflected Will Murray's intentions to place those novels in 1935 (and references that placed *Python Isle* in 1934), I can safely ignore chronological references in *Flight into Fear* which violated his intentions to place the novel in the late 40s.

A reference to Doc's presence in Moscow "before the war" (chap. 19) may also be an editorial oversight. Doc went on to say that the Soviets were "our side" then. The war may have been the Korean War in Dent's original manuscript, but now it would be interpreted as a reference to World War II. If the "war" was World War II, then the statement would only make sense if Doc had said "during the war." Another possible interpretation is that the "war" meant the Cold War.

Flight into Fear is a sequel to *The Red Spider*, but I can't place these novels back to back in a chronological arrangement. It was snowing in Moscow in *The Red Spider*, which indicates that its events happened during either autumn or winter. In *Flight into Fear*, returned to the United States after having spent about three months (chap. 5) as Dwight "the Face" Banner in Europe. It was now the autumn in New York (chap. 2): "It is a cold damp evening. Fall is coming on." The fall was very severe in New York because it was snowing (chap. 4).

Since other novels fall into the spring of 1948, it is necessary for Doc to have some recorded adventures *(Return from Cormoral, The Swooning Lady.)* in his own identity during the gap between *The Red Spider* and *Flight into Fear*. *Flight into Fear* discussed how Doc had been spending his nights in hotels for months to ward off Soviet assassination attempts (chap. 5). He was using hotels for unexplained reasons in *Return from Cormoral*. There were no references to Doc's usage of hotels in *The Swooning Lady*, but that adventure only took a day. Before the novel began, Doc could have slept in a hotel and then returned to his skyscraper.

By this chronological arrangement, it is assumed that Doc offended the Soviet Union in March, but that the assassins weren't chasing him until May (between the events of *The Angry Canary* and *Return from Cormoral*). Probably the Soviet espionage apparatus spent the month of April debating how to dispose of Doc.

In the course of *Flight into Fear*, Doc became involved in a plot to spy on atomic devices being stored in the Ural Mountains. Doc did hear rumors that atomic tests had transpired inside Russia (chap. 11), by he heard no first-hand accounts. Such statements gives the impression that the Soviet Union had the atomic bomb. It should be noted that the Soviet Union is generally considered to have developed the bomb in the autumn of 1949, the time when evidence became available that a nuclear device had successfully been exploded there. In *The Red Spider*, Lester Dent was deliberately vague about how far the Soviets got in their atomic program because that novel was written in 1948. However, the Soviet Union could have been manufacturing bombs without testing any of them in 1948 (Israel does that today), or maybe the testing was being done in such a manner that defied detection by the United States and its allies in 1948. Another possible explanation is that the facilities were being maintained for future use. In 1948, the Soviet Union would have realized that it was very close to building a bomb, and was just creating the location to stockpile them.

All of Doc's assistants were out of the United States (chap. 5).

212. The Green Master
Published: Winter 1949
1948: November 15-20 (6 days)
Author: Lester Dent

It was "late spring" in South America (chap. 9). This would mean late fall in North America. The novel ended on a Saturday (chap. 12).

A false story was concocted with the intention to lead Doc on a wild goose chase (chap. 3). Supposedly agents of an unnamed country had abducted a Spanish scientist, the creator of a new virus. The country was intended to be the Soviet Union.

Renny, Johnny and Long Tom were absent.

A New York police sergeant had earlier "told a presidential candidate off for jaywalking" (chap. 5). Considering that Lester Dent hailed from the same state as President Harry S. Truman, the presidential candidate was probably Thomas E. Dewey, who lost to Truman in the 1948 election. Dewey had also lost the 1944 election to Roosevelt. Dent had modeled the unsympathetic character of D.A. Einsflagen on Dewey in *The Invisible-Box Murders*.

213. The Frightened Fish
Published: July 1992
1949: Mid to Late January (9 days)
Author: Will Murray

The year of this novel was clearly given as 1949. General Tojo had been executed by the Allies "a few weeks before" (chap. 5). Tojo was hanged on December 23, 1948.

Ham read a newspaper indicating that the Chinese Communists had taken Peiping (chap. 5). That city surrendered on January 22, 1949. Ham read the news on the eighth day of the adventure. Ham and his companions had been isolated from news while taking a submarine trip. It is impossible to know how many days passed between the fall of Peiping and Ham's reading of the newspaper. Doc's submarine, the *Helldiver*, appeared in this novel, It had last been used in *Devils of the Deep*.

The Frightened Fish is a sequel to both *The Screaming Man* and *The Red Spider*. Jonas Sown, the villain from *The Screaming Man*, returned. On a more pleasant note, so did Seryi Mitroff and Mahli from *The Red Spider*, According to *The Frightened Fish* (chap. 9). *The Screaming Man* transpired "over three years ago" near "the end of the war." This reference is consistent with my placement of *The Screaming Man* in June 1945. *The Frightened Fish* (chap. 7) claimed that the events of *The Red Spider* took place "almost a year ago." This statement is consistent with the placement of *The Red Spider* in March 1948.

Renny and Long Tom were absent from *The Frightened Fish*. Like *Flight into Fear*, *The Frightened Fish* asserted that the Soviet Union had the atomic bomb (chap. 5).

See my discussion of *Flight into Fear* (entry # 211) for the historical difficulties with that statement.

214. Up From Earth's Center
Published: Summer 1949
1949: February (9 days)
Author: Lester Dent

The novel was set in the winter (chap. 1): "Winter came."

Renny was in Lubec, Maine, working on the survey involving "the Quoddy project for harnessing the resources of terrific Fundy tides" (chap. 1). Johnny and Long Tom were absent.

Doc may have found a doorway to Hell in this novel. I will not engage in any speculation regarding the demonic entities encountered in *Up From Earth's Center*. Some questions in life and literature are better left unanswered.

CHAPTER II
Apocryphal Adventures

This section deals with theories and pastiches involving Doc Savage with other individuals from fiction, and in one case, history.

The Persecution of Clark Savage Sr.: The Priory School Theory Expanded

Philip José Farmer created a colorful background for Clark Sr. in *Doc Savage: His Apocalyptic Life*. Clark Sr. was the individual whose real identity was masked by the alias of James Wilder in Sir Arthur Conan Doyle's "The Adventure of The Priory School." Wilder was the illegitimate son of an English duke. With the help of a local innkeeper, Reuben Hayes, Wilder kidnapped his younger half-brother from an English school. Wilder's motive in this crime was to force the duke to acknowledge him as the rightful heir to the title. However. Hayes murdered an innocent bystander, a teacher named Heidegger, during the abduction. Overcome by guilt, Wilder made a complete confession to his father and revealed the location of his half-brother. In the interim, the school hired Sherlock Holmes to investigate. Holmes discovered the whole truth, and arranged Hayes' arrest. As for Wilder, Holmes came to an agreement with the duke to permit him to flee England for Australia.

According to Mr. Farmer, James Wilder was really Clark

Sr., and the events described above transpired in the spring of 1901. Changing his mind about Australia, Clark Sr. traveled to America instead. A detail left out in Doyle's story is that the duke's illegitimate son was also married. Settling with his pregnant wife in the United States, Clark Sr. then went treasure hunting in the Caribbean. In September 1901 He discovered sunken treasure which would eventually earn him a $50,000 after the British government took its cut. It was suggested by Mr. Farmer that Clark Sr. and his associates may have found more treasure, but didn't report it order to evade British taxation. In November, Clark Jr. was born.

According to Mr. Farmer, the guilt of Clark Sr. over Heidegger's murder motivated him to embarked on the project where scientists and various experts would train his son to be a champion of justice. The difficulty with Mr. Farmer's theory is that it didn't take into account two key remarks in Lester Dent's original novels. In *Danger Lies East* (chap. 2), it was hinted that Clark Sr. "had possibly been a little cracked on the subject of crooks, particularly of the international sort." Then in *No Light to Die By* ("Statement of Doc Savage"), Doc himself made this statement: "My father, victimized by criminals, imagined that he could turn me into a sort of modern Galahad who would sally out against all wrongdoers who were outside the law, and who would aid the oppressed."

Doc's father was "victimized by criminals." Doc's statement hinted that these criminals harmed a lot of other people besides Clark's father. The earlier quote from *Danger Lies East* suggests that the criminals operated on an international scale. In order for Mr. Farmer's explanation for the origins of Clark Sr. to be accepted, the existence of this international criminal gang would have to be accommodated. The key to doing so is Reuben Hayes. As Mr. Farmer himself noted, no amount of hush money by the duke was going to keep Hayes silent once he was faced with the gallows. Mr. Farmer suspected that the duke might have connived in Hayes' escape. Possibly some ingenious ruse was used to fake Hayes' death on the gallows.

Books like *The Daughter of Fantomas* (Black Coat Press, 2006) by Marcel Allain and Pierre Souvestre have demonstrated that a phony execution was possible in the early twentieth century. After his escape, Hayes may have joined an international gang. This gang later learned of the Caribbean treasure throve unearthed by Clark Sr. Hayes persuaded his confederates to extort the money out of Clark Sr. through a vicious campaign of persecution during 1901-1902.

Who could be Hayes' confederates? There are really no suitable candidates in the Sherlock Holmes stories. Professor Moriarty died in 1891. His chief lieutenant, Colonel Sebastian Moran was arrested in 1894. Sherlockian scholars generally place the death of Charles Augustus Milverton, the master blackmailer, in 1899. What about other famous master criminals? When Millennium Publications was publishing comic book versions of Doc's adventures in 1991, a two-part story, "Doom Dynasty," claimed that a persecutor of Doc's forebears was Dr. Antonio Nikola. This Dr. Nikola was actually the creation of Australian mystery writer Guy Boothby (1867-1905). Nikola appeared in five novels: *A Bid for Fortune* (1895, also known as *Dr. Nikola's Vendetta* and *Enter Dr. Nikola*), *Doctor Nikola* (1896, also known as *Dr. Nikola Returns*), *The Lust of Hate* (1898), *Dr. Nikola's Experiment* (1899), and *Farewell, Nikola* (1901).

Despite the entertaining story told in "Doom Dynasty," we can rule out Dr. Nikola as an adversary of Doc's father. First, Nikola had a somewhat chivalrous side to his character, which would later be displayed by Sax Rohmer's Fu Manchu and Ra's Al Ghul from the Batman comic books. Second, the internal chronological evidence of the Nikola saga would indicate that the master criminal retired around 1898 to a Tibetan monastery, where he conducted experiments in immortality which would eventually claim his life.

If we need to choose the persecutors of Clark Sr. from another fictional source, then I would nominate the title characters from Jack London's "The Minions of Midas." This story can be found in London's *Moon-Face and Other Stories* (1906). The recorded crimes of the Minions of Midas happened during August 1899 to February 1900. The Minions were an organization that targeted Eban Hale, an American millionaire. Unless Hale agreed to pay the Minions twenty million dollars, they swore to kill an innocent person at regular intervals. Hale refused, and an innocent working man was slain. Hale called in the local police, the Pinkertons and the Federal government. These agencies were helpless against the Minions. Innocent people of all classes, sexes and ages were being assassinated. The pressure of the Minions' murderous extortion caused Hale to commit suicide. On Hale's death, his wealth was inherited by his secretary, Wade Atsheler. Unfortunately, Atsheler inherited the persecution of the Minions as well. Atsheler was also driven to take his own life. The story ended with the Minions still at large. Their activities had been extended to Europe, and they were in search of new victims.

Maybe in 1901, a recent recruit of the Minions of Midas, Reuben Hayes, set his confederates on Clark Sr., the recent discoverer of Caribbean treasures. Somehow Clark Sr. succeeded where the police and the Pinkertons had failed, and destroyed this international murder syndicate. Combined with the guilt that he already felt over Heidegger's death, his experience with the Minions unhinged the mind of Clark Sr. He became determined to make his son the nemesis of all criminals.

It may be that the Minions of Midas caused the death of Doc's mother. *The Invisible-Box Murders* claimed that Doc's strange upbringing was the result of a joint decision by his parents (chap. 3). However, *Waves of Death* (chap. 5) asserted the at Clark Sr. was alone responsible for the decision since Doc's mother "died in Doc's youth." According to *Cargo Unknown* (chap. 6), Doc's mother "had died when he was less than a year old." According to Philip José Farmer's *Doc Savage: His Apocalyptic Life*, Doc's mother perished when the schooner *Orion* sank in 1902. Maybe this naval disaster was the result of sabotage by the Minions of Midas.

Who headed the Minions of Midas? Jack London does not tell us. I think the answer may lie in one of Doc's adventures. The strange events of *The Spook of Grandpa Eben* were supposedly the work of the ghost of Eben "Wildbuck" Riggs, an unscrupulous American adventurer who traveled around the world in the 1890s and early 1900s (chap. 5): "At one time, he was president of a Central American republic, and another time he owned a whole oilfield in Oklahoma, and another time he got to be almost emperor of part of China." Riggs began his career as a lawyer. Kaiser Wilhelm II offered "a reward of a million dollars for his head back in the 1890s." Riggs must have committed crimes in the Pacific islands under the control of the Second Reich. Riggs "lost at least ten fortunes, and each one was more than a million dollars" (chap. 1). He carried a strange charm, "a tiny carving of a human head done in some shiny black metal." Supposedly, this black carving was "a drop of the devil's blood that had frozen." The carving was shaped like the head of a native of India. Riggs had a son, who later sired Wilmore "Billy" Riggs. Billy Riggs did not inherit any of his grandfather's criminal tendencies. Riggs died "thirty years ago" (chap. 5). The year would be 1913 based on my chronological placement of *The Spook of Grandpa Eben* were. Riggs "died at the head of an army of two hundred adventurers who were trying to kidnap the head Lama of Tibet" (chap. 1). Riggs was "killed in a battle."

Eben Riggs sounds like a colorful character. I suspect him of being the archenemy of Clark Savage Sr. Riggs would have been just as dangerous as Cadwiller Oldin, John Sunlight and Jonas Sown, Eben could have headed the Minions of Midas during 1899-1902. When Clark Sr. crushed his organization, Riggs fled to commit crimes elsewhere. Riggs' takeover of a Central American republic may have led Clark Sr. to search for the Valley of the Vanished in 1911. Clark Sr. must have been the man who caused Riggs' death in Tibet during 1913. Clark Sr. never told his son about his ongoing vendetta with

Eben Riggs.

Philip José Farmer's speculations about Doc's parentage and "The Adventure of the Priory School" can only be reconciled to the Sherlock Holmes saga if Doc was born in late 1901. For this reason, Mr. Farmer assigned Doc Savage's birth to November 12. 1901. Jeff Deischer has proven irrefutably that Doc celebrated his birthday in late May by an insightful analysis of *Peril in the North*. How does a disciple of Mr. Farmer's theories reconcile this unassailable truth?

My friend Art Sippo has conceived a wonderful theory which he posted on the Internet. Doc's father was trying to cover up his origins. It was not generally known that his wife was three months' pregnant when he fled England. The elder Savage pretended that Doc had been born in May rather than November. This deception was effective because Doc was an exceptionally large child.. Art's theory can be found at his website "Speculations in Bronze:" http://speculations-in-bronze.blogspot.com/

The Savage Reversion

The surname Savage does appear in the Sherlock Holmes stories. Sir Arthur Conan Doyle's "The Adventure of the Dying Detective" concerned the investigation of the murder of young Victor Savage. The murderer was Victor's uncle, Culverton Smith, a specialist in rare Asian diseases. Smith murdered Victor to secure a reversion. In other words, under the terms of a legal will, a property inherited by Victor would revert upon his death to Smith.

Sherlockian chronologists generally place this case somewhere during 1887-1890. I concur with the argument that the story transpired in 1887.

Victor Savage could be one of Doc's relatives. According to Philip José Farmer's *Doc Savage: His Apocalyptic Life*, Doc's great-grandfather was a scientist, who found the notebooks of Mary Shelley's Victor Frankenstein. The wife of this scientist was named Mavice Blakeney. Upon Mavice's death, Doc's great-grandfather could have married Culverton Smith's sister and fathered a son. This son was christened Victor Savage after Victor Frankenstein. Culverton Smith must have aided Doc's great-grandfather in his experiments based on Frankenstein's notebooks. Before his death, Doc's great-grandfather must have hidden the notebooks in one of his various properties. This piece of real estate was inherited by Victor Savage, but the terms of the will permitted the property to revert to Culverton Smith. Therefore, Victor Savage was slain by Culverton Smith in order to gain possession of Frankenstein's notebooks. Fortunately, Sherlock Holmes apprehended Smith before he could put the notebooks to diabolical use.

Who hired Sherlock Holmes to find Victor Savage's killer? Doyle does not tell us, but probably Victor Savage had left a widow. She must have gained possession of the notebooks. When Clark Savage Sr. became a doctor in the United States during the 1900s, she must have given him the notebooks. Years later, Clark Sr. shared the notebooks with his son. These notebooks must have been the basis for the experiment to resurrect a dead man with a new element, which took a decade to mature. Doc began this experiment with his father in 1926, and the eventual outcome of this scientific endeavor during 1936 is described in Lester Dent's *Resurrection Day*.

Clark Savage Sr. in Maple White Land

Clark Savage Sr. made a brief appearance in *Ironcastle* (DAW Books, 1976) by Philip José Farmer and J. H. Rosny. The novel has an unusual history. It is Mr. Farmer's translation and embellishment of a French science fiction novel, *L'etonnate Aventure de Hareton Ironcastle* (1922) by J.H. Rosny. The plot of the novel concerned a scientific expedition led by Hareton Ironcastle to a fantastic land in Africa. Besides giving a scientific explanation for the strange phenomenon observed by the expedition, Mr. Farmer inserted various references to the works of other writers.

The Baltimore Gun Club from Jules Verne's *From the Earth to the Moon* was featured (chap. 1). The Diogenes Club from Sir Arthur Conan Doyle's "The Adventure of the Greek Interpreter" was briefly mentioned. There are references to Phileas Fogg from Verne's *Around the World in Eighty Days* and Professor Porter, the father-in-law of Edgar Rice Burroughs'Tarzan. One of the members of Ironcastle's expedition, Sir George Curtis, was the nephew of Sir Henry Curtis (chap. 24), a character from H. Rider Haggard's *King Solomon's Mines* and *Allan Quatermain*.

Hareton Ironcastle claimed to know Joseph Jorkens (chap. 3), a teller of tall tales invented by Lord Dunsany. Ironcastle recalled an adventure with Jorkens involving a gorilla in Africa. The apes of Africa figured prominently in Dunsany's "The Showman" from *The Travel Tales of Joseph Jorkens* (1931). However, Ironcastle stated that he and Jorkens witnessed a strange incident involving a woman and a gorilla in Gabon. No such event transpired in "The Showman," but an event of this nature was briefly described by the protagonist of *Trader Horn* (1927) by A. E. Horn and E. Lewis. Mr. Farmer indicated his familiarity with Trader Horn in *Tarzan Alive* (1972). Perhaps Ironcastle, Jorkens and Trader Horn were in Gabon at the same time.

Ironcastle begins in 1920, and a previous expedition involving the title character was recalled. Ironcastle, together with Clark Savage Sr., had journeyed to Maple White Land, an Amazon plateau populated by dinosaurs (chap. 1). This lost land had been described in detail in Sir Arthur Conan Doyle's *The Lost World* (1912), where it was discovered by Professor George Challenger. Ironcastle and Savage attempted to capture specimens with an "air-gun," which fired electrical bullets capable of stunning the dinosaurs. The dinosaurs would then be transported out of Maple White Land by zeppelins. A volcanic eruption destroyed Maple White Land before this plan could be put into effect. Ironcastle and Savage barely escape.

According to *Doc Savage: His Apocalyptic Life*, Clark Sr. was searching for Maple White Land during 1917-18, while his son fought in World War I. Clark Sr. didn't learn about his son's military exploits until after the Armistice (November 11, 1918). A remark in *Escape from Loki* (chap. 3) asserted that Clark Sr. was "exploring deep inside Brazil."

According to Mr. Farmer, not all the inhabitants of Maple White Land were destroyed in the volcanic eruption. In *The Lost World* (chap. 13), Professor Challenger discovered a race of apes with red hair. *Doc Savage: His Apocalyptic Life* speculated that Chemistry was of this species. Somehow Chemistry fled the plateau called Maple White Land into the Amazon jungle. By implication, the same would be true of the similar apes discovered by Monk and Ham during *The Green Death*.

For the chronology of Professor Challenger's exploits, see "The Anomaly of Professor Challenger's Daughter" in *Rick Lai's Secret Histories: Daring Adventurers* (Altus Press, 2008).

Doc Savage and King Kong

In a short story entitled "After King Kong Fell," Philip José Farmer had both Doc Savage and The Shadow witness the demise of King Kong in New York during 1931. The story was published in two short story collections by Mr. Farmer, *The Grand Adventure* (Berkley Books, 1984) and *The Classic Philip José Farmer*, 1964-1973 (Crown Publishers, 1984). The film *King Kong* was released in 1933, and a novelization by Delos W. Lovelace of the screenplay by Merian C. Cooper and Edgar Wallace was published in 1932.

In the novel (but not the film), it was snowing in New York when the story opened. Both film and book mentioned that the *Wanderer*, the ship anchored in New York, had to leave quickly to beat the monsoons which affect sailing in the Pacific. These storms would normally erupt during January-February. Therefore, the early portions of the King Kong story would seem to be set in early January. The ship then traveled to the Panama Canal and across the Pacific to the island where the giant ape known as King Kong resided. After some harrowing adventures, Kong was captured and brought to New York where he was exhibited in a theater. He then escaped to meet his death on the Empire State Building.

It is not quite clear how much time passed between Kong's capture and his exhibition in New York. It would have taken some interval of time before Kong's captor, Carl Denham, could have arranged to book a theater in Times Square and mount a publicity campaign. Furthermore, American law may have required Kong to spent months in quarantine in order to ensure that he was not carrying any infectious diseases.

After all, quarantine was imposed on Chemistry when he was discovered by Ham in South America. In both the film and the novel, the denizens of New York seem dressed for cold weather.

In Mr. Farmer's story, people were living in the Empire State Building. The building was officially opened on May 1, 1931. Considering the clothing worn by the New York populace. The time could not be May or the summer months. It would have to be autumn. The story was told from the viewpoint of a young boy from Illinois. He was visiting New York with his parents, and couldn't wait to get back home to tell his friends in the seventh grade the sights he had seen. This trip to New York would seem to have taken place during a brief school recess. The most likely time would be during the Columbus Day weekend in October. I do not have any Doc Savage novels assigned to October 1931 in my chronology.

"After King Kong Fell" would have transpired during the long gap between *The Land of Terror* and *Quest of the Spider*. In "After King Kong Fell," Doc and his assistants drove up in a black limousine towards King Kong's corpse. Doc, who had been riding outside on the running board, got off and conferred with three officials present at the scene. The officials were Mayor Jimmy Walker, Governor Franklin Roosevelt and the unnamed police commissioner, who briefly appeared in Lovelace's novelization. Doc and his men were not present in the Empire State Building when Kong climbed it. Doc must have just returned from an unrecorded adventure. He probably just returned to New York by either plane or boat. Since the Hidalgo Trading Company wasn't built yet, then Doc must have taken the limousine from either an airfield or a harbor.

According to *Doc Savage: His Apocalyptic Life*, Doc knew Carl Denham, the man who had captured Kong. In fact, Doc had supplied Denham with the sleeping gas grenades that had been used to capture Kong.

The following should be noted. If the events of *King Kong* were not judged inside the context of Mr. Farmer's story, then the entire story of the giant ape would probably be chronologically placed in January-March 1932.

A major question is left unanswered in "After King Kong Fell." Whatever happened to Kong's corpse? It was only mentioned that Kong's body was put in an icebox until legal ownership could be figured out. The most likely explanation is that Kong's body was stolen. Possible suspects in the commission of such a crime would include Zanigew, one of The Shadow's most dangerous enemies. Whether Doc Savage and/or The Shadow investigated the theft of Kong's body is not known.

Doc Savage and the Thing From Another World

Albert Tonik's "A Doc Savage Adventure Rediscovered" from *Doc Savage Club Reader #4* (1978?) puts forth an amazing theory about Doc Savage and a classic science fiction story, John W. Campbell Jr.'s "Who Goes There?" (*Astounding Stories*, August 1938). The story was initially published under the pseudonym of Don A. Stuart. Campbell's story concerned a scientific expedition in Antarctica. The expedition discovered a frozen alien from outer space in the ice. The alien's ship had crashed in Antarctica millions of years ago. When the alien was defrosted, it was discovered to be alive. The alien had the power to copy other life forms. It could also split off parts of its body to copy more than one life form. The expedition was faced with the horror of being gradually murdered, and then replaced by duplicates that were parts of this monstrosity from another world. An expedition member named McCready came up with a scientific test to tell the real humans from the duplicates. Under McCready's leadership, the remaining humans destroyed the invader from the stars. Movie versions of Campbell's story were made in 1951 and 1982 under the title of *The Thing*. McCready's physical description will sound very familiar to any Doc Savage fan. He is described as "a man of bronze," "a looming, bronze statue come to life," and "a bronze giant of a man." He had bronze hair and a beard. Unlike Doc, McCready was not a master of many sciences, but only a meteorologist. He claimed to have studied for a M.D. twelve years earlier, and even began an internship. However, he then diverted into the field of meteorology.

McCready's height is given as six feet and four inches. This statement would not jive with Lester Dent's notes, which were published as *The Doc Savage Files* (Odyssey Publications, 1986). Doc's height was given as six feet and eight inches. Dent's notation would be consistent with a statement in *Hex* (chap. 13): "His head scraped the top of the vault, and the storage chamber was eight feet over six feet high." However. Dent's *The Man Who Was Scared* (chap. 13) had a police bulletin described Doc's height as being only six feet and four inches. Therefore, the height given for McCready is at least an acceptable (although probably inaccurate) height to be applied to Doc.

Mr. Tonik believed that Campbell's short story was a genuine Doc adventure that had been distorted to hide our hero's true identity. According to Mr. Tonik, Doc had "really" been in Antarctica under his real name. I would modify Mr. Tonik's theory. I think Doc assumed the identity for reasons of his own. References in the novel placed it in September. Spring was coming to Antarctica. Spring in Antarctica would mean autumn in New York. In my chronology, I have placed the start of Doc's longest exploit, *The Red Terrors*, in early September 1936. Doc left New York for nine weeks at the beginning of *The Red Terrors*. Reporters were hounding him, and Doc wanted to take a vacation. He didn't want to go to the Fortress of Solitude because he craved human company. He supposedly went to Chesapeake Bay to devise a way to prevent starfish from destroying oysters. Maybe he didn't go to Chesapeake Bay. He could have hired an actor to impersonate him and go there. Doc employed such a stratagem with an actor in *The Laugh of Death* (chap. 6). In that World War II novel, it was mentioned that Doc had an arrangement with a talent agency to have available "actors who could double for me and my associates." This arrangement had been in effect for "some time." An actor could have actually fooled the reporters while Doc actually assumed the identity of McCready. He grew a beard, and used his contacts in the scientific community and the Navy to become part of the Antarctic expedition of September 1936. He assumed the identity of a meteorologist, but he had to make up some story for his obvious medical logic. He fashioned the lie about only studying for an M.D. Doc hoped to only engage in scientific research. Instead, he found himself battling a creature from the stars.

Mr. Tonik had theories about two other characters in "Who Goes There?" Mr. Tonik suspected that a character named Van Wall was Renny. I can't find any strong evidence inside the story to indicate such a possibility. Another character, Van Norris was described as "all steel." Mr. Tonik believed Van Norris to be Richard Henry Benson, another pulp hero from a pulp magazine published by Street and Smith. Known as the Avenger, Benson's exploits were chronicled by Paul Ernst (writing under the house name of Kenneth Robeson). Despite some similarities besides Van Norris and Benson, I can't accept the argument that they were the same man. Unlike Benson, Van Norris had a stocky build. The internal chronology of Benson's own exploits would indicate that he had retired from both business and adventure by 1936 in order to travel with his wife and daughter.

Doc Savage and the Rocketeer

Doc Savage, Monk and Ham made appearances in *The Rocketeer* (Eclipse Books, 1985), an original graphic novel (i.e. comic strip) by Dave Stevens. The story was set in California during April 1938. Doc invented a rocket pack that would allow a man to fly.

Nazi agents stole the rocket pack, but it fell accidentally into the hands of Cliff Secord, an American pilot. Not knowing the true origins of the invention, Secord created the masked identity of the Rocketeer. Both Doc and the Rocketeer prevented the Nazis from stealing a new experimental aircraft. The novel ended with Secord still in possession of the rocket pack, and headed towards New York. This entire adventure lasted about nine days (I counted six days, and Secord spent an unspecified amount of time in the hospital).

Secord's further adventures were collected in *The Rocketeer, Volume II* (Dark Horse Comics, 1996). This second exploit is also known as "Cliff's New York Adventure." In New York, Secord met a man named Jonas, who was clearly meant to be The Shadow. This second adventure lasted three days. The first Rocketeer adventure formed the basis for the 1991 film, *The Rocketeer*. In the movie, the time was changed to October 1938. Doc and his assistants were replaced by Howard Hughes and FBI agents.

I would place the first adventure of the Rocketeer after *The Yellow Cloud*, a novel that I have assigned to late March 1938. In *The Yellow Cloud,* Doc was working closely with the U.S. military to test experimental aircraft. A group of international spies were trying to steal the new airplanes. The spies sold their services to the highest bidder, and were probably stealing the aircraft on the behalf of Nazi Germany. Doc smashed the spy ring. With apprehension of the spy ring employed in *The Yellow Cloud*, the Nazis must have realized that proxy agents would not be able to steal secrets from under Doc Savage's nose. The Nazis decided to risk their own agents to obtain American aviation secrets in *The Rocketeer* graphic novel, Monk was drawn perfectly by Dave Stevens. Ham looked too much like the way in which he had been depicted in George Pal's 1975 movie. Ham shouldn't have a mustache or a monocle. Ham was depicted with black hair in *The Rocketeer*. Lester Dent originally described Ham as having "prematurely gray hair" in *The Man of Bronze* (chap. 4). The artists of the magazine depicted Ham with dark hair. Eventually, descriptions of Ham with dark or brown hair appeared in the novels. Ham had "dark hair" in The *World's Fair Goblin* (chap. 9) and *The Lost Giant* (chap. 7). He was described as having "brown hair" while operating under the alias of Futch, in *Let's Kill Ames* (chap. 8). We can assume that Ham dyed his hair in several adventures. According to *Escape from Loki* (chap. 4), Ham's hair was black during World War I. It must have turned gray by 1931.

Doc's face was never fully shown in *The Rocketeer*. Doc was either in shadows, or wearing a helmet. Characters who may be intended to be Renny, Johnny and Long Tom appeared when Doc was interrogating a Nazi spy injected with truth serum.

Since the Rocketeer met both Doc Savage and the Shadow, it might be appropriate here to show how the activities of those two heroes interfaced with the alter ego of Cliff Secord. The dates given for The Shadow's activities on based on my *Chronology of Shadows* (Altus Press, 2007).

1938:   March   During March 8-18, The Shadow's epic battle with Zanigew, the great criminal mastermind, brought him to the shores of California during

	the events of Walter Gibson's *Shadow Over Alcatraz* (December 1, 1938). Wounded at the end of this adventure, The Shadow would remain in California to recover. During 18 days in the same month, Doc Savage had his final showdown with John Sunlight, which ended in the mountains of Asia *(The Devil Genghis)*.
Late March	Back in the United States, Doc was cooperating with the American military with developing new advances in aviation. For a period of 4 days, he fought a group of free-lance spies hired by Nazi Germany to steal aviation secrets *(The Yellow Cloud)*. Doc's defeat of this spy ring prompted the Abwehr, the German Military Intelligence organization, to make a fateful decision. Its own agents in the United States were ordered to directly intervene to secure the vital secrets, and risk the consequences of a direct confrontation with Doc Savage.
Late March-Early April	Fully recovered from his wounds, The Shadow foiled criminals who stole an experimental naval craft. This California adventure lasted 14 days, and was described in Gibson's *Death Ship* (April 1, 1940). The Shadow found himself in an uneasy alliance with Japanese spies, who were aware of his pose as Lamont Cranston.
Early April	During a period of nine days, the events of *The Rocketeer* unfolded in California. Nazi agents stole a rocket pack designed for the American military by Doc Savage. The invention fell accidentally into the hands of Cliff Secord, who created the costumed identity of the Rocketeer. Together with Doc, the Rocketeer foiled the Nazi theft of a new American warplane. Injured in the exploit, Secord would escape from the hospital with the rocket pack. He went to New York to find his estranged girl friend, Betty. In California, The Shadow heard about Secord's actions. Burbank, The Shadow's contact man in New York had been gathering information about a series of murders in which the victims were ex-carnival performers. Burbank discovered that Secord was acquainted with all the victims, and informed The Shadow by radio. The Shadow followed Secord back to New York. In order to shake the Japanese spies, his former allies from *Death Ship*, The Shadow dropped his Cranston identity and became the similarly hawk-faced Jonas.
April	During a period of 3 days in New York, The Shadow as Jonas manipulated Secord into helping him catch the brutal murderer of the ex-carnival performers *(The Rocketeer: Volume II)*. Back in New York, Doc Savage failed to become involved in the murder case investigated by Jonas and Secord. Doc was too preoccupied with uncovering a land swindle revolving around the Lincoln Tunnel *(The Giggling Ghosts)*. Doc's involvement in this case lasted eighteen days.
May	Doc smashed another gang of freelance (i.e. independent) spies in *Merchants of Disaster*. The Nazis had temporarily learned their lesson. Don't go head to head with Doc! The Shadow destroyed a spy ring working directly for an unnamed country, probably Nazi Germany, in Theodore Tinsley's *Double Death* (December 15, 1938). You would

think that the Nazis should have realized an important fact from their recent experience with Doc. Don't mess with New Yorkers! What Cliff Secord was doing, only the late great Dave Stevens knows!

Doc Savage and the Mystery of Rudolf Hess

Doc Savage's adventure, *The Golden Man*, is one of those strange cases in literature where life later imitates art. Dent's novel was submitted to the publishers in July 1940. The title character of the novel was Paul Hest, "chief of intelligence for… an unnamed country, not the United States" (chap. 18). Various hints indicate that Hest's country was really Germany, then at peace with the United States and at war with Great Britain. Hest went on a secret mission by airplane. An agent, working for another unnamed country (Great Britain), placed a bomb in Hest's plane. When the plane exploded, Hest parachuted out and landed in the Atlantic Ocean. The explosion gave him partial amnesia. A chemical carried in the plane causes a golden luminous glow in the ocean around Hest. An American ship picked up Hest, and he was perceived as a supernatural figure. American gangsters kidnapped Hest to use of the head of a phony religious cult. Doc freed Hest and brought his American captors to justice. Hest presumably returned to Germany.

It is not quite clear why Hest was called "the golden man" in the novel. Maybe the chemical changed his skin and hair coloring, or Hest was a natural blond. On May 10, 1941, another Nazi went on a real-life secret mission by airplane. Like the golden man, he was forced to parachute. The alleged surname of this individual, Hess, is suspiciously similar to Hest. Parachuting into Scotland, the Nazi was arrested by the British authorities. The prisoner initially identified himself as Captain Alfred Horn, but later professed to be Rudolf Hess, the Deputy Fuehrer of Germany. Yet, this individual was unable to remember details of Hess' life. The prisoner asserted that he was suffering from amnesia. The prisoner claimed to have been on a peace mission. His hope was to meet with prominent Britons and negotiate a settlement of the war. Instead, the British authorities simply incarcerated him for the duration. Hitler claimed to know nothing of the so-called Hess mission and condemned his former Deputy. Tried as a war criminal at Nuremburg during 1945-46, the German prisoner was sentenced to life imprisonment. In 1987, the prisoner committed suicide in Spandau prison.

We have secret two secret aerial missions, two cases of amnesia, and two surnames, which are virtually identical. Because of the similarities between Paul Hest and Rudolf Hess, we could pretend that they were the same person. The Spandau prisoner was born with dark hair. While Paul Hest was swimming in the Atlantic Ocean, the luminous chemical from the wrecked plane could have gotten into his hair and dyed it gold. Hest's hair would have begun to return to its natural color during the fourteen weeks when he was in the hands of American gangsters. His captors could have re-dyed his hair with chemicals of their own to maintain the illusion of Hest being a mystical being. The golden man was described as "very little above average size" (chap. 2). What is average size? If it's five feet and ten inches, then the golden man was about six feet tall, the exact height of the Spandau prisoner.

Among the duties of Rudolf Hess as Deputy Fuehrer was supervision of the Auslands Organizations, whose duties were to keep contact with German nationals abroad. He also controlled a similar organization called the People's League for Germans Abroad, plus the Nazi Party's Aussepolitisches Amt (foreign political department), and the Verbindungsstab, which kept files on government and civil service officials. Together, these various groups gave Hess his own private intelligent network independent of the Abwehr, the military intelligence unit headed by Admiral Canaris, and Heinrich Himmler's SS.

The simple theory would be that Paul Hest was really Rudolf Hess, and that he flew two unusual missions by airplane.

The difficulty with such a theory is that there is abundant evidence that the German parachutist from Scotland is not the real Rudolf Hess. The Deputy Fuehrer had wounds from World War I according to his medical records. The German parachutist did not show any evidence of such wounds when examined.

A theory first advanced in fiction by Anthony Boucher's "The Adventure of the Illustrious Impostor" in Ellery Queen's anthology, *The Misadventures of Sherlock Holmes* (1944), and later advocated in non-fiction by W. Hugh Thomas' *The Murder of Rudolf Hess* (Harper and Row, 1979) explained the medical discrepancy. According to the theory, the real Rudolf Hess was murdered in Germany by a political rival, possibly Heinrich Himmler. A double for Hess was then sent on this mission to England in order to hide the assassination and discredit the victim.

This evidence leads to a more complex theory linking the events of *The Golden Man* and historical reality. Paul Hest was Rudolf Hess' double. Their similarity in surnames suggest that they were distant cousins. Paul Hest must have impersonated Rudolf Hess on secret missions. Paul Hest was working for the Deputy Fuehrer at the time of *The Golden Man*. When Hest returned to Germany after his encounter with Doc, he somehow fell under the control of one of Rudolf Hess' enemies. Paul Hest's was then coerced to impersonate Rudolf Hess on the bizarre peace mission to Britain.

Doc Savage vs. Fu Manchu

The greatest contemporary fictional master criminal during Doc Savage's career was Sax Rohmer's Dr. Fu Manchu. The activities of this arch-felon spanned the years shortly before the First World War to the 1950s. In many ways, Doc Savage was sort of a good version of Fu Manchu. Like Doc, Fu Manchu was a master of many sciences. Both were surgeons.

Fu Manchu even had an ongoing enterprise equivalent to the Crime College. Fu Manchu abducted scientists from all over the world, and forced them to work in his secret laboratories.

Fu Manchu headed an international criminal organization, the Si-Fan, which was centered in Asia. It wouldn't be too difficult to pretend that many of Doc's foes with ties to Asia were leading officials in the Si-Fan. The list could easily include the villains from *Pirate of the Pacific*, *The Mystic Mullah*, *The Jade Ogre*, *The Majii*, *The Feathered Octopus* and *The Mountain Monster*. The treacherous representatives of a Chinese province in *Haunted Ocean* probably were Si-Fan agents. The Mystic Mullah created a poison from the venom of the neotropical rattlesnake (*Crotalus durissus*). How did a criminal from Outer Mongolia get a snake from Central America? Fu Manchu could have lent the reptile to him. Fu Manchu had a wide menagerie of creatures from around the globe. His favorite pet, a marmoset, was from South America.

The Si-Fan also had extensive operations in the Middle East. The crooks from *Murder Mirage* tried to sell their radioactive material to some mysterious group known as the Seven Companies Syndicate (chap. 18). This group could have been a front for the Si-Fan, which was ruled by a Council of Seven led by Fu Manchu.

In *Meteor Menace*, a Western scientist in Tibet went insane and became a maniacal master criminal named Mo-Gwei. In Sax Rohmer's *The Bride of Fu Manchu* (1933), it was revealed that Fu Manchu used a drug, the Blessing of the Celestial Vision, to reduce abducted scientists to a state of mental servitude. Perhaps Fu Manchu or his agents encountered the scientist from *Meteor Menace* in Tibet, and gave him the Blessing of the Celestial Vision. The scientist could have become Mo-Gwei to do the bidding of Fu Manchu.

It is surprising that Fu Manchu never attempted to abduct Doc because of his vast scientific knowledge. However, John Sunlight attempted to kidnap Doc and transport him to Asia in *The Devil Genghis*. It is possible that Sunlight was allied with Fu Manchu in this novel. John Sunlight was now justifying his crimes by espousing an idealistic philosophy of world peace. Fu Manchu was a misguided idealist who advocated similar positions. After Sunlight escaped from the Arctic following the events of *Fortress of Solitude*, Fu Manchu could have contacted him. With Fu Manchu's help, Sunlight could have established his Asian base with great ease and speed. Mention should be made here of the theory offered in Dafydd Neal Dyar's "Sunlight, Son Bright," from *The Doc Savage Club Reader* #8 (1979?). Mr. Dyar speculated that Fu Manchu was Sunlight's father. Fu Manchu's plan to foster a male heir in *The Bride of Fu Manchu* demonstrated that he had no sons. Sax Rohmer's novels only featured a daughter, Fah Lo Suee, who would have been born when her father was nearly sixty. It is possible that Fu Manchu had fathered one or two daughters long before the birth of Fah Los Suee. Sunlight may be descended from one of these hypothetical children. See "John Sunlight and the Si-Fan Succession" from *Rick Lai's Secret Histories: Criminal Masterminds* (Altus Press, 2009).

Like Doc Savage's adversaries in *The Munitions Master*, Fu Manchu supposedly murdered Adolf Hitler in the late 1930s. The alleged assassination of Hitler was recorded in *The Drums of Fu Manchu* (1939), in which the German dictator appeared under the alias of Rudolph Adlon. A reference to "the retirement from public life of the ruler of Turkey" (chap. 42) would imply that the novel was set in September 1937 (Prime Minister Ismet Inonu of Turkey stepped down on September 23, 1937). A remark about the recent resignation of "a prominent Cabinet Minister" (chap. 1) would seem to be a reference to the resignation of Prime Minister Stanley Baldwin in May 1937. The supposed liquidation of Hitler caused problems for Sax Rohmer when he wrote the sequel, *The Island of Fu Manchu* (1941), set in the early years of World War II.

Rohmer tried to sidestep the issue by brazenly claiming that the British Foreign Office had forced the events of *The Drums of Fu Manchu* to be falsified (*The Island of Fu Manchu*, chap. 36).

Doc Savage may have been responsible for Fu Manchu's greatest defeat. In *The Island of Fu Manchu*, the Si-Fan had accumulated a huge arsenal at a secret base in Haiti. Besides futuristic planes armed with disintegration rays, there were over a hundred similarly armed submarines. A reference to a naval battle in Skagerrak (chap. 12) places the novel in April 1940, when the British and the Nazis were fighting in Norway. Fu Manchu issued a warning to the Allies (Britain and France) and the then neutral United States. If they negotiated with the Si-Fan, then the weapons would be used against the Nazis. If the Allies refused to bargain, then the Si-Fan would use the weapons against them. Fu Manchu's dreams of power come to an end because the disintegration ray technology, utilized in various ways throughout his headquarters, had a strange affinity with lighting. Electricity was drawn from the sky by the disintegration rays, and the Si-Fan's Haitian base exploded. Fu Manchu survived, and continued his activities into the 1950s. However, his power never reached these heights again.

Sax Rohmer never explained Fu Manchu's escape from the Haitian fiasco in the subsequent stories. Probably he was able to flee in one of the Si-Fan's submarines.

Even though he was punishing his treacherous daughter by putting her in a state of catalepsy, he must have taken her with him. She reappeared in *The Wrath of Fu Manchu* (1973).

The lighting bolts were a very convenient *deus ex machina*. There may be more to Fu Manchu's defeat than a simple act of God. The British government dispatched Sir Dennis Nayland Smith to deal with the situation, and he was only victorious due to the fortuitous lighting storm. Wouldn't the United States have dispatched someone to Haiti? Who would be better qualified than Doc Savage?

My chronology does not explain where Doc Savage was in April 1940. I have placed *The Golden Man* in April-July 1940, but Doc was missing from the first fourteen weeks of that adventure. Why did it take Doc so long to track down Monk and Ham in a South American jail? Doc attributed the delay to a lie told about their whereabouts (*The Golden Man,* chap. 8). However, Doc had seen through such lies before. Something must have distracted Doc from searching for Monk and Ham. The United States must have sent Doc to Haiti. There he penetrated the Si-Fan's secret base. He sabotaged the disintegration ray technology to attract lighting, and consequently tricked Fu Manchu into destroying his huge arsenal when he activated the rays. After the Haitian episode concluded, Doc contacted his Crime College graduates to locate Monk and Ham. While Doc was waiting for his intelligence network to locate them, he spent time designing and modifying aircraft for the U.S. government.

Fu Manchu abducted scientists by injecting them with a drug that put people into a cataleptic trance. The scientist would be buried, and then Si-Fan agents would steal their sleeping bodies from graveyards and revive them. Fu Manchu's drug is very similar to a drug which Doc Savage discovered in Africa during *Birds of Death*. The people who owned the drug were descended from Egyptians (chap. 14). In *The Island of Fu Manchu* (chap. 34), Fu Manchu revealed that he had discovered the ingredients for his cataleptic drug in Egypt around 1880. The drug had supposedly been used by the ancient priests of Thebes. This drug, discovered by Fu Manchu in Egypt, must be the same drug used by an offshoot of the Egyptian civilization in *Birds of Death*. There is a conflicting origin story given for Fu Manchu's cataleptic drug in Rohmer's *The Golden Scorpion* (1919). Fu Manchu's drug, identified as F. Katalepsis, was supposedly derived from the venom of "the common black scorpion of southern India" (part 4, chap. 1). Probably Fu Manchu ran out of the ingredients discovered in Egypt, but realized that he could replace them by modifying scorpion venom from India.

Fu Manchu may also have been familiar with the Red Death, the poison used to kill Doc's father in *The Man of Bronze*. The symptoms of the Red Death are identical with the venom of the Scarlet Bride, a rare species of spider, which appeared in *President Fu Manchu* (1936, chap. 14). However, the Red Death in *The Man of Bronze* was derived from birds.

There is one last matter involving Doc and Fu Manchu that needs to be scrutinized. Doc Savage's father supposedly died from the Red Death in April 1931. Since he was at the *Fortress of Solitude*, Doc never examined his father's corpse. What if Fu Manchu found a cure for the Red Death? Si-Fan agents could have injected Doc's father with both the Red Death antidote and F. Katalepsis. After Clark Sr. was buried, the Si-Fan could have stolen his comatose body. Doc's father may not have really died in April 1931, but could have been taken prisoner by Fu Manchu.

There is The possibility of an epic confrontation in 1931 revolving around Doc, Fu Manchu, and two individuals with the habit of laughing in an eerie fashion. However, I will discuss that later in order to focus on evidence that Fu Manchu battled Doc Savage in the 1920s.

The Adventures of Doc Ardan

Jean-Marc and Randy Lofficier started Black Coat Press in 2003 for the larger purpose of translating major French works of science fiction and mystery into English. One of the works that the Lofficiers decided to make available in an English edition was *La Cite de L'Or et de la Lepre* (1928) by Guy d'Armen. Little is known about the author. In fact, Guy d'Armen is generally believed to be a pseudonym. The novel pitted a muscular Western scientist, Francis Ardan, against an evil Asian scientist, Dr. Natas (Satan spelled backwards). The similarity between Ardan and Doc Savage may have been apparent to a publisher in the 1940s who published French versions of the Doc Savage pulp novels in the 1930s. Doc Savage was altered into Franck Sauvage. The house name of Kenneth Robeson was replaced by Guy d'Antin, a name suspiciously similar to Guy d'Armen.

Taking a page from Philip José Farmer's *Ironcastle*, the Lofficiers "adapted" d'Armen novel and published it as *Doc Ardan: City of Gold and Lepers* (2004). As in *Ironcastle*, the French text was considerably altered to include literary crossovers. The character of Ardan was made more like Doc Savage. The Savage connections come from *Doc Savage: His Apocalyptic Life* rather than the pulp novels. For example, Ardan received a medical degree from John Hopkins University in 1926. Ardan is clearly marketed as a disguised version of Doc Savage. The adventure was set in 1927, and doesn't conflict with any of my chronological notations.

Similarly, Dr. Natas was transformed into an alias assumed by Rohmer's Fu Manchu. The name of Rohmer's character never surfaced in the English adaptation, but the parallels are clear. The physical description of Natas was changed, The original version of Natas possessed gray eyes and long white hair. He was now endowed with green eyes and a shaven skull. Despite these changes, Natas was very much in the style of Rohmer's creation. In fact Guy d'Armen anticipated certain developments of the Fu Manchu series. In his duel with Francis Ardan, Natas extolled the historical Lord Kitchener and manufactured synthetic gold. Fu Manchu did likewise. However, he didn't do these actions until *The Mask of Fu Manchu* (1932). For a detailed discussion of the premise that Ardan's enemy was Fu Manchu, see "Alias Dr. Natas" in *Rick Lai's Secret Histories: Criminal Masterminds*.

Another series of Ardan short stories appeared in a series of short stories by multiple writers in a series of anthologies published by Black Coat Press, *Tales of the Shadowmen*. Here is a checklist:

Volume	Year	Story	Author
1	2005	"The Vanishing Devil"	Win Scott Eckert
2	2006	"The Eye of Oran"	Win Scott Eckert (as Win Eckert)
		"The Star Prince"	Jean-Marc Lofficier and Fernando Calvi
3	2007	"Les Levres Rouges"	Win Scott Eckert

| 4 | 2008 | "The Reluctant Princess" | Randy Lofficier |
| 5 | 2009 | "Iron and Bronze" | Christopher Paul Carey and Win Scott Eckert |

The chronology of the story is as follows. "The Vanishing Devil" in 1949-51. Despite the title, "The Vanishing Devil is *not* a sequel the authentic Doc Savage novel, *Up from Earth's Center*. Instead, Ardan fought Dr. Natas again. "The Eye of Oran: was set in June 1946, and its sequel, "Les Levres Rouges," transpired in July. These stories could fit in my chronological arrangement by happening between the Doc Savage adventures *The Devil is Jones* (#195) and *Death in Little Houses* (#196). "The Star Prince" is a short vignette that could be set in any time frame. "The Reluctant Princess" took place in the 1920s (most likely somewhere during 1928-29). "Iron and Bronze" occurred in November 1929, which by pure happenstance falls into a gap in my chronology.

All of the stories utilize literary crossovers. There are too many to cite here, but "Iron and Bronze" was inspired by my article, "Zanigew the Killer," which can be found in *Rick Lai's Secret Histories: Criminal Masterminds*. I speculated there that one of The Shadow's adversaries, Zanigew, was in an earlier identity Harry Killer, the master criminal of Jules Verne's *The Barsac Mission* (1919). In the Doc Ardan story, Harry Killer was the villain. He wasn't explicitly identified as Zanigew, bur a similar name appeared in the text.

The Haunting of Doc's Daughter

Philip José Farmer's *Doc Savage: His Apocalyptic Life* was part of a broader landscape. Together with *Tarzan Alive* (1972), this biography of Doc Savage laid the foundation for the Wold Newton Universe, a theoretical construct that unites the great heroes of fiction. To briefly summarize the premise of those two books, a meteor landed near the British town of Wold Newton in Yorkshire during 1795. Present at the meteor strike were several prominent people including Baroness Orczy's the Scarlet Pimpernel and the main characters of Jane Austen's *Pride and Prejudice*. Radiation affected the genes of the spectators. Their descendants would later develop extraordinary skills and abilities. Intermarriage between later generations strengthen the genetic impact. These mutated genes were inherited by Tarzan, Doc Savage and other notables. Consistent with this premise are numerous novels and short stories written by Mr. Farmer. Among these works are *The Other Log of Phileas Fogg* (1973), *The Adventure of the Peerless Peer* (1974) and *The Dark Heart of Time* (1999). In the genealogies of these books, Tarzan and Doc Savage were cousins. Tarzan's family, the Greystokes, resided in Pemberley House, an estate that originally belonged to the hero of *Pride and Prejudice*.

Mr. Farmer had started a Doc Savage pastiche which was left unfinished. The novel was intended to be based on his Wold Newton speculations linking Doc Savage and Tarzan. In *Doc Savage: His Apocalyptic Life*. Mr. Farmer had asserted that Doc's real name was not Clark Savage Jr. but James Clark Wildman Jr. It is under the Wildman alias that Doc Savage appears in Mr. Farmer manuscript.

Completed by Win Scott Eckert, the novel has been published by Subterranean Press in 2009 as *The Evil in Pemberley House*. In many ways, Mr. Eckert was ideally suited for this task. He has consistently championed the concepts of the Wold Newton Universe on the Internet: http://www.pjfarmer.com/woldnewton/Pulp2.htm. Mr. Eckert has also written several short stories set in the Wold Newton Universe. Besides Mr. Farmer's Wold Newton biographies and novels, *The Evil in Pemberley House* has strong connections to the Doc Ardan series written by Mr. Eckert and other writers, The plot of the novel heavily used the Priory School theory discussed earlier.

Before beginning a discussion of the novel. I must add a word of caution. Unlike the other Wold Newton works by Mr. Farmer, *The Evil in Pemberley House* has graphic sexual content. Mr. Farmer clearly intended this novel to be the Wold

Newton equivalent of *A Feast Unknown* (1969), an early controversial Tarzan/Doc Savage pastiche that was contradicted by his later works. While Doc does not engage in any controversial sexual acts in *The Evil in Pemberley House*, the novel's heroine behaves in a very provocative manner.

According to *The Evil in Pemberley House*, Doc married in 1951. In the same year, he fathered a daughter, Patricia Clarke Wildman. Mr. Farmer's original manuscript never identified Doc's wife, but only described her as a reformed confidence trickster. She was possibly intended to be Travice Ames from Lester Dent's *Let's Kill Ames*. Mr. Eckert makes Patricia's mother a character from his Doc Ardan tales.

When Patricia was 22, she became the heir to Pemberley House. Traveling to England, Patricia became involved with a ghost that haunted the mansion. She also found herself targeted for death by a group of criminal conspirators.

The novel contained a supposedly "fictionalized" adventure of Doc in which he appeared under the alias of Francis Ardan. The exploit was supposedly published in a periodical devoted to the exploits of Saxon Blake, a British sleuth. Saxon Blake is a disguised version of Sexton Blake, a popular British detective whose career spanned the 1890s to the 1970s. The "Doc Ardan" tale was set in 1927 shortly before the events of *Doc Ardan: City of Gold and Lepers*. In the story, Doc visited Pemberley House and demonstrated knowledge of his father's role in "The Adventure of the Priory School."

As previously noted, Mr. Farmer claimed that Doc's father trained his son to be a superman solely out of guilt for his role in the Priory School murder. If this was true, then Doc's knowledge of all his father's motivations in 1927 would totally contradict assertions in several World War II pulp novels. These novel professed that Doc never understood the reasons prompting his father's decision. Doc didn't reveal any understanding of his father's motivations until the postwar novels (see the "**Note**" after entry #178). In my earlier discourse on the Priory School theory, I noted that it merits expansion to include the persecution by criminals suggested in *Danger Lies East* and *No Light to Die By*. The only way that I could reconcile *The Evil in Pemberley House* with Lester Dent's novels is to argue the following rationale. Doc realized after 1927 that there must be more to his father's story than just the events of the Priory School. Doc didn't find out the full details of his father's past until the mid-1940s.

There are some chronological comments in *The Evil in Pemberley House* that merit scrutiny. There are veiled references to two Doc Savage's pulp adventures (chap, 17). *Up from Earth's Center* was placed in 1948. My chronology puts that novel in 1949 to accommodate Will Murray's *The Frightened Fish*, but late 1948 is an arguable assignment for *Up from Earth's Center* The completed manuscript can not be faulted for using the 1948 date since it would accurately reflect Mr. Farmer's prior chronological judgments in *Doc Savage: His Apocalyptic Life*. However, the same is not true of an allusion to the events of *The Black, Black Witch*. This pulp novel was assigned to 1943 in *The Evil in Pemberley House*. In Mr. Farmer's original chronology, *The Black, Black Witch* was slotted to 1942. My chronology also designated 1942 as the year of the novel's events.

The Evil in Pemberley House cited two Antarctic expeditions. The first is by Johnny in1929 (chap. 17). The expedition was not described in any detail in *The Evil in Pemberley House* except that Johnny had "strange experiences" that defied explanation. This 1929 remembrance is clearly a nod to Mr. Farmer's theory that Johnny was William Dyer, the narrator of H. P. Lovecraft's "At the Mountains of Madness." I have already given my reasons for dismissing this theory (see the "**Note**" after entry #76). Therefore, I view this 1929 trip as totally separate from the 1930-31 Dyer expedition.

The Saxon Blake episode from *The Evil in Pemberley House* also cited a 1925 expedition to Antarctic (chap. 17). Doc was part of this scientific team. Patricia recalled that most of Doc's fellow expedition members were murdered by a monster. This is an acknowledgement of Albert Tonik's theory that Doc was

McCready from John W. Campbell's "Who Goes There?" I earlier argued that the story should be placed in 1936. Mr. Eckert has chosen 1925 in order to reconcile McCready's assertion about studying for an M. D. with *Doc Savage: His Apocalyptic Life*. Mr. Farmer stated there that Doc earned his medical credentials in 1926. Needless to say, I viewed the 1925 expedition as distinct from the one described by Campbell. Doc must have gone on Antarctic expeditions in both 1925 and 1936. His daughter must have confused the two expeditions. Wold Newton scholars are free to disagree with me and side with the versatile Mr. Eckert.

Despite bring an ardent admirer of Philip José Farmer. I have never accepted his assertion that Doc Savage's real family name is Wildman. I believe that Mr. Farmer was guilty of misdirection when he conceived this premise. Proof of this misdirection is that the name of Doc's family is Savage in both *Ironcastle* and *Escape from Loki*. I speculate that Mr. Farmer promoted this Wildman deception in order to feature Doc Savage's family under an alias in an unauthorized pastiche. Probably the real name of Doc's father was James Clarke Savage. Doc's father altered his name to Clark Savage when he settled in America.

CHAPTER III
Parallel Lives: Doc Savage and The Shadow

Of all the other fictional characters created in other series, The Shadow would be the most appropriate figure to meet Doc Savage. The views of Philip José Farmer and Will Murray on Doc Savage differ in many ways, but both authors agreed that Doc and The Shadow must have known each other. Will Murray had hopes to write the first novel to feature the authorized team-up. Both DC Comics and Dark House Comics have done licensed stories teaming up the two heroes, but pulp fans are still awaiting an original novel featuring the two greatest heroes of the 1930s. There are strong connections between the heroes. Both magazines were edited by the same people. .John Nanovic, the editor during the classic years of both magazines, fed similar ideas to the author of both series.

An example is the appearance of stories based on the reports that Paul Redfern, an aviator who vanished in 1927, was either the prisoner or ruler of a South American tribe. The Doc Savage series focused on the prisoner angle of these rumors in three novels (*The Mental Wizard*, *The Green Death* and *The Men Vanished*) in which explorers are held captive in the jungle. By contrast, the story about Redfern being the ruler of a lost tribe inspired one of the most startling revelations about The Shadow. In *The Shadow Unmasks* (August 1, 1937), The Shadow who had been impersonating Lamont Cranston for years, was revealed to be Kent Allard, an aviator who vanished in Guatemala. When he reappeared as Allard, The Shadow claimed to have been ruling a tribe of Xinca Indians in Guatemala during the period in which he had really been fighting crime in the United States. Although Walter Gibson drew on Redfern to fashion Allard, the writer openly acknowledged the earlier case of the missing Colonel Percy Fawcett as the primary basis for The Shadow's real identity. Fawcett and Redfern were usually linked together as references in the Doc Savage novels demonstrate.

Lester Dent may even have poked fun at Walter Gibson, the principal author of The Shadow series. An examination of various Doc Savage novels indicates that Lester Dent was sympathetic to the Soviet Union in the 1930s (see my discussion of *Fortress of Solitude*, entry #99). Walter Gibson was very antagonistic towards the Soviets, and had The Shadow slaughter communists in *The Red Menace* (November 1931) and *The Romanoff Jewels* (December 1, 1932). There were also hints that The Shadow had once been a Tsarist agent during World War I. *The Mystic Mullah*, Dent had Doc Savage meet a friendly and heroic communist spy. The surname of this Soviet agent was Gibson.

Doc Savage's probable relationship with The Shadow can be deduced from a careful study of *The Man Who Shook the Earth*. Doc formed an uneasy alliance with John Acre, the head of the Chilean secret police. Acre, a man with a hooked nose and an affinity for black clothing, may have been inspired by The Shadow. Although Doc worked closely with Acre, the bronze crime-fighter was disturbed by the Chilean official's disregard for the sanctity of human life. Doc's natural instinct was to distrust Acre.

Having written a chronological study of The Shadow, *Chronology of Shadows*, I intend to examine those periods of time when The Shadow and Doc Savage most likely would have crossed each other's path. I also intend to discuss other items that link Doc and The Shadow including a close relationship with a prominent New York City official. Philip José Farmer's *Doc Savage: His Apocalyptic Life* claimed that The Shadow as Kent Allard taught Doc how to fly a plane before American entry into World War I. Such an event is a chronological impossibility.

According to *The Red Menace*, The Shadow was a spy in Russia in the early months of the war during 1914. He was then working for a country other than Russia (probably Britain). To be assigned to Russia, The Shadow would have been a spy in Europe for at least two years before World War I. There is nothing in The Shadow series to suggest that Allard pursued his aviator career before World War I. His aviation fame came in the 1920s. The earliest time in which Doc could have met The Shadow is World War I.

Great Escapes in World War I

Philip José Farmer's *Escape from Loki* gave the details of Doc's activities during World War I. Doc and his men met in a German prison camp, and launched a daring escape. It took Doc and the others a month to reach Italian lines. We are only given hints of what happened to Doc during that month (chap. 21): "The tale of how they made it through the mountains while hundreds of men were looking for them, how they kept from starving from death, is a saga in itself."

Much of the details of The Shadow's World War I career can be extrapolated from *The Shadow's Shadow* (February 1, 1933) and *The Shadow Unmasks*. During the war, Kent Allard was a spy known as the Dark Eagle (or the Black Eagle). As the Eagle, Allard faked the crash of his airplane behind enemy lines in 1917. He conducted undercover operations against Germany until the autumn of 1918. Shortly before the war ended (November 11, 1918), Allard reappeared back in Allied lines. He falsely claimed to have been in a prison camp during his private campaign behind enemy lines.

During Allard's undercover activities of 1917-18, we are told by Walter Gibson that the Eagle helped Allied prisoners of war escape to freedom. Perhaps the Dark Eagle helped Doc and his fellow escapees during the month of travel through Austrian territory to Italy. In what prison camp did Allard falsely claim to have been a POW? Maybe he pretended to be a former inmate of Loki. If Allard utilize such a deception, the decision may have come back to haunt him years later. Doc would know that Allard was never held there. First, Allard would have re-appeared after lying about being held prisoner by the Germans. In 1937, Allard mysteriously came back after being supposedly lost in Guatemala for twelve years. Doc may have concluded that Allard was lying again, and deduced the real reason for Allard's absence since 1925.

The Men Who Brought Down Al Capone

Although I will later speculate on the identities of criminals who fought both Doc Savage and The Shadow, one criminal appeared in both series. Actually fictionalized versions of a real-life crime lord were fashioned in both series. Al Capone provided the inspiration for both Pal Hatrack in *The Purple Dragon* and Nick Savoli in Gibson's *Gangdom's Doom* (December 1931). Doc's duel with Hatrack supposedly happened in 1929. I have offered the theory that Doc was responsible for Hatrack's real-life counterpart, Capone, allowing himself to be arrested on a concealed weapons charge in that year. Capone was fearful that Doc would send him the Crime College.

Gangdom's Doom was based on the Chicago election of April 8, 1931. In that election, Capone's candidate, incumbent Big Bill Thompson, lost to Anton Cermak.

The election eroded Capone's power in Chicago, and helped to pave the way for his conviction on tax evasion in October. In Gibson's novel, The Shadow disrupted the criminal operations of Savoli (alias Capone) so much that he was totally unable to rally his forces to win the election. The election took place shortly after The Shadow's departure from Chicago. I place the novel's events in March 1931.

The Capone surrogates fashioned in these pulp novels suffered different fates than the man on which they were modeled. By 1940, Hatrack had died in prison. Savoli supposedly jumped bail after being indicted. In real life, Capone was convicted in the autumn of 1931. In November 1939, Capone, no longer in control of his mental faculties due to the debilitating effects of syphilis, was released from prison.

Let us take a brief detour back to historical reality. Unfair credit has been given in television shows and movies to Elliot Ness, who led raids on Capone's breweries, for causing the fall of Al Capone. The Special Investigations Unit of the IRS prepared the case against Capone. This group was headed by Elmer Irey, and his subordinate, Frank G. Wilson, conducted the investigation of Capone's finances. The efforts of the various government agents investigating Capone were coordinated by George E. Q. Johnson. In the opinion of Laurence Bergreen, author of *Capone: The Man and the Era* (1994), Johnson was most deserving of the title "The Man Who Got Capone." However, pulp fans should fell free to theorize that Johnson had some help from Doc Savage and The Shadow.

Doc's Decision to Kill No More

In his second recorded adventure of the 1930s, *The Land of Terror*, Doc totally lost all sense of restraint in combating crime. He butchered criminals with no regard to the consequences. The most revealing episode of that novel was when Doc recklessly released the Smoke of Eternity just to have the pleasure of killing the evil Kar. Doc destroyed the whole of Thunder Island with its scientifically priceless population of dinosaurs just to kill one man. If you read the novel carefully, it will become blatantly clear that Doc only needed to chase Kar into the path of a carnivorous dinosaur in order to eliminate him.

The death of his father followed by his tutor Jerome Coffern had totally unhinged Doc. He was becoming a ruthless avenger of evil. This transformation had happened by the end of July 1931. The next known exploit of Doc was in June 1932, *Quest of the Spider* Doc's was still capable of slaying opponents, but his violent method had toned down significantly. Over the next five months, Doc would tune his methods of crime-fighting to become totally non-lethal. What cause Doc to change? He did take a trip to the Fortress of Solitude before *Quest of the Spider*, but meditation alone for weeks may not explain Doc's change of heart. He may have come into contact with The Shadow during the gap between *The Land of Terror* and *Quest of the Spider*. In fact, there is evidence that they participated in at least two cases together. Doc would have eventually been repelled by The Shadow's brutal activities. The Man of Bronze would have looked at the Knight of Darkness, and asked himself some poignant questions: Is this what I will become? A maniac who wipes out scores of criminals? A man who laughs at the suffering of misguided human beings? Doc's answer would have been to take solace in his Hippocratic Oath by affirming the sanctity of human life in all his future deeds.

The Colossal Steamship Swindle

In order to answer the point raised by Philip José Farmer about the rapid construction of a hospital between *The Man Who Shook The Earth* and its sequel, *Meteor Menace*, I had to imagine a hypothetical Chilean millionaire for whom Doc performed an earlier service. In Gibson's *The Wealth Seeker* (January 15, 1934). The Shadow as Lamont Cranston asserted that one of his friends was Pascual Cordillez, "the Chilean mine owner" (chap. 9).

In Gibson's *The Embassy Murders* (January 1, 1934), reference was made to an unrecorded adventure in South America. In 1931, The Shadow was responsible for the death of Alvarez

Menzone, swindler and murderer in Caracas, Venezuela (chap. 18). The fact of Menzone's death was unknown to the outside world. Menzone was in Caracas floating a fraudulent plan for a steamship line (chap. 12). In *Chronology of Shadows*, I placed this unrecorded adventure in September-October 1931. The Shadow was absent from New York for months according to *Double Z* (June 1932), a novel which I placed in November 1931. Reporter Clyde Burke "had received no orders from The Shadow during these recent months" (chap. 4). From Venezuela, The Shadow could have proceeded to Chile where he befriended Pascual Cordillez. Another possibility is that Cordillez was visiting Venezuela. I believe that Cordillez was also the Chilean millionaire who later built the hospital for Doc Savage. Doc and The Shadow must have been uncovering a huge swindle being perpetrated in South America involving steamship lines. They both befriended Cordillez during this period. Doc's ownership of an Atlantic steamship line, mentioned in *The South Pole Terror* (chap. 15), probably resulted from this unrecorded adventure.

Alvarez Menzone was probably just a pawn of more dangerous criminals. Since The Shadow impersonated Menzone years later in *The Embassy Murders*, he probably impersonated Menzone after killing him in order to trace his hidden masters. There are two masterminds from The Shadow series who could have been behind this gigantic fraud. The first in Isaac Coffran, a villain who battled The Shadow in *The Eyes of The Shadow* (September 1931) and *The Shadow Laughs* (October 1931). Coffran escaped after these two battles, which I placed in 1930. He never appeared in any future Shadow novels. This unrecorded case may have resulted in the end of his criminal career.

The second villain is Zanigew, the mastermind from *Shadow Over Alcatraz* (December 1, 1938). Although he only appeared in that one novel, it was clearly stated The Shadow had felt the hand of Zanigew as a hidden force in some of his earlier unrecorded exploits. "Dying crooks" had uttered the name "Zanigew" to the Shadow (chap. 2). Perhaps one of these crooks was Coffran. Zanigew was a physical giant of a man. He could have given Doc Savage as tough a fight as Bruze from *The Sargasso Ogre*. Although The Shadow didn't see Zanigew until *Shadow Over Alcatraz*, nothing would prevent Doc from physically confronting Zanigew. Due to his mistrust of The Shadow, Doc could have withheld a description of Zanigew from his rival crime-fighter.

If we are to believe Philip José Farmer's "After King Kong Fell," both The Shadow and Doc Savage returned to New York from South America in early October to witness the aftermath of a startling event at the Empire State Building.

The Limehouse Masterminds

As discussed in my "**Note**" following "The Sniper in the Sky" (entry #23), there was ample evidence of an unrecorded Doc Savage adventure in Britain during the gaps between the summers of 1931 and 1932. During this advent, Doc gained the eternal gratitude of both the British Secret Service and Scotland Yard. The Shadow had an unrecorded adventure in England during December 1931. This exploit was alluded to in *The Man from Scotland Yard* (August 1, 1935). Inspector Eric Delka of Scotland Yard recalled The Shadow's exploit (chap. 7): "Dimly Delka could remember rumors of strange events in London years before. Of a fight down in Limehouse way in which a cloaked avenger had wiped out a horde of ruffians to save a squad from Scotland Yard." Doc and The Shadow could both have been in England investigating crimes in the Limehouse district of London. We are now presented with an extraordinary possibility. The Limehouse angle raises the stakes considerably for this unrecorded adventure. An incredible confrontation between the forces of good and evil could have transpired in December 1931.

One was an idealist who abducted other individuals in order to brainwash them into his service for what was perceived as the greater good. The other was a merciless pragmatist who laughed at the death of his enemies. I am not describing Doc Savage and The Shadow, but the two greatest criminals of Limehouse. Both were adversaries of Scotland Yard, and one had been sought by the British Secret Service as well. Both were created by Sax Rohmer.

As you probably already guessed, the first criminal is Fu Manchu. I have already described many possible connections between him and Doc in the "Apocryphal Adventures" session. The only other thing that should be noted here is that Fu Manchu's whereabouts in 1931 are totally unknown. Cay Van Ash's "A Question of Time" in *The Rohmer Review* offered strong arguments that the events of *The Mask of Fu Manchu* (1932) transpired in 1930. The next chronological case involving the insidious mastermind was *The Bride of Fu Manchu* (1933). Fu Manchu gave a discourse on world politics in that novel (chap. 23). When coming to Germany, He only commented on President Von Hindenburg (called "Von Hindenburgh"). Hitler wasn't even mentioned. In April 1932, Von Hindenburg had defeated Hitler in a presidential election, but the elderly president would appoint the Nazi leader to the post of Chancellor in January 1933. Fu Manchu observed that incumbent Herbert Hoover "makes way for Franklin Roosevelt." The presidential campaign of 1932 would have begun in July 1932 with the nomination of Roosevelt as the Democratic candidate. Hence, *The Bride of Fu Manchu* happened in 1932.

The second Limehouse criminal is Marquis Yu'an Hee See. He only appeared in one novel, *Yu'an Hee See Laughs* (1932). The novel takes place in an unspecified year shortly before the month of March (chap. 1). Early 1931 would seem to be the likely time of the novel. Presiding over an empire of drugs and wholesale murder, the Marquis lacked the chivalry demonstrated by Fu Manchu. Like many a Doc Savage villain, he utilized a submarine in his schemes. He eluded justice at the end of this novel. The Marquis used the alias of Mr. King, a name adopted by an earlier Limehouse mastermind in Rohmer's *The Yellow Claw* (1915). The earlier Mr. King, never described by Rohmer, supposedly drowned in the Thames, but his body was not recovered. If the Marquis was actually the earlier Mr. King, then he was almost certainly allied with Fu Manchu. Rohmer's *The Golden Scorpion* (1919) suggested that Fu Manchu and the original Mr. King were agents of the same secret society. Fu Manchu would have escaped any battle with Doc Savage and The Shadow in 1931, but Yu'an Hee See could have perished.

In *Pirate of the Pacific* (chap. 12), Renny recognized a species of Asian jungle spider, whose bite was fatal. Fu Manchu used such creatures, particularly the Scarlet Brides from *President Fu Manchu* (1936).

The Shadow's Experiments in the Rehabilitation of Criminals

Although The Shadow killed criminals without hesitation, he did display some interest in the peaceful rehabilitation of criminals. The Shadow had convinced minor criminals to mend their ways in *Kings of Crime* (December 15, 1932) and *Road of Crime* (October 1, 1933). I placed *Kings of Crime* in the summer of 1932 and *Road of Crime* in the spring of 1933. The most famous case of The Shadow's rehabilitation experiments happened in *The Broken Napoleons* (July 15, 1936), a novel assigned to December 1935. The Shadow was now abducting criminals in large groups, and conducting them to an island in the West Indies. There the criminals were being rehabilitated under the direction of criminologist Slade Farrow. The Shadow first met Farrow in *The Green Box* (March 15, 1934), a novel placed in January-February 1934.

The logical assumption would be that Farrow persuaded The Shadow to establish this island. Nevertheless, the evidence of *The Sealed Box* (December 1, 1937), a novel assigned to July 1937, would totally refute this argument. *The Sealed Box* (chap. 4) told of an unrecorded adventure that happened five years earlier. This exploit would have occurred in 1932. Traveling to the town of Southbury, The Shadow discovered that Larry Sherrin had embezzled a large sum of money from his employer, Richard Whilton.

Sherrin intended to frame others for the embezzlement, and to use the money to establish himself as the leader of a gang of robbers. Although The Shadow uncovered Sherrin's villainy, he was extremely merciful towards Sherrin. With the knowledge of Richard Whilton, The Shadow imprisoned Sherrin on the island in the West Indies. There Sherrin would be rehabilitated. I placed the episode with Sherrin in April 1932. It was not until five years later that Sherrin was allowed to return to the United States.

The Shadow's meeting with Sherrin happened before Slade Farrow arrived on the scene in 1934. The Shadow's island must have been operational before Farrow became its supervisor. Farrow's involvement permitted The Shadow to dramatically expand his island prison. Here is a brief chronological summary of The Shadow's activities mentioned in this discussion .

1932:	April	The Shadow spared Larry Sherrin, and incarcerated him on a remote island.
	Summer	The Shadow rehabilitated another criminal, Herbert Carpenter, but doesn't utilize the island *(Kings of Crime)*.
1933:	Spring	The Shadow rehabilitated another criminal, Graham Wellerton, without use of the island *(Road of Crime)*.
1934:	Jan.-Feb.	The Shadow met Slade Farrow *(The Green Box)*.
1935:	Dec.	Farrow was supervising the island prison to which The Shadow was shipping mass amounts of crooks *(The Broken Napoleons)*.
1937:	July	Sherrin was released from the island *(The Sealed Box)*.

If The Shadow didn't get the idea for his island from Farrow, then who inspired him to take an interest in the rehabilitation of criminals through such a radical means? The answer has to be Doc Savage. Doc's Crime College had been in operation since at least 1929. If crooks in *The Annihilist, The Purple Dragon, The Flying Goblin* and *The Talking Devil* could have learned the secret of the Crime College, then The Shadow could also have unearthed the truth. During their adventures together in 1931, the two heroes could have debated the merits of the Crime College. To The Shadow, the destruction of a man's personality by brain surgery would have been no different than the taking of a man's life. After Doc's surgery, the man had mentally been murdered to all intents and purposes. Doc may then have challenged The Shadow to create a rehabilitation method that was better. The Shadow toyed with his island idea in April 1932. He put at least one criminal, Larry Sherrin, there before largely ignoring the whole proposed enterprise. The Shadow didn't even bother to use the island when rehabilitating two minor crooks in *Kings of Crime* and *Road of Crime*. The Shadow needed the proper supervisor to make this grand scheme practical. It wasn't until two years later that The Shadow found such an individual, Slade Farrow.

The Shadow may have gotten the idea for a remote island location for his rehabilitation center from one of Doc's enterprises. In Laurence Donovan's *The Men Who Smiled No More* (chap. 2), it was mentioned that several Crime College graduates were given jobs in the nitrates mines of a Pacific island chain. Doc was on the board of directors of the company that owned the islands. On the other hand, The Shadow may have gotten the idea for his private island rehabilitation center from British adventurer Bulldog Drummond, who had utilized a private island prison for communist spies and agitators in H. C. "Sapper" McNeile's *The Black Gang* (1922). Drummond's prison, however, was used for rigid punishment rather than benign rehabilitation. The inspiration for an enlightened method of rehabilitation could only have come to The Shadow through his contact with Doc Savage. Doc was almost certainly aware of The Shadow's island operation. Although Doc would have viewed the whole enterprise as an inferior version of the Crime College, it would have convinced the bronze adventurer that The Shadow was capable of pursuing constructive paths in his war on crime.

Other Possible Common Enemies

Some villains may have fought both Doc Savage and The Shadow, but never the two together. One such candidate would be Merry John Thomas, Doc's antagonist in *Cargo Unknown*. Thomas had been a big shot in New York and Chicago during Prohibition. Doc, who had been fighting gangsters since 1929, never heard of Thomas when the two met in the closing days of World War II. My *Chronology of Shadows* argued that The Shadow established his New York base in 1928. Perhaps fear of The Shadow caused Thomas to abandon a life of crime in that year. By World War II, Thomas' retirement fund had been exhausted, and he was forced to resume a criminal career.

The Shadow visited Moscow in an unrecorded adventure in November 1932. He was returning from this adventure in *Murder Trail* (March 15, 1933), a novel placed in December 1932. Perhaps The Shadow tangled with Frunzoff Nosh from *The Red Spider*, who had been active in Soviet politics since the 1918 Uritsky assassination. Makaroff from *Terror Wears No Shoes* was probably active at this time as well.

Cadwiller Olden, Doc's antagonist from *Repel* (*The Deadly Dwarf*), had been operating as a criminal for at least "two years" (chap. 12) before encountering *The Man of Bronze*. Maybe Olden crossed the path of The Shadow earlier. Olden's demise in his battle with Doc is far from conclusive. Will Murray dropped strong hints of Olden's possible resurrection before the new paperback novels were suspended. Maybe Olden was being considered as the villain of Will Murray's proposed novel teaming up Doc and The Shadow.

The Mystery of Judge Crater

There are conflicting solutions offered for the actual disappearance of Judge Joseph Force Crater in the adventures of The Shadow and Doc Savage. Crater had vanished on August 6, 1930. In Gibson's *Double Z*, Crater appeared under the alias of Judge Tolland. When the novel opened, Tolland had been missing for "fourteen months" (chap. 1). Tolland had voluntarily vanished because he was fearful of the master criminal known as Double Z. If the fictional Tolland disappeared around the time of his real-life counterpart, then the novel would have been set in either October or November 1931 (I chose the later month). *Double Z* tracked down Tolland, murdered him, and then had the judge's body secretly buried.

In February 1937, Doc would find Judge Crater held prisoner in Greenland during the events of *Devil on the Moon*. Crater was being held captive by the Man in the Moon, an international spy who imprisoned people with valuable information. How could Doc meet Crater six years after his murder by Double Z? Double Z may have been preparing an actor to impersonate Judge Crater. With Crater secretly buried, the impostor would appear and take Crater's place. However, Double Z's death at the hands of The Shadow forced the impostor to go into hiding. The Man in the Moon then captured the impostor under the mistaken belief that he was the real Crater.

Overlords of the Green Shirts

Both Doc and The Shadow had cases with villains based on Horia Sima, a fascist leader who disappeared from Rumania in January 1941. Sima's political party, the Iron Guard, was know as the Green Shirts. In *Peril in the North*, the Sima surrogate was called Mungen. In Theodore Tinsley's Shadow novel, *Gems of Jeopardy* (September 1, 1941), Sima appeared under the alias of the Colonel. Like Mungen, the Colonel fled to the United States. The Colonel didn't fare well on his arrival on American shores. He was murdered by an indigenous criminal, Mr. X.

Since the real Sima later surfaced in Germany and migrated to Spain, it's probably best to envision Mungen and the Colonel as Sima's top lieutenants in the Green Shirts.

The Hidalgo-Guatemala Connection

The Shadow reappeared in 1937 in his identity of Kent Allard. This story is told in *The Shadow Unmasks*. Allard had disappeared in Guatemala in 1925. Allard pretended to have been lost in the jungle for the last twelve years. He had actually been fighting crime as The Shadow during those years. By this time, Doc Savage was almost certainly aware that The Shadow impersonated Lamont Cranston. Doc would have come into contact with The Shadow in his Cranston identity in 1931. Doc's intelligence network consisting of Crime College graduates could have been used to track the movements of the true Lamont Cranston in various parts of the globes. Doc would have realized that The Shadow was not truly Cranston.

When Allard reappeared, Doc would have harbored suspicions. As discussed earlier, Doc probably was well aware of Allard's strange disappearance in World War I, and the false POW camp story spread by Allard to cover his activities as the Dark Eagle. Although Dent's notes indicate that the fictional Central American republic of Hidalgo was based on Nicaragua in *The Man of Bronze*, the description of Hidalgo in *The Golden Peril* (ghosted for Dent by Harold A, Davis) more closely matches Guatemala. If Hidalgo was really Guatemala, then Doc could have used his contacts in the government and the Valley of the Vanished to investigate Allard's story. There can be little doubt that Doc discovered the truth about The Shadow's real identity.

Mention should be made of Daniel Swartzinski's theory in

"The Mended Eagle" from *Echoes #25* (June 1986). Various hints were offered in the early Shadow novels that the cloaked crime-fighter had been disfigured during World War I. Gibson abandoned this plot line, but it has always been speculated that Allard may have received plastic surgery shortly before the events of *The Shadow Unmasks*. Mr. Swartzinski's theory was that Doc Savage performed the plastic surgery on Allard's face. Doc was certainly qualified to perform this operation. Doc was described as a "master" of plastic surgery in *The Mystery on the Snow* (chap. 26). However, I strongly doubt that The Shadow would have desired that his secret identity be made known to Doc. Also The Shadow would not desire to be put in the uncomfortable position of owing such a huge debt to Doc. The two adventurers would have been rivals and occasionally uneasy allies. My own theory is that Allard performed the plastic surgery himself after mastering an ancient Aztec method of plastic surgery encountered in Gibson's *Six Men of Evil* (February 15, 1933).

If you looked through the pages of The Shadow series, there are references to Hidalgo in *The Crime Crypt* (June 15, 1934) and *Cyro* (December 15, 1934). In these novels, Hidalgo was not meant to be the fictional Central American republic from the Doc Savage series, but the real-life Mexican state of the same name. In *The Crime Crypt* (chapters 1-2), a crook named Martin Havelock pretended that his illegal wealth came from silver mines in Hidalgo. The title villain of *Cyro* (chap. 12) actually owned mines in Hidalgo. The mines were supposedly filled with gold, but they had failed to produce that valuable commodity (chap. 22). Cyro attempted to steal a treasure of gold doubloons retrieved from the wreck of a Spanish galleon. Cyro's scheme was to pretend that the stolen gold had come from his non-productive mines in Hidalgo. The activities of Havelock and Cyro demonstrate that it was common practice among master criminals of the 1930s to have some knowledge of mines in Hidalgo. Doc Savage must have been aware of this criminal trend. Consequently as part of a misinformation campaign, he named his warehouse the Hidalgo Trading Company instead of the Guatemala Trading Company. Crooks would eventually learn of the warehouse's existence. There were also rumors about Doc's secret source of wealth circulating in the underworld. Although the criminals of *White Eyes*, *The Golden Peril*, *Poison Island* and *They Died Twice* managed to pursue solid leads about Doc's gold supply, other criminals were probably misled by the sign on Doc's warehouse. These foolish crooks blindly looked for the gold in the Mexican State of Hidalgo, and found only a false trail.

The Shadow would have known that Doc's gold supply was really in Guatemala. The Mayans in Guatemala would never have revealed any information about the Valley of the Vanished, but Kent Allard had the loyalty of a tribe of Xinca Indians in that country. The Xincas must have spied on the Mayans, and relayed all pertinent information to The Shadow.

Who was the Police Commissioner?

Doc Savage generally received remarkable cooperation form the individual holding the title of New York police commissioner. In the early novels, the police never interfered in Doc's activities. Every policeman knew Doc by sight. He was permitted to violate speeding laws. Prisoners were allowed to be kept in his custody for eventual transfer to the Crime College.

The police commissioner was only named twice in the Doc Savage series. *The Invisible-Box Murders* featured Commissioner Stance, who had embarked on his career as a cop pounding a beat in Gravesend. His depiction as "acting head of the police department" (chap. 3) would imply that he was a temporary holder of the office. In *The Whisker of Hercules* (chap. 5), the commissioner's surname was given as Boyer.

In The Shadow series, the police commissioner is a major supporting character. For most of the series, he was the impulsive and domineering Ralph Weston, a snob who cultivated the city's financial elite. During 1934-35, Wainwright Barth, a thoroughly incompetent official, replaced Weston for lengthy periods. After 1935, Weston remained commissioner into the late 1940s.

In order for Doc and The Shadow to coexist, then Weston must be assumed to be the police commissioner in the overwhelming majority of Doc's exploits. The reference to Commissioner Boyer in *The Whisker of Hercules* can be easily dismissed. Boyer could be an alias for Weston just as certain world leaders in Doc Savage were given false names. However, the following other matters need to be reconciled:

1) In December 1934, the police commissioner's background was supposedly that of a policeman who rose through the ranks (*White Eyes*, chap. 21). The background doesn't seem to fit Weston, who was an officer in World War I. Weston's snobbery is incompatible with the background of a hard-boiled professional policeman. It is inconceivable that Barth was a policeman promoted on merit. The description of the commissioner in *White Eyes* only fits Stance.

2) In September 1935, Doc's relations with the police department deteriorate due to a change in police commissioners (*The Vanisher*, chap. 13).

3) During July 23 to August 2, 1936, a change of commissioners resulted in another temporary suspension of Doc's honorary commission (*The Whistling Wraith*, chap. 15).

4) During September 13-17, 1940, A career policeman named Stance was the commissioner in *The Invisible-Box Murders*.

When I read The Shadow novels in submission order, I saw that Barth only replaced Weston for three intervals. Of course, various factors forced me to rearrange the submission order to get a coherent chronological order. Still, I only ended up with four absences by Weston. Ralph Weston first appeared in *Hidden Death* (September 1932). In this novel, Weston had his first meeting with Detective (later Inspector) Joe Cardona. The impression was given that Weston had only been commissioner for a short period. I placed the events of *Hidden Death* in March 1932. This is the known career of Ralph Weston based on my observations in Chronology of Shadows. I have indicated in bold characters the events from the Doc Savage series that raise questions.

1932:	March	First known appearance of Ralph Weston.
1934:	Jan.	Weston left New York to organize the National Police of the South American country of Garacua (actually the Caribbean island of Cuba). Barth replaced him during this absence. A military coup in Garacua (Cuba) happened during Weston's visit. The new government felt that the presence of a prominent American in their government might lead to charges of "Yankee Imperialism" from the political opposition. A cordial understanding was reached with Weston by the Garacuan authorities, and Weston returned to New York to resume his duties. Barth stepped down as commissioner.
	Late June	The political situation stabilized in Garacua (Cuba), and Weston accepted a second invitation from the indigenous authorities to reorganize the National Police. Barth became commissioner again.
	Early Dec.	Someone with a totally different background than Weston or Barth was police commissioner. This person was a career policeman, who dealt with Doc Savage.
	Late Dec.	Weston returned from Garacua (Cuba) to become commissioner again. Barth had earlier left on a trip to Europe.
1935:	Late Feb.	Weston left New York for supposedly a long vacation in the Caribbean. Weston spent some time in Bermuda, but he really might have been sent to the Caribbean by the United States in order to be close to Cuba and monitor political events there. Back from his European trip, Barth became commissioner again.
	June	Weston was again commissioner. He must have returned to New York in either May or June (None of the Shadow novels placed by me in May identified the commissioner by name).
	August	Barth was again commissioner. Weston's absence was unexplained.
	Early Sept.	Weston was again commissioner. He would remain in this position for the remainder of The Shadow series.
	Mid-Sept.	A change of commissioners caused problems for Doc.
1936:	July 2-Aug. 2	A change of commissioners caused Doc's honorary commission to be suspended.
1940	Sept 13-17	Stance, a career policeman, was "acting" police commissioner.
1949:	June	Last known appearance of Ralph Weston as police commissioner.

This chronological arrangement answers one of the points raised earlier by the Doc Savage series. It was the replacement of Barth by Weston in September 1935, which resulted in Doc's problem with his honorary commission in *The Vanisher*. If a circumstance arose when Weston and Barth were both absent, who would be the commissioner? The answer is probably a high-ranking career policeman named Stance. The description of the commissioner in *White Eyes* fits Stance. Barth must have been gone in early December 1934. Most likely, Barth had already embarked on his European trip, and Stance was temporarily assuming the position until Weston's return. In *Chronology of Shadows*, I assigned Gibson's *The Golden Quest* (May 1, 1935) to five days in early December 1934. The novel does not mention the police commissioner, and the events would be chronologically concurrent with *White Eyes*. The events of two Shadow novels overlap the events of *The Whistling Wraith*. These novels are *Loot of Death* (February 1, 1937) and *Murder House* (March 15, 1937). *Loot of Death* transpired during July 17-24,1936, and *Murder House* during July 28 to August 2, 1936. The police commissioner did not appear in *Loot of Death*. In *Murder House* (chap. 7), an unnamed police commissioner informed Inspector Joe Cardona by letter to take a vacation of two weeks. This commissioner's surname was never given. He may not have been Weston. Ralph Weston could have taken a summer vacation, and left someone else, probably Stance, temporarily in charge. It was Weston's temporary replacement who caused the problem with Doc's honorary commission in *The Whistling Wraith*.

We are now left with Stance's appearance in *The Invisible-Box Murders* during the second half of September 1940. *Chronology of Shadows* has the events of two Shadow novels, *The House on the Ledge* (April 15, 1941) and *Mansion of Crime* (March 1, 1941), assigned to the second half of September. Neither novel featured an appearance by Commissioner Weston. Stance could have filled in as commissioner when

Weston began a vacation in the middle of September

Since all the discrepancies regarding police commissioners have been resolved, the relationship between Doc Savage and Ralph Weston can be properly evaluated. Weston probably became commissioner in January 1932. He was not the commissioner during the events of *The Man of Bronze* and *The Land of Terror*. Those adventures transpired in 1931. He was also not the commissioner when King Kong climbed the Empire State Building in the same year. However, Weston was the nameless commissioner for most of the series beginning with *Quest of the Spider*. In February 1932, Weston was seriously injured. Fortunately, Doc Savage was there to prevent his death (*The Phantom City*, chap. 7): "It was well known that Doc's magical skill at surgery had once saved the life of the police commissioner." Weston's first meeting with Cardona happened a month after this operation. Weston would show his gratitude in to Doc in many ways. Weston granted Doc and his men honorary commissions in the New York police department. The rank of these commissions was originally captain, which was later modified to inspector. During the tenure of Weston's predecessor, traffic cops had been told to fully cooperate with Doc: "New York City traffic policemen had been instructed by their chiefs to give every assistance to this remarkable man of bronze" (*The Land of Fear*, chap. 10). Weston granted Doc authority to use a regulation police siren in his car (*The Polar Treasure*, chap. 5). The siren had first appeared in *Quest of the Spider* (chap. 11), where it was described as "newly installed." At Weston's orders, all policemen were shown a picture of Doc and given orders to assist the bronze adventurer in every way (*Quest of Qui*, chap. 6). An order bearing Weston's signature was posted on the bulletin boards of all precinct stations (*The Mystery on the Snow*, chap. 10). The order directed that "Doc Savage was to receive every cooperation, and no questions asked."

In May 1934, Weston set foot in the Hidalgo Trading Company during the events of *Cold Death* (chap. 24). Laurence Donovan described Weston as "a stocky red-faced man." Considering that Weston was an extremely impulsive and excitable individual," the adjective "red-faced" would be apt. However, Weston was not "stocky." Donovan must have confused Weston with Inspector Cardona, who was stocky. Considering that Donovan made mistakes like claiming that Habeas Corpus originated from Australia instead of Arabia, his physical description of the police commissioner should not be viewed as totally accurate.

The strong friendship between the police commissioner and Doc became disrupted by Weston's heavy involvement with Cuba during 1934-35. Weston left Cuba in December 1934 just when Doc arrived there during the events of *White Eyes*.. When Weston returned to the Caribbean in late February 1935, he did some investigating of strange rumors about activities at a Cuban sugar plantation. Although Weston could find no conclusive proof, he correctly suspected that Doc had been illegally smuggling gold into Cuba. Doc had abandoned this operation after the events of *White Eyes*. This discovery led Weston to become extremely suspicious of Doc. Weston feared that Doc might now be smuggling gold into the United in violation Gold Confiscation Act (1933) and other Federal laws. Under Barth, Doc's good relations with the police continued.

When Weston returned from his trips to Cuba and the Caribbean, strong questions started to be asked about Doc's activities. It was perhaps understandable that Weston was becoming somewhat paranoid. In the course of his adventures with The Shadow, famous criminologists, as well as respected members of the elite Cobalt Club, had been exposed as master criminals. If these other prominent men were exposed as criminals, what about Doc Savage? These suspicions of Doc were fueled by Stance, who was probably the deputy commissioner of the New York police department Weston's relationship with Doc reached their low point in September 1935 when Weston returned from a brief unexplained absence (possibly another trip to Cuba). On the flimsy evidence of planted fingerprints, Weston ordered a police dragnet directed against Doc (*The Vanisher*, chap. 13). Weston should have remembered that an earlier gang of crooks had used fake fingerprints to frame Doc in *The Spook Legion* (chap. 11). When Doc proved his innocence in *The Vanisher*, Weston felt extremely embarrassed. He vanquished his paranoid suspicions, and renewed his friendship with Doc. However, Stance continued to view Doc with unease. While briefly replacing Weston in *The Whistling Wraith* and *The Invisible-Box Murders*, Stance would cause serious problems for Doc.

Evidence of Weston's renewed faith in Doc can be found in *The Purple Dragon*, an adventure set in August 1940. Convincing evidence had been planted against Monk and Ham, which made them look like the murderers of a young woman. Doc convinced Weston that his assistants should be released in his custody by arranging a telephone call to the supposed victim (chap. 17). Weston never heard this woman's voice before, but he believed her statements because Doc guaranteed her veracity. Monk and Ham were released. In *Terror Takes 7* (chap. 6), Weston delayed an Assistant District Attorney's efforts to get Doc's commission revoked even though the bronze adventurer was a murder suspect.

Sometimes false evidence and public pressure, however, gave Weston no option but to pursue Doc. A major example was when Weston reluctantly led a posse of nineteen prominent men to capture Doc in *The Mindless Monsters* (chap. 13). According to Alan Hathway's *The Headless Men* (chap, 9) and *The Mindless Monsters* (chap. 8), Weston had promoted Doc to an honorary deputy police commissioner. The promotion would have happened by September 1939, the time of *The Headless Men*. Doc's commission remained upgraded until at least the events of *The Mindless Monsters* in October 1939.

However, Stance eventually convinced Weston to downgrade it back to inspector. If Stance was the real deputy commissioner, then we can assume that he was made extremely uneasy by Doc's title. Doc's rank was an inspector in September 1940 during *The Invisible-Box Murders* (chap. 3).

Whatever Doc's problems with Weston and Stance, there is nothing which suggests that The Shadow intervened to augment Doc's trouble with the police. The Shadow may have lectured Doc that this was the price paid for acting against crime in the open. The Shadow had much less problems with the police because most of the time they refused to acknowledge his existence publicly. The Shadow also let Weston and Cardona get most of the credit for the cases that he solved.

Other New York Crime-fighters

Philip José Farmer's *Doc Savage: His Apocalyptic Life* claimed that Doc Savage coexisted in New York with other heroes besides The Shadow. These heroes include Rex Stout's Nero Wolfe and two pulp heroes, the Avenger and the Spider. Mr. Farmer even briefly mentioned that Leslie Charteris' the Saint, who spent a considerable amount of time in New York during the 1930s, also coexisted with Doc and the Shadow.

The New York police commissioner did appear in the Avenger series, but he was unnamed. Both the adventures of Nero Wolfe and Saint featured New York commissioners whose names are not Weston, Barth, Stance or even Boyer. The commissioners from these series are minor supporting characters. In order to pretend that these characters exist in the same fictional universe, then the references to the identity of the police commissioner in the novels by Stout and Charteris would need to be reconciled with both the exploits of Doc Savage and The Shadow. The commissioners encountered by Wolfe and the Saint either are Weston, Barth or Stance acting under different names, or there are one or two other fellows to be thrown into this game of musical chairs. Such an intellectual exercise is outside the scope of this present discussion.

The Spider series is an entirely different manner. Commissioner Stanley Kirkpatrick is a major supporting character whose activities can not be reconciled with Weston, Barth and Stance. In fact, the entire Spider series can't be reconciled with the adventures of Doc Savage and The Shadow. The crimes committed in the Spider series were so incredibly violent that one can not imagine either Doc or The Shadow idly sitting back in order to let another hero routinely handle such cases. Thousands of New York resident perished in several novels. Last but not least, the Spider is too much like The Shadow. The two crime-fighters even dressed similarly. One can not imagine the New York Police relentlessly hunting the Spider while pretending that The Shadow doesn't exist. However, one could reconcile the New York police department's policies towards the Shadow and the Saint. Like the Spider, the original version of the Saint in the 1930s was that of a vigilante who ruthlessly executed criminals above the law. Both Scotland Yard and the New York police department were trying to pin these murders on the Saint. The Saint's methods of crime-fighting are very distinct from those of The Shadow. If a vigilante openly feuding with the police is needed to be added to a fictional milieu inhabited by both Doc Savage and The Shadow, then the Saint, rather than the Spider, is that man.

The Men Who Would Be Khan

If Doc and The Shadow were rivals, then so were their most infamous adversaries from the 1930s. Both John Sunlight and Shiwan Khan, who fought The Shadow four times, were running around the Chinese province of Sinkiang posing as modern-day incarnations of Genghis Khan. Shiwan was a direst descendant of Genghis Khan. Sunlight's ancestry is a mystery. Maybe he also was a direct descendant of the Mongol conqueror. For speculation regarding this possibility, see "John Sunlight and the Si-Fan Succession" from *Rick Lai's Secret Histories: Criminal Masterminds*.

The Prevention of the Fourth Reich

Both Doc and The Shadow halted plans to have a future leader of a Fourth Reich. Doc prevented Hitler's escape from Germany in *Violent Night* (*The Hate Genius*). In *Death Has Grey Eyes* (April 1945), The Shadow ended the career of a young Nazi smuggled into the United States for the purpose of being the next Fuehrer. I place *Violent Night* in June 1944, and *Death Has Grey Eyes* in September-November 1944. The evil Jonas Sown, the secret ruler of the Axis powers, was probably behind both schemes. Sown must have originally wanted Hitler to escape. Under a new identity, Hitler would help Sown establish a new Reich probably in South America. When Doc foiled Hitler's escape in June 1944, Sown then turned his hopes on a young Nazi whom he was secretly training. The Shadow removed this proposed new Fuehrer from the scene permanently in November 1944. This was the same month in which *Rock Sinister* took place. As noted in my discussion of that novel, Sown may have exposed a prominent South American leader to his emotion charging device in January 1943. This exposure caused the South American leader to plan a fascist takeover that Doc averted in November 1944. Sown must have been trying to prepare the South American base for his Fourth Reich. With his plans for a Fourth Reich foiled, Sown fled Europe in December 1944. Sown eventually decided to seek control of the Communist Bloc in 1949, when Doc defeated him once and for all in *The Frightened Fish*.

Here is a brief chronological breakdown of the important events relative to the foiling of the Fourth Reich. The comments about the Shadow's activities during December 1943 to August 25, 1944 are based on references in *Death Has Grey Eyes* (chap. 20)

1943:   Jan.   The President of Uruguay suffered a strange illness shortly before the end of his term. It is suspected that Jonas Sown brought about this illness by exposing the foreign leader to his mind-altering device.

	Dec.	The Shadow secretly arrived in France to conduct secret operations against the Nazis.
1944:	June 6	The Allies landed in Normandy.
	June	Hitler attempted to escape Europe, but Doc Savage captured him in Switzerland *(Violent Night)*. Unfortunately, Jonas Sown dispatched Otto Skorzeny on a successful mission to free Hitler from his Allied captors in Switzerland.
	Aug.25	The Shadow was in Paris when Allied troops liberate it.
	Sept.	The Shadow went to Germany to investigate a plot to plant Hitler's successor inside the United States *(Death Has Grey Eyes,* chap. 1). Jonas Sown was almost certainly behind this scheme.
	Oct.	The Shadow returned to the United States.
	Nov.	In the United States, The Shadow destroyed the schemes of the man chosen as the next Fuehrer *(Death Has Grey Eyes,* chapters 2-20). In Uruguay, the country's ex-president attempted a fascist takeover *(Rock Sinister)*. Doc Savage crushed this plot (Lester Dent altered the names of the South American politician and his country, as well as pretending that the scheme's chief operative was still in office).
	Dec.	Sown fled Europe.
1945:	June	Doc forced Sown to destroy his emotion charging device *(The Screaming Man)*.
1949:	January	Death of Jonas Sown *(The Frightened Fish)*.

Clubland Heroes

If Doc and the Shadow needed to meet, they probably would choose some neutral ground. The Shadow wouldn't go to the eighty-sixth floor, nor would Doc go to the Shadow's sanctum. Perhaps they met at a club where both were members. As Lamont Cranston, The Shadow belonged to the exclusive Cobalt Club. Doc would never join such an organization. It was populated by greedy snobs. Doc was president of the Scientific Club (*The King of Terror*, chap. 1). The Shadow would never have joined a club over which Doc exercised control.

Even more restrictive than the Cobalt Club was the Midas Club, where Ham Brooks lived (*The Man Who Shook The Earth*, chap. 2). In order to join, you must have five millions which you made yourself. Money received through an inheritance didn't count. Although The Shadow had probably done this financial feat during his impersonation of Lamont Cranston, it is doubtful that he would want to join the Midas Club. The Shadow wanted to be near Commissioner Weston in order to pump him for information. It would be impossible for Weston to join the Midas Club. The Shadow also wanted to keep an eye on the large number of criminal masterminds who joined the Cobalt Club. No criminal in his right mind would join the Midas Club. What crook wants to live near one of Doc's principal assistants? In short, there were no material advantages for The Shadow to join the Midas Club.

There is the Explorers League, an organization mentioned in *The Men Vanished* (chap. 1) and *Pirate Isle* (chap. 1). At least Doc and Johnny belonged to this club. The Shadow could join this organization twice. First, he could gain a membership by impersonating Cranston. It's possible that the real Cranston was already a member when The Shadow coerced him into complying with the assumption of his identity. Second, The Shadow could join in his real identity of Kent Allard. Famous explorers and noted scientists could be found every night in the Explorers League. The Shadow would want to join this club for two reasons. First, he would view the members as his peers.

Second, he could gather valuable information about scientific advances and recent museum acquisitions A lot of The Shadow's cases involved either the theft of new inventions or museum artifacts. This would be the ideal place for the two crime-fighting rivals to meet.

It could also be assumed that Clark Savage Sr. was also a member of the Explorers League. Besides Johnny, Doc's other assistants were probably members as well. Lester Dent's Explorers League was based on a real-life organization, the Explorers Club, which has its main headquarters in New York. The following is the history of the real-life Explorers Club:

1904 The club was founded by Henry Collins Walsh "to further general exploration, to spread knowledge of the same, and to encourage ex-

	plorers in their work by evincing interest and sympathy, and especially by bringing them in personal contact and binding them in the bonds of goods fellowship."
1905	The club held its first meeting on October 25 in rented rooms at 23 West 67th Street.
1912	The club moved into its first home at 345 Amsterdam Avenue.
1922	The club moved to 47 West 76th Street.
1928	The club moved to 544 Cathedral Parkway.
1932	The club moved to 10 West 72nd Street
1965	The club moved to 46 East 70th Street.

In *The Crimson Serpent* (chap. 4), Doc attended a meeting of the Scientific Adventurers' Club in Chicago. The Shadow also visited Chicago on occasion and may have joined the club as either Lamont Cranston or Kent Allard. The Scientific Adventurers' Club is based on the Adventurers Club of Chicago founded in 1911 by Major W. Robert Foran. The club still exists today, and its address is 714 S. Dearborn, Unit 6, Chicago, IL 60605.

Savage Family Secrets

The Shadow and Doc both had adventures in London. There is a club there which is one of the more unusual associations for men. It is called the Savage Club, and has existed since 1857. It was founded by a group of inspired celebrants at the Crown Tavern. Nobody knows for certain how the club got its name.

The most accepted explanation for the naming of the Savage Club is that it was christened in a jocular fashion after Richard Savage (1698-1743), a minor poet. He was also a blackmailer and a convicted murderer. In 1727, Savage was found guilty of fatally stabbing a man during a fight in a brothel. Savage was sentenced to death, but he escaped the gallows due to the influence of his literary friends. They successfully convinced the King to pardon Savage on the grounds that his violent act was really self-defense. Savage eventually died in a debtors' prison in Bristol. Richard Savage is only remembered today because his friend, Dr. Samuel Johnson, wrote a famous biography about him.

The story about Richard being the source of the club's name can be found in Percy V. Bradshaw's *'Brother Savages and Guests': A History of the Savage Club 1857-1957* (W. H. Allen, 1958). This assertion is denied in Stephen Fiske's "The Club Title," which was published together with other articles by Savage Club members in *A Savage Club Souvenir* (1916). Fiske gives three other contrary explanations. One popular story asserts that it was named after Henry Savage, a writer. Henry Savage was "a penny-a-liner," who was discovered dead from starvation in Covent Garden Market. The location of Savage's demise was a center of the most abundant food in London. According to Fiske, the Club's founders viewed the incident of a man starving among heaps of foods as tragically ironic. They supposedly formed the Savage Club "to immortalize this terrible incident of London life." Another story claims that the club got its name from a joke that journalists, poets and artists are really "savages." A fourth version of the story merely stated the name Savage Club was chosen because it was less pretentious than the alternatives (the Addison Club, the Goldsmith Club or the Johnson Club) under consideration. According to Wikipedia on the Internet, there is yet another explanation for the Savage Club's name, a waitress at the Crown Tavern referred to the patrons as "that bunch of savages!" Most of the Club's members are writers, doctors, lawyers, actors, musicians and artists.

Neither the poet Richard Savage nor the writer Henry Savage should be confused with Colonel Richard Henry Savage (1846-1903). An American engineer, diplomat and novelist, Colonel Savage inspired Henry Ralston, the business manager of Street and Smith, to authorize the creation of fictional heroes christened Doc Savage and Richard Henry Benson (the Avenger). Colonel Savage's connection to Doc Savage and the Avenger was revealed in Will Murray's "The Forgotten Doc

Savage." This article was first published in Mr. Murray's *Secrets of Doc Savage* (Odyssey Publications, 1981).

I have a different explanation for the christening of the Savage Club. The logo of the club features a Plains Indian. According to Pat Savage in *I Died Yesterday* (chap. 3), her grandfather was noted Indian fighter in "the northwest." Pat's grandfather could have been in western Canada when news of the California Gold Rush reached there in 1849. Pat's grandfather could have joined the large groups of Canadians who traveled to California through Oregon. During the trek through Oregon, these Canadian prospectors came into conflict with the Bannock Indians and Shoshone Indians. In 1857, Pat's grandfather could have been one of the celebrants at the Crown Tavern in England. A writer may have commented on the irony of a man named Savage having fought "savages" in Oregon. Pat's grandfather may have retorted that his Indian opponents were noble and chivalrous. Furthermore, Pat's grandfather would have stated that the writers of London were the true "savages" of the world. From this remark, a discussion resulted which led to the formation of the Savage Club. Possibly this discussion also mentioned the notorious Richard Savage and the ill-fated Henry Savage.

According to Philip José Farmer's *Doc Savage: His Apocalyptic Life*, Pat's grandfather was a noted British scientist who committed suicide in prison in the late nineteenth century. Mr. Farmer does not give the year of this misguided scientist's death, but he apparently perished before the birth of Doc's father in the late 1870s. Doc's great-grandfather had been arrested in connection with criminal experiments revolving around the secret notebooks of Victor Frankenstein. In *I Died Yesterday*, Pat stated that she and Doc have a common grandfather, but *Violent Night* (*The Hate Master*) identified her as Doc's "distant" cousin (chap. 2). Mr. Farmer attempted to reconcile the discrepancy by identifying Pat's grandfather as Doc's great-grandfather. It is possible that Pat's grandfather was both an Indian fighter in North America during the Gold

Rush of 1849 and an imitator of Victor Frankenstein in the 1870s. Perhaps this scandal caused members of the Savage Club to obscure the role of Pat's grandfather in the adoption of the name for the club. Pat Savage must have only known about her grandfather's activities in 1849. She had no knowledge of his dangerous experiments in the 1870s.

The Savage Club professes to welcome "solitary men or irrelevant characters, kind or quirky ones." Among its members was John Dickson Carr's Dr. Gideon Fell (see the short biography of Fell written by Carr for Anthony Boucher's anthology, *Four-&-Twenty Bloodhounds* (1950)), and journalist Edward Malone (from Doyle's Professor Challenger series). The club has certain rules that all members must obey. Guests of members are forbidden to buy drinks. No one may enter the bar wearing an overcoat under penalty of buying a round of drinks. I'm not sure what happens if a guest of a member wears an overcoat in the bar. The most famous American to set foot inside the Savage Club was Mark Twain. He once requested that the Savage Club store two cases of bourbon for him until he returned. Twain died in 1910 before he could claim his liquor. Despite Twain's death, the Savage Club felt honor bound to preserve the bourbon in storage for him. The bourbon was destroyed, alas, during a World War II air raid. The club encourages odd and eccentric behavior. Members are encouraged to tell stories at the drop of a hat. The Savage Club has certain similarities to the Billiards Club featured in Lord Dunsany's stories of Joseph Jorkens.

It is highly doubtful that Doc would join this club even though the name might have attracted him. Doc was a very serious person with generally little time for horseplay (his behavior in *The Freckled Shark* was an exception to this rule). However, The Shadow had certainly been known to enjoy a good laugh. He could have joined this club when he was posing as an Englishman named Clifford Gage during World War I and the 1920s. The Clifford Gage identity appeared in *The Black Master* (March 1932). The Shadow would have been intrigued by the secret origins of the Savage Club's name. He could have investigated, and found the skeletons in Doc's family tree. Maybe some indiscreet member of the club accidentally blurted out the truth to The Shadow. The information obtained by The Shadow would involve the bizarre experiments of Doc's great-grandfather. The Shadow might have wondered who had possession of the Frankenstein notebooks. Further investigations would have led The Shadow to Clark Savage Sr. The Shadow would have wondered if Clark Sr. was the correct individual to possess such knowledge. The Shadow then would have investigated the origins of Clark Sr., and learned the reasons why he had authorized the unusual training of his son. The Shadow would have discovered all this vital information in the 1920s.

Clark Sr. must have shown the Frankenstein notebooks to his son in 1926 in order to begin the decade long experiments which culminated in 1936 during *Resurrection Day*. However, Clark Sr. would not have revealed to his on the details of their notorious ancestor's experiments in the 1870s. Doc Savage probably assumed that his father had gained possession of the notebooks in the course of an adventure rather than as a family legacy. If The Shadow discovered the secrets of Doc's family, then he didn't reveal them to Doc until April 1945 (see the "**Note**" between entries 178 and 179). My chronological investigations have led me to believe that Doc learned about his father's secrets during a London visit at that time. In *Chronology of Shadows*, I have only allocated five days in April 1945 to one of The Shadow's recorded adventures, *A Quarter of Eight* (October 1945). It is possible for The Shadow also to have gone to London in April 1945. The Shadow could have been the person who informed Doc about his father's past.

Why The Shadow withheld the information for so long would be anyone's guess. Perhaps The Shadow felt that the information could hurt Doc's feelings, and the bronze adventurer was better off not knowing. Another possible explanation is that The Shadow may have been hoping to use that information at an appropriate time to manipulate Doc into collaborating with him. As The Shadow stated in *The Black Master* (chap. 20), he would do anything, including resorting to crime, if "the end justified the means." Maybe The Shadow needed Doc's help in London during April 1945, and the information about Doc's family enabled the Knight of Darkness to compel The Man of Bronze to comply with his wishes.

CHAPTER IV

The Literary Works of Clark Savage Jr., A Partial List

In addition to his many accomplishments, Doc Savage is a well-known author whose literary output includes the following:

1) *The Armor Plate Value of Certain Alloys* (*The Terror in the Navy*, chap. 1). It is described as "a thick book full of fine print and intricate mathematical computations."

2) *Atomic Research Simplified* (*The Green Death*, chap. 2).

3) A number of surgical treatises (*The Devil Genghis*, chap. 10). At the start of *The Awful Dynasty* (chap. 1), Doc was writing a "treatise on a new type of brain surgery."

4) A book on corporate law (*The Yellow Cloud*, chap. 10). This book confirmed Ham's suspicion that Doc's legal knowledge was superior to his own.

5) A book on philosophy and psychology (*The Gold Ogre*, chap. 2).

6) A book on "electrolysis phenomena" (*The Goblins*, chap. 10).

7) A short book and a few scientific articles on Amazon and Guinea (Guiana) dialects (*TheDerelict of Skull Shoal*, chap. 13).

You will not find these works in any libraries, they exist only in the imagination of Lester Dent, Harold A. Davis and William G, Bogart. One wonders if Doc ever wrote an autobiography. Renny Renwick apparently wrote an autobiography. In this book, Renny mentioned the fight with the old man from *The Terror in the Navy* (chap. 10). Renny was also the author of various articles for the engineering journals (*Satan Black*, chap. 10). Renny wasn't the only one of Doc's assistants to have authored an article or a book. Long Tom had at least one article published by a technical magazine (*The Land of Terror*, chap. 6). Johnny wrote several articles for scientific magazines (*The Awful Egg*, chap. 6), as well as a book on geological movements with a horizontal component (*Mystery Island*, chap. 4).

CHAPTER V
Chronological Checklist

1. 1918: March 31 to mid-July (107 days)—*Escape from Loki*
2. 1928 (1 day)—"Monk Called it Justice" (radio play)
3. 1929: April (1 day)—"The Box of Fear" (radio play)
4. 1929: June (1 day)—"The Phantom Terror" (radio play)
5. 1929: December (1 day)—"The Red Lake Quest" (radio play)
6. 1930: February (1 day)—"Needle in a Chinese Haystack" (radio play)
7. 1930: March (1 day)—"Mantrap Mesa" (radio play)
8. 1930: April (1 day)—"The White-Haired Devil" (radio play)
9. 1930: May (1 day)—"Poison Cargo" (radio play)
10. 1930: June (1 day)—"The Evil Extortionists" (radio play)
11. 1930: June (1 day)—"Death Had Blue Hands" (radio play)
12. 1930: July (1 day)—"Find Curly Morgan" (radio play)
13. 1930: July (1 day)—"The Sinister Sleep" (radio play)
14. 1930: August (1 Day)—"Radium Scramble" (radio play)
15. 1930: August (1 day)—"The Too-Talkative Parrot" (radio play)
16. 1930: August (1 day)—"The Growing Wizard" (radio play)
17. 1930: September (1 day)—"The Blue Angel" (radio play)
18. 1930: September (1 day)—"The Green Ghost" (radio play)
19. 1930: October (1 day)—"The Impossible Bullet" (radio play)
20. 1930: October (1 day)—"The Oilfield Ogres" (radio play)
21. 1931: May (25 days)—*The Man of Bronze*
22. 1931: June 12-July 8 (27 days)—*The Land of Terror*
23. 1932: August (1 day)—"The Sniper in the Sky" (radio play)
24. 1932: Early April (1 day)—"The Southern Star Mystery" (radio play)
25. 1932: June (7 days)—*Quest of the Spider*
26. 1932: Late June to late July (35 days)—*The Polar Treasure*
27. 1932: Very late July to mid-August (22 days)—*Pirate of the Pacific*
28. 1932: Late August (4 days)—*The Red Skull*
29. 1932: September (13 days)—*The Lost Oasis*

30. 1932: Late September to Mid-October (28 days)—*The Sargasso Ogre*
31. 1932: Late October (4 days)—*The Czar of Fear*
32. 1932: November to early December (40 days)—*The Phantom City*
33. 1932: December (9 days)—*Brand of the Werewolf*
34. 1933: Early January (6 days)—*The Man Who Shook the Earth*
35. 1933: January-February (50 days)—*Meteor Menace*
36. 1933: Early March (5 days)—*The Monsters*
37. 1933: Mid-March (8 days)—*The Mystery on the Snow*
38. 1933: April (23 days)—*The King Maker*
39. 1933: Early May (8 days)—*The Thousand-Headed Man*
40. 1933: Mid-May (4 days)—*Fear Cay*
41. 1933: Mid-May (2 days)—*Death in Silver*
42. 1933: First half of June (10 days)—*Python Isle*
43. 1933: Late June (3 days)—*The Sea Magician*
44. 1933: August (1 day)—"Black-Light Magic" (radio play)
45. 1933: August (7 days)—*The Squeaking Goblin*
46. 1933: Late September to October (32 days)—*Land of Always Night*
47. 1933: Early November (2 days)—*The Annihilist*
48. 1933: November 7-21 (15 days)—*The Mystic Mullah*
49. 1933: December (10 days)—*Red Snow*
50. 1934: January (7 days)—*Dust of Death*
51. 1934: February (27 days)—*The Spook Legion*
52. 1934: Early March (4 days)—*The Secret in the Sky*
53. 1934: March-early April (15 days)—*Spook Hole*
54. 1934: April (1 day)—"Fast Workers"
55. 1934: April (1 day)—"The Fainting Lady" (radio play)
56. 1934: May (3 days)—*Cold Death*
57. 1934: Late May (2 days)—*The Roar Devil*
58. 1934: Early June (10 days)—*Quest of Qui*
59. 1934: Mid-June to earl July (15 days)—*The Jade Ogre*
60. 1934: July to early August (29 days)—*The Majii*
61. 1934: August (10 days)—*The Fantastic Island*
62. 1934: September 1 to October 10 (40 days)—*Mystery Under the Sea*
63. 1934: October 15-18 (4 days)—*The Seven Agate Devils*
64. 1934: October 23-24 (2 days)—*The Midas Man*
65. 1934: November (3 days)—*The Metal Master*
66. 1934: Early December (5 days)—*White Eyes*
67. 1934-35: December to early March (82 days)—*The South Pole Terror*
68. 1935: March (7 days)—*Haunted Ocean*
69. 1935: Late March (3 days)—*Mad Eyes*
70. 1935: April (19 days)—*He Could Stop the World*

71. 1935: Late May (4 days)—*Land of Long Juju*
72. 1935: First half of June (3 days)—*The Men Who Smiled No More*
73. 1935: June 16-20 (5 days)—*Murder Melody*
74. 1935: July 4-13 (10 days)—*Murder Mirage*
75. 1935: August (3 days)—*The Black Spot*
76. 1935: Late August (7 days)—*The Terror in the Navy*
77. 1935: Mid-September (6 days)—*The Derrick Devil*
78. 1935: Late September (5 days)—*The Vanisher*
79. 1935: October (5 days)—*The Land of Fear*
80. 1935: December (8 days)—*The Mental Wizard*
81. 1936: January 3-February 28 (57 days)—*Resurrection Day*
82. 1936: March to early April (38 days)—*Repel*
83. 1936: Mid to late April (15 days)—*The Motion Menace*
84. 1936: April 30 to July 14 (76 days)—*Ost*
85. 1936: July 23 to August 3 (12 days)—*The Whistling Wraith*
86. 1936: August (17 days)—*The Sea Angel*
87. 1936-37: September-January (140 days)—*The Red Terrors*
88. 1937: February (13 days)—*Devil on the Moon*
89. 1937: Early March (6 days)—*The Golden Peril*
90. 1937: March 15-27 (13 days)—*The Pirate's Ghost*
91. 1937: May (15 days)—*The Munitions Master*
92. 1937: May 25 to June 4 (11 days)—*The Feathered Octopus*
93. 1937: June (17 days)—*The Forgotten Realm*
94. 1937: Early July (2 days)—*The Living Fire Menace*
95. 1937: July 12-14 (3 days)—*The Mountain Monster*
96. 1937: Mid-July to August (42 days)—*Mad Mesa*
97. 1937: October to early November (33 days)—*The Submarine Mystery*
98. 1937: Late November (4 days)—*The Green Death*
99. 1937-38: December to very early January (31 days)—*Fortress of Solitude*
100. 1938: March (18 days)—*The Devil Genghis*
101. 1938: Late March (4 days)—*The Yellow Cloud*
102. 1938: April (18 days)—*The Giggling Ghosts*
103. 1938: Early May (5 days)—*Merchants of Disaster*
104. 1938: Mid-May to early June (20 days)—*The Flaming Falcons*
105. 1938: Second half of June (5 days)—*The Freckled Shark*
106. 1938: Early July (6 days)—*The Crimson Serpent*
107. 1938: July (15 days)—*The Gold Ogre*
108. 1938: July 30 to August 2 (4 days)—*Tunnel Terror*
109. 1938: August (5 days)—*The Angry Ghost*
110. 1938: August 25-26 (2 days)—*World's Fair Goblin*
111. 1938: September 4 to October 24 (51 days)—*Poison Island*

112. 1938: Early November (7 days)—*The Stone Man*
113. 1938-39: December 11 to January 13 (34 days)—*The Dagger in the Sky*
114. 1939: First half of May (9 days)—*The Other World*
115. 1939: Second half of May (3 days)—*The Spotted Men*
116. 1939: Early June (6 days)—*Hex*
117. 1939: July (4 days)—*The Devil's Playground*
118. 1939: Late July-early August (15 days)—*The Men Vanished*
119. 1939: August 21-September 5 (16 days)—*Bequest of Evil*
120. 1939: Mid-September (5 days)—*The Headless Men*
121. 1939: September 21-23 (3 days)—*The Evil Gnome*
122. 1939: Early October (2 days)—*The Mindless Monsters*
123. 1939: Mid-October (3 days)—*The Boss of Terror*
124. 1939-40: December to early January (36 days)—*Devils of the Deep*
125. 1940: January 23 to March 2 (40 days)—*The Awful Dynasty*
126. 1940: March 6-13 (8 days)—*The Flying Goblin*
127. 1940: Second half of March (11 days)—*The Awful Egg*
128. 1940: Early April (3 days)—*The All-White Elf*
129. 1940: April (after the 9th) to July (109 days)—*The Golden Man*
130. 1940: August 1-3 (3 days)—*The Purple Dragon*
131. 1940: Early August (3 days)—*The Pink Lady*
132. 1940: Late August (5 days)—*The Green Eagle*
133. 1940: Early September (3 days)—*Mystery Island*
134. 1940: September 13-17 (5 days)—*The Invisible-Box Murders*
135. 1940: September 19-25 (7 days)—*Birds of Death*
136. 1940: October 9-13 (5 days)—*Men of Fear*
137. 1941: March to April (47 days)—*The Magic Forest*
138. 1941: May 10-11 (2 days)—*The Rustling Death*
139. 1941: Late May (3 days)—*Peril in the North*
140. 1941: August (12 days)—*Pirate Isle*
141. 1941: August (6 days)—*The Speaking Stone*
142. 1941: Early September (6 days)—*The Man Who Fell Up*
143. 1941: September 16-24 (9 days)—*The Too-Wise Owl*
144. 1942: Very late April (2 days, possibly April 29-30)—*The Three Wild Men*
145. 1942: Early May (3 days, possibly May 2-4)—*The Fiery Menace*
146. 1942: Second half of June (12 days)—*The Laugh of Death*
147. 1942: Early July (4 days)—*The Time Terror*
148. 1942: July (7 days)—*The Talking Devil*
149. 1942: Early August (4 days)—*The Goblins*
150. 1942: August 12-14 (3 days)—*Waves of Death*
151. 1942: Second half of August (2 days)—*The Mental Monster*
152. 1942: September 23-24 (2 days)—*Mystery on Happy Bones*

153. 1942: October 6-16 (11 days)—*They Died Twice*
154. 1942: October 19-28 (10 days)—*The Devil's Black Rock*
155. 1942: November (6 days)—*The Black, Black Witch*
156. 1943: January 3-10 (8 days)—*The King of Terror*
157. 1943: Early March (4 days)—*The Running Skeletons*
158. 1943: Mid-March (9 days)—*Hell Below*
159. 1943: Late March (5 days)—*The Secret of the Su*
160. 1943: April 5-7 (3 days)—*The Three Devils*
161. 1943: April (8 days)—*Death Had Yellow Eyes*
162. 1943: Late May (6 days)—*The Pharaoh's Ghost*
163. 1943: June (7 days)—*The Man Who Was Scared*
164. 1943: July 26-30 (5 days)—*The Spook of Grandpa Eben*
165. 1943: Early September (3 days)—*The Whisker of Hercules*
166. 1943: Mid or Late September (6 days)—*The Derelict of Skull Shoal*
167. 1943: October 7-12 (6 days)—*According to Plan of a One-Eyed Mystic*
168. 1943: December (5 days, after the 7th)—*The Shape of Terror*
169. 1944: January (4 days, before the 14th)—*The Lost Giant*
170. 1944: March (27 days)—*Jiu San*
171. 1944: April (4 days)—*Weird Valley*
172. 1944: May (2 days)—*The Terrible Stork*
173. 1944: June (3 days, probably after D-Day (June 6))—*Violent Night*
174. 1944: Early July (9 days)—*Satan Black*
175. 1944: September (2 days)—*Strange Fish*
176. 1944: October (4 days)—*The Ten Ton Snakes*
177. 1944: November (5 days)—*Rock Sinister*
178. 1945: March (20 days)—*Cargo Unknown*
179. 1945: May (3 days, after V-E day (May 8th))—*The Thing That Pursued*
180. 1945: Early June (3 days)—*The Wee Ones*
181. 1945: June (16 days)—*The Screaming Man*
182. 1945: Early July (6 days)—*King Joe Cay*
183. 1945: Mid-July (2 days)—*Terror Takes 7*
184. 1945: August 1-2 (2 days)—*Trouble on Parade*
185. 1945: August (5 days)—*Se-Pah-Poo*
186. 1945: Late August (7 days)—*Terror and the Lonely Widow*
187. 1945: Mid September (4 days)—*Colors for Murder*
188. 1945: September 23-26 (4 days)—*Fire and Ice*
189. 1945: December 5-9 (4 days)—*Measures for a Coffin*
190. 1945: Mid December (2 days)—*Three Times a Corpse*
191. 1946: First half of January (12 days)—*The Exploding Lake*
192. 1946: Late January (6 days)—*Danger Lies East*
193. 1946: March (2 days)—*Death is a Round Black Spot*

194. 1946: April 1-10 (10 days)—*Five Fathoms Dead*
195. 1946: May (2 days)—*The Devil Is Jones*
196. 1946: July (2 days)—*Death in Little Houses*
197. 1946: September (8 days)—*Target for Death*
198. 1946: Late October (2 days)—*The Disappearing Lady*
199. 1947: January (12 days)—*The Death Lady*
200. 1947: February 1-2 (2 days)—*No Light to Die By*
201. 1947: April (2 days)—*The Monkey Suit*
202. 1947: May (3 days)—*Let's Kill Ames*
203. 1947: June (3 days)—*Once Over Lightly*
204. 1947: July (1 days)—*I Died Yesterday*
205. 1947: September (17 days)—*Terror Wears No Shoes*
206. 1948: Late January (2 days)—*The Pure Evil*
207. 1948: March (13 Days)—*The Red Spider*
208. 1948: April (7 Days)—*The Angry Canary*
209. 1948: May (3 Days)—*Return from Cormoral*
210. 1948: June (1 day)—*The Swooning Lady*
211. 1948: October (13 days)—*Flight into Fear*
212. 1948: November 15-20 (6 days)—*The Green Master*
213. 1949: Mid to Late January (9 days)—*The Frightened Fish*
214. 1949: February (9 days)—*Up From Earth's Center*

CHAPTER VI
Alphabetical Entry Cross-Reference

The following is a list of the novels and radio plays in alphabetical order. Next to them is the entry number for easy reference. Please note that the entry number is not a page number.

According to Plan of a One-Eyed Mystic: 167
The All-White Elf: 128
The Angry Canary: 208
The Angry Ghost: 109
The Annihilist: 47
The Awful Dynasty: 125
The Awful Egg: 127
Bequest of Evil: 119
Birds of Death: 135
The Black, Black Witch: 155
"Black-Light Magic" (radio play): 44
The Black Spot: 75
"The Blue Angel" (radio play): 17
The Boss of Terror: 123
"The Box of Fear" (radio play): 3
Brand of the Werewolf: 33
Cargo Unknown: 178
Cold Death: 56
Colors for Murder: 187
The Crimson Serpent: 106
The Czar of Fear: 31
The Dagger in the Sky: 113
Danger Lies East: 192
The Deadly Dwarf: See *Repel*

"Death Had Blue Hands" (radio play): 11
Death Had Yellow Eyes: 161
Death in Little Houses: 196
Death in Silver: 41
Death is a Round Black Spot: 193
The Death Lady: 199
The Derelict of Skull Shoal: 166
The Derrick Devil: 77
The Devil Genghis: 100
The Devil Is Jones: 195
Devil on the Moon: 88
The Devil's Black Rock: 154
Devils of the Deep: 124
The Devil's Playground: 117
The Disappearing Lady: 198
Dust of Death: 50
Escape from Loki: 1
"The Evil Extortionists" (radio play): 10
The Evil Gnome: 121
The Exploding Lake: 191
"The Fainting Lady" (radio play): 55
The Fantastic Island: 61
"Fast Workers" (radio play): 54
Fear Cay: 40

The Feathered Octopus: 92
The Fiery Menace: 145
"Find Curly Morgan" (radio play): 12
Fire and Ice: 188
Five Fathoms Dead: 194
The Flaming Falcons: 104
Flight into Fear: 211
The Flying Goblin: 126
The Forgotten Realm: 93
Fortress of Solitude: 99
The Freckled Shark: 105
The Frightened Fish: 213
The Giggling Ghosts: 102
The Goblins: 149
The Gold Ogre: 107
The Golden Man: 129
The Golden Peril: 89
The Green Death: 98
The Green Eagle: 132
"The Green Ghost" (radio play): 18
The Green Master: 212
"The Growing Wizard" (radio play): 16
"The Impossible Bullet" (radio play): 19
The Hate Genius: see *Violent Night*
Haunted Ocean: 68
He Could Stop the World: 70
The Headless Men: 120
Hell Below: 158
Hex: 116
I Died Yesterday: 204
The Invisible-Box Murders: 134
The Jade Ogre: 59
Jiu San: 170
King Joe Cay: 182
The King Maker: 38
The King of Terror: 156
Land of Always Night: 46
Land of Long Juju: 71
The Land of Fear: 79
The Land of Terror: 22
The Laugh of Death: 146

Let's Kill Ames: 202
The Living Fire Menace: 94
The Lost Giant: 169
The Lost Oasis: 29
Mad Eyes: 69
Mad Mesa: 96
The Magic Forest: 137
The Majii: 60
The Magic Island: See *Ost*
The Man of Bronze: 21
The Man Who Fell Up: 142
The Man Who Shook the Earth: 34
The Man Who Was Scared: 163
"Mantrap Mesa" (radio play): 7
Measures for a Coffin: 189
Men of Fear: 136
The Men Who Smiled No More: 72
The Men Vanished: 118
The Mental Monster: 151
The Mental Wizard: 80
Merchants of Disaster: 103
The Metal Master: 65
Meteor Menace: 35
The Midas Man: 64
The Mindless Monsters: 122
"Monk Called it Justice" (radio play): 2
The Monkey Suit: 201
The Monsters: 36
The Motion Menace: 83
The Mountain Monster: 95
The Munitions Master: 91
Murder Melody: 73
Murder Mirage: 74
Mystery Island: 133
Mystery on Happy Bones: 152
The Mystery on the Snow: 37
Mystery Under the Sea: 62
The Mystic Mullah: 48
"Needle in a Chinese Haystack" (radio play): 6
No Light to Die By: 200

"The Oilfield Ogres" (radio play): 20
Once Over Lightly: 203
One-Eyed Mystic: see According to Plan of a One-Eyed Mystic
Ost: 84
The Other World: 114
Peril in the North: 139
The Phantom City: 32
"The Phantom Terror" (radio play): 4
The Pharaoh's Ghost: 162
The Pink Lady: 131
Pirate Isle: 140
Pirate of the Pacific: 27
The Pirate's Ghost: 90
"Poison Cargo" (radio play): 9
Poison Island: 111
The Polar Treasure: 26
The Purple Dragon: 130
The Pure Evil: 206
Python Isle: 42
Quest of Qui: 58
Quest of the Spider: 25
"Radium Scramble" (radio play): 14
"The Red Lake Quest" (radio play): 5
The Red Skull: 28
Red Snow: 49
The Red Terrors: 87
The Red Spider: 207
Repel: 82
Resurrection Day: 81
Return from Cormoral: 209
The Roar Devil: 57
Rock Sinister: 177
The Running Skeletons: 157
The Rustling Death: 138
The Sargasso Ogre: 30
Satan Black: 174
The Screaming Man: 181
The Sea Angel: 86
The Sea Magician: 43
The Secret in the Sky: 52

The Secret of the Su: 159
Se-Pah-Poo: 185
The Seven Agate Devils: 63
The Shape of Terror: 168
"The Sinister Sleep" (radio play): 13
"The Sniper in the Sky" (radio play): 23
The South Pole Terror: 67
"The Southern Star Mystery" (radio play): 24
The Speaking Stone: 141
Spook Hole: 53
The Spook Legion: 51
The Spook of Grandpa Eben: 164
The Spotted Men: 115
The Squeaking Goblin: 45
The Stone Man: 112
Strange Fish: 175
The Submarine Mystery: 97
The Swooning Lady: 210
The Talking Devil: 148
Target for Death: 197
The Ten Ton Snakes: 176
The Terrible Stork: 172
Terror and the Lonely Widow: 186
The Terror in the Navy: 76
Terror Takes 7: 183
Terror Wears No Shoes: 205
They Died Twice: 153
The Thing That Pursued: 179
The Thousand-Headed Man: 39
The Three Devils: 160
Three Times a Corpse: 190
The Three Wild Men: 144
The Time Terror: 147
The Too-Wise Owl: 143
"The Too-Talkative Parrot" (radio play): 15
The Too-Wise Owl: 143
Trouble on Parade: 184
Tunnel Terror: 108
Up From Earth's Center: 214
The Vanisher: 78
Violent Night: 173

Waves of Death: 150
The Wee Ones: 180
Weird Valley: 171
The Whisker of Hercules: 165
The Whistling Wraith: 85
White Eyes: 66
"The White-Haired Devil" (radio play): 8
World's Fair Goblin: 110
The Yellow Cloud: 101

Made in the USA
Lexington, KY
05 September 2010